THIS PRINCESS KILLS MONSTERS

THIS PRINCESS KILLS MONSTERS

The Misadventures of a Fairy-Tale Stepsister

A NOVEL

RY HERMAN

THE DIAL PRESS
New York

The Dial Press
An imprint of Random House
A division of Penguin Random House LLC
1745 Broadway, New York, NY 10019
randomhousebooks.com
penguinrandomhouse.com

A Dial Press Trade Paperback Original

Library of Congress Cataloging-in-Publication Data
Names: Herman, Ry, author.
Title: This princess kills monsters / Ry Herman.
Description: New York, NY : The Dial Press, 2025.
Identifiers: LCCN 2025000687 (print) | LCCN 2025000688 (ebook) |
ISBN 9780593733080 (trade paperback) | ISBN 9780593733097 (ebook)
Subjects: LCGFT: Queer fiction. | Fantasy fiction. | Romance fiction. | Novels.
Classification: LCC PR6108.E75 P75 2025 (print) |
LCC PR6108.E75 (ebook)
LC record available at https://lccn.loc.gov/2025000687
LC ebook record available at https://lccn.loc.gov/2025000688

Printed in the United States of America on acid-free paper

2 4 6 8 9 7 5 3 1

BOOK TEAM: Production editor: Cara DuBois •
Managing editor: Rebecca Berlant • Production manager:
Nathalie Mairena • Copy editor: Katie Herman •
Proofreaders: Shasta Clinch, Alissa Fitzgerald, Megha Jain

Title-page art: 4zevar/Adobe Stock

Book design by Alexis Flynn

The authorized representative in the EU for product safety and compliance is Penguin Random House Ireland, Morrison Chambers, 32 Nassau Street, Dublin D02 YH68, Ireland. https://eu-contact.penguin.ie.

For my parents,
who read me bedtime stories
and did all the voices

Then her father said to her, "Dearest child, why art thou so sad? Thou shalt have whatsoever thou wilt." She thought for a moment and said, "Dear father, I wish for eleven girls exactly like myself in face, figure, and size."

—Jacob and Wilhelm Grimm,
"The Twelve Huntsmen" (1812),
translated by Margaret Raine Hunt

THIS PRINCESS KILLS MONSTERS

PROLOGUE

The Tale of the Twelve Hunters,

as It Has Been Inaccurately Recorded

You might have heard the story of the twelve hunters during your childhood. It's in the same book as the fables about the princess imprisoned in the tower, the children who found a gingerbread house, and the woman who lost her shoe at a party.

Although the story was based on true events, they were recounted by those who half remembered them to those who had never witnessed them at all. Unlike the other tales, it is frequently skipped or ignored. Which is a great pity, in my opinion, because I am in it.

As it has come down through the ages, it goes something like this:

Once upon a time, when the world was younger and the stars burned a little more brightly, a prince was engaged to a woman he loved beyond measure. She loved him just as much in turn. Many were the occasions they would sit together, speaking of nothing but how deeply they loved each other.

"I love you," he would proclaim—and proclaim it he did, for

this was in the days when it was considered poor form to merely "say" something, and everyone was required to proclaim, declaim, avow, or otherwise speak more ostentatiously. So: "I love you," he would proclaim.

"I love you more," she would avow.

"That is impossible, for I love you most of all," he would declare. "There can be no love that is greater than mine."

"But my love for you *is* impossible," she would counter, "because I love you even more than the greatest amount of love one person could ever feel for another. I win."

"You cheated," he would sulk.

"You still lost!" she would gloat. "Suck on your loss, loser."

And then they would make out.

One day, right in the middle of this nonsense, when they were eagerly anticipating the argument's aftermath, a messenger arrived with an urgent message.

"What is it?" the prince snapped.

"I am sorry to interrupt your daily, um . . . conference with your lady love," the messenger apologized, "but your father is gravely ill, on the very point of death, and wishes you to come to his side immediately."

"Oh, my goodness! I will go to him at once. My darling," the prince exclaimed as he turned to his lady, "I must depart for my own kingdom. Take this ring to keep me in your memories. I shall return to you as soon as I can."

"Take as much time as you need," she responded, accepting the ring. "Your ailing father needs you. I will wait, if I must, until the seas run dry."

"You will not have to wait, for I will make my way back to you, though my path be barred by a thousand armies."

"If those armies should impede you, I will wait for you until the sun shrivels to an ember."

"But I shall not be impeded, though the world itself crack in twain!"

And so on.

Once their vows had scaled to satisfyingly ridiculous heights, the prince threw himself astride his loyal destrier and galloped to his father's side. So quickly did he ride that despite the long distance, poor roads, bad weather, and occasional attacks by horrible monsters, it took him only two months, which really was pretty good time, considering. But in spite of his haste, when he arrived, his father, the king, was gasping his last. He had held out until his son's arrival only through sheer force of will.

"My son," his father rasped, his words faint, "I am glad I could see you one final time. I beg of you, swear to me you will fulfill my dying wish."

"Of course!" the prince sobbed. "Anything!"

"Then I ask you to marry the princess of the mountain kingdom far to the east."

"I shall!" the prince vowed, then added, "Wait, what?"

But the king had passed into the realms beyond mortal knowledge and spoke no more.

The prince was crowned king soon thereafter. He delayed fulfilling the vow for as long as he was able, but once the mourning period for his father had ended, he felt compelled to abide by his promise. He sent a message to the east to propose for the hand of the princess of the mountain kingdom. His suit was accepted and the engagement proclaimed throughout their lands.

Only then, when he could put it off no longer, did he send a letter to his former fiancée. For so ashamed was he that, rather than face her in person, he broke up with her by post.

The lady was not pleased.

She did not, however, pine, or weep, or lock herself in a darkened room while minstrels played sad music for her in the courtyard. Such was not her nature. She stormed through her father's house in a rage, shouting at all and sundry. She ranted, and raved, and hurled crockery against the wall so she could hear the gratifying smash. Her father was at first understanding of her shock and grief, but when her fury did not abate as the weeks grew into months, he became alarmed.

In an effort to placate her, he asked, "My dearest daughter, is there anything which would please you? For you may have whatever you wish."

His daughter ceased shouting. Lost in thought, she lowered the earthenware soup bowl she'd been about to throw, turning it over and over in her hands.

At length, she answered, "If that is so, Father, then I would like you to find eleven girls who appear exactly identical to me in every respect."

He stared at her in surprise. "I was envisioning something more along the lines of a puppy."

"Eleven girls," she repeated, her fingers whitening as her clutch on the bowl tightened, "who appear exactly identical to me in every respect."

"Very well, I'll find them!" he promised. "Just . . . just put the bowl down, all right?" For his supplies of crockery were running very low.

He searched throughout the land until eleven women were found who met his daughter's requirements. When they arrived, she had a dozen identical huntsmen's outfits made to their size. The eleven girls changed into these clothes, and she donned the twelfth outfit herself. Thus attired, she bid farewell to her father, and the women rode off together.

"Goodbye!" he shouted after them. "Have fun doing whatever it is you intend to do with eleven eerily similar women disguised in men's clothing!"

As you may have guessed, the twelve of them arrived many weeks later (bad roads, miserable weather, etc.) at the court of the former prince, now king.

"Hello, strange king whom I have never met!" the lady

greeted him. "Have you any need of huntsmen? For we twelve are mightily skilled at hunting and eager to put ourselves at your service."

"Is that so?" The king did not recognize her, thanks to her cunning disguise, but he found he was much taken by the appearance of these strangers. "I must say, you are exceedingly handsome fellows."

"Are we really?" the lady inquired smugly.

"Remarkably so. Just to my taste, so to speak."

"Imagine that," replied the lady.

"Obviously, I could not refuse a request from such a group of attractive, I might even say enticing—"

"You're beginning to make this a little weird," she informed him.

"Sorry. What I meant to say is, of course I shall accept your service. I hereby declare you to be the King's Huntsmen!"

And thus they were welcomed into the court with great celebration.

Now, as you are no doubt already aware, the king had a talking lion who knew all manner of secret things.

Oh, did the talking lion never come up before? You'd think such a phenomenal creature would have been brought to your attention right away, not suddenly dropped into the middle of the story like this. And you might, in addition, reasonably expect a quick explanation of why the king had this talking lion, and how it knew secret things, and so forth. But you will not receive such information, not in this version of the tale.

So—for unknown reasons, there was a talking lion. One day, apropos of nothing in particular, the lion pronounced to the king, "You believe you have twelve huntsmen serving at your court."

The king was understandably perplexed. "I know I have twelve huntsmen."

"You do not," the lion averred.

"I assure you that I do. I have seen them. I was there when they were taken into my service. In fact, I hired them myself."

"You do not have twelve huntsmen. They are women."

"They cannot possibly be women," the king scoffed. "They wear trousers. Women do not wear trousers. Honestly, I'd have thought you knew that. What kind of magical talking lion are you?"

"They are women," the lion explained, "who have *put on trousers* in order to *disguise the fact that they are women*."

The king was dumbfounded by this remarkable statement and stood in silent shock for several minutes.

"If that is true, then prove it," he commanded, once he had regained his wits.

"Hm. We could spy upon them whilst they are naked, perhaps."

"That idea makes me curiously excited, but no. It seems rude. What else have you got?"

The lion considered. "We shall scatter some dried peas around the room and summon the hunters to your presence. Men step firmly when they walk and would smash the peas beneath their boots. Women hop and skip and spring about and would roll the peas across the floor."

"Really?" The king was dubious.

"Oh, yes. It's a well-known fact. I have theorized it's an evolutionary adaptation designed to keep floors free of vermin. The men stamp any insects flat into the floor, and then the women sweep them aside to the corners. It's explained in more detail in my book, *A Natural History of Humans*."

"Hmph," muttered the king. "We'll see."

Despite his skepticism, the king took the lion's advice and arranged for the plan to be enacted. But a servant who was fond of the huntsmen overheard the discussion and went to tell them of it.

"The lion wants the king to think you're girls!" he warned them.

"How ridiculous," the lady laughed.

"I know! You wear trousers!"

The lady conferred with her fellows once the servant had gone. "When the time comes, you must step firmly on the peas. Resist any womanly impulses to gambol or caper."

"Can we not scamper? Or even prance?" one of the girls beseeched her.

"You must not prance, no matter how powerful your prancing instinct," the lady ordered them. "Be brave."

The following morning, the king called the huntsmen to court. But the twelve disguised women stomped into the room, taking such solid steps that every pea was smashed to bits beneath their boots.

"You wished for something, my king?" the lady queried.

"Not really," he hedged. "I just wanted, uh, to say hi."

"Hi."

"Hi there."

"Hello."

They smiled at each other inanely for a while until the lion cleared his throat and the king, coming back to his senses, dismissed them.

"Well, it looks like I was right and you were wrong," the king scolded the lion. "Wallow in your wrongness, Lion."

"Someone must have warned them," the lion growled. "They knew you were testing them, so they imitated the insect-stamping walk instead of using the insect-sweeping walk. Give me another chance."

"You may have one more chance, but then I will waste no more time on this farce. Choose some final trial."

The lion pondered. "All right—here is a plan that cannot fail. Have twelve spinning wheels set up around the room, and summon the hunters to your presence. Being women, they will naturally be drawn to them. Any man would simply ignore them."

"Really?" The king was once again dubious.

"Oh, yes. Female humans are invariably obsessed with spinning, whereas male humans are repulsed by anything of the sort. I have hypothesized this is because humans are actually a kind of enormous spider. It goes back to the days when the women would use their spinnerets to produce webs so they could trap their prey, whereas men would only employ them to swing from tree to tree. Of course, your spinnerets are mostly vestigial now."

"That is a compelling theory," the king admitted.

"It explains the insect stamping, too. It's all in my book. I can send you a copy if you like."

The king took the lion's advice and commanded that the spinning wheels be brought in. However, the servant who was fond of the huntsmen once again overheard the plan and went to tell them of it.

"Oh, no!" cried one of them when she heard what was in store. "How can we possibly resist the powerful allure of treadle-operated textile-production devices?"

"We must once again be brave," their leader exhorted them. "Treat them as you would a less beguiling apparatus. Behave as if they were not designed to seductively twist plant fibers into thread."

The following morning, the king once again called the huntsmen to court. But the twelve disguised women walked past the spinning wheels without paying them any mind.

"What do you wish of us, my king?" the lady entreated.

"Uh, I wished for something, yes," the king extemporized, realizing that calling them in for no apparent reason was beginning to look rather odd. "I wished . . . to organize a hunt today!"

The lady bowed to him. "Then it shall be done."

Once they had left, the king frowned at the lion. "They are clearly men. They didn't even glance at the spinning wheels once. Admit to your lies, you lying liar."

"I am no liar!" the lion roared. "Someone must have warned them! They knew you were testing them, so—"

"Silence!" bellowed the king. "I will hear no more of this nonsense!" And he strode off to join his huntsmen on their hunt, leaving the lion behind to grumble under its breath about ungrateful kings who don't know how lucky they are to have a magical talking lion hanging around all day questioning people's gender.

"Ah, what a lovely day for a hunt!" the king opined as he rode with his hunters through the vast forest. "Just me and my twelve manly companions. Manly men doing manly things in a manful way. Let us idly scratch at our testicles whilst we pee standing upright together."

"Um, sure," asseverated the lady—and I am very sorry she asseverated it, but I am rapidly running out of synonyms.

As she was wondering how she could best excuse herself from these activities, a messenger greeted them, which to her immense relief distracted the king from his itchy balls.

Her relief was short-lived, however, for what the messenger had to report was this: "My king! Your bride, the princess of the mountain kingdom, has at last arrived! She has reached the border of the kingdom and will be here shortly."

Upon overhearing this, the lady fainted dead away, falling off her horse.

Distraught by the notion that his cherished huntsman had been injured, the king ran over to help. As he removed the huntsman's gloves—for as everyone knows, when someone has fallen unconscious, you must take off their gloves immediately—he noticed she was wearing the ring that he had given to his true love. Peering at her face, he recognized her at long last.

His heart was touched, and he kissed her. As she opened her eyes, he said, "I am yours, and you are mine, and nothing shall ever part us again." And yes, he simply said it, much to the amazement of everyone present.

Turning to the messenger, he added, "Go and tell the princess of the mountain kingdom to return to her own land. I cannot marry her, for I have a bride already."

Smiling at him through tears, still dizzy from her fall, the lady murmured, "I win."

After the wedding celebration, the king grudgingly admitted that the lion had told the truth and made sure that the lion's book was widely disseminated. *A Natural History of Humans* proved to be a great delight for the minority of scholars who agreed humans are a kind of enormous spider. And they all lived happily ever after.

That is the story as it is currently told. But savvy readers may perhaps have noticed it doesn't make a lot of sense.

What, exactly, was the endgame of the lady's plan? Why did it require finding eleven identical duplicates? What was up with the gender-essentialist lion? Did the king really not recognize his one true love until he noticed the ring? And what on earth did the princess from the mountain kingdom think of all this?

That last one, at least, is a question I can address.

Because I am the princess from the mountain kingdom.

PART I

MY EVIL STEPMOTHER

CHAPTER ONE

The Irritating Riddle of the Sphinxes

I was going to get myself eaten. I could tell. It was just one of those days.

The field beyond the low rise was guarded by three stone sphinxes. A sphinx, as you might be aware, is a terrifying creature with the head of a woman, the body of a lion, and a mouth full of sharp fangs it uses to rip off the limbs of slow-witted travelers. When found in nature, sphinxes are about as large as a cow. Whoever had sculpted their likenesses here hadn't been concerned with realism, and all three were roughly the size of a barn.

Whether made of flesh or made of stone, sphinxes adore riddles and games. The best way to avoid losing any limbs is to correctly answer whatever they ask. But in this case, I was having a difficult time figuring out what the question was in the first place. So far, I had managed to determine that one of them always lied and one of them always told the truth—although I wasn't entirely certain which one was which—while the third one, for some reason, only recited nature poetry.

I remembered there was a way to solve this kind of puzzle, but I couldn't for the life of me recall what it was.

"Will you answer this question with a lie?" I asked.

"No," said the first sphinx, grinning to reveal its pointed stone teeth.

"No," the second sphinx replied as well.

"A lone fallen leaf / Floats across the placid pond / Autumn has arrived," said the third one.

I'd been hoping one of the sphinxes would say it was lying, get caught in a paradox, and . . . I don't know. Explode, maybe.

There might have been no solution at all. I didn't think the third one was working quite right. It was noticeably more chipped and weathered than its fellows, and its nose had fallen off. If it had been a patient of mine and not a statue, I would have diagnosed it with late-stage syphilis.

Treat with a carefully measured mixture of arsenical compounds and elemental bismuth, I thought automatically. *Keep watch for signs of toxicity; the medicine can be as dangerous as the disease unless the dosage is precise.*

But the sphinx was not my patient, statues could not catch syphilis—or at least, I very much hoped they could not—and arsenic would have had little effect on natural erosion. I didn't treat patients anymore anyway. To be honest, I never really had; I'd only assisted my mother and father in their work.

My job was to go on nonsensical quests and solve annoying puzzles. Although I'd been failing at that here, and I was beginning to fear my wits were about to prove fatally slow.

"You have two questions remaining," said the first sphinx.

"And then," said the second, "we will not eat you."

It was probably unreasonable to hope that the first one was the liar and the second was telling the truth.

"A blanket of snow," said the third, "Untouched by morning footsteps / Glitters like granite."

"That's hardly a relevant verse at the moment," I told the sphinx with a huff. "It's not even cold yet. There won't be any snow for months."

It tried to sniff disdainfully through its missing nose, scrunching its face up so tightly that a few more pebbles cracked off and fell to the ground.

The day was, in fact, bright and clear, a crisp morning in early autumn that for once promised no rain. A lone cloud stretched across the sky, a thick white line with wisps reaching out from the center in straight, regular rows. It looked like the spine and ribs of some enormous skeleton suspended in midair. Behind the sphinxes, a single row of trees topped the rise, their leaves just beginning to show the first hints of red and gold. And beyond, on the other side of the slope, spread a broad flat field overrun by tall, yellowing grass.

Which made the sphinxes a problem, because I was supposed to plough that field and sow it with teeth.

A thousand teeth, to be precise. I had no idea why; my stepmother hadn't bothered to explain. She never did before sending me or my sisters off on one of her bizarre quests. But when the queen says go, you go. I had tried refusing once, and it wasn't an experience I cared to repeat anytime soon.

All three of us, Jonquil and Calla and me, had been assigned the tooth task. But my stepmother hadn't told any of us where the field was, if she even knew. Calla, my younger half sister—we're a blended family—had set off for the east. My stepsister, Jonquil, the eldest, had set off for the west. Both of them left their spouses behind at the palace and traveled far and wide across the earth in search of the proper location.

I, in the meantime, decided to get a start on the tedious process of gathering a thousand teeth. After a few days spent dickering with dentists, I didn't have anywhere near enough, so I started going door to door. As it turns out, people exhibit a wide variety of reactions to a stranger asking if they happen to have any spare teeth lying around, but none of them could be described as delight.

The sphinxes were waiting for my next question with unconcealed impatience. "If I asked whether I could just walk past you, what would you say?" I hazarded in ill-considered desperation.

"I would say no," said the sphinx I thought was telling the truth, crouching down and lashing its tail.

"I would say yes," said the sphinx I thought was lying, rearing up and stretching its claws.

"The sun-dappled grass / Beneath the windblown branches—"

"I get it," I told them with a tired sigh. "One more question and then you'll eat me. Or maybe you won't. Or maybe you'll describe the ocean waves crashing against the rocky shore."

"Oh, that's a good one!" said the sphinx with no nose.

"Feel free to use it if you want." Perhaps playing muse to the sphinx would help somehow. It seemed unlikely.

I had managed to obtain enough teeth for the ploughing, although only because I'd had a lucky break the week before. In the middle of my tooth-collecting rounds, I'd been accosted by a fairy who accused me of trying to muscle in on her turf. She'd been gathering children's teeth for centuries. In exchange, she left small coins under their pillows. An odd hobby, but the habits of fairies were often difficult to understand. For instance, my sister-in-law, Gnoflwhogir, made necklaces out of the left ears of her enemies. I tried very hard not to be Gnoflwhogir's enemy.

When I explained my quest to the weird orthodontic fairy, she forgave my effrontery and took me down a road made of teeth and through a gate made of teeth to her mansion made of teeth so we could sit on her tooth couch and drink tea from a pair of enormous hollowed-out molars pulled from some young giant's mouth. She was eager to off-load her surplus, honestly.

But even so, she refused to let me have any unless we made some kind of trade. Some further chat revealed she was almost out of under-pillow coins; she didn't earn any income apart from teeth, which made me question her business model.

I went out to fetch some money for her and came across a cave where a troll was hoarding an enormous pile of small change. He was primed to eat me until I mentioned I was willing to strike a deal for cash, and he revealed that he was a collector of rare manuscripts with a desperate desire for first editions. It ended up turning into a whole . . . thing, and by the end I had traded the jewels of a princess (my earrings, since I am a princess, technically) for a fiddle that played itself for a goat with a golden fleece for a musty pile of handwritten pages for a sack full of coins for a whole lot of teeth. As an added bonus, the fairy directed me to the field where the teeth needed to be sown; she was an expert on all matters dental.

She didn't mention the stone sphinxes, though. And by the time I discovered their presence, I was utterly exhausted from travel and dealmaking.

But exhausted or not, I had a task to perform. I was about to take a stab at my final question—one that I was fairly sure would result in my being chomped to bits—when I noticed the field had begun ploughing itself.

I watched in astonishment as neat furrows opened in the dirt, in lines as even and parallel as musical staves. They ripped right through the grass and undergrowth without pause. In less than a minute, anyone would have thought a farmer with a team of oxen had been working the field over for days on end.

I opened my mouth to ask if that was supposed to be happening and then snapped it shut just in time. That would have been a depressingly bad final question to get eaten for.

"Hi, Melilot!" came a voice from behind me, startling me so much that I jumped.

"Calla," I said, closing my eyes.

I had a half-formed hope that if I didn't look at her, my younger sister would turn out not to be there after all, her voice merely a hallucination brought on by stress and fatigue.

"How's your quest been going?" she asked, persistently real. "Have you been getting on well with the sphinxes?"

"Swimmingly." I swung around, wrenching my eyes back open and plastering a smile on my face. "We've become the best of friends."

"A lie!" said Probably Truthful Sphinx.

"The truth," said Probably Lying Sphinx.

"On the pebbled coast— / Hold on, I've nearly got this— / Roaring, foam-tipped surf . . ." No-Nose Sphinx trailed off and pouted as it ran out of haiku syllables.

Calla grinned at me, no trace of malice on her face. There never is. I felt like an ass for wishing her away. Don't get me wrong. I like my sisters. I love my sisters. But it would be nice if once, just once, they got hopelessly lost on one of our assigned tasks and utterly failed at it, while I came home with every problem solved and all the spoils of victory neatly wrapped up in a bow. Maybe then the queen would stop treating me like the broken cauldron she never quite got around to throwing out. The way she'd treated me ever since she released me from my tower prison.

Calla, as usual, looked like she had been sleeping in a hay barn—and very possibly she had been, although I've also seen her look that way after a comfortable night in her own bedroom. Mysterious stains spotted her surcoat, and so many holes riddled her kirtle that it was less kirtle than hole. My own well-worn traveling clothes were pristine in comparison. Pieces of straw flecked her uncombed hair, and speaking of her hair . . .

"You've got birds," I said, "nesting on your head."

She nodded slowly, making an effort not to wake them. "Yes. They're starlings. The little one is Antonio Frühvogel-

Featherington, and the bigger one is Tweet. Aren't they adorable?"

They were. The pair of them were fast asleep and nestled together, tucked heads resting one atop the other. I was relieved it was only birds taking a nap on her head this time. I've seen her infested with naked mole rats. Or even beetles, which is rather off-putting. Calla loves all of nature's creatures and would never think to evict a friendly beetle from her hair just for being a beetle. No matter what, however, she always somehow smells like a fresh spring breeze. It's almost obnoxiously pleasant.

Beneath the birds and above the tattered clothing, Calla looks more like me than our other sister does. That isn't really surprising, since Calla and I share one parent, while Jonquil isn't related to me by blood. Jonquil inherited the queen's looks; my older sister is statuesque, with hair that cascades down her back in long dark plaits—although unlike the queen, she bears angry scars around her neck and all her joints. Calla is on the smaller side, and she and I share the tight curls and dimpled smile that we both received from our father. But Calla has my stepmother's eyes, and I, of course, do not. I also try to keep my hair cropped a bit shorter than Calla's since mine tends to grow spontaneously when I'm under stress. If I let it go untended, I start to trip on it.

"So," I said, "I'm guessing you're behind the magic self-ploughing field."

"It's not magic," she replied. "Some earthworms agreed to do me a favor."

"Of course they did." Peering more closely at the roiling earth in the middle distance, I could just make out the wriggling mass of them as they churned their way through the soil. As a plan, it was disgusting but effective. I was glad she wasn't carrying any of them in her hair. "How did you manage to make friends with earthworms?"

"I rescued one from being eaten by a bird."

"You saved one worm, and every worm on earth became your sworn friend for life?"

"Well . . . yes."

If I had tried to save a worm from a bird, all I would have gotten was pecked. In Calla's case, the only surprising thing was that she hadn't enlisted an army of gophers and moles as well.

"I suppose all we have to do now is get past the sphinxes and sow the teeth, then," I said.

"Oh, well, that's . . ." She sounded almost embarrassed. "That's taken care of, really."

"What do you mean, it's taken care of?"

I glanced over at my sack of teeth and found it lying empty and flaccid on the ground.

"Remember that bird I rescued the worm from?" Calla said. "I didn't want to leave the poor thing hungry, so I helped it out. One thing led to another, you know how it goes."

Over the field, a whole flock of starlings fluttered through the air, wheeling into dense clusters that immediately broke apart again. Tiny white objects rained from their beaks—my carefully collected teeth, I assumed. As far as I could tell, not a single bird was diving down to grab a worm. Calla must have negotiated a truce.

"So I managed to accomplish absolutely nothing on this quest," I said. "As usual."

"This again?" Calla sighed. "Don't be ridiculous. It was a quest for teeth, and you literally found the teeth."

"You could have done that. Anyone could have done that."

"Well, you also kept the sphinxes from attacking us."

I frowned. "How . . . did I do that, exactly?"

"My comrades, look!" shouted Probably Truthful as it noticed what was going on in the field. "We have been tricked!"

"This lack of betrayal shall not be met with instant death!" bellowed Probably Lying as it crouched to spring.

"A storm in the air— / Its sharp and pungent odor / Heralds the thunder!" threatened No-Nose.

Calla's eyes widened. "I thought you said you were getting on well with them! You didn't ask them the question?"

"What question?"

"The question that makes them not attack us!"

"Calla, tell me what the confounded question *is*. I've still got one more!"

"You ask the first one what the second one would say if you asked what isn't the right thing to say to keep them from—Eek!"

She ducked just before a stone claw swung through the air where her head had been. The claw slammed into a tree, which shuddered, tilted, and toppled over, showering us with dirt as its roots ripped out of the ground. Antonio Frühvogel-Featherington and Tweet woke with startled chirps. They launched themselves out of Calla's hair and took wing.

The birds had the right idea. "New plan," I said. "Run."

I grabbed Calla's hand, and we dashed away. The stone sphinxes bounded after us. The ground trembled with their every step. I might have had one question left, but it didn't look like I was going to get a chance to ask it.

A tail as wide as a barrel lashed toward me, arcing over the sphinx's head like a scorpion's sting. It missed by only the barest of margins as I threw myself to the side. My hair sprouted a few inches in panic.

"Help!" Calla screamed. I turned, thinking she was calling for me, but then a swarm of buzzing black-and-yellow darts flew into the sphinxes' eyes. The monsters roared and shook their heads, batting at the blinding clouds around them.

"Wasps?" I asked.

"I lent them a hand a while back," Calla panted. "Long story, no time, keep running!"

I revised my opinion—there were worse things than earthworms she could have had in her hair.

The wasps weren't going to distract the sphinxes for long. No-Nose had already figured out wasps couldn't do much against stone. It charged forward again. The other two wouldn't be far behind.

"If we can find somewhere to hide—" I began, but I didn't get any further before No-Nose gathered itself for a tremendous leap. The stone sphinx sprang, blotting out the sun as it sailed over our heads. It landed in front of us with a sound like a building collapsing and smiled its sharp-toothed smile.

"Crickets are chirping," it growled rather incongruously. I heard the others catching up behind us. "On a sultry summer night—"

An earsplitting screech rent the air, and something huge crashed into the side of the sphinx, bowling it over. "Ow!" it cried out. "That really hurt!"

"Get on!" my older sister, Jonquil, yelled from the back of her dragon as it dipped low. "Now!"

The dragon's scales glittered with iridescence, red and blue and green, as they caught the sunlight. Calla and I didn't have to be asked twice. We sprang on, careful not to put a foot through the delicate wing membrane. The two of us scrabbled at the ridge of the dragon's spine, trying to find a place to cling to as it hurled itself back into the air.

One of the trailing sphinxes took a lunge at us. It fell well short, its tail snapping off when it smashed onto the ground. The dragon swiveled its long, snakelike neck and unleashed a gout of flame at our pursuers. Heat seared my arm as its fiery breath narrowly missed its own passengers. I tried to shift out of the way and nearly fell off.

The fire engulfed the tailless sphinx while I struggled to find my balance again on the shifting scales. Dead, crisped wasps dropped from the air around it. Calla made a noise of distress in the back of her throat. I wasn't sure how I should feel. They had defended us valiantly, but . . . wasps.

The sphinx seemed little affected, its stone face merely blackened a bit. "You will escape our wrath!" it roared after us. "We will not chase you to the ends of the earth and beyond!"

"Maybe that's the truthful one," Calla suggested optimistically.

"Thanks," I said to Jonquil, more grudgingly than she deserved. "For coming to save us."

Jonquil shrugged.

Unlike both Calla's garments and my own, her clothing was immaculate in spite of whatever adventures had brought her here on dragonback. There wasn't a speck of dirt on her highly impractical gown; she was riding the dragon sidesaddle, and I've got no idea why she didn't slide right off.

Of course, you could drop her in a mud pit, and she'd come out spotless. I was certain she used some kind of magic for it. I'd always thought it pointless, wasting a spell that way, but as the oldest, she felt that there were standards she needed to uphold.

"I'm glad to be of help," she said, "but that's not why I'm here."

My brow furrowed. "You didn't come to rescue us?"

"No. You've been summoned to Skalla. The queen wants to see you immediately."

"Seriously? Now?" My stepmother's sense of timing was as maddening as ever.

Very few people could send lifesaving assistance in my direction, whether intentionally or by accident, and somehow leave me feeling miffed about it. Only my immediate family, really.

I finally managed to get a solid grip on the dragon and peered over the side to see if the sphinxes were still trying to follow us. In the field below, babies were beginning to grow out of the ground where the teeth had been planted. Weird.

"So what does she want with us?" I asked. "Did she come up with another quest before this one was even finished?"

"She doesn't want to see all three of us," Jonquil said. "Just you."

"Oh," I said, my throat going dry. "Crap." A private audience was never, ever a good sign.

Being devoured by a sphinx would have been safer.

CHAPTER TWO

A Modest Proposal

The palace of the sorceress-queen of Skalla has walls of stone with neither mortar nor join, rising smooth and unbroken to the sky. The whole thing was hewn out of the living rock of a mountain by giants, who carved the chambers and corridors over the course of a single day in exchange for whatever it is that giants like. Magical geese? Golden apples? That's what they prefer in the stories, but plus-plus-plus-size socks sound more practical.

The interior of the palace is a maze of twisty hallways and irregular rooms. The passages lead up to dizzying heights in towers that used to be crags or peaks and down to suffocating depths in dungeons that were once vast natural caverns. Outside, at the base of the mountain, the queen's expansive gardens flourish, and beyond those, spreading out in all directions in an almost perfect circle, lies the town that lives under the sway of Skalla's dread ruler. From a distance, it looks like a small wooden ring that's been tossed onto a stone peg.

The town-that-lives-under-the-sway, etc., is a remarkably

prosperous and happy one. As I trudged toward the palace, I passed well-kept homes with brightly painted doors and hordes of small children playing games that mostly involved running around and shrieking. A town protected by the sorceress-queen is a well-protected town, indeed; the last princeling looking to wage war here left with his army dispersed by dragon flame. His eyeballs remained behind, impaled on the shrubbery. Invading Skalla is unwise.

So is stealing anything from the queen's gardens. The penalty for filching her flowers is death. Well, all right, it's technically death; the sentence can be reduced by plea-bargaining. The last person to fall afoul of the law, a merchant who stole a rose, only had to send his youngest daughter to board with us for the summer. Nice girl, very popular with the furnishings—always willing to stop for a chat with a lamp or a clock. Jonquil flirted with her shamelessly (this was before my sister was engaged to Gnoflwhogir), but I think the girl ended up marrying a bear? So don't steal any plants, lest you be saddled with a bear for a son-in-law. Or some other disagreeable fate.

The gardens are beautiful, though. Even on an early autumn day, the beds were a riot of bright colors, abloom with crocuses and dahlias, cyclamen and begonias. I inhaled the delicately scented air as I meandered through. When I was a child, I lived right outside the gardens, in a little cottage. Before my mother died. Before my father remarried.

The gardens were the reason I'd asked Jonquil to drop me off outside the town instead of flying me up to the turrets on the dragon. I felt in need of calming before I met with my stepmother.

I climbed up the thousand steps that led from the base of the mountain to the entry of the palace. Tired and rather sweaty, I passed through the antechambers with their winding staircases leading to all parts of the interior. At last, I stood before the great bronze doors. Beyond them, the queen was lying in wait for me, perched on her obsidian throne.

The pair of ogres standing on guard screamed, "HALT!" Ogres are noisy in general, every footfall a stomp and every word a bellow. "WHO DARES," they thundered in unison, "TO BEG FOR AN AUDIENCE WITH THE MIGHTY QUEEN, THE FELL SORCERESS OF SKALLA, THE—"

"Hi, guys," I said. "How's it going?"

Femus crouched down—both of the ogres were a good twelve feet tall and bulging with muscles in unlikely places—and squinted the single bloodshot eye above the bridge of his nose. "MELILOT? OH, GOOD, YOU'RE HERE. SHE'S WAITING FOR YOU."

Humba and Femus had known me since I was a small child, but ogres are not known for either their visual acuity or their brainpower. Squeeze a piece of cheese and tell them you're crushing a rock in your fist, and they'll fall for it every time. The "audience with the mighty queen" speech had taken them months to memorize. They were quite nice, though, once you got to know them. Happy to get a box off a high shelf for you.

"Any idea what she wants from me?"

"NO, SORRY," Humba lisped through his tusks. "SHE HASN'T SAID."

"I suppose that's not much of a surprise."

He nodded in agreement. "HOW WAS YOUR TRIP?"

"Oh, the usual," I told him. "Tedious tasks, confusing riddles, brushes with death."

"SOUNDS LOVELY," Femus said. "MEET ANYONE TASTY?"

"Not this time, no."

His question was not intended as a euphemism. When I described the ogres as being nice, I should have added this was only true if no-eating-people rules were strictly enforced. The deal in my stepmother's kingdom was that they could have as much food as they wanted as long as it didn't talk. They tended to be a bit wistful about the taste of human flesh and were always encouraging me to give cannibalism a try. Thus far, I had declined.

"I shouldn't keep her waiting," I said. "Let me through?"

I took a steadying breath and squared my shoulders as Femus pulled open the heavy doors. As always, they made a horrendous noise as they scraped against the floor. I suspected my stepmother had designed them that way. She does love creating a certain ambiance for her visitors.

Once I was past the threshold, the doors shut behind me with a clang.

The throne room is nearly half a mile across, a huge windowless cavity in the heart of the palace lit by flickering torchlight, with only scattered pillars keeping the top of the mountain from crashing down and crushing everyone within. The obsidian throne squats in the exact center like a spider lurking in its web. My shoes clacked against the mosaic tiles that covered the floor, scenes of beasts and battles picked out in sharp, unfaded colors, blood reds and bile greens. Stories from the queen's life. Who had placed them there? Surely not the massive hands of giants.

My stepmother was waiting for me, still as the surface of a pond on a windless day, as I approached the throne. I knelt before her, my hands pressed against the cool tiles, my face to the floor.

She said nothing.

Until she spoke, I was obligated to wait at her feet. My attempts to ignore the practice during my adolescence had not gone well. Today, my only act of defiance was that I hadn't bothered to change out of my sweaty traveling clothes. My stepmother would just have to deal with the stink. She might be able to command my presence, but I could choose not to be presentable.

Minutes passed. I tried not to fidget. What did she want with me this time? It was impossible to predict what schemes might have bubbled up from the depths of her peat-bog mind. Her plans could take years to form and slowly rise, until they burst at the surface with a viscous *gloop* that left everyone around her smelling bad.

Perhaps I would be asked to bring her a dragon's smallest toenail again. Or gather starlight in a bucket, which is even harder than it sounds—it bounces right out unless you can clap a lid on fast enough. Or maybe I'd be given a task with a clear purpose for once, like slaying some monster that was threatening the townsfolk and laying waste to the turnip crop. A deadly basilisk, perhaps. I'd venture out to find it, and a magical talking fox would warn me not to stay at the brightly lit, expensive inn; he'd advise me to take a bed at the miserable, gloomy one instead. My sisters would ignore the warning, but I would listen. . . .

My knees were aching. Whatever I had expected, it wasn't to be left waiting for all eternity, head bowed, while she sat in ominous silence. I'd have bruises in the morning.

To prepare a salve for bruises, I recited in my mind, *collect arnica flowers when they are just beginning to bloom. Store them in a jar of oil for four weeks, strain out the blossoms, and combine the oil with beeswax.* By which time my bruises would have long ago faded, so there wasn't much point.

Neither of my sisters was foolish enough to ignore magical talking foxes, anyway. If a deadly basilisk was getting at the turnips, no doubt one of them was already taking care of it, and we'd have deadly-basilisk stew for supper.

I began to count the colored tiles set into the floor. *One, two, three* for the black tiles forming the backward-facing leg of a goat-headed demon. *Four, five, six* for the red tiles depicting the gore dripping from its maw. *Seven, eight, nine, ten, ele—*

"The king of Tailliz," my stepmother said, "has asked for your hand in marriage. I have agreed."

I'd been midway through the hindquarters of a hippogriff. The quivering light from the sconces gave it the illusion of motion, as if it were about to leap up and bite my hand.

My first thought was *I'll have to leave Skalla. The king of Tailliz isn't going to come and live here.*

My second thought was *If I run away, I'll need to start the moment I walk out of this room, while there's a chance it might take her by surprise. Straight out the front gate and no looking back.*

My stomach cramped into a tight knot. It was a struggle to keep my breathing even and controlled.

I looked up. "Hasn't he been married a couple of times already?" I asked with what I felt was admirable composure—only a slight tremor on the last word. "And he doesn't lack for children, the last I heard. Surely he has no great need of another bride."

I did not add that the king of Tailliz was, as far as I could remember, three times my age. That argument was unlikely to have any effect on her judgment. No argument would, not once her decision had been made. Try sometime to convince the queen she doesn't actually need the smallest toenail of a dragon. See how far you get. And then, once you've been released from your doorless tower prison, watch as your sister rides by on a grateful dragon cured of its painful hangnail and handily saves your kingdom from an invading army.

My stepmother hadn't even had the grace to look smug about it.

She always turned out to have excellent reasons for her bizarre, complicated, wheels-within-wheels plans. Although she'd never bother to tell you what they were. Or shield you from the consequences of carrying those plans out. Jonquil had been dismembered and beheaded while fighting a grootslang in the Summerlands. She's fine now. Except for the scars. And the nightmares.

"You are thinking," my stepmother said, "of King Estienne. He is king no longer. He has died after a lingering illness. His son, Gervase, sent word to ask for your hand."

That did not make me feel any better about the situation. If anything, it troubled me more. I knew something of Estienne from my occasional lessons in statecraft. Tailliz was one of a dozen or so small kingdoms on the shores of the western sea, and its aging king had been a peaceful and conservative monarch, although one of no particular note. His son was scarcely more than a name to me, a footnote on a list my tutors had made me memorize in case I ever had cause to travel west.

Which now, I supposed, I did.

She rose from the obsidian throne and walked toward an oval mirror that hung from a nearby pillar. When she tapped the glass, her reflection was replaced by a forest scene. Dense trees and underbrush and, in the far distance, a castle on an island in the sea. Tailliz?

Now that she was no longer sitting, it was permitted for me to stand as well, much to the gratitude of my throbbing knees. As a princess, I had been given years of training in grace and deportment, so I was able to lurch to my feet with only a tiny bit of a stagger.

"Why is this happening so rapidly?" I asked. "Is he that desperate for an heir? Does he know I barely count as a princess?" I wasn't even in line for the throne; that was reserved for the queen's blood relatives. Calla sometimes grumbled that this was unfair to me, but I had a hard time believing it would ever matter. I expected that my stepmother would still be ruling Skalla hundreds of years after I had perished of old age.

I thought I remembered Gervase had been a younger son at the time of his birth. Some of his siblings must have died. That didn't seem like a promising portent. What had they died of? Could I be heading into danger of some kind?

My stepmother's eyes remained fixed on the scene in the mirror. "It is possible he is unaware of your parentage. He did not ask for you by name."

"How charming. What did he request, then? Any spare girls you might happen to have lying around?"

"He specified his bride should be of age and as of yet unmarried."

"What luck," I spat, "that I qualify."

"Yes." Her reply contained no acknowledgment of my sarcasm. She did not turn from her contemplation of the forest in the glass. Her features might as well have been carved out of the same raw mountain rock as the palace. She seemed as ageless and eternal as the columns supporting the ceiling, and her expression was just as impenetrable.

He must have dispatched a messenger immediately after his coronation if I was hearing about his proposal before I'd even known Tailliz had changed rulers. I hadn't been out on the tooth quest for more than a few weeks. What was the cause of all this speed and urgency? It was odd that my stepmother had accepted so quickly. Had the messenger already been sent back with her agreement?

And without mine. My assent had been neither asked for nor required.

Since I was the queen's stepdaughter, my fate was shaped by the obligations of politics and the caprices of sorcery, not by lesser concerns like my own preferences. I'd always assumed my marriage wouldn't be of my own choosing. I'd hoped, though, that I would at least have some say in the matter.

My sister Jonquil was married to a fairy princess from the Summerlands. It was a political arrangement, accompanied by a trade agreement reducing the tariffs on honey, blood, and hen's teeth and containing a codicil that stopped the theft of babies and their replacement by changelings, an issue that had brought Skalla and the Summerlands to the brink of war. But Jonquil and Gnoflwhogir had had a chance to meet, and fight a grootslang together, and save each other's lives before the treaty was finalized.

Calla's fate sounded worse on the surface; when she turned eighteen the year before, the queen had offered her hand to all comers in a contest, as if she were a prize cow. But for all practical purposes, she'd made a love match. Technically, Liam had won the competition by crossing the world and sailing the seas and bringing back a golden feather from the undying firebird. Everyone knew, though, that Calla had liked him better than any of the others and had blatantly cheated to help him out. The queen pretended not to notice. Calla is the baby of the family and can get away with things that would see me clapped into the tower again in an instant.

My fate, it appeared, was to be shipped off to some complete stranger, with no opportunity to make my own choice. As usual, I was about to be stuck with the worst of three bad deals.

I had my suspicions as to why things tended to turn out that way. And just where I stood in my stepmother's regard. I was an afterthought. I always had been. At best, a disappointment. At worst, an irrelevancy.

The middle child. The only one with no blood relationship to the queen; when she took my father as her consort, the daughter from his previous marriage came along as part of the bargain. I was the least magical of her three children. Not so enchanted, or enchanting, as Calla, so beloved by nature's creatures that mice do her sewing and raccoons wash her dishes. Not so powerful in spell craft as Jonquil, who turned herself into a lake once when she was courting Gnoflwhogir. A whole lake. With ducks. Where did the ducks come from, I ask you?

When I tried to turn into a lake, I only managed to transform myself into a puddle. That was after hours of effort that left my ears ringing. It goes without saying I failed to produce any waterfowl. And I doubted anything would ever strengthen my power—not the Golden Key, or True Love's First Kiss, or a hair plucked from a devil's tail. A sow's ear will not become a silk purse no matter how much effort goes into the sewing. My greatest achievement as a sorceress thus far was making my hair grow, which, as you might imagine, has limited utility. But I was burdened with a stepmother who routinely performed six impossible acts before breakfast and had little patience for those who couldn't. In the face of that unattainable standard, I'd only ever had two options: Try to live up to it, and fail. Or try to rebel against it, and fail even harder.

My stepmother moved away from the mirror and reached over to cup my chin with her fingers, turning my head until her storm-cloud-dark eyes met mine.

It took every ounce of my self-control not to flinch. I'm not sure what shocked me more—her touching me or her meeting my gaze. She didn't generally do either. She seldom looked at people. She looked around them, above them, and very often through them, her attention fixed on matters far beyond their petty understanding.

If there was a time, during my childhood, when I'd longed for her to hug me, that feeling had withered away years before. Now I mostly hoped she would leave me alone. Possibly after first telling me I was as capable and worthy as my sisters. And as long as I was imagining the preposterous, maybe then she'd grant me three wishes and a magic porridge pot.

"Melilot," she said. "I would like you to trust me."

I was unable to stifle a short nervous laugh.

Five heartbeats passed before she released my chin. Her eyes slid away from mine, which honestly came as a relief.

Was she serious?

I couldn't afford to trust her. Not when Jonquil still had scars circling her neck and joints, ragged marks that never faded. Not with my stepmother's history of poisoning, of trickery, of dark and dangerous magic.

My stepmother, queen of Skalla and Sorceress of the Mountain, had been on that black burnished throne for a long, long time. Threats to her kingdom and impediments to her rule were dealt with. Pawns were put at risk whenever necessary. After the tower, I had tried to accept being a pawn for fear that if I did not, she might begin to see me as an impediment.

My trust had never been required by her before. I wondered why she was asking for it now.

"If you told me why you were sending me off," I said to my stepmother, "if you told me anything, for once, then I might believe it wasn't simply because you can't stand the sight of me."

"And what would I tell you? I see a thousand thousand futures where you go and a thousand thousand futures where you do not. To speak of the one I desire most is to well-nigh guarantee it will never come to pass."

"A very convenient excuse for not saying anything."

"Yes."

I sighed. There would be no answer. I didn't know why I'd tried. "Will that be all, or did you want something else of me? Perhaps you need a pin fetched from the bottom of the ocean or a hundred lost pearls gathered in a night?"

She gestured my dismissal. I turned and walked off, all the long way across the throne room and out through the great bronze doors. Humba and Femus, seeing the anger plain on my face, said nothing as I tried to slam the doors behind me. They weighed a quarter ton together, so I was only able to push hard enough to produce a quiet thump. Even the horrible squeal sounded muffled. I am no ogre.

Senseless rage would do me no good. I clenched my teeth until my breathing slowed, and I was able to think rationally about what was happening.

If I was going to run, this was the time. Maybe I could make a go of it, at least for a while. I might stumble across a cave full of robbers or a cottage full of dwarves and keep house for them in exchange for a place to stay. Which didn't strike me as being a wonderful life, but there was a chance I wouldn't utterly hate it. I was no stranger to cleaning up messes—it was a useful habit in a place where Calla's helpful animals were constantly rampaging through on one errand or another. It sounds cute until you find what the rats have left on your floor and the doves have left on your bedsheets.

But even if I found somewhere to hide, how long would it be before my stepmother showed up with a clever disguise and a shiny red apple? I'd probably end up lying in a glass coffin until the trump of doom. Or at best, I'd find myself engaged to a different prince. One with a tendency toward necrophilia. The coffin kissers are the worst.

The queen had tamed giants and destroyed armies. I doubted it would take an eternity for her to track me down. Running away would only be putting off my fate, not escaping it.

Instead of heading down the thousand steps to the town, I went up to my room to prepare for the journey to Tailliz.

· CHAPTER THREE

My Siblings Offer Marital Advice

"If there's a locked room King Gervase doesn't want you to look at," Jonquil said, raising her voice to be heard over the cacophony of chirps, hisses, and yips, "you might want to stay out of it until we're over there for a visit."

"Wrong!" declared her wife, Gnoflwhogir. "Open the door immediately. Open every door! Find his secrets, steal his treasures, drink his wine!"

Jonquil rolled her eyes. "Don't expect a quick rescue, is all I'm saying."

"I'm not going to need a—"

"Tailliz is too far for me to get there right away," she went on as if I hadn't spoken, "even on dragonback. And Mother never lends me the seven-league boots. But if you do the exact opposite of anything my wife tells you, there's a chance you might lead a quiet life."

Gnoflwhogir snorted, succinctly expressing her contempt for the very concept of a quiet life, and rolled off the bed. She landed with a thump on the pile of rejected dresses that Liam,

Calla, and Calla's swarm of furred and feathery animal friends had tossed out of my closet and onto the floor. A couple of chipmunks who'd nearly been crushed by Gnoflwhogir's sudden drop scurried into a corner and chittered at her angrily.

Fairies can be difficult to deal with, although I'm sure they find mortals similarly frustrating. The fae folk consider logic, reason, and self-restraint about as appealing as a pile of dead bugs. Less so, come to think of it, since fairies have been known to make lovely dresses out of butterfly wings. This notorious aversion to common sense may explain their propensities for tooth buying, child stealing, ear collecting, and so on.

Jonquil was often driven to distraction by Gnoflwhogir's impetuousness, while Gnoflwhogir regarded Jonquil as rather unadventurous. They had fierce arguments every now and again, and I'd needed to comfort Jonquil in the aftermath more than once. Nonetheless, the magnetism that had locked their gazes together when they first met had never lessened. Possibly it helped that Gnoflwhogir was six feet tall and muscled to match, with hair the color of jade, flawless skin a few shades lighter, and the large, reflective eyes of a nocturnal predator. She always looked like she was about to pounce on you, whether to bite you or give you a kiss. Jonquil was equally as lovely, for that matter—though I suspected Gnoflwhogir admired Jonquil's dismemberment scars even more than her figure, particularly since Jonquil had acquired them while keeping the grootslang from chomping on her spouse-to-be.

As soon as my sisters and their spouses heard about my engagement, they'd come to my room. It hadn't taken long for them to get word—the throne room is too big to keep entirely free of insects, and a humble ant had overheard everything that passed. Ants are terrible gossips. Calla knew about the proposal before I was all the way up the stairs, and she promptly shared the news with Liam, Jonquil, and Gnoflwhogir.

By the time the late afternoon sunlight was slanting through my bedroom window, the four of them, along with a horde of weasels and bluebirds and squirrels, had assembled to help me gather items for my trousseau. The floor was a crush of small creatures ferrying lace gloves and silk scarves, while birds fluttered back and forth with earrings in their beaks. I was sorting through my own underthings, since that wasn't a task I wished to leave to a random squirrel. Squirrels have awful taste; they're as bad as magpies—the shinier it is, the better. If I let them choose it, my lingerie would be nothing but sequins. As it was, I'd need to double-check the shoes that night to make sure I was leaving with a few pieces of practical footwear and not a rodent-selected collection of silver, ruby, and glass confections.

At least the squirrels weren't peppering me with unnecessary advice. My relatives were failing to observe the same courtesy.

"If he comes to you only in the dark, and you wonder if you've married some kind of terrible beast, never try to get a look at his face," Jonquil told me.

"I know," I said.

"No fetching a candle while he's asleep, it'll just end in tears."

"And," Calla began, "if it turns out that he *is* some kind of terrible beast—"

"I know!" A tiny hedgehog was taking a nap in my underwear drawer, so I delicately removed it and handed it over to her.

"—then remember you don't have to put up with any crap from him," she continued without pause as she slipped the hedgehog into her hair, where it joined a family of wriggling dormice. Animals never poop in her hair, by the way, no matter how many of them are living there. They reserve that for other places. Like my underwear drawer. "You can break whatever his curse is without being a doormat," she said. "Always stand up for yourself."

I sat down heavily on the bed. "That's not what I'm worried about."

"What are you worried about, then?" Jonquil asked. "Spinning wheels? Flax stalks? Getting stuck to a goose? If you do your best not to touch anything suspicious—"

"Touch everything suspicious!" Gnoflwhogir urged, baring a grin full of needle-sharp teeth. "Kill anyone who tries to stop you!" Her fingers reached for the great claymore she usually kept strapped to her back, but she hadn't brought the sword to my bedroom. Her hand dropped, brushing fondly across her necklace of left ears instead. They looked very much like dried apricots. "Stab yourself with every spindle," she advised me. "Put your hand on every goose. Be bold, be bold!"

"But not too bold," Jonquil cautioned, frowning.

Lest that your heart's blood should run cold, I mentally recited—the traditional instruction given to women who might be about to marry murderous villains. "For goodness' sake, Jonquil, I'm aware of the common difficulties new brides face." Why was she reminding me of poems I already knew by heart? Why was she warning me about overly adhesive geese? My stepmother had given me the same practical education as my sisters. "I know what to do if my husband-to-be is invisible, or quadrupedal, or has a rotting pile of maidens' corpses in his castle."

"None of that will happen in Tailliz, hen," Liam said, speaking for the first time. He came from Ecossia, and a trace of his homeland's accent lingered in his gently rolled *r*'s and the soft glottal stops of his final *t*'s. "Well, maybe the pile of bodies, but I doubt it. Tailliz hasn't any magic to speak of. Not a single sorcerer's been born there in over a century." He tucked another dress into the carved wooden chest. The ferret lurking inside busily folded it up. "There's a talking lion who's counseled the royal family for generations, and I've heard rumors about odd things in the woods. But no more than that."

"Odd things in the woods?" I asked.

He shrugged. "There's been talk of animals behaving strangely. And some that aren't natural. Misshapen. At least, there was talk of it a few years ago. I've not been out that way in a while."

Calla looked concerned at the thought of unnatural animals. I was concerned myself, although not for the same reasons. I'd been on enough quests to know that unreliable, offhand rumors can turn out to be of crucial importance.

Liam was the best informed of any of us about the western kingdoms. Ecossia is an island country not far across the straits from Tailliz. It's a wild land of hills and bogs, best known for strange enchantments, fierce warriors, and fluffy sheep. He had the characteristic Ecossic look to him—red-orange hair, a strong chin, and freckles, along with paler skin than anyone of Skallan heritage—but he was neither an enchanter nor a warrior. Nor was he a sheep, obviously.

He was also not, I suspected, the minor Ecossic prince he'd claimed to be when he came seeking Calla's hand. Based on his knowledge of fabric and couture, my best guess was that he'd been a tailor. He made my sister happy, though, and that was what mattered. Besides, his expertise ensured there was a judicious eye on the dresses going into my trousseau.

Liam handed a beribboned blue ball gown to a trio of snakes, who grabbed it with their mouths and dragged it awkwardly across the floor to the chest. "So what are you worried about, then?" he asked.

I wandered over to the window and placed my hands on the sill, squinting at the dying daylight. Surprisingly, the room behind me went quiet, the mice and hamsters silencing their squeaks and the flutter of wings dying down as the birds settled themselves on curtain rods or bedposts.

They were probably expecting me to express my feelings by bursting into song, as Calla sometimes did. Which meant they were going to be sorely disappointed. I have yet to improvise a stirring ballad on a moment's notice.

"What if I go all the way there and I don't like him?" I said.

"Or what if he doesn't like me? What if I can't stand living in Tailliz and miss being here every single minute for the rest of my life?"

The sun was setting behind the crags of the western range, turning the sky pink and gold. The long, low clouds were tinged with the same colors. I had seen this same view, or one very much like it, nearly every night I was home since I'd moved to the palace with my father years ago. Even when I'd been far away—whether out traveling or locked in a lonely tower—this had always been what I'd returned to when the quest was over or the punishment was done. The mountain range, seen through a bell-shaped window set in the smooth, dark wall of a chamber carved by giants. The place where I lived, just across the hall from my sisters.

My breath was knocked out of me in a single, involuntary cry as Jonquil and Calla simultaneously embraced me on both sides.

"No matter what happens, you can come here to visit for as long as you want," Jonquil said. "And we'll go out there. All the time. I'll steal the seven-league boots if I have to."

"And if you don't like him," Calla added, "or if he's such an oaf that he doesn't like you, then tell him he can take his crown and shove it."

"Yes!" Gnoflwhogir shouted from the floor, one pointed ear twitching excitedly. "Straight up his ass! Force it in yourself if he refuses!"

I grinned once I got my breath back. "I doubt the queen would approve of that."

"You've said no to her before." Calla wasn't grinning. She looked as serious as I'd ever seen her. My own smile slipped off my face. "You're practically the only one who ever has."

"And I got locked up for my trouble." I shook my head. "She won't let me get away with something like that again."

"It might not turn out badly," Calla said. "She's not as heartless as she wants everyone to believe. You never seem to realize that."

Jonquil made a noise of assent. "I've always thought it's how she keeps herself on the throne. She tries to be so terrifying that no one will dare to challenge her."

I'd heard them make this argument before. To me, it seemed like a distinction without a difference. "So you're saying she isn't completely merciless. She just acts completely merciless at all times."

"She doesn't, though. Not always," Calla said. "You were in the tower, but here you are now, walking free. Unpoisoned, unensorcelled, and unharmed. Maybe you could say no again, if you wanted to. If you needed to."

"Could I?" I asked. "Without an even worse result? Are you certain of that?"

She hesitated. While she was deciding on her reply, I backed out of my sisters' embrace. They reluctantly let me go.

The noise and bustle in the room resumed. I pretended to once again become fascinated by the contents of my underwear drawer. It was full of spiders now. I hoped they had better taste than squirrels.

It was easy enough for Calla to tell me to defy the queen. She got what she wanted without needing to. And Jonquil was too dutiful to refuse any request her mother made of her. Neither of them had ever put their foot down and said, "Enough. I won't. No."

All three of us had suffered in the queen's service—Jonquil by far the most. If it hadn't been for fairy magic fueled by Gnoflwhogir's burgeoning affection, my older sister would still be in bloody pieces strewn across the grassy hillocks of the Summerlands. But neither of my sisters had ever faced the queen's direct and personal wrath.

I'd taken what had happened to me as a warning. A year and

a day of imprisonment was a light sentence by her standards. All I'd had to face was the loneliness. The boredom. The humiliation when my misguided attempt at escape had only proved that my judgment was as poor as she'd always thought. The self-loathing I'd felt after watching someone fall, down and down and down, into the piercing thorns of the rosebushes I had grown. Self-loathing because I should have felt anguish and horror when the thorns stabbed out his eyes, but I hadn't.

And of course, I'd also had to face the knowledge that my refusal to obey my stepmother's commands had ultimately been pointless. That I was merely a cog in her machine. One she'd handily replaced when I proved defective. After she'd clapped me in the tower for my insubordination, she'd simply assigned my task to Jonquil, who completed it more quickly and easily than I ever could. My defiance meant nothing to my stepmother because I meant nothing to her. She'd made it plain she could snuff me out like a candle in a hurricane whenever she wished.

Calla believed my fears of poisoned apples and glass coffins were overblown. That my previous punishment had been light not because it was meant as a warning but because the queen regarded me as her daughter and wished me no harm. But even Calla wouldn't go so far as to say my fears had no basis whatsoever.

"It's possible that you'll like him, you know," Jonquil said. "Gervase."

Possible, yes, but it wasn't anything I could count on. "I suppose."

"Kill Gervase in his sleep," Gnoflwhogir muttered from the carpet. A rabbit sniffed at her necklace of ears, wrinkled its nose, and moved on.

"Or that you'll like Tailliz," my stepsister continued, trying to ignore her wife.

"Slice his throat." Ignoring Gnoflwhogir was difficult. "Drip poison in his ear."

"Perhaps you'll like it more than here," Jonquil tried once again.

I gave up on trying to shake the spiders out of one of my lacier pieces and shut the drawer. "So far all I've heard is that it's magically backward and haunted by unnatural creatures. Oh, and they take advice from a talking lion. Is the lion nice?"

"No," said Liam.

"You can see why my enthusiasm isn't exactly unbounded."

"It can't possibly have nothing whatsoever to recommend it, can it?" Calla turned to Liam in appeal. "Surely you know something worthwhile about Tailliz. Or Gervase."

He pondered for a moment before he answered. "It's a lovely country, Tailliz," he said at last. "Forests full of massive trees, fifty times your height, so wide at the base a dozen people couldn't clasp hands around them. And Gervase is well liked, both in Tailliz and elsewhere. He was engaged to an Ecossic lady, before . . ." Liam's voice trailed off. I assumed he meant before Gervase broke it off to send a proposal in my direction. The situation had no doubt changed now that Gervase was king rather than umpteenth in line to the throne.

How, I wondered, was his previous betrothed feeling tonight? Most likely, no one had asked her. With a throne in the offing, it mattered very little how she felt, or how I felt, or even how Gervase felt.

"Anyhow," Liam continued, "there aren't stories of him kidnapping women to make them spin straw into gold. Or drowning any wee bairns prophesied to marry someone inconvenient. He likes hunting, I think. I've heard he has a healthy stable of horses and a good pack of dogs." His brow creased as he considered, and then he reached in his pocket and took out a slender sewing needle and a spool of silk thread. He held them out to me. "Here. You should take these. Keep them on you if you can."

I looked at them in confusion. "In case my clothing tears during a hunt?"

He shook his head. "No. You'll need them if you're ever attacked by wolves."

It's easy to harbor the illusion that Liam is the normal one in the family, until you talk to him for more than five minutes. I took the needle and thread.

I still didn't have much to go on regarding Tailliz and Gervase. Tall trees and a king fond of hunting. I supposed it was conceivable that the two of us would get along. Hunting wasn't my favorite activity, but I knew enough about it that he wouldn't think I was a complete ignoramus. My mother and father had served as attending physicians at more than a few hunts; it's amazing how many accidents can happen when an angry boar confronts a skittish horse.

Perhaps I wouldn't mind living there. The decision to go might have been taken out of my hands, but once I was out from under my stepmother's thumb, maybe I'd find a way to make a fresh start. Forge my own path at last.

"He can't be the worst person in the world if he likes horses and dogs. I guess I'll find out the rest soon enough." I plucked a satin chemise out of the paws of a badger and edged my way around the other furry creatures crisscrossing the floor. "Is there still room for this in the chest?"

There wasn't a great chance I'd find happiness in Tailliz. But a sliver of hope is better than no hope at all.

PART II

HOW TO GET LOST IN THE WOODS

CHAPTER FOUR

Going Places Is Bad, and You Shouldn't Do It

The thing you're never told about traveling is that it's horrible. Uncomfortable, dangerous, smelly, and itchy.

My pumpkin turned carriage lurched violently, jouncing its way over another bump. A freezing draft whistled straight through the unglazed window, the cold air numbing my face. I shivered in my cloak and drew up the riding hood. It was a good cloak, my favorite—thick wool dyed a cheerful scarlet—but it didn't do much to ward off the chill.

When the weak late-autumn sun bothered to peek out from behind the clouds, little of its light filtered down to the forest floor. The road wound through a dense wood. Dark, gnarled trunks rose from a thick mat of dropped needles and dead leaves gone black with damp. Occasionally one of the great trees Liam had spoken of drifted by, an enormous tower of shaggy red bark that rose above the forest canopy like a pillar holding up the sky. We had to be in Tailliz now, or close to it. A solid month after setting out from Skalla, we were finally nearing our destination.

A drizzle started pattering down from the gray clouds. Again.

Leaning toward the window, I tried for the fourth time that day to begin a conversation. "How much longer until we get to the castle, do you think?"

The unconvincing facsimile of a guard riding alongside the carriage stared off into the middle distance, while his (much more convincing) facsimile of a horse plodded stolidly onward. Only a few telltale signs, like rounded ears, gave away that the horse wasn't really a horse, but no one would mistake the enameled flesh and rough-hewn features of the guard for anything human. His face looked like someone had attacked a chunk of ivory with a chisel.

For a full minute, the guard remained as speechless as the scrimshaw carving he resembled. Then at long last he muttered, "Don't know."

I made another attempt. "I'm looking forward to a warm bed. And a bath. I know you don't sleep, but do you bathe? I mean, I imagine you're used to a good going over with a toothbrush every night and morning, but—"

The carriage clattered over a particularly jarring dip in the road. My teeth clacked together sharply. I nearly bit my tongue. I was grateful to Jonquil for enchanting the pumpkin, but she had neglected to make it well sprung. It rattled me around like dice in a cup every time a wheel dropped into a rut.

I don't hate nature. I like the outdoors. Some of it. In limited doses. After journeying east of the sun and west of the moon on my stepmother's orders, I have seen vistas that defy the imagination with their grandeur. I have stood on a high, windswept cliff top so close to the stars that I could see them performing the joyous pirouettes and cartwheels that make them twinkle. I have descended into a cave so deep I could hear the buried gemstones singing their slow, thrumming songs. I have trudged across cotton-candy clouds to giants' castles, swum up waterfalls, and trekked over the glaring white plain of trackless ice that stretches across the rooftop of the world.

But however beautiful a place might be, that doesn't necessarily mean you'd want to spend the night there. I am not good at sleeping in uncomfortable conditions; I toss and turn on anything even slightly hard or lumpy. The plain of ice was miserable. I hardly got any sleep at all, and then as an added, special agony, I woke up every day with my hair frozen to the ground. Nothing says "Good morning!" like a chunk of your hair ripping free from your scalp when you sit up.

The trip to Tailliz wasn't as bad as that. During the day, the pumpkin coach kept the rain off me. My poor driver and guards were soaked whenever there was a downpour, and we got caught in more than one during the monthlong journey. I'm not sure they cared, since they'd been grown out of the teeth Calla's birds had sown. I doubt anyone who used to live in a mouth is fussy about getting wet.

As usual, my main source of discomfort was the nights. The lands between Skalla and Tailliz were wild and unsettled, as you might have guessed from the state of the roads. We came across exactly two villages along the way. Neither was large enough to have an inn, but both times we were allowed to sleep in a barn provided by a terrified but well-paid farmer. Every other night, I'd either tried to doze off while sitting bolt upright in the too-narrow coach or taken my chances in the wilderness. Needless to say, whenever I decided on camping, it rained. My longing for a good night's sleep had grown desperate. And the less said about the bathroom arrangements, the better. You'd think that after all the questing, I'd have gotten used to it at some point, but I never did. Even without frozen hair, each new venture into the unknown was a fresh horror of wet clothing, restless nights, and shitting in the great outdoors.

It would have taken scarcely any time to get to Tailliz using the seven-league boots, by the way. But there was only one pair of those in Skalla, which meant the queen reserved them for the most important of endeavors. My marriage, apparently, did not qualify.

So it wasn't terribly surprising that as we neared the end of our journey, juddering through the mighty forests Liam had described, I was in a thoroughly bad mood.

He'd been right about the trees, though. If anything, he'd failed to capture their magnificence. Over the past week of travel, a scrubby woodland had transformed into a close-packed forest, and then one morning the great trees had begun to appear, their trunks stretching into the distant sky. Far up in their heights, sprays of branches that must have been as broad across as houses dwindled into tiny circles of green against a cloudy gray background. I wondered how much damage they would do if they ever went walking. Even ordinary trees can defeat evil wizards who dare to engage in unsustainable logging practices, and a king in Ecossia famously lost both his throne and his life when the local woods started wandering around.

"Do you think we've crossed the border into Tailliz yet?" I shouted out the window at the guard, who had drifted a bit farther from the carriage. Possibly he had done so to get away from my efforts at starting a discussion. A noncommittal grunt answered me.

"The castle might only be a few hours from here," I continued. "Or perhaps a day? Not another week, I hope. One more week without a proper bath and they'll smell me coming when we're twenty miles off."

This time I received no reply whatsoever. I shrank back on my hard wooden seat. Perhaps I should have recruited an ogre or a river hag to join my guard. Anyone willing to have a conversation. I wasn't sure why the teeth found talking such a chore. You'd think that teeth would be more prone to chattering.

But then, what did I know about teeth? Perhaps they disliked dampness as much as I did, and they weren't feeling talkative because they'd spent the entire journey wet and miserable.

Maybe they longed for nothing but dry silence and had hated being teeth in the first place. No one, I imagined, ever asked for their teeth's opinion on the subject before growing them in their mouths.

I leaned partway out the window to ask if he remembered being a tooth, if he'd been a contented tooth, but before I could, something moving too fast for me to see it ripped my guard off his horse. An instant later, there was a wet crunch.

He hadn't had time to scream.

The carriage shuddered as something slammed into its side, toppling me back inside before I had a chance to figure out what was going on. My head hit the wall with a crack. I could hear the horses shrieking out in front and the fluttering and cawing of local birds fleeing the area. I had no idea what was happening. Trolls? Robbers?

Unnatural creatures in the woods?

More than ever, I regretted bringing only the teeth along as guards. Teeth are tough, as you probably know if you've ever been bitten. But there are tougher creatures in the world. And transfigurations have vulnerabilities. They tend to lapse back into their original forms if they're damaged enough.

Speaking of which, a misty glow was limning the inside of the carriage. It grew brighter as another slam shook the vehicle. Something wooden snapped and broke. The enchantment wasn't meant to stand up to this kind of punishment. If I didn't get out quickly, I'd find myself trapped inside a pumpkin shell—or worse. Transformation spells can go haywire when they break. It could mistakenly try to revert the coach's contents along with the coach. Myself included. I had no desire to spend the rest of my days as a pumpkin seed.

My surroundings were already beginning to shrink and turn an alarming shade of orange. I pushed at the door handle, which turned slick and pulpy under my hand. Caught halfway between a door and a vegetable, it was too solid to break but too pumpkiny to open. The walls were closing in, threatening to crush and smother me in pumpkin flesh before the spell even had a chance to transmogrify me. The window was too small to squeeze through by then, no bigger than a clenched fist.

My hair had grown to nearly waist length while I hunted for an escape, bursting out from my head and filling the shrinking space with brown curls. I could feel it getting tangled in seeds and stringy fibers. In a panic, I threw my whole body at the door, once and then again. On the third blow, it shattered. I tumbled out onto the ground, landing in an awkward splay on the wet leaves. Behind me, the carriage collapsed into a mangled pile of skin and pulp.

Rain dampened my cloak. A spray of broken teeth fanned out in front of me on the ground. Fragments of molars, bicuspids, and incisors—the remnants of my guards. I hoped they'd been as insensible to pain as the pumpkin-carriage and hadn't felt a thing. Out of the corner of my eye, I saw a handful of mice scurrying off into the woods—the horses, too, had returned to their original state.

Beyond them, something shifted on the ground. A paw the size of an ogre's mallet, covered in dark gray fur.

I spat a leaf out of my mouth and scrambled to get my feet back under me. Then I thought better of it and slowed my movements, not wanting to look like prey.

I raised my eyes to get a look at what had slaughtered my guards and discovered a creature with the low-slung body of a wolf—if wolves were the size of bison. Or had eight legs. Too many black, lidless eyes were crowded onto its face. Two hairy appendages extended from the sides of its canine muzzle. They twitched toward me. It snarled, lips curling to reveal a pair of curved fangs dripping with strings of dark, viscous fluid.

Behind it there were two more, and others were stalking in from the sides. Half a dozen? More? There were probably some I couldn't see.

The rain fell harder, fat droplets trickling from the canopy of branches overhanging the road. Water slid down my face and neck. My panicked hair growth had knocked my hood off. I didn't reach up to pull it on. Better to get wet than risk setting them off.

Whatever they were. "I've seen wolf spiders before," I whispered, "but you're the first spider wolves."

There are rules about this sort of thing. There's always a way to prevail, by being kind or clever or humble or brave. You can guess the answer to a sphinx's riddle, outwit an ogre, bargain with a witch. But this was a creature I'd never heard of, not in all my travels. I was at a complete loss. And this time, I wasn't likely to get three guesses to figure it out.

The monster nearest to me growled and scuttled closer. The motion was unnerving. Nothing that looks like a wolf should scuttle. I took an involuntary step back, my foot landing with a squish in the smashed vegetable mess that used to be a carriage.

"Nice, uh, doggie spider?" I tried. "Spoggie? Who's a good spoggie?" It didn't stop growling. The spiny hairs on its back stiffened like the hackles of an enraged dog. Calla would have had them all gazing at her adoringly by this time, eating pumpkin seeds out of her hand.

I slowly backed away, around the pumpkin and past the tree line, hoping they might lose interest once I was hidden from sight by the underbrush. Dead, damp plant matter squelched under my shoes. The spider wolves followed, slinking around the trees, low rumbles and high-pitched chitters emanating from their throats in eerie concert. I tripped and stumbled over the uneven ground, just catching myself before I fell.

One of them skittered nearer, its fangs protruding from its jaw, too large for its mouth. "My," I said, "what big teeth you have."

Leaving the road had been a bad idea. In my fright, I had forgotten that it's dangerous to stray from your path, into the unknown. Hemmed in by tangles and thickets, I'd only made it that much harder to run.

Trying to be like Calla hadn't worked. Jonquil, I imagined, would simply have done her lake trick. That was worth a try. Assuming the creatures were willing to stare at me menacingly for a few hours while I made the attempt.

Become water, I told myself. *Become cool, clear, rippling, wet. Do not think. Be. Water does not think. Water does not—*

The spider wolf leapt for my throat.

Traveling is horrible. Never let anyone tell you otherwise.

CHAPTER FIVE

The Mysterious Masked Men

I raised my arms in a futile effort to ward off the attack, and I was bracing myself for the agony of fangs piercing my flesh when a masked man in green grabbed the leaping spider wolf by the leg and slammed it into the ground.

It yowled. Or at least it did until he followed that up with a punch to its head that resounded with the sharp crack of breaking bone.

My mouth dropped open, and I stood there blinking in shock.

The man's flame-red hair and pale skin, visible below the green domino mask, put me in mind of my brother-in-law, Liam. Who was this? Where had he come from?

"I could use some help here!" he shouted into the woods as another spider wolf jumped onto his back. Four pairs of claws ripped through his shirt, drawing blood.

"Can you hold it still, Sam?" another voice called out in reply. Both of them had accents like Liam's, too. "Clem almost has a shot!"

"Hold it still," the man in green muttered. He twisted around to make a grab for the monster's body. "Maybe I should wrap it up and put a wee bow on it, too."

Its fangs snapped at his face. They missed by only a fraction of an inch. His muscles bulged with strain as he struggled to hold the creature off. This was a beast capable of ripping the heads off my bone-solid, enamel-coated guards. I had trouble believing any ordinary person stood much of a chance against it.

Nonetheless, he somehow managed to wrap his arms around it. He kept it pinned long enough for an arrow to come whistling out of the woods and bury itself in the monster's ear.

In the meantime, I had done absolutely nothing but stand there, astonished. I pulled myself out of my paralysis as he dropped the creature to the ground. Behind him, another spider wolf poised to spring.

"Hey, ugly!" I shouted, scooping up a pile of rotting leaves and needles from the forest floor. It whipped its head around, and I hurled them at its face. It flinched back, dirt and detritus showering its unblinking eyes. That distracted it sufficiently for my rescuer—Sam, I supposed—to grab it around the throat and squeeze.

"Thanks." He flashed me a brilliant smile. The spider wolf thrashed beneath him.

"I should thank *you*!" I winced as its claws pierced his flesh. The green shirt was rapidly darkening with blood. I cast about for a better weapon than a pile of leaves—a rock, a fallen branch, anything.

Several other spider wolves were lying prone and bloodied nearby, most of them pincushioned with arrows. Two more masked men in green backed toward me, one with a sword at the ready and one with an arrow nocked in a bow. Both were as redheaded as my rescuer. Between the masks and the hair, I was having difficulty telling them apart. The swordsman walked with a slight limp. One leg of his breeches was streaked with fresh blood at the knee.

I picked up the biggest stick I could find. The remaining spider wolves—more than I would have liked—prowled in a wide circle around us, weaving between the trees. They slunk low, crawling in twitchy fits and starts in their unsettling insectile way.

"What are they doing?" I asked.

"Keekin' at us till we bolt," said the one with the bow.

"I'm sorry, what?"

"They're waiting for us to break and run," explained the one with the bloody knee. "We'll be easier to pick off that way. We've seen them do this before."

I bit my lower lip in worry. That wasn't promising. It might mean the creatures were as intelligent as they were vicious.

Sam dropped the spider wolf he'd been throttling and joined our small group. "Where's Harry?" he asked, his eyes on the circling monsters.

"He's aff tae git th' ithers," his bow-wielding friend replied. "They'll turn up soon. Mibbie."

"No matter how fast he runs," Sam said, "it'll take too much time."

"Do you have a weapon?" I asked, prepared to offer the stick I held clenched in my shaking hands. He was likely to do more good with it than I would.

He shook his head. "No. But I'm brilliant with my fists."

"If you're sure." I was dubious. He was clearly strong—inhumanly strong if he was able to wrestle these monsters and win—but he wasn't invulnerable. I glanced at his shredded, bloodied shirt, wondering how much longer he could last.

One of the spider wolves ventured closer and was nearly beheaded for its trouble when the swordsman took a swing at it. It retreated, growling.

"Should we try to pick off a few?" Bloody Knee asked, dropping into a readied stance.

The bowman—Clem if I'd heard right—grimaced. "If they git crabbit enough, they'll a' charge in at wance."

"Maybe so," Bloody Knee said. "But they're going to do that soon either way."

Sam turned to me. "Can you even the odds? That piece of wood—what can you do with it?"

"Hit them on the head?" I said, puzzled.

"Could you maybe . . . turn it into an enchanted spear?" he asked. "Or make it fly and fight on its own? Or transform it into a wooden man, with mighty oaken fists?"

I took a half step back in sheer surprise. The answers were, in order: no, definitely not, and maybe—if I had a year's time and a lot more luck animating plant matter than I'd ever had before. I narrowed my eyes. "What makes you think I can do any of that?"

"You're a sorceress, aren't you?"

I was about to reply that I wasn't a very good sorceress and ask how he knew I was a sorceress in the first place when I was cut off by the twanging of a bow. Another of the beasts had prowled closer. Clem's arrow had pierced its vitals before I'd noticed it was coming.

Who were these people?

Clem took no more than a moment to survey his work. "Sam," he said, "she cannae dae it. She's nae th' princess."

"Of course she is," Sam argued back. "Who else could she be?"

"Princesses dinnae travel alone, oan foot, wi' thair locks a' in a fankle."

I wasn't sure what a fankle was, but I didn't think he was giving my hair a compliment. "I've been on the road a long time," I muttered. "And it's been a very hard day."

"We can figure out who she is later," Bloody Knee said tightly.

"Although if she's the savior who's supposed to rescue Tailliz from peril, I'm guessing she'd have done more than throw a few wet leaves."

If I was the *what* who was supposed to *what*?

"We have," he continued, "more urgent matters to deal with."

He motioned his head toward the spider wolves. They had given up on trying to make us run. Instead of circling, they crouched down, the joints of their spidery legs sticking up above their backs. Dozens of gleaming black eyes fixed on us. A low, constant growl came from all around, making the hairs on the back of my neck stand up.

Clem loosed an arrow as they lunged for us. "Och, bugger m—" he began, but they were at our throats before he could finish.

Everything became a dizzying frenzy of motion. One of the monsters stumbled and dropped, an arrow in its throat. A sword flashed to my right, trailing dark blood as it carved deadly arcs through the air. Sam was suddenly in front of me, snatching two spider wolves out of the air midleap, one in each hand, and smashing them to the ground. A third sailed past him, though, its jaws wide and aimed at my face. Inside its mouth, sharp, chitinous ridges clicked together in anticipation.

I shoved the branch down its throat.

Black liquid bubbled up in its mouth. It made a strangled gagging noise as it crashed into me. Its momentum carried it forward, knocking me flat on my back. The air was forced out of my lungs. I struggled to breathe while the hairy limbs at the sides of the creature's muzzle scrabbled at my face, and its four front paws raked my shoulders and sides, ripping gouges in my flesh. Then it shuddered and lay still.

The end of my stick was poking out of its skull. It had been driven through by the creature's own immense weight. The weight that was, at that moment, pinning me to the ground, making me an easy target for the next one to come.

As I strove to wriggle out from under it, something lifted the monster off me and tossed it to the side. I looked up to see Sam smiling. He reached a hand out to help me up.

"Thanks," I said, hauling myself to my feet. "Again."

"We're making a habit of rescuing each—"

The rest of what he was going to say was lost in a pained bellow as Sam went down under a torrent of fur and claws and fangs. I screamed. The attacking monsters were a tangle of limbs. How many were there? Four? Five? This time, I didn't even have a few wet leaves.

As I flailed uselessly at one of the beasts with my fists, I saw a blur at the edge of my vision, like a flaw in a clear glass window. Before I could blink, the blur reached Sam, stabbing a spider wolf in one of its huge upper eyes. The beast shrieked and snapped at whatever it was, but the blur was never where the spider wolf expected it to be. It shifted out of reach with a speed that my eyes couldn't follow.

A stiff wind blew out of nowhere, nearly toppling me over again. While I fought to keep my balance, I heard an odd crackling sound below me.

Frost spread across the ground like a cascade of spilled milk, turning the black leaves white.

Someone grabbed hold of my arm, keeping me upright. Sam had somehow gotten free from the pile of spider wolves. He was covered with blood and nearly unrecognizable; I only knew it was him because he didn't have a sword or a bow.

For a moment, I thought the monsters attacking him had vanished, but then I saw them rolling away, blown aside by the wind like so many tumbleweeds. Sam braced himself against a tree to keep us from tumbling right along after them.

The wind abated as abruptly as it had arrived. Bloody Knee rushed in, slashing at the dazed monsters. The blur zipped from one to another, leaving death in its wake. Within moments, the creatures besetting Sam had been hacked to pieces.

I looked around at a scene of unimaginable carnage. I was surrounded by slaughtered spider wolves—peppered with arrows, stabbed, or killed in far less natural ways. A few of them had been frozen in place mid-snarl like some strange new kind of taxidermy, their fur iced over. As I watched, a final one plummeted from a tree branch, crashed into the leaf litter, and lay still.

To my great surprise, we seemed to have won.

CHAPTER SIX

In Which Everyone Lies a Lot

I shivered. The air had grown bitter cold, frigid as the plain of ice at the top of the world. My damp clothes had turned stiff and cracked when I moved.

Sam swayed on his feet, half-faint from shock and blood loss. Now I was the one lending a supportive hand.

"Is everyone all right?" the blur asked, flickering back and forth like a child who couldn't keep still, its words as rapid as its movements.

"Take your leg off, Harry," Bloody Knee said, limping up to join the rest of the group. "We can hardly see you. Where's Kit got to?"

"Here." Another masked man in green stepped from the trees.

"Good work with the wind there." Bloody Knee's Ecossic accent was lighter than the others', with the faintest hint of a Tailliziani lilt. I wondered if he'd been in the country longer. "Max, put your hat on before we die of a chill."

"Oh, right," said another of them. "Sorry." He pulled out a bycoket hat, pointed in the front like a bird's beak, and jammed it down slantwise on one side of his head until it covered his left ear. The air temperature immediately began to rise, the aching cold warming to a normal autumn chill.

The blur, in the meantime, shifted a bit and resolved into yet another man in green, one leg detached from his body and clutched in his hands.

Well. I'd seen stranger things.

Looking around, I counted six of the masked men in green. Half a dozen men who appeared astonishingly similar to one another, now that I took the time to study them more closely. True, there were some obvious differences—one had a hat, one had a bow, one was holding his own leg—but they all were the exact same height and build. They all had hair of the same flame-red hue, cut to the same length, and their complexions were the precise same shade of pale. Six pairs of eyes shared the delicate blue of a forget-me-not. Even the freckles beneath their domino masks speckled their cheeks in roughly similar patterns.

Their looks and speech marked them as Ecossic. They could have been Liam's identical sextuplet cousins. Why were they here?

Masked men in the woods were usually robbers.

Which meant I couldn't trust them simply because they'd rescued me. You would not believe the lengths some villains are willing to go in order to get you to lower your guard. Child-eating witches will swear up and down that they are innocent old women who happen to admire the architectural properties of gingerbread. Wolves can make a surprisingly convincing case that they are your grandmother. Well, ordinary wolves can. If they had eight eyes and legs, that would be a bit of a giveaway.

I didn't have the faintest idea who these people were or what they wanted. And if life under my stepmother's rule had taught me nothing else, it was that I shouldn't put my faith in anyone without knowing what their motives were first.

"I'm a little scratched up, and so is, uh, the lady here," Bloody Knee said, indicating me. "I think Sam got the worst of it."

"I'll be fine," Sam murmured, shifting more weight onto me. I grunted, my knees nearly buckling. "I just need . . ."

I eased Sam onto a fallen log. "Stitches," I said. "Rather a lot of them."

Sam mumbled something incoherent in response. His wounds were deep, especially the ones low on his left side. They looked bad—far worse than the shallow cuts on my shoulders or the ones on Bloody Knee's leg if he was still walking on it without wincing.

"Does anyone have any alcohol?" I asked. "The stronger the better."

"Aye." One of them passed me a flask. "We cuid a' dae wi' a wee dram efter that."

I could tell which one that was, at least. "It's not for drinking." I took the needle and thread out of my dress pocket. Good thing I'd kept them there rather than storing them in the chest with everything else. Just in case I was ever attacked by wolves. It's always a good idea to pay attention to my brother-in-law's cryptic comments.

I used whatever was in the flask to sterilize my sewing tools as well as I was able. It smelled like kerosene. Clem tutted at the waste.

"It lowers the risk of infection," I said. "Take your shirt off, Sam."

"No!" Bloody Knee said. "He . . . needs to keep warm, surely. So he doesn't go into shock."

Spare me from the ignorant medical opinions of amateurs. But the whole lower half of Sam's shirt was so shredded it hardly mattered, so I didn't bother to argue. Better not to lose the time.

I poured the remaining contents of the flask over Sam's wounds. He hissed in pain. When they were as clean as I could reasonably get them, I put the needle against his skin.

Push it through at a ninety-degree angle, close to the side of the wound. Don't go too far in; keep it just above the fat. Rotate clockwise. The needle should come out straight across from the first hole. Make a loose knot, and then tighten it until the flesh just closes.

Sam clenched his jaw when the needle went in but made no further sound. The others crowded close, watching suspiciously, but relaxed when it became apparent I knew what I was doing.

"What a mess." The man in the bycoket hat shook his head. "I told you we shouldn't have split up. And we should never have left the others behind."

"If we hadn't split up, we might never have found her," Bloody Knee replied.

The others? What others? *Move down a quarter inch, and make the second stitch. And then the third.* Were there more of them somewhere? How many identical masked men could there be?

"Who have we found, come to that?" said the man holding his leg in his arms, hopping forward to get a better look at me. He glanced over my bedraggled, bloodied clothes and the mess of pumpkin entrails in my hair. "That's a pretty red cloak she's wearing beneath all the mud, but it's hardly a silken gown. Is this really the princess?"

"Nah, she isnae," said Clem.

"She might be," Sam muttered.

"Why don't we ask her?" Bloody Knee said, turning to me. "Who are you?"

"Before I answer," I responded, carefully pulling thread through flesh, "who on earth are you?"

Bloody Knee's eyebrows crawled up above his mask like two indignant scarlet caterpillars. "We're the people who just saved your life. It's a bit ungracious to refuse us your name."

I tied off a stitch and gestured for his sword. "Help me with this? I didn't bring scissors."

He drew his blade and gently sawed through the thread.

"Thank you," I said. "For everything. I'm grateful for your timely arrival, truly. But that being said"—I took a deep breath—"you are a group of armed men. You appear to have been roving through the forest looking for a wealthy noblewoman. I would very much like to know your intentions before we proceed any further."

There was a moment of silence while they blinked at me, and then Hat On Ear burst out laughing so hard he had to sit on a stump.

"She thinks we want to rob her!" he managed to gasp out as the others turned their perplexed stares on him.

"Yes," I admitted. "It's the masks, really." I began stitching anew, working on another deep gash. Sam's fingers tightened on the log.

My suspicions had been eased somewhat by the gales of hysterical laughter, but the possibility remained that it was all a ploy.

"We're not highwaymen," Bloody Knee said. "We have no intention of robbing anyone."

"I see." I didn't add that theft wasn't my greatest worry. Abduction seemed far more likely. Saving my life would have had little point if all they wanted was jewelry, but a corpse has no value to kidnappers seeking a ransom. Or, of course, there was a chance they wanted to take me to their lair and force me to keep house for them. That would be a problem; my stepmother might believe I'd gone with them voluntarily, to avoid the marriage.

Direr possibilities existed as well. I couldn't discount them. But the men in green had made no threats, and if I was any judge of character, they didn't strike me as the worst sort of villain.

"We're King Gervase's huntsmen," Bloody Knee told me. "Now, are you the princess or not?"

"Huntsmen," I repeated.

"Yes."

"So you're out for a hunt then, I suppose?" I looked up from my stitchery and glanced around. "Without horses, hounds, or hawks."

He hesitated only for a moment. "We were questing for the stag."

"All six of you." Looking for tracks was normally a task for a single person and a dog. "And isn't that usually done before breakfast?" Overhead, the light gray clouds had dimmed to dark gray with the arrival of twilight. I turned my attention back to the task at hand. I needed to finish while I could still see what I was doing.

"Our hunting methods are unorthodox but"—he gestured toward the piles of dead spider wolves—"very effective."

A fair point. I nodded in acknowledgment. "And are the masks also part of your unorthodox approach?"

"Masks," said Detachable Leg smoothly, "are the latest fashion at the court of Tailliz."

"Really. So before I arrive, should I borrow one from you, so I can fit in?"

"It's the latest court fashion we are trying to start," he amended. "It'll catch on eventually."

"This is beside the point," Bloody Knee said. "We don't have to explain ourselves to you. We are duly appointed officials of the king. So, I will ask one final time—are you the princess?"

They were hiding something, that much was obvious. Their story was so full of holes that a real hunting party could have ridden straight through it. Which meant I had to decide whether I would be better served by telling the truth or by matching their lies with one of my own.

There is a school of thought that says telling the truth is always the best policy. According to this doctrine, liars inevitably end up tangled in their own web of falsehood and soon enough suffer a suitably ironic punishment. Cry wolf, and you will be devoured, with none coming to your aid; cut off your toes to change your foot size, and all you'll get is a painful limp and a blood-filled glass slipper. Which can't, incidentally, have been pleasant for the next person to try it on.

The truth-tellers, meanwhile, will be seen for the pure souls they are and always come out on top in the end. They'll win by virtue of their virtue, so to speak.

This is complete nonsense. The next time a giant asks whether you are a delicious, edible mortal woman or some kind of oddly shaped rock formation, try giving the first answer and see what happens. So my judgment was that until I had more information about my current situation, deception was the better part of valor.

I finished off a final stitch and patted Sam on an unwounded patch of shoulder. "There. That should do for now." He sighed in relief and gave me a crooked, if pained, smile.

I turned to Bloody Knee.

"If I am a princess," I said, "then where is my retinue? My servants? My guards? Where is my carriage?"

The masked men had already made half my argument for me. They'd noticed I was out alone and had little besides the sturdy clothes I'd been wearing for the journey, now somewhat torn by the claws of monsters. Nothing but scattered teeth remained of my traveling companions, and there'd been no sign of my gowns and jewels and squirrel-selected shiny shoes in the remains of the enchanted carriage; presumably, they were pumpkin innards now. Never, ever leave anything important inside a dying spell.

"For that matter," I continued, "if I were the mighty sorceress you're apparently expecting, then why would I need to be rescued from a few, um . . ." I glanced over at the tangle of monstrous corpses. "What were those, anyway?"

"We've been calling them spider wolves," one of them said.

"Because otherwise they'd be wolf spiders, and that's already a thing." He held a finger to one nostril and blew through the other. A blast of wind lifted up the carcass of a spider wolf. It danced around in the air for a few moments before it dropped with a squishy thud.

"Ah," I said, disquieted. "But anyway, no. Not a princess. I hope you weren't counting on meeting her today."

Bloody Knee's shoulders relaxed with such stark, obvious relief that I felt slightly insulted. I'd thought I might see disappointment or perhaps suspicion, but not that. He really hadn't wanted to meet the princess. To meet me. I wondered why.

"Well then," he said. "If you aren't the princess, who are you?"

"Her handmaiden, of course," I answered. "No more than a minor noblewoman from the court of Skalla." Lies are best concealed within as much truth as possible. "I've been sent out in advance to make sure everything is properly arranged for the wedding."

"I see." He frowned thoughtfully, but if he had any doubts, he didn't express them aloud.

"My horse was chased off by the spider wolves before you arrived." That was also reasonably close to the truth. I hoped the mice were doing well, wherever they were; they'd been Calla's friends. "So if you're King Gervase's huntsmen, might you be willing to escort me to the castle?"

"Aye, of course," Sam said, rising a bit unsteadily from the log. "We'd be happy to."

"Even though you'd have to give up on your stag?"

"Stag?" he said.

"The one you were tracking," I reminded him, "when the spider wolves attacked."

"Obviously, your plight takes precedence," Bloody Knee cut in. "We might want to wait until morning to travel, though." He glanced up at the darkening sky. "It's a full day's journey from here."

"If we have to, I suppose." A night facing unknown dangers with people I didn't entirely trust wasn't exactly what I'd been hoping for.

Sam seemed less than thrilled with the notion as well. "Shouldn't we be on our way? What if more of those things come?"

Bloody Knee shook his head. "Then better that they come when we're in a good defensive position and not wandering through the woods in the dark."

"But, Jack—"

"Oh!" I said. "You're a *Jack*! Why didn't you say so in the first place?"

My muscles unknotted as the bulk of my tension drained away. Bloody Knee's name was the most reassuring piece of news I'd had since my rescue.

Everyone knew that you could rely on a Jack—or a Hans, or an Ivan, depending on the local naming conventions. They weren't likely to be outright villains, even if they weren't always heroes. These so-called hunters might be lying about who they were, but if their leader was a Jack, my chances of being kidnapped, robbed, abandoned, or forced to scrub dishes had dropped considerably.

He looked discomfited. "It's . . . a nickname, really. You shouldn't make too much of it."

"Isn't it usually a nickname?" I asked. "For John, or Jonathan? Or maybe James? I don't see why that makes any difference."

"Let's git awa' fae thae deid beasties and mak' camp," Clem interjected. "Afore we lose th' light athegither."

We left the bodies of the spider wolves behind, pressing into the forest for perhaps another half an hour before we topped a low, clear hill that, being slightly less boggy than the lower land around it, was judged a suitable place to spend the night.

By then, the clouds were clearing, and the first stars of evening glimmered in the sky. The hunters who were well enough to help moved to busy themselves, gathering the driest leaves they could find for bedding and the driest branches for a fire. Clem and The Nose Blower constructed a lean-to with a blanket they'd produced from somewhere. They all worked together in a way that spoke of long practice.

Sam wanted to pitch in, too, at first, until I described exactly what would happen if he pulled out his stitches and sepsis set in. Since the rest of them appeared to have things well in hand, and I feared I'd only be in the way, I sat next to him on a flattish rock and let them get to it.

I readied myself for at least one more horrible night in the wilderness. Although if they truly did intend to get me to my destination the next day, it might be the last one.

"What's your name, princess's handmaiden?" Sam asked, turning toward me. His jaw clenched as his stiffening, bloody shirt pulled away from his wounds. "Since I'd rather not have to refer to you as 'Princess's Handmaiden.'"

"At least it's better than 'Detachable Leg' or 'The Nose Blower,'" I muttered.

"Sorry, what?"

"Nothing," I said. "You can call me Clover."

"That's a bonnie name." His smile made me wish it were actually mine.

"So . . ." I cast about for a way to turn the conversation to any subject but me. "Have you been a huntsman long?"

"Not as long as all that. I've been with Jack since the beginning, though."

"The beginning?" My forehead wrinkled. "The beginning of what?"

"That, I'm afraid, is a rather long story."

"Is it a good story?"

"It's filled with mystery, magic, adventure, and danger," Sam assured me.

"The kind where every word is proclaimed or avowed?"

"Exactly."

"Sounds intriguing," I said. "And we have all night, it seems."

I made myself as comfortable as I could on a hard rock in a damp forest on a chilly autumn evening. Exhaustion dragged at my eyelids, but I wasn't likely to get much sleep in those conditions. And if I was going to spend the night wide awake, wearing torn and bloody clothing, surrounded by strangers, and lying my head off, there was no need for me to be bored as well.

"Once upon a time . . ." Sam began.

CHAPTER SEVEN

The Tale of How Two Became Six

Once upon a time, when the world was younger and the leaves were a little greener, there lived a fellow we shall call Jack. Jack was not his name, precisely, but it was close enough as makes no never mind, so Jack is what we shall call him.

Jack had been disappointed in love, for his betrothed had spurned him for another. But Jack was not the sort who would collapse in despair and let fate toy with him however it wished. So he conceived of a brilliant plan.

"As step one of this brilliant plan, I shall search every hill and vale in the country of Ecossia," he pledged, "until I find eleven others who appear exactly identical to me in face, figure, and size."

"Wait," I interrupted. "He did what? Eleven people exactly identical to— What possible purpose could that serve? What was he trying to do? Discredit his rival? Win back his love? How were eleven other Jacks supposed to help with that?"

"I've barely begun," Sam said. "Perhaps your questions will be answered later on."

I gestured for him to proceed.

"I shall search every hill and vale," he pledged, "until I find eleven others who are identical to me in face, figure, and size."

With that in mind, the first person he approached, sensibly enough, was his twin brother.

Jack found his brother in the forest, where that mighty fellow had just finished plucking up six trees as easily as if they were blades of grass.

"What in the world are you doing?" Jack questioned his twin.

His brother tied one of the trees in a pretty bow around the other five. "I'm gathering some of these twigs for our dear old dad. The winter will be cold and damp, and he might need the wood for his fire."

Jack rolled his eyes. "You're such a fucking show-off, Sam."

"Oh, you're Jack's brother?"

"I am, aye. And it isn't the first time I've been dragged into a ridiculous scheme like this one because of it. You're yawning. Should I let you sleep?"

"No, no. I'm not going to be able to sleep in the middle of a forest, anyway. What exactly, by the way, is the ridiculous scheme you've been dragged into?"

He ignored my question and went on.

"Sam, I need your help," Jack entreated. "As you know, my heart has been sliced into pieces like a bruised, mealy apple, its very core ripped out and the remnants laid upon a crust of misery, to be baked into a pie of sadness after being sprinkled with the cinnamon of despair."

"Now I'm hungry," Sam complained.

"I have conceived of a bizarre plan whose first requirement is that I seek out eleven others who are identical to me in face, figure, and size. I believe this is my one and only chance, for I am far too weak, useless, and pathetic to succeed without help. And you are the person most like me in all the world, except stronger and handsomer and overall better in—"

"You really are his brother, aren't you?"

"—every way. What do you say, Sam? Will you help me?"

"Aye, of course," Sam agreed graciously, as was his wont. "I can never refuse you. Let me drop these wee sticks off first, and then we shall be on our way."

And so the two of them set off.

"Do you always go along with every wild idea he dreams up?" I asked.

"I'm fine with following his lead. Jack enjoys being the romantic hero. I'm content with a supporting role."

"Really?" Thanks to my family, I had some experience feeling like a secondary character in my own story. I can't say I enjoyed it.

"It's all for the best," Sam said. "Jack's never steered me wrong."

"If you say so." His wounds seemed to argue otherwise, but I refrained from pointing this out.

They decided the next person they should recruit to their cause was their cousin Clem, the famed hunter, as Clem's resemblance to the pair was so strong that as children they had oft been called by the wrong names at family gatherings. Or at least, they had been until Clem opened his mouth, for he had been raised in the high hills and spoke in their manner.

When they approached Clem's land, they found the man in question standing atop a ridge with his bow, peering into the distance with an arrow nocked and drawn.

"Hello, Clem—" Jack began, stopping when his cousin shot a sharp glare in his direction.

"Shhh," he whispered. "Ye'll friten it aff."

Jack lowered his voice. "What are you hunting?"

"Twa miles awa', a flea is sittin' oan an oak tree branch. Ah'm wantin' tae shoot tis left yak oot."

Clem loosed his shot, and a minute later, they heard the faint but unmistakable cry of a flea being half blinded by an arrow hitting its left eye.

"You did not."

"I may be embroidering the tale somewhat," Sam acknowledged.

"Any more embroidery and it'll have more stitches than you do."

He chuckled and flashed a rather charming grin before continuing.

Jack and Sam put their case to Clem, and he immediately agreed to join their cause.

Now, while the three of them had other close relatives, none fit the bill; they were all too short, too tall, too slender, too stout, or otherwise unsuitable. So the three of them set out across the land in search of additional companions.

After many miles of walking, they came upon a curious sight—seven windmills whose sails were racing around at tremendous speeds, in spite of the calm weather.

"That's strange," Jack commented, approaching the windmills. "I wonder if—"

But we are never to know what he wondered, for as soon as he came within a few feet of a windmill, a mighty wind picked him up and sent him tumbling arse over teakettle down the hill.

Unable to account for this narrowly focused gale, the three travelers moved on. Two miles from the windmills, however, they came across a man sitting in a tree who, as it happened, appeared identical to Jack, Sam, and Clem in face, figure, and size.

"That's quite a coincidence, isn't it?"

"Well, perhaps not completely identical in face." Sam tapped his mask. "He only needed to be close enough for this to finish the job."

"It still seems unlikely. He had the same eye color? Jawline? Complexion? Ear shape?"

"Ecossia is an island. Most of us are related. Before a couple starts courting, they have to consult a special chart to make sure they aren't each other's grandparents."

"Is that possible?"

"It's not even unlikely. My second cousin made a mistake with the chart and ended up accidentally marrying himself."

"I see." I tried to nod, and my head drooped until my chin touched my chest. I wrenched my head back up, my eyes snapping open.

"Are you sure you're not too tired for this?"

"I'm fine."

The man in the tree was holding one nostril shut and blowing through the other. Bewildered, the three travelers asked what he was doing.

"Two miles away, there are seven windmills," the man explained, "and I'm blowing on them so they spin around."

Jack remained perplexed. "Your breath is so mighty you can turn seven windmills at once, and you are only using it to . . . turn seven windmills at once?"

The man shrugged. "Everybody needs a hobby."

The man introduced himself as Kit.

"Jack, Sam, Clem, and Kit? I'm having trouble telling you apart. Do any of you have a two-syllable name?"

"That's why we took them. Makes it even trickier to tell who's who. Just remember that I'm the handsome one."

"The handsome identical duplicate?"

"I have a very handsome bearing. My posture is unmatched."

"It was the first thing I noticed about you. *What excellent posture,* I thought as the spider wolf was attempting to bite your head off."

When Jack and Sam and Clem let the windmill blower know what they were about—

"Wait. . . . If those are all assumed names, then what's your real one?"

"Sam," said Sam.

When Jack and Sam and Clem let him know what they were about, Kit agreed to join them.

The search continued without luck for several days. While they ran into many travelers, all of them were too burly, too delicate, too dark haired, too blond, or otherwise unsuitable. But then they came across a man in a field standing on one leg. He had taken his other leg off and set it on the ground. Except for that single small oddity, he was identical to Jack, Sam, Clem, and Kit in face, figure, and size—or at least, as close enough in face for it to make no difference.

Jack glanced from the attached leg to the unattached one and back again. "I suppose that's convenient for scratching your foot."

"This is the only way I can stand still," the man elucidated.

"When I use both legs, I run so quickly that the fastest bird cannot keep up."

As soon as the others explained their plan, this man, named Harry, agreed to join their ranks.

"Two syllables! At last."

"The rest of us thought it was too fancy, but he couldn't be dissuaded."

"I will also note you still have not explained this mysterious plan to me."

"Oh, haven't I?" His expression was a picture of blameless innocence.

The five of them resumed the quest. They had traveled together for perhaps a week when the weather turned. Although summer had not yet ended, an unseasonable chill pervaded the air, and snow started to whirl down from the sky. It fell thicker and faster and soon became a blizzard. They began to worry for their very lives, for none of them were dressed for winter, and they were out on the road and far from shelter.

While they were debating what to do, they stumbled across a man sleeping outdoors, dusted with snow, and snoring loudly. In his slumber, his hat had fallen from his head and lay half-embedded in a nearby snowdrift. Fearing the stranger would freeze to death before nightfall, the five companions shook him awake.

"Oh, my goodness!" he cried out. "I fell asleep with my hat off. I guess there's *no bed* like a *snow bed*!" Harry slapped his one attached leg and chuckled with delight at the jest, but the others remained silent, for they did not see the humor in it or, indeed, realize any joke had been attempted.

The odd fellow stuck the hat skew-whiff on his head so that it covered his left ear. The snow ceased falling, and the temperature began to rise.

"Let me guess—he was identical to Jack, Sam, Clem, Kit, and Harry in face, figure, and size?"

"Got it in one. Should I stop now?"

"What? No. Why?"

"You just slid right off the rock."

I had. When had that happened? And for that matter, how was I comfortable enough to start dozing off on the bare ground? His voice was so soothing, though.

He offered me a hand, and I drew myself up, brushing dirt and leaves off my cloak. "Please continue. I want to hear how it ends."

Max—for that was his name, or at least we will choose to pretend so—became a member of the group as soon as he heard what was afoot.

The six of them journeyed for weeks together and had many adventures. However, at this point Jack's plan had run into a snag, for even in Ecossia, it had become difficult to find others who were like enough to them in looks. A month passed, but every single person they came across was too scaly, too feathered, too fetal, too dead, or otherwise unsuitable.

"Too what?"

"We were really scraping the bottom of the barrel by that point."

But just when Jack had nearly lost hope, in a town at the southern edge of the island, he saw six men passing through a market. They were as indistinguishable from each other as six pips in a pear and likewise similar to Jack and his fellows.

Jack grabbed the arm of a nearby costermonger. "Who are those six men? For it is urgent that they join my cause, and follow me about, and dress in green, and wear masks, all for reasons I have no intention of revealing in the present narrative."

"You were never planning on telling me? You're mean."

Sam gave a remorseful sigh. "I wish I could tell you, really. But I promised Jack I'd keep his secrets."

"Mean," I murmured, swaying where I sat. I put down a hand to steady myself so that I wouldn't fall off the rock again.

"Begone with you, for I have costers to mong," the costermonger sneered, "and I do not have the time to answer foolish questions." But once Jack had purchased a few costers, the peddler became more amenable. "Those are the six siblings of our duchess," our hero was informed. "As odd a family as ever you'll find. When the eldest brother speaks, frogs and toads leap out of his mouth. And where the next eldest walks—"

"Yes, yes," Jack cut him off. "I'm sure they're all extraordinary. But where do they live?"

"Why, up in the castle that sits upon yonder hill."

And he pointed to a great, dark edifice that squatted on the hillside. In shape, it resembled a malevolent toad, its gate a gaping maw that made our heroes feel uncomfortably like flies.

Undaunted, Jack and his friends soon presented themselves at the castle, where they were greeted by none other than the duchess herself.

"My brothers shall not go with you," she advised them, "for they are dear to me, and I wish to keep them by my side. But I will make you this offer instead—if one of you can beat me in a footrace, you shall leave with as great a reward as the strongest among you can carry. If you fail, however, then you shall all be beheaded instead."

Jack was puzzled. "Do you make this same offer to every group of strangers that drops by?"

"Yes, actually."

"Why?"

The duchess shrugged. "Everybody needs a hobby."

"We agree to your terms!" Jack declared, for during that short conversation, he had already conceived of yet another ridiculous plan.

And there shall the tale be paused, for the sun has long since set, and we must travel when morning arrives.

"No, wait. You shouldn't . . ." I was having trouble finding words. "You can't end it there."

"Your eyes have been closed for the last five minutes. I'll tell you the rest another time. Listen, we've not got any blankets or pillows. Perhaps you might—"

"Mm," I said. Or something equally coherent. I leaned my head against Sam's shoulder and fell asleep.

CHAPTER EIGHT

The Forest Primeval—and Also Repulsive

I ran through a hallway made of teeth. It twisted around like a corkscrew, leaving me unsure whether I was running on the floor or the ceiling. If it was the ceiling, I'd fall off as soon as I stopped, but there was no time to double-check. I was late for my deportment lesson, which was taught by a particularly irascible swan-maiden. She'd fly into a rage if I wasn't there on time, and I had no desire to be pecked again.

The teeth bit into my bare feet as I hurried along, because I was naked. I must not have had time to put any clothes on. The swan-maiden would not be amused.

Swan-maidens have no business teaching deportment, anyway. It doesn't take much skill to stretch out your neck when your neck is already five feet long. I'd argued to my stepmother that we'd learn more from, say, a frog prince. Someone who'd really had to work at it. But she'd ignored me.

When was I going to reach the lesson room? The hallway stretched on and on. So many teeth. Endless teeth. Was this truly a hallway, or was it a mouth? It began to close in on me.

Biting down. It was going to chew on me for hours, like a piece of stringy gristle. I had to get the teeth planted in the field right away, or they were going to—

"Melilot!" Jonquil shouted. "Slow down."

I turned and saw her behind me, struggling to catch up. "There's no time!" I said. "We're late enough as it is."

She was fully clothed, I noted. Typical. Little Miss Dutiful would never show up nude in a classroom. She'd meet my stepmother's impossible standards or die trying. Again.

Jonquil rolled her eyes. "We're not late for anything. This is a dream."

A dream? What nonsense. This was just an ordinary day where I was running naked through a hallway that was also a mouth because I was late for my . . .

Oh.

I stumbled to a halt, and Jonquil caught up to me, panting. She glanced at me once, her eyes widening, and then carefully looked in any direction but mine.

"Did you want to put some clothes on?" she asked. "It's just that, when I bring Calla in, you'll be the only one not wearing anything. So if that would make you feel awkward . . ."

"What does it matter? You're not real. She won't be, either."

"Oh, no, I'm actually here."

"You are?"

"I spent the last month learning how to dreamwalk so we could visit you. Surprise!"

"You learned to dreamwalk in *one month*?" Entering the dreams of others was unfathomably difficult magic—the kind that wizened, ancient witches sometimes achieve after a lifetime spent staring at constellations and chicken entrails, struggling to unlock the secrets of the universe. Of course Jonquil had worked it out in a few weeks.

Unless I was only dreaming she'd dreamwalked here? No, she was too . . . steady. She didn't fit in with the rest of the scenery, like an oil portrait dropped into a smear of watercolors. The teeth shifted and twitched in the corners of my eyes, sometimes a hallway and sometimes a mouth, and sometimes the walls were green or sparkly or Thursday. But Jonquil remained Jonquil, never once becoming a platypus or a hat rack.

I looked around in search of a tapestry I could wrap around myself, but the walls remained bare of anything but dentition. "I'm not sure where I can find a—"

"Dream," Jonquil reminded me.

Right, how dense could I be? I concentrated, getting my thoughts under control, and a gown draped itself over me.

In the meantime, Jonquil looked over her surroundings with a fascinated air. "Are you still fretting over the tooth quest? I didn't think it was that traumatic, as they go. Is it the near disaster at the end that bothers you? Or just handling all those teeth?"

"Do not," I growled, "psychoanalyze me based on a single dream you have invaded."

"I was only trying to help."

"Melilot!" Calla cried, throwing her arms around me. "I missed you!"

Her boots were muddy, and her skirt was unraveling at the hem. How was she so disheveled even in a dream? She couldn't have gone to bed in those clothes.

I softened a bit as I hugged her back. My sisters had been thinking of me and had wanted to see me, so they'd found a way. If their method happened to involve powerful, intrusive magic, that was par for the course in my family.

"So, are you in Tailliz?" Calla asked. "Have you met King Gervase? What's he like?"

"No, not yet. I'm still on the road."

Well, off the road and in the woods. I was about to mention that when Jonquil said, "Have you had any trouble along the way? Anything we should know about?"

I hesitated.

I could tell them about the spider wolves, describing my rescue and possible ongoing abduction by masked men. And no doubt my sisters would come racing to my aid.

But for perhaps the first time, I didn't need their help. I had survived the spider wolves, and I had deceived the hunters or robbers or whoever they were. I was managing things well enough on my own, doing fine without my sisters intervening. Which was not something I got to experience much, if ever.

It was far from certain my sisters would share my opinion of events. Jonquil had asked if I needed any help within five minutes of appearing in my dreams, which neatly summed up how she thought of me. The moment they heard about my circumstances—stranded in the woods with strangers—they would be convinced I'd made my usual muddle of things. They'd set off to pluck me out of danger.

Whether I wanted them to or not.

I shrugged and lifted my chin, looking Jonquil in the eye. "Sorry to disappoint you, but it's been a rather boring trip. Although honestly, you might have thought to put a spring arrangement in the carriage and some cushions on the seats."

"Pumpkins are very resistant to suspension systems!" she replied, too defensively. Had I hurt her feelings? I'd only meant to deflect the conversation. "Turning plant matter into metal requires a fundamental restructuring—"

The walls began to shudder, teeth falling all around us like hailstones. One bounced off my nose and rattled to the ground.

"What's happening?" Calla asked, nearly falling over as the floor heaved like a flapping tongue.

"I think she's waking up," Jonquil said. "Melilot, take care. I'll do my best to bring the rest of the family along next time, so . . . try to be decent?"

"Next time, you should knock first!" I shouted over the noise of the dream collapsing.

Jonquil waved goodbye as she faded from my view. "We'll see you when the celestial spheres are aligned again!"

Maddeningly, I was somehow both relieved and saddened their visit was coming to an end. "Wait," I began. "How long before—"

My eyes blinked open to find a masked face looming above mine. A hand was on my shoulder, gently shaking me awake.

"It's dawn, Not The Princess. Time to rise."

I tried to figure out which one of them it was, but it wasn't easy, especially with the vestiges of a toothy hallway still dissipating from my mind's eye. The hunter didn't sound like Clem, and both his legs were on. . . . Could it be The Nose Blower? What was that one named? Kit, I thought. Or maybe this was Bloody Knee. Jack. He was wrapped in a cloak to ward off the morning frost, so I couldn't see if there were bloodstains on his breeches. Once Jack got around to changing his trousers, identifying him was going to be even more difficult.

If this turned out to be an abduction, I would have to learn how to tell them apart. I might be spending a great deal of time with them while I waited to be ransomed. Or for my stepmother to show up with a poisoned apple.

"Come on," whoever it was said. "We've got a long walk to the castle."

All around me, the men were striking the camp, kicking dirt over the last embers of the fire, or pulling on their boots and gloves. They'd already donned their masks. I wondered if they'd slept in them.

The man who'd woken me turned away to finish dressing, and before he got his gloves on, I noticed a gold ring on his fourth finger. A wedding band? Or an engagement ring, perhaps. According to Sam's story, Jack had been betrothed and then abandoned. If that was Jack, interesting that he was still wearing it.

Where was Sam, anyway? I only counted five of the huntsmen, and none of them had a half-shredded shirt.

That was when I heard a snore from behind me and noticed my head was cushioned by something softer than I might have expected. I half raised myself up and turned to see it had been Sam's stomach. He was still asleep. With his mask on.

Had he served as my pillow for the whole night? And had I slept the whole night through? That never happened.

I prodded him with a finger. "Wake up, sleepyhead."

The snoring stopped. "Every part of my body," he said without opening his eyes, "hurts. I think I'll just stay right here forever, if you don't mind."

"The sooner we get going, the sooner we can get you real medical attention. And maybe," I added, "don't fight monsters with your bare hands."

"I'll keep that in mind the next time I save your life."

"If you do, I might not have to save you from bleeding out afterwards."

"We'll likelie be able tae shift mair quickly," Clem said from off to my left, "wance the twa of ye finish flirting."

Sam made a sputtering noise that did not rise to the level of words. I blushed.

We gathered for a quick breakfast of hard bread and cheese, and I took some time to observe the men. The one who'd woken me up had definitely been Jack, I decided—he was still walking with a bit of a limp. For that matter, while Sam remained cheerful, he was barely capable of standing upright.

I tried to remember the names from the story. Hat On Ear was Max. Detachable Leg was Harry.

Identifying them was going to become impossible if more of them turned up at some point. "Where are the rest of you? The ones you mentioned yesterday?" I asked. "Are those the duchess's brothers?"

"Aye," Sam said. "We've got the full dozen now. But we left them at Castle Tailliz. Someone needed to stay behind and guard the king."

"Guard the king?" I frowned. "Why would huntsmen be guarding the king? Shouldn't the king's guards be the ones doing the guarding?"

There was a pause, and five of them swiveled their heads to look at the sixth, who rose carefully to his feet. Jack again; he wasn't putting any weight on his bad leg.

"Sam misspoke," he said. "He meant they stayed behind to serve at the king's pleasure, in case he wanted to hold a hunt today. And we should return as soon as possible. For the same reason. Let's go."

Sam, who was fidgeting in embarrassment, said nothing in reply. The group's ringleader had chastised his loose-lipped subordinate into silence. The others likewise remained speechless as they finished gathering their belongings. Jack's word on the subject, it appeared, was final.

It would have been nice to change into something less covered in blood and dirt. With all the lovely dresses in my trousseau turned into so much mulch and pumpkin seeds, I was beginning to appreciate the utility of Jonquil's clothes-cleaning magic. The destruction of my garments might have helped me sell my story, but I was desperate for anything dry.

When we decamped, we didn't make our way to the road, much to my surprise. Instead, Jack forged a path through the forest itself. It seemed like an excellent way to get lost. Which in turn seemed like an excellent way to get killed. Even ordinary woods can hold untold dangers if you venture too far from the known routes, and these woods were far from ordinary. But none of the hunters protested. I hoped they knew what they were doing.

We trailed along behind Jack, except for Harry, who affixed his leg back on and darted ahead to scout whenever he was able. The rest of us tromped leadenly through the leaf litter and mounds of fallen needles, eternally plodding up steep rises or down precipitous slopes, often forced to detour around the massive trunks of the great trees. Jack had to use his sword to hack his way through dense underbrush more than once. It was slow, tough going, especially with some of us wounded. I hung back with Sam and helped him along as best I could. My progress wouldn't have been much faster than his, anyway, not in a dress whose hem was intent on catching on every bush we passed and thoroughly inappropriate shoes that were soaked through within minutes. Perhaps it was just as well I'd had no ball gowns available.

Walking through the woods should have been much more uncomfortable than traveling in the coach. I was wet, filthy, terrifyingly deep in a trackless forest, and not without my own injuries. The gouges in my shoulder where the spider wolf had raked me ached abominably. Even my good red cloak was failing me, the wind whistling through more torn rents than I was capable of fixing with what was left of Liam's spool of thread.

Nonetheless, I was finding the journey noticeably more pleasant. The huntsmen's silence ended soon after we set out, and the chatter of voices was a relief after weeks in the presence of no one but a troop of taciturn teeth. I found a smile drifting onto my face as I listened.

Or rather, I did once I became used to the horrific aberrations we periodically glimpsed peering out at us from the trees.

At first glance, many of them weren't obviously abnormal. The bird tottering on a tree branch didn't look unusual to me until I noticed it was perching on the backward-bent legs of a cricket, so thin they barely held it up. I flinched back, but the hunters only regarded it warily, then carried on when it did nothing.

"Most of them are harmless," Sam told me. "You can go weeks without seeing any deadly beasts, sometimes."

"Which beasts are the deadly ones?"

"Any that try to bite you. Even the wee ones." He considered for a moment. "Especially the wee ones. Some are extremely poisonous."

That didn't make me feel safe, exactly, but once we'd passed a few of them without incident, I stopped shying from every shadow. Most of the monstrosities looked more ill than dangerous: Squirrels with the heads of cats, too heavy for their bodies, chins dragging on the ground as the poor creatures staggered sideways to pull them along. A mouse crawling on a carpet of centipede limbs, with thin membranous wings poking uselessly out of its shoulder blades, endlessly fluttering without enough strength to lift it off the ground. They might not have been deadly, but they still made me shudder in dismay.

We came across far more of the creatures than I would have expected from the mere rumors Liam had described. Had their numbers increased since the last time he'd passed this way, years before? Or did few travelers venture this deep into the woods—and fewer return to tell the tale?

I hoped not, especially when it remained a mystery why my masked companions had chosen to plunge headlong into the forest's heart.

CHAPTER NINE

Ask Not for Whom the Hamster Screams

After a while, I began to spot the differences among the huntsmen—they might have looked much the same in their domino masks, but they weren't at all similar otherwise. Jack remained inscrutable to me, but the rest were coming into sharper focus.

"Hey, Harry," said Max—Max was the one who liked to tell bad jokes. "Did you know I can cut down a tree just by looking at it?"

"No," said Harry. "Really?" Harry was the one who liked to hear bad jokes.

"It's true! I saw it with my own eyes!"

Harry guffawed, while Clem looked pained. "Eejits," he muttered. He was the one who hated bad jokes.

Kit hardly said anything, although he frequently turned aside to hold a finger to his nose and blow the autumn leaves into swirling gyres, grinning too widely whenever he did. I was beginning to find him slightly unnerving.

Sam, when he was up to talking, mostly asked me questions

about my life, which I fended off. I did the same to him, and he returned the favor.

I thought about what Clem had said and decided that flirting was an accurate way to describe what Sam and I had been doing. Practically since the moment we'd met. I liked Sam. His easy smile and his sense of humor. His attentiveness, despite his own injuries. I liked him rather a lot.

Which was perhaps not a feeling I should have been allowing to germinate when I was set to be married to someone else, and the consequences of endangering that engagement could be severe. I'd been fixated on my stepmother sticking me in a glass coffin if I defied her will, but that was only one of many possibilities. She might turn me into a bird and lock me in a cage instead. Or put me to sleep for a hundred years behind a wall of thorns.

Assuming the huntsmen's intentions toward me were not nefarious, and I was being taken to the castle as they claimed, then whatever was going on between Sam and me would have to end as soon as I revealed my true identity. A pang of loss struck me at the thought, which was ridiculous considering I had known him for less than a day. But it would have been nice to find out what might have developed if I had really been a handmaiden named Clover trading veiled glances with a hunter named Sam.

Or even if I were a princess who'd been abducted by an attractive outlaw. I had heard of successful relationships with stranger origins.

Perhaps, I thought as we stopped at the bank of a wide river, I could still hold out some hope I was being kidnapped. Our insanely dangerous route through the forest couldn't possibly be the easiest way to get to the castle. It seemed far more likely to lead to a robber's den. Criminals might brave the dangers lurking in the woods to avoid a prison sentence—or a noose.

"I'm fairly sure we can ford it," Jack said, staring into the swift-flowing water. "I don't think it's too deep."

A virulently purple fish with the extended eyestalks of a slug poked its head out of the river, blinked at him, and then disappeared again with a quiet plop.

"Maybe not," said Sam. "We don't know what's in there."

"I can blow the rest of you across," Kit offered.

Before I could point out what a terrible idea that was, Clem shook his head. "Och, ye dafty! We'd break oor arses oan they rocks."

An argument immediately broke out, all of them talking at once.

"I'll freeze the water so solid, the fish will think they're already in the icebox—"

"—freeze us to death, more likely—"

"—shoot an arrow wi' a rope tied tae it—"

"—worst idea I ever—"

"—if Sam can punch out a tunnel underneath—"

"—if I can *what*?—"

"—we should throw Harry's leg over to the other side—"

"—drink the river dry—"

"—somehow learn to teleport—"

"—no, no, levitate—"

"—teleport!—"

"—levitate!—"

"—won't even work, it's not flying, you can't go sideways—"

"Or," I shouted over them, "we could make our way to the road! Where I imagine there is a nice, solid bridge over this river."

Silence fell over the group. "There is," one of them admitted after a moment. "But . . ."

I sighed. "We aren't going to the castle, are we?"

"We are!" Sam said.

"It's fine if we're not. You're a nice enough bunch, for criminals, and it's not as if there's a lot I can do about it, anyway."

Jack leaned against a tree. "We're avoiding the road because we've already been ambushed there. Going back to it would be pressing our luck."

"Ambushed?" I said. "Who ambushed you?"

"I'm surprised you have to ask, considering you've got their claw marks in your shoulders."

"Oh."

I'd assumed the spider wolves were just a local hazard, the kind of danger that might beset any unwary soul wandering through the woods. "Ambushed" implied the attack wasn't a matter of chance. That it had been planned.

Planned by whom?

"The spider wolves—they've been hunting you?" I asked.

"Yes, lately. Although they first showed up a year or so before we entered into the king's service." Jack's gaze wandered away from mine. He seemed to be looking at nothing in particular. Or perhaps at something no one else could see. "When Gervase was still a prince, his eldest brother was torn to bits by a pack of them while he was out on a hunt, along with almost the whole of his hunting party. It was assumed to be bad luck, an unfortunate encounter with the dangers of the wilderness. There'd been rumors about strange things in the forests of Tailliz for years, after all.

"His next-eldest brother, however, was carried off by an enormous horned bird only a few months later. The family held on to the belief he might be alive until they found his arms and legs scattered across a clearing. Another brother was dragged shrieking into a hole by something with too many teeth, and then their father died a lingering death after being bitten by a furred snake with fins." His eyes returned to mine. "Since taking our position as Gervase's huntsmen, we've had to fend off assaults by all of those creatures, as well as things that were almost, but not quite, bats, rats, cats, badgers, and hamsters."

"Hamsters?" I asked.

"I can assure you that a screaming twenty-foot-tall hamster is not a foe for the faint of heart. No one knows why these things are happening, or how, or what is causing them, or when they will strike next. So while the forest may be full of oddities these days—"

"You're choosing to stray from the path," I said. "You brave the dangers of the unknown for the concealment that it offers."

He nodded. "We avoid the road as much as we can and vary our routes. And until we know the cause of the attacks," he added with a faint smile, "we also treat any strangers we happen upon in the woods with the gravest suspicion."

"Jack," Sam protested, "you can't possibly believe she—"

"I'm giving her the benefit of the doubt, for now," Jack said, "because she was attacked herself and injured in the bargain. Which would be quite a risk to take if it was only to deceive us. But I am looking forward to what is, I'm sure, the very reasonable explanation for why Skalla sent a wedding planner out on her lonesome, without a guard, companion, or chaperone, into the notably dangerous wilderness between the two countries." He sketched me a quick bow. "And now, if you please, we should make our way across this river."

Drat. And I'd thought my story had been so believable, too. I suppose once someone's been beset by monsters in the woods a time or two, they learn to be more wary thereafter.

It was eventually decided that Max would freeze the river while the rest of us waited a safe distance back, and soon we were sliding our way across slick ice. I found myself more than a little bit nervous during the crossing. If anything was going to leap out of the forest and attack us again, we were presenting it with a prime opportunity as we inched forward, one firm push away from being flat on our backs. But nothing came to bite our heads off.

All things considered, I no longer regretted avoiding the road.

In fact, the rest of the journey passed without incident. When the late afternoon sunshine cast a warm orange glow on the few leaves still clinging to their branches, we clambered out of a small gully, and the towers of a castle heaved themselves into view.

Jack gestured toward it with a flourish, as if it were his and he were presenting it to us for our entertainment and delight. "Castle Tailliz. The stronghold of King Gervase."

At long last, I had arrived.

PART III

YONDER LIES THE CASTLE

CHAPTER TEN

I Am Greeted with a Toad to the Face

Castle Tailliz was not as breathtaking a sight as the soaring giant-carved spires of my stepmother's palace. It wasn't very big, as castles go, but it was imposing in its own way: a solid, pugnacious-looking edifice designed for defense and not pretending otherwise. The castle took up the whole of a small island in the center of a half-moon-shaped bay, the walls rising straight up from a high cliff face of white stone. Narrow-windowed towers loomed over the ramparts at every sharp corner. A single wide bridge leapt across the bay on soaring arches, connecting the castle proper to a stout keep on the mainland.

We at last rejoined the road, which wound ahead through a cluster of houses and farms lining one side of the bay before it reached the keep. The capital city of Tailliz, presumably, as unimpressive as might be expected of the capital of any minor, unimportant kingdom.

Something about it seemed not quite right to me. I wasn't sure why until we got closer.

No smoke rose from the thatched roofs, and no fishing boats

plied their trade in the water. When we reached the outskirts of the village, I saw no one in the fields planting crops of winter wheat or washing their clothes in the small river that poured into the bay. No children played in the street. The buildings stood eerily silent around us; our footsteps on the cobbles were the only sounds not made by wind or surf. The paint on the walls was peeling. Fences slumped in disrepair. As far as I could tell, the place was deserted and had been for some time.

The first time I came across anything in Tailliz that didn't strike me as an ominous portent, it would come as a very pleasant surprise.

Had the villagers been eaten by monsters? Surely the hunters would have said something. They appeared to be unconcerned by the emptiness of the village and made no comment as we passed through.

Jack led us to the keep, where the gate was warded by a formidable portcullis and huge ironclad wooden doors that might each have been carved from the great trees in a single piece. Any army with plans to take Castle Tailliz would have a tough job of it.

Of course, the assaults on the kingdom weren't being made against the walls. They were being made against any who dared to venture outside of them. This was a country under siege by an unseen enemy, even if no sign of that siege showed in the placid, unruffled waters lapping at the seashore.

And it was, according to my stepmother's design, going to be my home from that point on. Or at least, it would be my home once I admitted to my true identity. The idea failed to fill me with a swell of happy anticipation.

I wondered briefly if the castle would turn out to be as empty as the village, but I was quickly disabused of that idea. "Hallo, the keep!" Jack called up to the gatehouse.

"Hallo, the huntsmen!" a voice replied. "Which one are you? Is that Jack I hear?"

"Indeed, it is."

"Glad you're back at last. We were getting worried!"

It was reassuring to find the castle inhabited—although that destroyed any remaining shreds of my theory that I had been kidnapped by bandits. I hadn't been taking the idea all that seriously by that point, anyway. Whatever secret had led the hunters to don masks and accost young women in the woods, it wasn't that.

A soldier poked his helmeted head over a parapet. "What's that you've caught for us there? A fat deer? A succulent boar?"

"Alas, neither," Jack replied. "'Tis a girl."

"Oh, is it? And how does she taste?" Riotous laughter echoed from above.

"The ogres always thought I'd be delicious," I said. "But then, they say that about everyone."

Jack blinked at me. "A very strange girl," he muttered. Sam grinned.

Soon the small troop of soldiers standing guard (all human—no ogres, dragons, or transfigured teeth here) raised the portcullis and let us through. From there, a trek across the long bridge led us through another gate and into a courtyard within the castle walls.

A very crowded courtyard. The bridge had been silent save for the cries of seabirds and the slosh of the waves against the stone supports. Here, noise assaulted my ears, and my vision was blocked by the great mass of people crammed into the yard. My nose was likewise overwhelmed. The scent of unwashed people mixed with a strong smell of horse and dog; I imagined stables and kennels lurked somewhere nearby. As we pressed through, I saw that crudely constructed shelters had been erected haphazardly throughout the courtyard, springing up from the ground like mushrooms. Most were rickety structures, made of whatever material had come to hand—loose lumber, boxes and barrels, blankets to keep out the rain. Sheep and cows were packed shoulder to shoulder in rough pens, adding their noise to the general clamor. Cookfires had been lit wherever there was enough room. There must have been a few hundred people jammed into the cramped space.

"So this is where the villagers got to," I said, relieved. They hadn't been devoured. They'd sought shelter behind the stout castle walls.

"No one wants to take their chances with the monsters," Sam said.

Hundreds of refugees. My notion of a country under a siege hadn't merely been a colorful metaphor. I'd been more correct than I'd known.

The Tailliziani packing the courtyard were a varied lot, with hair that could be anything from ash blond to so black it was nearly deep blue and complexions that ranged from almost as pale as my Ecossic escort to almost as dark as my sister Jonquil. Pretty much what I'd expect in a kingdom on the western shore that, as I recalled from my lessons, had a reasonable lumber trade during the months when the coast was navigable. Dynastic marriages weren't the only reason foreigners came here. Which didn't guarantee I'd be welcomed to the court with open arms, but at least I wouldn't be an inconceivable oddity solely because I spoke with a different accent.

It took us an age to pick our way through the courtyard, as the pathway weaving between the structures shifted with the crush of people, sometimes vanishing before our eyes.

"Gervase has tried to make room for as many as possible." Sam surveyed the makeshift campground, his lips drawn into a grim line. "As much as the court nobles have allowed him to, anyway."

"Allowed?" I said. "Isn't he the king?"

"Aye, but . . . it's complicated."

"The Great Hall is over here," Jack broke in as we approached a pair of doors leading to the castle's interior. "We'll find you an escort to the women's wing and let the king know you're here."

"An escort to the what?"

Before we could proceed any further, we came to a halt as half a dozen men fought their way out of the press and approached us. All of them were dressed in green and wearing masks. I was unsurprised to see they each bore the stamp of an Ecossic lineage and were in fact identical in appearance to my traveling companions. The duchess's brothers had come to rejoin the rest of their peculiar fraternity.

The two groups greeted each other with boisterous cries and joyous hugs, and I immediately lost track of who was who.

"We were expecting you last night," one said, talking loudly to be heard over the noise. He paused, taking in our torn clothing and assorted bloodstains. "What happened?"

"Nothing that couldn't be overcome by a nip of frostbite," another replied. Max? Yes, he had the hat. "What about here?" he asked. "Anything attack while we were gone?"

"No, but there's something you should—"

One huntsman had been looking me up and down the entire time, frowning. "Who's this?" he spat. "Is this the princess?"

A toad leapt out of his mouth and smacked into my face.

I batted at the creature as it busily crawled up my hair. It was large and surprisingly heavy. "Excuse me. Did you just *spit a toad* at me?"

"Serves you right," he said. "I hope it gives you warts." As if to emphasize the point, he spat again, ejecting a tiny, colorful frog onto my shoe. It hopped away into the crowd. I dearly hoped it wasn't one of the poisonous ones.

"Jude, we've talked about this," another hunter said with thc weary air of frequent repetition. "Don't spit amphibians at people. It isn't polite."

"I'm doing it for Jack!" the frog spitter protested.

"Look at her," said the other one. "Would any princess be so bedraggled? Her dress is all over muck."

The toad croaked loudly in my ear.

My interest in the rest of their argument was nonexistent. Nor did I care what imagined grudge Jude held against a princess he had never met. For whatever reason, while wounds, exhaustion, and a desperate need for a bath hadn't pushed me over the edge, a toad in my hair was the final straw.

I wrenched the toad off my head, painfully ripping out the tangle of hair it clung to, tossed it aside, and stalked off toward the Great Hall, forcing a path through the multitudes in the way. Some of the huntsmen shouted after me and ran in pursuit, but the crowd closed in my wake, slowing them down. One almost managed to reach me before he was cut off. The villagers' boots crushed the flowers that sprung up under his feet where he walked.

I ignored that and ignored the shouts, which soon faded into the rest of the noise.

Enough was enough. The huntsmen's secrets and dislikes and strange powers were of little consequence now that they had brought me to the king. I had no need to wait in the "women's wing," whatever that was, until the king deigned to call for Clover the handmaiden. It was time to drop the disguise and present myself as I was.

I didn't know what my husband-to-be was going to make of me in my current state, and I didn't much care. I wasn't the one who'd asked for this wedding. If he was shocked to find his bride straggling in encrusted with blood and dirt, he could damn well learn to live with it. It probably wouldn't be the last time it happened, given my luck and my history, so I figured I might as well start as I meant to go on.

I threw open the double doors to find a large room, its high wooden ceiling held up by broad smoke-blackened beams. Dust motes danced in the dying sunlight that slanted through a dozen west-facing lancet windows. Before me were the backsides of a pack of nobles in richly dyed clothes, scarlet and gold and vermilion and indigo, like a flock of bright birds. I caught glimpses of their faces as they turned to talk with one another, and I noted that none appeared to be wearing masks. The "latest fashion at the court" had decidedly failed to catch on.

A clear avenue led across to the other side of the room, where the top of an ornate throne peeked up above the elaborate feathered hats. Heads swiveled in my direction as I strode boldly ahead.

And then something rolled under my shoe, and my foot slipped out from under me. I landed on my arm with a sickening crack.

I yelped in surprise at the sharp stab of pain, which quickly dulled to a low, aching throb. Around me, the murmurs of the crowd ceased.

In the silence, a deep, sonorous voice spoke. "That," it said, "clearly proves my hypothesis. We have here before us, in this very hall"—the voice paused for dramatic effect—"a woman!"

CHAPTER ELEVEN

The Lion's Test

"Thank you for stating the obvious, Lion," a different voice snapped. "I could have told you that. Do you have any idea why she's here?"

From my vantage point on the floor, I saw a circle of faces hovering over me, white teeth splitting mustaches and beards into amused grins.

"She should not be here at all," said the first, sonorous speaker. "This is a grave breach of protocol. In the third chapter of my book, you will find—"

"We know the rules. Someone send for Angelique, she'll sort this out. And give that woman some air. I think she's hurt."

Murmurs of assent arose from the assembled gentry. The assorted beards above me pulled back, leaving me staring at the high ceiling. I regarded it for a few moments, then rolled my head to the side. A pair of slippered feet approached, scattering tiny round green balls across the flagstones.

Why was the floor covered in dried peas?

"Are you injured?" A woman knelt beside me, placing a cool hand on my shoulder. Long blue-black hair brushed against my cheek.

I looked up into a gentle smile and a wide-set pair of warm brown eyes. "I . . . My arm. I don't know if it's broken or only bruised."

For a simple fracture, I thought, *manipulate the ends of the broken bone until they line up properly. This will hurt. A lot. Splint the arm to hold the bone in place. Allow six to twelve weeks for the injury to heal.*

The woman's forehead knitted with concern. "Can you wiggle your fingers?" She ran her hand down my sleeve. "Maybe you should stay on the floor for the moment."

"That doesn't sound like a bad idea," I replied.

"Who are you? From your accent, I'm guessing you're from Skalla?"

The tromp of heavy footfalls sounded behind me, and I looked back to see one of the hunters entering the room.

"Her name is Clover," he said.

Blood on his breeches. Jack.

"She's come to see to the wedding arrangements on behalf of the Skallan princess," he added. "Monsters attacked her in the woods."

"Did they?" The woman examining my arm narrowed her eyes. "And your merry band just happened to be there to rescue her, I take it? That's rather a coincidence."

"A very fortuitous one," he agreed. "I can't imagine Skalla would have taken her death well. They might have gone so far as to call off the marriage."

The woman was poised to say more, but before she could, the nobles watching the exchange melted away as fast as a herd of antelope fleeing from a predator. And in their wake, the predator stepped forward.

If you have ever seen a lion up close, you know they are big. Bigger than you would expect, even if you are expecting something big. And the kingdom's talking lion was larger than that.

He was easily ten feet long from his nose to the tip of his tail. Most of that was solid muscle. His head overtopped the height of the tallest people in the crowd. His shaggy mane shaded from tawny at the forehead to a dark brown around his powerful shoulders. An incongruous set of spectacles perched precariously on his nose.

The lion looked at Jack and frowned. Lion mouths are not human mouths and do not readily shape themselves into human expressions. When you spend time with a cat, though, which having a sister like Calla makes inevitable, you quickly find out they have their own ways of expressing pleasure, or anger, or disdain. And the feline expression he wore at that moment was, unmistakably, a frown.

"You did not disturb the peas when you walked," the lion rumbled.

"Peas? What peas?" Jack asked, glancing down. "Oh, are there peas on the floor? How odd."

"You have altered your behavior. But when your fellow conspirators enter the room—"

As if on cue, eleven more masked men in green poured through the door, walking with a heavy, deliberate tread, stamping on the peas. One of them frowned in puzzlement when he saw me on the floor. Sam, I guessed, the moment before I confirmed it by checking his claw-torn shirt. If they'd stopped to change their clothes, I'd no doubt have been at a complete loss.

"You must have been warned about the test!" the lion said. "Who warned you?"

"Or perhaps," someone new cut in, stepping out from behind the great cat, "your ridiculous test has failed, Lion. Admit you were wrong, and leave it be."

"I was not wrong!" the lion protested. "I will find a better test!"

The man walking around the lion wore clothes no finer than those of the other nobles. But my attention was drawn to the gold circlet, studded with jewels, making a dent in his curly black hair.

My first view of King Gervase, my intended husband, was from the floor. I could see up his nose.

His gaze locked with Jack's. "You're back."

"Yes." Jack seemed likewise unable to tear his eyes from Gervase. "Are you all right?"

"I'm fine. There were no incidents here." The king glanced at the bloodstains spotting Jack's breeches. "But you're hurt."

"Just a scratch."

I took the opportunity to study my betrothed. There was nothing obviously wrong with him. He had a long, narrow face with a prominent nose. Thin lips framed by a neatly trimmed mustache and beard. Olive-toned skin and dark eyes. Not entirely to my tastes, but it was a face I might get used to in time. If I had to.

"What happened?" he asked Jack.

"Nothing important. A minor skirmish."

That was something of an understatement. "I'd hate to see a major one, then," I said. "I could have died."

The king finally deigned to look in my direction. To do him credit, his tone was apologetic as he crouched down to talk to me. "I'm sorry you had to go through that," he said. "And that you have received further injuries here."

"Injuries?" Sam asked. "What injuries?"

"She slipped on the peas," the dark-haired woman explained.

Sam scowled at the lion belligerently, his hands clenching into fists at his sides.

"Did I hear right that you've come about the"—the king

paused—"the wedding arrangements? With the princess of Skalla?"

His mouth curled down at the corners. He looked no happier than Jack had been at the prospect of Princess Melilot. Was anyone pleased by this marriage?

"What did Jack say your name was?" he asked.

I hesitated.

This would have been the perfect time to reveal my true identity. Whatever secret the huntsmen were hiding, they had kept their word and delivered me safely to the castle. All I had to do was declare myself, and I would surely be cosseted, fussed over, wined, dined, and made comfortable.

Something Jack had said when he entered the room, however, niggled at my mind.

Monsters attacked her in the woods.

Attacked *her*. Not *us*. Me. And he was right. The trap had been laid for a traveler on the road. The road a princess arriving from Skalla was almost certain to take. Even after Jack had told me the monster attacks were planned, I'd still assumed I'd merely been in the wrong place at the wrong time. But what if, instead, it had been an attempt on my life?

An assassination attempt, targeting me. The real me, Melilot, not Clover the handmaiden—because no one makes plans to eliminate handmaidens who don't actually exist. Was there someone who did not want this wedding to take place? So much so that murdering a foreign princess was a reasonable alternative?

"Clover," I said. "My name is Clover. And before the princess arrives, I think we need to have some words about your health and safety standards. Will there be any peas on the floor in the wedding venue?"

At that, the king's face cracked into a rueful smile. "I assure you that won't be an issue. And I hope your arm isn't hurt too badly." He straightened out of his crouch and turned to the woman hovering over me. "Angelique, would you see that our guest's needs are taken care of? Make sure that includes a visit to the chirurgeon."

"Of course. Are you able to stand?" she asked me, offering a hand. Since I didn't think lying on the floor for the rest of time would be the best of choices, I accepted her help and let her pull me up by my uninjured arm.

"We'll discuss the wedding plans when you've had a chance to rest," Gervase said. "In the meantime, please make yourself welcome in my kingdom. I wish you could have had a better introduction to it, but things have been"—he searched for the right words—"somewhat unusual, of late."

"So I've heard," I muttered as Angelique led me off. Sam took a step after us, but Jack put a hand on his shoulder and shook his head.

"Finally, the sanctity of the Great Hall is restored," the lion rumbled. "Or partially restored, at any rate . . ." He began complaining once again that his test had been interfered with, whatever that might mean, and the interrupted argument between him, the king, and the huntsmen resumed as the assembled nobles murmured and tittered behind us.

There was too much happening that I didn't understand. Huntsmen in masks, a king unhappy to wed the bride he'd sent for. Peas all over the floor.

The only thing certain was that someone had enemies here. And it was entirely possible that the someone in question was me.

CHAPTER TWELVE

The Princesses and the Peas

Angelique unlocked a small door at the back of the Great Hall with one key among dozens on a ring.

A stinging pain jabbed at my foot every time I took a step. I couldn't remember how I'd hurt it. I limped along after her into a windowless passage lit by smoky sconces.

"The sanctity of the Great Hall?" I asked. "What was that about?"

"Our lion is hundreds of years old and considers himself the keeper of our ancient traditions." Angelique rolled her eyes. "He's written some fantastically boring book explaining them. You weren't supposed to be in the hall at all. I'm only allowed in myself on a technicality."

I wondered how many of these "traditions" there were and how easy it would be to violate them by accident. It would probably be a good idea to find a copy of that book, however dull it might be.

We climbed up a short flight of steps, and I made the mistake of grabbing for the banister with my injured arm. I swore under my breath and jerked it back.

"The chirurgeon will see to your arm. And the rest of your injuries," Angelique said, looking over my various cuts and bruises. "After that, perhaps a bath?"

"The very suggestion," I replied, "makes me want to kiss you."

She laughed merrily. "Surely you don't mean that."

"I think you underestimate just how desperately I want a bath."

"Then that was rather forward of you," she said, smiling as she gazed at me through half-lidded eyes. "Not to mention verging on scandalous."

Oh, dear. I hadn't intended to be suggestive. My doomed flirtation with Sam had been bad enough without my also attracting the interest of . . . who was this, exactly? The keys suggested an upper servant of some kind. "Er, are you the chatelaine here? Will I be consulting with you about the wedding arrangements?"

"Something like that," she said. "I'm Gervase's older sister."

My eyebrows shot up in surprise. "I didn't know the king had a sister." She hadn't been on the list of names I'd had to memorize during my lessons. And in Jack's story of the attacks on the royal family, she'd gone entirely unmentioned.

"You're not alone in that." Her smile didn't drop. "No one but Gervase ever seems to remember I exist. We had different mothers, and mine produced no male heirs, so hardly counted."

"A surplus stepdaughter? I know how that goes."

I took a moment to study her. I could see the resemblance to the king, now that I was looking for it. In her features, that narrow face and jutting nose had settled into something more harmonious. Perhaps that was the contribution of her disregarded mother. In all honesty, Angelique was a bit more to my taste than King Gervase. I still wouldn't have been leaping with joy if

I'd been forced into an arranged marriage with her. But I might not have been quite so disgruntled about my fate.

She studied me right back, with a look that felt like it was piercing through every last one of my secrets.

Definitely more to my taste.

Oh, dear.

I lurched away, breaking our gaze, and pain shot through my foot again as my weight fell on it. It didn't feel like an injury; more like a rock in my shoe. "Hold on for a second."

When I slipped the shoe off my foot and upended it, a pea rolled out. I brushed at my clothes, and a few more peas escaped from where they'd hidden in the folds and pleats of my skirt, dropping to the floor with faint, dull tinks. I'd probably be shedding them for days.

I sighed. "Wonderful. If any of these end up in my mattress, it'll keep me awake all night." And I'd so been looking forward to a comfortable bed.

"Really?" Angelique tilted her head, intrigued.

I nodded. "Sensitive skin."

"What a remarkable coincidence—it's the same for me. Any lump in the bedding might as well be a boulder."

"What were the peas for, anyway?"

My shoe back on, we made our way through the passage. The noises of a castle drifting from afternoon to evening echoed through the hall: the rhythmic clank of a blacksmith pounding on an anvil, the baying of dogs longing to be released from their kennel, a snatch of drunken song.

"The peas are another of the lion's strange notions," Angelique said as she ushered me through an archway. "He has some kind of fixation on the king's huntsmen. I'm not clear on the details, but he's convinced they're hiding something."

"I can't think what gave it away. The masks, perhaps?"

Angelique chuckled. "Nothing gets past our lion. Anyway, he's been devising tests to prove his claims."

"And the peas were supposed to show . . . ?"

"I haven't the slightest idea."

"What does the king think of all this?"

"Gervase thinks the keeper of our ancient traditions has lost his mind. He won't refuse to set the tests, though. It was already causing talk that he took twelve masked strangers into his service. He can't afford to alienate the court any further."

"He can't?" It was hard to imagine my stepmother caring if she alienated the whole of Skalla. "Why not?"

Angelique paused. Her gaze flicked around the empty corridor, as if to make sure we were alone, before alighting back on me.

"He's scarcely been king for two months. The troops are more loyal to their barons than to him. And the times are . . . tense." Her mouth tightened into a thin hard line. "Watch your step while you're here, wedding planner. And if you ever feel the need to flee, let me know. I might be able to help."

She turned on her heel and strode onward. I followed, wondering exactly what kind of snakes' nest my stepmother had shoved me into.

When we reached the chirurgeon's surgery, it proved to be an untidy chamber deep in the bowels of the castle, reeking with horrible odors. The chirurgeon himself was a white-haired man with dirt crusted under his fingernails. He didn't bother to wash his hands before examining me. I disliked him immediately, and the feeling soon became mutual.

He diagnosed my arm as sprained rather than broken and bound it competently enough. The haircut he offered was quick, rough, and uneven, but it still came as a relief since, after everything that had happened, my hair reached below my waist and was impossibly tangled, not to mention matted with pumpkin debris. It had become so heavy that I felt like I was floating with it gone.

But then, the chirurgeon took offense when I refused a poultice for the scratches on my shoulders. When I sniffed it, it smelled distinctly of pig dung. Since I likewise turned down the offered courses of leeches, laxatives, and purgatives, we fell into an argument while Angelique looked on with amusement.

"You," he snapped, "are a silly cow who's going to choke on her excess bile!"

"I'll take my chances with that rather than bleed, shit, and vomit myself to death under your tender care." I had a vague notion my responses might be a bit out of character for a handmaiden, but I couldn't bring myself to stay silent. Very little offends me like subpar medical practice.

"If the two of you are done quarreling," Angelique said drily, "might I ask for another treatment?"

The chirurgeon recovered the tattered shreds of his dignity and turned to Angelique with a much more solicitous air.

"How have your headaches been lately, my dear?" he asked.

"Not so bad as they sometimes are," she replied. "I've nearly recovered from yesterday's."

He nodded and examined her skull for a few minutes before smearing a paste on her forehead that smelled of garlic and wormwood. I judged it harmless, though it was also completely useless. But I had to clench my jaw to keep from objecting when he applied a leech to her inner elbow. She wasn't my patient. At least he hadn't attempted to drill a hole in her head.

He waited until the paste grew crusty, then rinsed it off and told her if she came again the next day, he would prepare a lozenge. I shuddered to think what might be in it.

"Have you suffered from headaches long?" I asked when we were back out in the hall.

"Since I was a child. Some days I can't get out of bed." She shrugged. "The chirurgeon does what he can, but nothing works well."

"Where does it originate?" I couldn't help myself. "What part of the head, I mean. And are they ever accompanied by nausea or distorted vision? Or by sensitivity to light and sound?"

"What an odd little duckling you are," she said. "How did a handmaiden come by such strong opinions about medicine?"

I'd been right—I was being too assertive about this. I'd have to be more careful. "My parents were . . ." I hesitated. What made the most sense for the persona I'd created? Very few nobles become doctors, even the kind of minor noble who'd be chosen as a handmaiden. The chirurgeon certainly hadn't struck me as being among the aristocracy. "They were interested in such matters," I said. "Patrons of the local academy."

"How fascinating." She stopped before a stout wooden door and unlocked it with a key from her ring. "Here we are. The women's wing. We'll see about that bath and then find you a bed. One without any peas in the mattress."

I hoped a warm bath could be arranged, but I sorely needed any bath at all, even a cold one. And a bit of soap would be better for my injuries than pig dung.

"By the way," I said as I stepped through the door, "why exactly do you have a 'women's wing'?"

CHAPTER THIRTEEN

Spinning My Wheels

"Once upon a time," said the oldest of the Yvettes, "when the world was younger and the mountains soared a little higher, there was a sorceress-queen whose daughter was the most beautiful maiden in the land."

I pricked my finger with my embroidery needle and gave a yelp. Sewing fabric was a very different skill from stitching flesh, and my facility with the latter had not transferred as well as I might have hoped.

The circle of women, from adolescent to elderly, turned as one and glared at me for the interruption. I ducked my head in apology.

The eldest Yvette cleared her throat and resumed. "The queen had declared that anyone who wished to woo her daughter must first complete an impossible task or else perish. But a prince had heard tales of the maiden's great beauty and set off to win her hand in spite of the danger. One day, as he was riding to the sorceress-queen's lands, he saw what he thought was an enormous haystack. When he got closer, he realized it was a man with a stomach the size of a small mountain, who had lain down there to rest. 'Take me into your service!' the man importuned the traveler. 'For whenever I take a deep breath, I become three thousand times larger than this.' The prince thought he could make use of such a miraculous talent and agreed to take the man on. After a while, the two of them came upon a fellow who had covered his eyes with a bandage. 'I can never remove my blindfold,' he repined, 'for my gaze is so devastating that whatever I look at shatters into pieces. . . .'"

I found my attention drifting; the tale sounded a great deal like one I'd heard before. Although there was little enough for my wayward attention to land on. There wasn't much to do in the quarters set aside for women, other than sew and listen to stories.

My cunning disguise had turned out to be the worst possible choice. A full week after my arrival at the castle, I had absolutely nothing to show for it. My investigation into who might be trying to murder me had made no progress. I'd scarcely seen Gervase and had no notion of whether I should be pleased or dissatisfied to be his fiancée. For that matter, I hadn't made much headway with the wedding plans that were my purported reason for coming.

The problem should have struck me earlier. I hadn't found it odd that the hunters were all men; identical duplicates, after all, are required to be identical. But the same had been true of the guards at the gatehouse and the nobles in the Great Hall—all men. If nothing else, the lion's sneering disdain at my presence might have given me a hint.

Say what you would about my stepmother—and I always did—she was not of the opinion that women were only fit for childbearing and child-rearing. She might be happy to trade away a daughter like a rug, but prior to the trade, she wanted that daughter put to the best possible use in her service. I had traveled enough on her various quests, however, to have discovered there were many countries where this was not the case. Pawn that I might have been in Skalla, there were places where I wouldn't be considered a playable piece at all. And Tailliz, it appeared, numbered among them.

The burden here seemed to fall most on unwed noblewomen of marriageable age. In other words, precisely the guise I had chosen. Had I announced myself upon arrival and wed Gervase, I would have had the run of the castle along with the duties and privileges of a queen. Had I claimed to be a humble goosegirl seeking a flock of waterfowl to tend, I would have had more freedom to come and go as I pleased. But the traditions of Tailliz dictated that noblewomen be cloistered behind stout walls, rarely seen until they emerged for an arranged marriage.

The reasons for this remained obscure to me, although apparently they were detailed in the lion's book. I had failed to obtain a copy; few of the women knew how to read, so books were not kept in their quarters. And my questions on the subject received contradictory answers when they weren't contemptuously dismissed. I was left unsure whether it was presumed the women would be assaulted by ruffians, infected with disease, or driven to fornicate like bunnies the moment they were let out of doors. Perhaps all three at once.

My attitude toward Tailliz, which had not been optimistic to begin with, became darker with each passing day. I was offended not only by the treatment of women but also by the blatant waste of space during a national emergency. While the women's wing was crowded—noble families from every part of Tailliz had lingered in the capital after Gervase's coronation, as keen as anyone else to seek the safety of the castle walls—the rooms weren't so packed that they couldn't have sheltered a few of the villagers who'd been sleeping outdoors.

In the mornings, the inmates of the women's wing were allowed to take the air on a wide balcony, hidden from the masses in the courtyard by a filigreed wooden screen. We peered through cutouts shaped like flowers and diamonds to watch the daily hunting party set forth. Cheers erupted from the crowd as the king, his lion, and his band of masked hunters sallied through the gates, accompanied by a din of clattering horseshoes and baying dogs. I tried to pick out Sam from among their ranks; I was fairly certain I could tell which one he was, although I wasn't sure what made him stand out. Perhaps it was his posture. Did he, I wondered, ever think about me?

"I'm surprised there are any hunts," I'd remarked to Angelique on the first day. "Aren't they concerned about being ripped apart by the horrors in the forest?"

The young blonde next to Angelique—Yvette, I later learned she was called; I soon discovered most of the ladies were named Yvette, along with a sprinkling of Yvonnes—gave me a glare so baleful that if she'd had a shred of magic in her body, it would have flayed my skin off. Angelique merely smiled.

"They never go the same way twice," she told me. "No one can predict which route they'll take through the woods."

Jack's strategy of straying from the known paths was being put to heavy use, it seemed. "Does it work?"

"It's been weeks since the last attack on a hunting party. Well," she added, "at least until the one that beset you."

"I wouldn't think that makes it safe enough to risk the king."

The smile faded from her lips. "My brother can be brave to the point of foolishness. If the hunts must take place, then he insists upon joining them."

I was about to ask why the hunts had to take place at all, but the answer occurred to me before I opened my mouth. With the farmers huddled within the castle walls, the daily hunts were likely one of the few regular sources of food remaining. The animals the villagers had brought with them couldn't possibly feed everyone. But a single stag could provide a hundred meals and a wild boar almost as many. The king and his huntsmen were risking their safety to make sure no one starved.

After that morning, I scarcely saw Angelique. In the absence of a queen, she had been given special dispensation as the king's sister to leave the women's quarters and fulfill the role. Her debilitating headaches kept her confined in her chambers the rest of the time. And I, in the meanwhile, spent my days finding out what unmarried upper-class women in Tailliz did with their lives:

Sit.

Spin.

They spent most of the day assembled in the largest room in the women's wing, a circular chamber with a great stone hearth, crouched over spinning wheels or needle and thread. To make the time pass more quickly, they told stories like the one Eldest Yvette was sharing now. She was the most frequent storyteller and had been granted permanent possession of the most desirable seat, next to the fire. I had gathered she was the king's great-aunt, and I wondered if the other Yvettes had been named in her honor.

It shocked me that so many of the ladies took the dire, deadly risk of spinning thread so cavalierly, endangering their very lives for the sake of clothing, bedding, and tapestries. But I supposed if the king and his huntsmen were going to throw themselves in the path of horrible monsters, the ladies of the court felt they could do no less. And it was, of course, as necessary a task as gathering food. I came from a realm where clothing was fashioned by other means, and my travels abroad had been more concerned with magical quests than textiles. It had never occurred to me that in a place where sorcery was uncommon, enormous daily energy had to be expended in order to prevent an outbreak of mass nudity.

However much I admired their bravery, I couldn't bring myself to join them. The first few days, I had the excuse of my sprained arm. After that, I insisted, I needed to repair the slashes the spider wolves had left in my beloved red cloak. But when that was done with, they tried to sit me in front of a spinning wheel, and I flatly refused. I was happy to embroider, sew, and knit, especially as there was little else to occupy my time. Pricked fingers, I could live with. But some lines I wouldn't cross, not with the habits of a lifetime warning me off.

"The princess was convinced her new husband was a swineherd," Eldest Yvette recited, her story coming to its end, "and tended the pigs with him for a week, until she thought she could stand it no more. But one day while he was out, a pair of strangers came to the farm. 'Come,' they urged, 'we will take you to your husband.' They led her to a palace where the prince stood in wait, dressed as befit his station. She did not recognize him until he kissed her. 'I had to endure much to be with you,' he admonished her, 'and now you have likewise endured much to be with me.' And they lived happily ever after."

The ladies around me murmured their appreciation. Personally, I thought the prince had behaved like an ass. Although admittedly the princess had tried to set him on fire earlier on in the tale, so forcing her to feed hogs for a week might not have been the worst punishment imaginable. I had my doubts about their future happiness together.

During the chatter that followed the storytelling, I turned to the Yvette to my right. "I was wondering," I said, "if you might be able to help me with something."

Righthand Yvette sucked her cheeks in as if she were being forced to chew on a lemon. "Oh?" Her gaze remained locked on her whirring spinning wheel. My carefully schooled expression, friendly, open, and ingratiating, was completely wasted.

I forged ahead nonetheless. "I find myself a bit lost in the politics of Tailliz," I confessed. "When my lady arrives, I hardly know what to tell her. Does the king—"

"I know nothing of such matters," she said. "You must make your inquiries elsewhere."

"Attend to your sewing," said the Yvonne to my left, a tall, imperious woman. "Smaller stitches. Don't be sloppy."

"Thank you," I said with an admirably straight face, "for gifting me with your wisdom." I stabbed my needle into the cloth. I refrained from telling her she might be more appreciative of my "sloppy" wide stitchwork if I were doing my best to close off one of her arteries without tearing right through it.

She narrowed her eyes, trying to determine whether or not I was being sarcastic. I showed her a sweet smile. I considered giving her the appellation Giant Fucking Asshole Yvonne. But that, I decided, would be too mean.

I went with Snotface Yvonne instead.

For the twelfth or thirteenth time that day, I had to remind myself I was attempting to gather information and therefore not in a position where I could cheerfully throttle them all. And if Snotface had let slip anything useful, even in the course of yet another snub, I would have been grateful for the privilege of being insulted. As usual, though, my latest bid to ascertain whether the king had any enemies—or indeed, learn anything else—had smashed straight into a brick wall.

Possibly, the Yvettes and Yvonnes knew as little as they claimed, their lives so constrained that the vagaries of the court were outside their experience altogether. But I doubted it. These were the sisters and daughters of barons and dukes, and at the very least, they had spent their childhoods outside of these walls. They had to have some idea which of their relatives hated each other.

The simple truth was they didn't like me.

I wasn't sure why. They did not strike me as irredeemably ill-natured; like people anywhere, they could be charming or disagreeable depending on their mood. But with the exception of Angelique, they invariably treated me with contempt. It had not escaped my notice that my seat was far from the hearth. In a draft.

It might simply have been that I was a foreign interloper with foreign beliefs and assumptions. They seemed rather dismissive of such things. I was far from certain that was the case outside the bounds of the women's wing, where ships from other lands brought visitors with trade goods up the coast every summer, and Ecossic hunters were lauded as heroes. But hereditary nobles could be an insular lot. And their insularity probably didn't diminish when they were literally walled off from the rest of the world.

I tried again, on a different topic, with the futile hope I would eventually win them over. My previous attempts to fulfill my self-imposed role as a wedding planner hadn't met with any great success, but perhaps the eighth time would be the charm. "Regarding the marriage ceremony," I began, "who might I talk to about—"

"The ceremony," Righthand Yvette informed me, "will be the ancient Tailliziani rite of matrimony."

"The unexpurgated version," a younger Yvette said—Snotface Yvonne's daughter, I thought? She was the one who had glared at me on the balcony when the hunt set off the first morning. "All seven hours of it."

I couldn't repress a wince. "Seven?" I somehow doubted the bride was going to be given any breaks to have a snack. Or go to the bathroom.

"Nothing less will do for a royal wedding," sniffed Righthand Yvette. She still hadn't looked up at me, and her foot never paused on the treadle. I eyed the whirling spindle nervously and did my best not to draw back.

"And of course," said Baleful Glare Yvette, "it will be held in the castle courtyard."

"Ah," I said. "Perhaps there should be a backup plan? Since a whole village is currently packed into that courtyard."

A pair of affronted glances were my only reply.

"Or even just in case of rain?" I added.

They somehow managed to look more affronted than before.

None of this was unusual. Any suggestions I made were generally met with silent horror, silent outrage, or outraged, horrified silence.

Gervase had never bothered to send for me to discuss the wedding, despite what he'd said when we'd met. Possibly there was simply no need. According to the denizens of the women's wing, everything had already been planned to the minute to account for the ancient traditions, precedents, and political squabbles of Tailliz. The tiniest of details had been decided in advance, from who would be sitting with whom to who would decidedly not be sitting with whom. My sole contribution, both as foreign planner and eventual bride, was to muck all of this up by my very presence.

"Will Princess Melilot," asked Eldest Yvette, "have any opinions regarding the decorations?"

"It depends," I said, receiving a harsh sneer in response. "Why do you ask?"

Eldest Yvette did not deign to reply.

That kind of question, I had discovered, was a trap. If I stated that Princess Melilot had any preferences as to, say, food, they were outraged that the menu required a change. If I stated that Princess Melilot had no preferences as to food, they were horrified that they had no way of catering to her tastes. It was the same for every other matter, and I ended up attempting to give both answers at once, creating the impression of a princess with strong yet nonexistent opinions on colors, flavors, flowers, music, and dancing who would arrive with a retinue numbering somewhere between none and infinite, all of whom would insist on sitting, standing, or kneeling at the front, at the back, or possibly in the sea.

I was spared further conversation when Eldest Yvette launched into another story and the rest of the group fell silent. This one was about a princess who demanded her suitor spend the night with a bear. Insufferable princesses getting their comeuppance was the theme of the day. It was clearly meant as a pointed commentary about my "mistress." I wondered if they thought they were being subtle.

I had never been asked to contribute to the storytelling sessions, although they must have been tired of tales they already knew. It was just as well. The audience would not have been the friendliest, and I would have been too tempted to tell one about a disguised woman suffering through trials until her enemies were vanquished. Perhaps the one with the swans. Or the dead horse. Or the donkey that pooped gold.

Instead, I bent my head over my embroidery and spent the rest of the afternoon in silence, daydreaming now of Sam's grin, now of Angelique's gaze, and sometimes only of solitude.

CHAPTER FOURTEEN

I Learn Why Everyone Hates Me

The following morning, Angelique at last made another appearance, joining the rest of us on the balcony to watch the king and his hunters depart. While the cheers were still ringing in the air, she pulled me aside, maneuvering me into a room no bigger than a closet. Since the shelves lining the walls were half-filled with candle stubs, mopheads, and assorted bric-a-brac, a closet is probably exactly what it was. We were pressed close. I could smell her perfume. Rose and jasmine, with a hint of cinnamon.

She looked exhausted, her face drawn, tension at the corners of her mouth and eyes. I recognized the expression; my parents' patients had often tried to disguise the extent of their pain. Angelique's headaches might have lessened enough for her to get out of bed, but they hadn't let up entirely.

"Have you tried putting a cold, damp cloth on the back of your neck when you feel a headache coming on?" I could no longer in good conscience leave her to the tender mercies of the chirurgeon. "It sometimes helps if you put a few drops of peppermint oil on it."

Her brow drew down in puzzlement. "What? No."

"You can also try taking ginger extract, or feverfew."

"I don't—" She stopped and began again. "That's not what I brought you here to talk about."

"Are you sure you don't want to, though? Those remedies might not work, but they have more of a chance than wormwood smeared on your forehead. Or leeches." I shuddered.

She shook her head, then stopped, grimacing. Her hand rose to press against her temple. The motion clearly hadn't done her pain any favors. "You are so very odd. Now, listen: There's a matter we need to discuss."

She glanced into the hallway, to make sure the rest of the ladies had passed out of earshot, and then shut the door, leaving us in the dim light that crept in around the edges of the frame. I was beginning to wonder exactly what her intentions were. And whether I should object if an assignation in a closet was what she had in mind. But that didn't strike me as her style.

"The others," she said, "think that you've been putting on airs."

"They do?" I racked my brain for what I might have been doing. Did I have some princessy habit giving me away? "Why would they? Do you?"

"I'm not certain." She looked me up and down with that keen gaze of hers. "Why won't you spin?"

I gaped at her in bewilderment; the answer to that question seemed obvious to me. "Are they blaming me for not sharing the risk?" I refrained from pointing out that Angelique did as little spinning as I did; being the king's sister, I imagined, had its privileges here.

She blinked. Whatever answer she was expecting, that wasn't it. "The risk? What on earth are you talking about?"

"The risk of death? Or a hundred years of sleep? Or any curse, really."

A long pause followed before she spoke again. "Are you . . . are you worried that our spinning wheels are *enchanted*?"

"Aren't you?"

"That doesn't happen here!"

Now that I gave the matter a moment's thought, I realized that without any sorcerers, witches, or evil fairies in Tailliz, the concern simply wouldn't exist. I'd been avoiding anything with a spindle for so long it hadn't occurred to me that the fear of them might not be universal.

"In Skalla, no one would touch one," I said. "They've been banned for a century or more."

"Because of the terrible peril," she replied evenly, "of spinning wheels."

"They're ridiculously easy to enchant. It's got something to do with the combination of rotating bits and stabby bits. They suck up dark magic like nobody's business and spit it out on anyone so unlucky as to brush past. I thought you'd just accepted it."

"You thought we'd accepted chancing death every time we want to make a shirt?"

"Well, I mean . . . you need the shirts, don't you?"

Princess Angelique let out a long breath. "So very, very odd. What do you do for shirts in Skalla? Surely someone's needed new clothes in the last hundred years."

"Fairy godmothers are popular. And the fae folk can weave dresses out of cobwebs and moonlight." They did have a tendency to dissolve back into cobwebs and moonlight if you tore them, which could be embarrassing at a dinner party. "My sister gets birds and mice to make most of her clothing. There's all kinds of methods, really."

"Fascinating." She did not sound particularly fascinated. "But be that as it may, everyone here assumes you consider spinning beneath you. Handmaidens spin. Embroidery is reserved for ladies of higher station."

"It is?" So much for my powers of observation. I'd worked out that seats by the fire were a sign of status, but it had escaped my notice that the chores were structured by class position. It might have been easier if I'd been able to work out whether a baron's daughter ranked higher than a viscount's sister in Tailliz—assuming I could even keep track of which Yvette was which.

"I'll let the others know you have strange foreign customs," Angelique decided. "They'll think you're somewhat dim, be delighted by their own superior ways, and forgive you. I won't mention the part about enchanted spinning wheels." She turned and reached for the door handle, but then she hesitated and looked back at me. "You know a fair bit about magic, don't you?"

"Some," I said, wondering where this was headed. "It's a basic survival skill in Skalla."

"Are you a sorceress yourself?"

It was my turn to hesitate, unsure how the truth would be taken. Sorceresses were not well regarded everywhere, and if you took my stepmother as an example, it was not a prejudice altogether without cause. But Angelique appeared to be more curious than concerned.

"A very minor one," I confessed. "But yes, I have a little of the talent for it."

She nodded sharply, as if something she'd already suspected had been confirmed. "In that case . . . how would you feel about joining the hunts?"

The proposal took me by surprise. "I thought women weren't allowed to go hunting here."

"Women, yes, but . . ." She waved her arm in a dismissive gesture. "You're a Skallan sorceress. It's not the same thing. I'm sure I can arrange permission for it, and it would make everyone feel so much safer. The king got engaged to a Skallan in the first place for his own protection, after all."

I stood there open-mouthed as that piece of news hit home. Again and again, this conversation was leaving me flat-footed, struggling to catch up with things I should have figured out days before. I was beginning to feel as dim as Angelique planned to portray me. Jack had said outright that the Skallan princess was supposed to save Tailliz from peril. To be fair, I'd been distracted at the time by the monsters trying to eat me.

Gervase had broken off his previous engagement and sent out to Skalla for a bride because the situation had grown desperate, and the Skallan royal line was seething with sorcery. If either of my sisters had been sent along, he'd have been getting a good deal out of the bargain. But my sisters were both married, so he'd wound up with me instead. The least of us all. So far, my efforts to defend Tailliz against the terrors that beset it had consisted of beating a few of them with a large stick.

I wanted to go on the hunts. By then, I was desperate to grasp at any excuse to escape from the claustrophobic boredom and hostility of the women's wing. But if I was charged with the defense of the king and failed miserably at it, I doubted warm regard would be my reward.

Angelique was still waiting for my reply. "I'm not sure how much I can do," I said. "I'm not as powerful as"—I almost said "my stepmother" but caught myself in time—"as you might hope. I wasn't being modest when I said my talent was a small one. I can't magic my way past a few animated statues to plough a field."

"Animated what?"

"It's a long story, never mind. My point is, my capacities are strictly limited."

She plucked a metal bowl off a shelf and toyed with it. It reflected the dim light, casting strange shadows across her face. "Even a tiny bit of magic would make me feel infinitely better if I knew for certain it was on the king's side. It would only be until the princess arrives, so you won't have to do it for very long. I doubt you'd be in much danger."

When I didn't answer, she tossed the metal bowl into the depths of the closet with a clatter and put her hand on my shoulder. It still stung from my not-completely-healed cuts, so I had to make an effort not to flinch.

She brought her face close to mine. Her eyes were wide and vulnerable, and I could feel the warmth of her breath on my cheek. "Please," she whispered. "I'm begging you. My brother is out there every day with only those strange masked men to protect him."

It wasn't in me to ignore such a plea. Or at least, I found I couldn't refuse one that came from her. "All right. If it would mean that much to you."

She pulled away and turned her face to the side—embarrassed, I imagined, by how much of herself she'd just revealed. She took a moment to regain her composure. When she looked at me again, all traces of distress were gone from her face. Only her exhaustion remained. "Just do whatever you can. I'm glad someone will be out there to keep an eye on the huntsmen. You can't trust someone who hides their true self."

And with that, she flung open the closet door and swept off down the hall. I trailed along in her wake.

She'd cajoled me into agreeing so quickly I'd barely had time to think, but as I considered the idea, I realized joining the hunt might end up being well suited to my own purposes. I'd learned little about any murder plots while sitting around with a needle and thread, bored and browbeaten in the sewing room. And accompanying the hunt would also give me time to observe my husband-to-be. Spending the day out hunting with him would surely give me a better idea of what he was like.

But that was reasoning after the fact. I'd agreed to go because Angelique had asked me.

And for that matter, for all my rationalizing about getting to know Gervase, I wondered if it was the chance to see Sam again that had exerted the greater pull on me.

PART IV

A-HUNTING WE WILL GO

CHAPTER FIFTEEN

An Inopportune Interruption

In the warm darkness, a pair of arms wrapped themselves around me. A pair of lips sought mine. I responded eagerly, sliding my hands beneath clothing, feeling the play of muscles under skin. I pulled myself closer until our bodies were pressed together.

Behind me, someone cleared their throat uncomfortably. Someone else tried without success to suppress a giggle.

I leapt away from my lover, embarrassment heating my face. I couldn't believe I'd been caught kissing . . . kissing . . .

Who had I been kissing?

That could wait. "Who's there?" I shouted, groping about for anything I could use as a weapon. There were assassins lurking in the kingdom. If they had come for me, I didn't want to face them empty-handed.

"Um, we're very sorry to intrude," my older sister said, "but we thought it might be important."

"Jonquil?" I peered into the darkness. "What are you doing here? And where are you? I can't see a thing."

"You can if you want to. It's—"

"Oh, just give her some light," Gnoflwhogir interrupted. "By the time you explain, she'll be awake."

I heard her hands clap together, and the space was immediately illuminated.

"The space" was the best way to describe it. What the light revealed wasn't a chamber of the castle; it was a featureless black void. My feet rested on nothing, and nothing lay overhead. There were no walls for as far as I could see, only more nothingness, extending into infinity for all I knew. I found it somewhat puzzling that I could see the featureless black void better now that it was well lit.

Joining me in the nothingness, standing at odd angles—slantwise, perpendicular, or even upside down—were my sisters and their spouses.

The obvious explanation occurred to me. "I told you to knock first."

"I tried," Jonquil said, "but there was nothing to knock on."

"Which makes it a very boring dream," Gnoflwhogir complained. "No décor whatever. Are you always this single-minded when you—"

"Darling," Jonquil said. "Stop."

Jonquil looked almost as discomfited as I felt. At least I was wearing clothes this time; things hadn't yet progressed to the point that I'd removed any. Gnoflwhogir seemed impatient, and Calla had both her hands over her mouth, her brown cheeks dimpling as she futilely tried to hide a smile. As for Liam, his attention was focused on something over my shoulder.

"That . . ." he said. "That isn't me, is it?"

"What?" I turned to look. The figure I'd been kissing was waiting there motionless. "Of course that's not you!"

"It's all right with me if it is," Calla said. "I don't mind. No one can help what they dream."

"It isn't!" I insisted. Did my sister think so little of me? Did she assume I was jealous of everything she had, no matter what it was? "I mean, just look at it. That looks nothing like Liam."

I could, in all honesty, see where the confusion came from. My dream lover had bright red hair—a bit more flame red than Liam's, but my family had no idea I'd met a dozen other redheads recently. But while it had Sam's hair, it also had Angelique's proud nose. Beyond that, its body was somewhat amorphous, mostly broad hands, full lips, and . . . other parts both masculine and feminine, with the rest of it fading into foggy obscurity.

It reached out to stroke my cheek, but I was no longer in the mood. "Please go now," I said. Its plush mouth pouted, but it dutifully slunk off into the darkness. I felt bad about that, which was silly, considering it was a figment of my overheated imagination.

"Was it Gervase, then?" Calla asked. "Because that wasn't what I expected the king of Tailliz to look like."

"I'm not going to discuss it," I replied. "Didn't you say you were here for something important?"

"Yes." Jonquil looked relieved that the topic of discussion had changed. "Gnoflwhogir came down with a bout of prophecy. It might be about you."

"She did? What was it?" Fairy prophecies are never to be taken lightly. They can provide a timely warning of grave danger. They are also, however, highly annoying.

Fairy prophecies tend to come in the form of the most appalling possible doggerel, with some repetitive meter that makes them stick in your head for hours. More aggravating still, they're rife with ambiguities and double meanings. The very worst kind fulfill themselves at your expense when you try to avoid them—if you get a prediction that your son will kill you, and you throw your baby out the window to prevent it, then you've all but guaranteed that in twenty years' time, a "stranger" will murder you on the road. Even the less obnoxious ones are easy to misinterpret. Cross that river to wage war, and I'll destroy a vast empire, you say? Great! Oh, you meant I'd destroy *my own* empire. Whoopsie.

But while fairy prophecies have their perils, ignoring them is catastrophically foolish. One way or another, they always come true.

Gnoflwhogir closed her eyes and took a deep breath. "The king will ride—"

"Er," I said, "would you mind turning right side up before you continue? It's just, it's distracting this way."

She popped one eye back open. "I am not upside down. You are the one who is upside down."

"Darling," said Jonquil in a tone that implied there would be an argument later if Gnoflwhogir persisted.

The fairy sighed and rotated herself until she was only at about a ten-degree tilt from my perspective. Good enough, I supposed. I gestured for her to continue.

She began again:

The king will ride.
His future bride,
Disguised, will join the royal hunt.
The ground will shake; the earth will quake,
The woods become a battlefront.
Your love one breath away from death
And clinging by his fingertips—
If you would save him from the grave,
The answer lies upon your lips.

In the silence that followed, I tried to make heads or tails of it. It certainly sounded like it was meant for me—the king's future bride, riding beside him in disguise. But what of the rest of it? Was there going to be an earthquake? And if there was, what in the world could I say that would help?

"So, you can see why we stopped by," said Calla, "as you're the only one among us who's about to marry a king."

"Or is ever likely to," Jonquil added.

Liam frowned. "I'm a prince. I could be a king someday."

"Of course you could, sweetling," Calla said, reaching up at an odd angle to pat the probable tailor on the shoulder. "But I can hardly be your *future* bride, can I? Although," she went on thoughtfully, "I suppose you might marry Melilot if I died."

"Right. That's why I wanted to know if I was the dream lover she was—"

"First, that's morbid," I told them. "Second, that's gross, and third, no it wasn't!" I'd have stomped my foot, but there wasn't anything to stomp it on.

"The poem made it sound like her love is a king already," Calla pointed out, as calmly as if she hadn't just discussed her husband marrying her sister after her death. "So that would make it Gervase, wouldn't it?"

Would it? I'd hardly met the man. Although that might matter little if our love was a foregone conclusion foretold by prophecy. Which is yet another reason prophecies suck. They make you feel like a doll being played with by some omnipotent child. As if an inescapable force were going to mash me up against Gervase and shout, "NOW KISS!"

"All of this is beside the point," Jonquil said, trying her hardest to salvage the conversation. "What we really want to know is, do you need our help again?"

"Do I need . . . ?" I narrowed my eyes. That little "again" she'd thrown in rankled.

"We couldn't imagine why you would be disguised," Calla said, "or heading to a battle in the woods, but if it is about you, and you want us to step in, just give the word."

Four different faces regarded me from the endless void. Dark or pale or brown or green, sideways or upright or angled, small or large—distance was hard to judge in the emptiness, and I couldn't tell whether they were very close or simply very big. But either way, they shared a single expression.

Concern.

And it drove me livid with rage.

I didn't want their pity. Or their sympathy. Or, least of all, a rescue. Again. Again, again, Jonquil could fuck right off back to Skalla with her "again."

Apparently, they found it inconceivable that I was capable of handling a quest as simple and straightforward as "go and get married." People get married every day. Women who can't speak for six years while they sew nettle shirts get married. Men who never bathe or cut their fingernails and sleep in bear skins get married. My stepmother got married, more than once, even though taking her for a bride sounds about as safe as sticking your hand in a steel trap and hoping it decides not to snap shut; I suppose my father must have loved her, as baffling as I found it. While I might have failed to measure up to her example in every other respect, surely I could muddle my way through a wedding ceremony. Even a seven-hour-long one.

And yes, all right, my attempt at achieving marital bliss wasn't going spectacularly well thus far. That didn't mean I wanted anyone to come and fix it. Couldn't they leave me this, at least? Couldn't they leave me anything?

"I don't think the prophecy is about me," I said. "I've got no reason to don a disguise, and I don't intend to join any royal hunts. They don't hold royal hunts here, anyway."

Jonquil cast a sidelong glance in my direction. "I thought King Gervase was supposed to be a keen hunter. Always out with his beloved horses and dogs, wasn't that right?"

Drat. I'd forgotten to keep my lies close enough to the truth. "Oh, he was. But that was before he became king. Now he's too busy with, uh . . ." My mind went blank for a moment as I tried to remember what non-sorcerous monarchs did all day. I doubted Gervase spent his time turning his enemies into frogs. "Meetings and things," I supplied at last. "Perhaps the rhyme is about someone Gnoflwhogir knows in the Summerlands?"

My sister-in-law pursed her lips. "I hadn't heard King Oberon was looking for a seventh bride. But he might be."

"You should check," I said.

She nodded sharply, green locks of hair whipping forward and then back again. "Of course. From the sound of it, someone is in great danger."

I opened my mouth to agree, but then I hesitated. She wasn't wrong. *Your love one breath away from death*. It occurred to me that rejecting their offers of help might be a mistake.

But it was my words that were supposed to rescue my love from death—whoever my love might be. My words. Not theirs.

While I was considering that, their faces and bodies began to stretch and distort. They blinked in and out of sight like fireflies on a dark summer night.

"You're waking up," Jonquil said through her pulled-taffy mouth, her words sounding distant. "Quick, give us a hug before you go."

My rancor toward them diminished. I had no idea when the celestial spheres would be aligned again—whatever that meant—and I did appreciate their visits, even if they couldn't help being their overbearing selves. I wrapped my arms around each of them in turn, holding tight as their limbs went rubbery and whipped out of control. It was a bit like trying to wrestle with angry snakes, although angry snakes don't try to whisper last-minute wedding-night advice in your ear.

"Thanks for the needle and thread," I said to Liam as I hugged him. By the time I reached him, he was barely more than a suggestion of a torso and face. "They came in very handy. Pity you can't give me anything useful in a dream."

He gave me a quick kiss on the cheek and winked at me. "Maybe I can't, hen," he said, "or maybe I can."

He vanished, and the quality of the darkness changed from the nothingness of nowhere to the more familiar black that lurks behind closed eyelids.

I opened them to discover that my chamber in the women's wing was scarcely brighter lit. Morning had not yet come; the sky outside the narrow window remained a deep purple. But I was wide awake and not likely to fall back asleep anytime soon. I tossed aside the bedclothes and arose. Although the moment my feet touched the cold stone floor, I reconsidered getting out of bed, then or ever again. When I managed to convince myself I couldn't stay wrapped in warm blankets for the rest of my life, I untied a borrowed silk scarf from around my hair and got dressed, careful not to wake any of the Yvettes who shared the room with me. The air was filled with snores. Heavy scents of perfume and powder wafted up from their nightclothes.

My outfit for the day's hunt was evidence of a debate I had not been party to. I had been provided with riding boots and leggings, but since that was not considered appropriate clothing for a woman in Tailliz, I had also been given a long skirt to throw over them. However, someone must have pointed out this rather defeated the purpose of the leggings; I could not possibly ride astride in a full skirt and would fall off my horse if it went into a gallop while I was riding sidesaddle—Jonquil might have been able to stay poised on the back of a flying dragon while wearing an elaborate gown, but that was not a skill possessed by many. So as a compromise, my skirt had been slit up the back and hastily finished—the stitching around the slit was obviously new. Women's riding clothes were such an alien concept here that they had to be improvised.

Leaving the women's wing without permission or an escort was, of course, also on the long list of forbidden activities. But I decided that if one of the rules had stopped applying to me, I might as well act as if they all had. I was heading out with the hunting party anyway come the dawn. There didn't seem to be much point in spending the intervening hours pacing to and fro in an overfamiliar room.

I threw on my newly mended red cloak and made my way to the viewing balcony, where I wedged myself through the gap between the screen and the wall and clambered down. Fifteen feet of roughly hewn stone wasn't much of a challenge for someone who had once climbed a glass mountain to fetch a fruit (it wasn't worth the trip—its peels cured all wounds, which was nice, but it was mealy and rather sour).

In the courtyard below, almost everyone was still asleep, animals and humans alike. I wandered between the banked cookfires and ramshackle shelters, stepping carefully so as not to accidentally tread on anyone sleeping on the bare ground, and drew my cloak in closer. The air was chilly, even with the castle walls blocking the ocean breezes.

Would the villagers still be huddled in the castle's shadow when autumn gave way to winter? Once again, I resented the waste of space in the women's wing. Surely at least some of the younger girls shivering in the cold could have bedded down there, if the taint of male presence was too offensive to Tailliziani tastes. I would have to bring it up with Gervase whenever I finally admitted to my true identity, if he was the kind of king who would listen to his queen, rather than treat her as nothing but a prop or a broodmare. Perhaps today I would have a chance to find out.

My goal in crossing the courtyard was finding the stables; since I was up, I thought I'd let the horses become accustomed to me before the hunt. It's never a bad idea to get to know your horse—I'd learned that much from Calla. I might not be able to beguile them into adoring me the way that she did, but the better acquainted we were, the less likely I was to be bucked off.

I'd had some experience being thrown from a horse. Back when my stepmother had sent me to search for the finger bone of the Deathless One, I'd ridden bareback on the Wild Stallion of the Taiga. His tail and mane were made of flame, and he could cross a thousand leagues in a single day. He also had a nasty temper.

For the hunt, I had been promised a gentle bay mare. I probably should have taken that as an insult, yet more evidence of the Tailliziani disdain for my gender. But to be honest, it hadn't been very pleasant to ride bareback on a wild stallion with a tail and mane made of flame. Between the sore ass and the burned bosom, I'd regretted it for days afterward. A gentle mare would suit me fine.

The stable was dark, close, and smelly, with dozens upon dozens of horses dozing in their stalls—duns and bays, grays and chestnuts. A few of them blinked open their eyes and snorted curiously when I came in.

"Hello, horses," I whispered. There were more than I'd expected, and I wasn't sure which one was mine. "I didn't bring any food for you, but I'm friendly, and, um . . . I smell good, maybe?"

"You do," a voice agreed from the darkness.

I spun around, startled, wondering for an instant if there was a talking horse in Tailliz to go with the talking lion. But a moment later, one of the huntsmen stepped into view, masked and red-haired and clad in green.

There was something about his grin I thought I recognized.

"Sam?" I asked.

"Hello, Clover," Sam replied. "You've changed your hair."

"It was too tangled to do anything but cut it off. Did you like it better long?"

"I like it both ways."

"Really?"

"Well . . ." He hesitated. "It's a bit choppier now."

I'd hoped a week of growth might have undone some of the damage, but apparently it hadn't. I silently cursed the chirurgeon to whatever fate awaited bad hairdressers.

"I'm surprised to see you up so early," Sam added, "and, um, so freely out and about."

"I couldn't sleep," I said. "And I didn't want to wait for permission."

He chuckled. "Rule breaker."

"Sometimes. Not when my stepmother gives me an order." I changed the subject. "What about you? Why are you here before the break of dawn?"

"Nerves, I suppose." He patted the flank of a drowsy horse. "We've been doing well so far by never taking the same route twice, but there's always the chance we'll run into something nasty."

"You're not wrong about that. I had . . ." I hesitated. My family seemed a bit too difficult to explain, especially for Clover the handmaiden. "I had an oracular dream. Something is going to happen, on one of these hunts. The ground will shake."

"An earthquake?" His hand went still, until the horse nuzzled his ear, and he resumed his attentions to it.

"Not necessarily." I didn't want to overinterpret, not when fairy prophecies carried the risk of double meanings. If I definitively stated it would be an earthquake, then holes full of jagged teeth might open beneath our feet instead, as I remembered had happened to one of Gervase's brothers. Although if I said the prophecy meant that, it would probably turn out to be an earthquake.

"Should we call off the hunt for today?" Sam asked.

"Only if you want to risk being killed by your own son in twenty years."

"What?"

"Sorry. I just meant trying to avoid it would be a bad idea."

Sam frowned. "It doesn't sound like the prophecy is a very useful one, then."

"That's how they go sometimes."

"Well," Sam said philosophically, "if there's nothing to be

done about it, there's no use in worrying." He nodded toward the horse he was stroking. "Have you met your trusty steed yet?"

"No. Is this her? She's pretty. What's her name?" The reddish brown of her coat shaded into black at her mane and tail, with a broad white blaze trailing down her muzzle from the forehead.

"She's called Poma," Sam said. "It's the old Tailliziani word for apple. She loves them."

"I wish I'd brought one."

He reached into his pocket and pulled out a bright red pippin. "Saved it from my dinner. I always like to have treats for them."

He carved off a slice with a knife and handed it to me. I grinned and held it out in the palm of my hand. Poma grabbed it with her lips and eagerly chewed. The dinners in Castle Tailliz were a bit spare these days, so I was glad the mare appreciated Sam's sacrifice.

The sky outside was still dark. It would be a while yet before the hunt began.

"You know," I said, "you never finished that story you were telling me."

"You fell asleep."

I dragged a bale of hay over and sat on it as if it were a bench, then looked up at him with wide, expectant eyes; I was clearly awake now. He laughed and handed the knife and apple over to me so he'd have his hands free to gesture as he talked.

"So, where did we last leave our heroes?" he asked.

"The duchess had just challenged you all to a death race, and Jack had accepted."

"Ah, that's right."

Poma's eyes were fixed on the apple in my hand. I cut another slice for her while Sam resumed the tale.

CHAPTER SIXTEEN

The Tale of the Duchess's Challenge

Once upon a time, etc., etc., brokenhearted man, identical duplicates, windmills, snowstorm, castle that looked like a big toad . . . and there we are.

"My brothers shall not go with you," the duchess avouched. "But I will make you this offer instead—if one of you can beat me in a footrace, you shall leave with as great a reward as the strongest among you can carry. If you fail, however, I'll cut off your heads."

"We agree to your terms!" Jack affirmed, for he had already conceived of yet another ridiculous plan.

It was decided that the first to bring water back from a distant well would be declared the winner. A crowd gathered to watch the race. Jack slapped Harry on the back and announced, "You're up."

"Harry . . . that's Detachable Leg, right?" It had been over a week since I'd traveled with the huntsmen, and I'd started to lose track.

"That's the one."

"Got it. Please, go on."

The duchess picked up a pitcher, and Harry fastened his leg on and grabbed one as well. They commenced the race at the very same moment, but a mere eyeblink later, Harry could no longer be seen. He ran so fast that to the crowd, it seemed as if the wind had rushed past them. The duchess was only a little way along when he made it to the well, filled up his pitcher, and started his return journey.

He'd run very far by then, and when he was halfway back, he was overcome with exhaustion. Feeling assured of his victory, he put down his pitcher, took off his leg, and stretched out for a nap. But he was fearful he might oversleep and lose the race, so he decided to make himself an uncomfortable pillow out of a horse's skull that was lying close by.

My forehead wrinkled. "A horse's skull."

"It's what he used."

"He rested his head on a convenient . . . horse's skull."

"This is the part of the story you find unbelievable?"

"I'm familiar with bloodthirsty nobles and death races. Horse-skull pillows are weird."

Meanwhile, the duchess, who was a speedy woman herself—easily as fast as the fastest of ordinary people—was rushing back from the well. When she noticed her opponent lying there asleep, she cackled, overturned his pitcher, and ran on.

"Soon their heads will decorate my wall," she chortled. "Six identical heads at one go—what a coup! I will be the envy of all the other head-collecting duchesses."

All would have been lost had Clem not positioned himself at the top of the castle's tallest tower for the best view of the race. With his keen eyesight, he'd seen everything that had passed. Taking careful aim with his bow, he shot the horse skull out from under Harry's noggin without so much as severing a single one of the runner's hairs. Harry woke with a start.

"Oh, my goodness!" Harry yelped, realizing his water had been spilled. "I must hurry, or I shall lose both the race and my head!"

Quick as a wink, he whisked on his leg, sprinted to the well, refilled the pitcher, and made it to the finish line the moment before the duchess stepped across.

"I'm glad I made an effort at the end there!" he trumpeted as the crowd cheered him. "What I was doing in the beginning could hardly be called running at all."

The duchess stamped her feet in rage over her loss and began plotting to renege on her promise. "How wonderful that you have defeated me," she grated out through clenched teeth. "We must celebrate your victory. Come with me, so you may eat and drink your fill!"

She brought the six of them to a room that had an iron floor, and iron doors, and windows set with iron bars. In the middle of a room was an iron table groaning under the weight of iron platters full of delicious food. "Go on in. Have as much as you like," the duchess encouraged them.

While the six men were tucking into their meal—

"You went into a room with an iron floor and bars across the windows? That didn't make you suspicious?"

"Did you miss the part about the delicious food?"

"Is that all it takes for you to traipse right into an obvious death trap?"

"I am highly motivated by delicious food."

While the six men were tucking into their meal, the duchess shut and locked the doors, then stomped downstairs to the kitchen to see her cook.

"Those wretched men tricked me!" she fulminated. "Light as great a fire as you can beneath the iron floor. Soon they shall see I never, ever lose a bet."

The cook complied, and the iron room began to grow warm. At first the men took little notice, placing the blame on the blazing summer sun striking the castle walls and the spiciness of the food upon their plates—

"Yes, because both of those things are likely to make the floor heat up."

"I generally don't assume that people have a murder room installed above the kitchen," Sam replied. "Who does that?"

"I would guess not very many," I admitted. To be fair, the murder room in my stepmother's palace was underneath the catacombs, nowhere near the kitchen at all. It didn't see a lot of use; no one dared to make assassination attempts on her anymore.

After a short time, the room was hot indeed. Becoming uncomfortable, the men tried to get out, only to find the doors locked and windows bolted shut. They soon realized that the duchess had concocted an evil plan and meant to do them harm.

"What can we do?" moaned Harry. "I cannot run through a locked door."

"An' ah cannae shoot aff an iron snib wi' an arrow," confessed Clem.

"Nor will a strong wind cool the room nearly enough," lamented Kit, for by that time the heat was unbearable, and it was clear they would not survive much longer.

"But I can cause a frost so deep the fire itself will freeze!" And with that declaration, Max whipped off his hat.

"Wait," I said. "If you have the strength to carry six trees, couldn't you have just broken down the door instead?"

"I let Max have his moment; I'm generous that way. Also, I was still eating."

The temperature dropped as frost fought flame. But soon it was clear the fire was losing the battle. Within five minutes, the air had cooled from broiling to roasting. Within ten minutes, it was merely sultry. Within twenty, it had become brisk. After half an hour, the room was so cold that the soup on the table froze solid in the bowls, rather to the dismay of the one among them who hadn't finished his meal yet.

At this point, the duchess flung open the door, only for her jaw to drop when she saw that her unwelcome guests had failed to perish.

"I must say your hospitality is appalling," Max complained, jamming his hat back down over his ear. "It's freezing in here! You might at least have warmed the place up."

By this time, the duchess wanted nothing more than to get rid of them. "You've had your meal," she grumbled. "Now be on your way!"

"Ah, but what of our reward? You promised as much as the strongest among us could carry," Jack reminded her.

"Fine!" the duchess snarled. "Take what you wish and be gone!"

And once she had said that, Sam strode toward the duchess's brothers, who had been observing the proceedings from the hallway. He scooped them up, three under each arm, enacting the final part of the plan Jack had conceived that morning. And our heroes walked out the castle gate with a chorus of cheerful farewells.

"And what did the six brothers have to say about that?"

"Believe me, they were only too glad to get out from under the thumb of the murder duchess."

The duchess was outraged, and in her fury she gathered together her troops in the courtyard. "Bring me my brothers!" she commanded. "And the thieves!"

The travelers had not gone far when they were overtaken by two regiments of cavalry. "You can have no chance against us," their commander observed. "Give over the brothers of the duchess, and surrender."

"Surrender?" bellowed Kit. "Never! Instead, you shall dance about in the air!"

He put his hand to his nose, closed one nostril, and blew a long breath out through the other. The horses were tossed neighing to the sky; the soldiers were blown through the air like dandelion seeds. They were flung hither and yon, some to the mountains, some to the valleys, and some to the plains. A sergeant, suffering from nine wounds, begged for mercy—

"The sergeant received nine wounds from the wind?"

"There might have been a running pitched battle across the whole of Ecossia before the final stand, but I'm cutting things short. It's nearly dawn; the hunt will be starting soon."

The sergeant begged for mercy. As he seemed like a reasonable fellow who did not deserve death merely for obeying his mistress, Kit let him land without further injury.

"Now return to your duchess," Jack ordered, "and inform her that her brothers are quite content to wear masks, and dress alike, and follow me around all the time for deeply mysterious reasons which I shall not divulge."

I stuck out my lower lip in what I hoped was an appealing pout. "You still won't tell me?"

"Maybe another time," Sam said. "When we're not about to be interrupted."

The sergeant ran back to tell the duchess what had passed, warning her that if she sent any more troops, they would likely find themselves tossed about through the air as well.

"I can see there is no defeating these great heroes," she griped, "especially the one called Sam, with his mighty and admirable posture. My brothers are out of my clutches forevermore. Let us be finished with this business and be content!"

And so the twelve men passed out of Ecossia and into another tale.

CHAPTER SEVENTEEN

The King and I

At first light, the other huntsmen filed into the stable. Sam was swept away in a bustle of greetings and preparations. Bows were strung, saddle pads were put in position, and everything was checked and rechecked to ensure a successful hunt without mishap or injury. King Gervase came in last, a pair of large brown dogs panting at his heels. The horses paid the dogs no mind, apparently long used to the commotion and noise of their smaller companions.

Somewhat to my surprise, Gervase strolled over to Poma's stall, stopping to give her mane a ruffle. My intention was to learn more about my fiancé that day, but I hadn't expected him to approach me so quickly or easily. I'd thought to observe him surreptitiously.

He did not speak for a few long moments. I waited for him to begin any conversation; my history with my stepmother had left me cautious around monarchs. I took the time to look him over as the seconds ticked by. He had traded his sumptuous court robes for practical hunting gear. It was expensive, rich leather and close-knit wool, and the bejeweled circlet remained perched on his head, but it was clear he took hunting seriously and expected dirt, damp, and blood to be part of it.

"I see you've met your horse," he said. "Does she meet with your approval?"

"Very much so, Your Majesty. A fine animal. And well named."

"That she is."

He produced an apple of his own, and Poma leaned her head against him affectionately as she munched it. My horse was going to be too well fed to do more than waddle if anyone else came in with the same idea.

While Gervase appeared content to let the conversation end there, my need to give him a warning won out over my caution. "Listen. There's something you should know."

He regarded me curiously while I recounted the heavily fictionalized "oracular dream" that I'd already described to Sam—with both similar explanations and similar omissions.

Afterward, the king frowned. "If trying to interpret it is useless, and trying to avoid it is pointless, then I don't see what's to be done about it."

I gave a helpless shrug. "Neither do I."

"Then I suppose we should proceed as if—" He broke off as one of the dogs leapt on his leg in excitement. With an apologetic smile, he turned to bring it to heel, firmly but with no sign of impatience.

Fond of horses and dogs. There were worse recommendations for a future spouse.

"I've been wondering," I said, "why you haven't summoned me to discuss the wedding arrangements."

His smile faltered for a moment. "Because I've been remiss in my duties."

"I certainly didn't mean to imply—"

He waved my objection aside. "I have. Your mistress will be here soon, I imagine?"

"Yes, I . . . suppose she will."

Though I hadn't been thinking about it when I brought the subject up, he had given me a reminder that there was only so long I could maintain my pretense. Suspicions would surely arise if the princess didn't make an appearance before the snow made the roads impassable. The truth would have to come out then.

"I should see to my own steed," Gervase said. "But we'll talk about this more. Both the wedding and your prophetic dream. I promise you that." He gave me a stiff nod and strode toward the stall of a large chestnut courser.

I decided I had best get a saddle on Poma. She waited patiently while I went through the process, and I was just tightening the girth when I heard a frosty voice behind me.

"So," it said, "you're a witch after all."

"A sorceress," I said as I turned around. "Not the same thing."

One of the masked hunters was standing so close I flinched away. He was watching me through narrowed eyes. No hat, two legs, and he hadn't launched any frogs at me.

"Jack?" I hazarded.

He bowed his head ever so slightly in acknowledgment, his face remaining hard as a gravestone. "Sorceress, witch—what's the difference?"

"That depends. Do you mean in an academic sense, a religious sense, or a folkloric sense?"

He blinked, taken aback. It was a tricky question, to be fair. If you're not familiar with the professional jargon, the differences between a sorcerer, witch, magician, wizard, and warlock can be difficult to follow.

"For example, if you go by folklore," I said, "witches eat people. I don't."

He shook off his confusion and resumed his narrow-eyed gaze. "Whether you do or you don't, I find it interesting you failed to bring the matter up the day we rescued you. If," he added, "we did, in fact, rescue you."

I ground my teeth together, feeling foolish for not foreseeing this. Jack had wondered from the beginning if I was deceiving him, and now that I'd admitted to being a sorceress, he had yet more reason to believe I'd been hiding other things as well. The difficulty, of course, was that he was right. It was just that the things I was hiding weren't nefarious, sorcerous plans. Or wickedly cannibalistic ones, for that matter.

"I'm a very minor sorceress," I said. "It hardly seemed worth mentioning."

"And how, pray tell, does one distinguish," he asked coldly, "between a minor sorceress and a—" He stopped short as a tentative hand tapped him on his shoulder.

For some reason, I once again had no difficulty telling it was Sam.

"Jack. I, um . . . I thought we talked about this."

Jack whirled to face his brother. "We did. And we agreed her behavior was suspicious."

"Well, aye, that's true," Sam conceded. "But also . . . not. Evil masterminds don't slip on a handful of peas and break their arm, do they?"

"It wasn't broken," I protested. "Only sprained."

Jack ignored me. "You said you would follow my lead on these things."

"On the mission." Sam shifted uneasily under Jack's glare. "Are you sure this is part of the mission?"

"Of course it is! She's been keeping secrets—"

"And no one who keeps secrets," Sam said to his masked sibling, "can ever be trusted, is that it?"

That did little to calm Jack down. "If you trust her, with everything that's been happening, you're a fool. A fool who's fallen for a pretty face. I can't believe you'd break faith with me over *that*!"

"No one's breaking faith with anyone!" Sam insisted. "You're still in charge here, Jack. It's only, she's been in the castle for days—"

"And now here she is on the hunt," Jack replied, his face dark. "We'll see how safe that makes us. The last time she was with us is the last time we were attacked. Stop acting like a mooncalf. Stay on your guard. And don't doubt I'll be watching you, witch," he threw at me as he stomped off, muttering to himself. Sam gazed after him, looking distraught.

The argument had made Poma skittish; she pranced in place, and her ears flicked back and forth with anxiety. I stroked her across the withers to settle her. "A pretty face, am I?"

"Well, you . . . That is, I mean, er . . ." Sam coughed.

I smiled into Poma's mane, where he couldn't see. "Thanks for defending me. I know you don't like going against your brother."

"I don't suppose you'd care to tell me whatever else you've been keeping from us?" he asked cautiously. "Or even why."

"Maybe another time," I said, echoing his words from earlier. If I ever decided to reveal my identity to someone, it wouldn't be in a crowded stable where any would-be assassin could overhear.

"A plausible explanation might help smooth things over with Jack."

I turned back around. "Would it? He seems intent on making me the villain."

Sam rubbed at the bridge of his nose. "You'll have to forgive him. Jack isn't usually so unreasonable. But it's been hard on him, all this. The constant threat, and . . . and everything else."

"Surely it's been difficult for everyone." I thought about the crowded courtyard packed with terrified farmers.

"It has," Sam agreed. "But Jack has a particular . . . He's got a good excuse for being . . ."

I waited. Poma snorted into my hair.

The fanfare sounded with a blare of trumpets. "Time we were off," Sam said, sketching a quick bow before he headed for his own horse. "Good hunting."

"Good hunting." I hooked my foot into the stirrup and swung astride, taking a moment to arrange my split skirt around the saddle.

We rode out into the courtyard, the packed masses making way before us. It was odd, leaving with the hunt that day—being watched by the crowd instead of watching along with them from the balcony. Had I caused a panic in the women's wing when I wasn't in my bed that morning? Well, they had to know where I was now.

If Princess Angelique was observing from above, I couldn't see her behind the filigreed screen. It was just as likely it was one of her headache days, and she wasn't there.

I found I was attracting more than my share of stares. I wasn't sure whether it was because I was a sorceress, simply because I was a woman, or both. It felt peculiar to be garnering the most attention in a hunting party that included a bespectacled lion, prowling back and forth in the courtyard and making the nearby horses prance nervously away. But I supposed the crowd was long used to the lion by then.

Across the bridge, the great ironclad doors opened, and the portcullis rose. Overhead, a dark bird circled. Something clutched in its talons glittered in the early dawn light. But we were thundering over the bridge before I had a chance to see more.

Cheers rang out from the assembly behind us as the doors swung closed again. Within minutes, we had galloped through the abandoned town and slowed to enter the woods.

The horses' hooves crunched through leaves and needles. It was a brisk late-autumn day. The air was dry and chill, carrying the promise of winter. It was warmer than the mountains at this time of year, though. Back home, fat flakes of snow would have already turned the peaks white and begun to drift onto the steep paths and sloped rooftops lower down.

We wove our way deeper into the trees, turning to the left or right according to some timetable I couldn't figure out. My sense of direction abandoned me not long after the castle vanished from sight. Within half an hour, I was helplessly lost. I hoped someone knew how to find the way back.

"When the princess arrives," said a huntsman behind me, "we should give her a fairy-tale wedding."

"What do you mean?" asked his companion.

"Leave her in the woods with a bag of breadcrumbs!"

That would be Max and Harry, I had no doubt. Clem swore at them in dialect too thick to be comprehensible, although the intent was clear. Their nonsense felt strangely comforting. If I was heading into the depths of the forest again, at least I was headed there with the same band of rogues as last time.

For the most part. We were a sizable hunting party. Armed guards, seated atop dauntingly large destriers, accompanied the king and his twelve huntsmen. And there was also, of course, one enormous lion. Sight hounds and scent hounds loped alongside us.

Given our random route, it would be impossible to hunt in the usual way, with additional dogs strung out through the woods at predetermined points. No one had bothered to tell me what we were doing instead. No one had given me a weapon, either, not so much as a cudgel to club small game.

It wasn't long before we encountered the peculiar denizens of the forest of Tailliz. Up a small slope, I spied what I thought was a stag, until I noticed it had no fur and the tentacled proboscis of a star-nosed mole. It bounded away in fright as we came close. None of the hunters tried to bring it down. The dogs didn't give it chase, either, but whined in dismay, crouching low on their haunches until it disappeared.

Once it was out of sight, King Gervase surprised me for a second time by maneuvering his courser next to Poma and matching my pace. On his other side, one of the huntsmen drew his own steed close by and watched me warily. The lion was never far from the king, either, and I could feel Poma tense as the great cat approached. I would have to handle her carefully to keep her from shying. I wondered whether Gervase planned to keep his promise to discuss our wedding plans. It seemed an odd topic for the present circumstances, but I imagined that rulers often had to multitask. My stepmother certainly never aimed for one goal when it lay in her power to aim for seven.

That wasn't what was on his mind at all, as it happened. "So, sorceress," he said. "If we are attacked on this day, what can you do to offer us protection?"

I blew out a sigh. This would be a short conversation; there was so very little to say.

"Almost nothing, Your Majesty," I admitted. "My greatest magical talent is rapid hair growth."

He looked at me blankly. "Hair growth?"

"I suppose it might confuse the kind of creature that is bewildered by a hat. Let us pray we are attacked by a parrot or a small dog."

He laughed. A nice laugh—cheerful, loud, and unrestrained. I liked it.

The lion, on the other hand, remained unamused. "Small dogs," he sniffed, "are an unlikely threat. And easily defeated by other means. We would not need to employ your dubious ability."

"She knows that, Lion," the king explained patiently. "It was a joke."

"I fail to see the humor in poor tactics."

"I tried to tell Princess Angelique I wasn't a very powerful sorceress," I said, "but I'm not sure she cared to hear it. Surely the huntsmen must have told you how useless I was in the battle against the spider wolves."

"Some of my huntsmen," Gervase responded, his eyes sliding to the one riding next to him, "have their own opinion about those events." The man in green looked away without replying.

The lion drew his mouth into a snarl. "Huntsmen," he growled. "You have no huntsmen." His teeth were bared. Poma would have bolted if I hadn't kept a tight hold on her reins.

"I told you to speak no more of that," the king said. "Your test failed."

"But—"

"Enough!"

Silence descended, although only over the small group near me. Farther off, I heard laughter and chat. One of the huntsmen grinned as he snatched Max's hat off, making the temperature drop until Max managed to grab it back again.

We rode on, passing through a wide, stony glade dotted with wildflowers. Towers of worn rock poked out of the ground like stretching fingers. The morning sun had risen higher in the sky by now, although it did little to warm us. My breath frosted in the chilly air. The wind blew the grasses into undulating patterns that glittered in the light like ocean waves. Overhead, birdlike creatures wheeled through the sky on wings of feather or skin or chitin, shrieking and screaming.

"What is the princess like?" Gervase asked me.

"I— What?"

"The Skallan princess. You are her handmaiden, are you not?" He studied his horse's ears. "All I know is her name. And that only because your queen mentioned it in her reply to my letter."

I hadn't expected the question. It had never occurred to me that Gervase would be just as curious about me as I was about him.

"You needn't reply if your answer would do discredit to your loyalty," Gervase said when I failed to respond.

He had taken my silence to mean Princess Melilot was so awful I didn't want to speak of her aloud.

"Nothing like that!" I said. "I was merely . . . considering where I should start. She's, she's . . ."

What could I say? What did I know about myself?

"She's the middle child of three," I said at last. "And has always felt it. Neither one thing nor the other, not the eldest, not the youngest, just there. Awkward and out of place, like a puzzle piece that doesn't quite fit."

After I said it, I wanted to bite my tongue. I wished it came more naturally to describe myself another way—as the most beautiful, the most powerful, the sweetest, or the cleverest.

The king had a thoughtful expression on his face. "I see. I was the youngest child myself. A late arrival. My brothers were too old to be jealous, so they fussed over me instead. And my sister grew used to me, in time."

"You received all the available attention, then."

"Oh, yes. So you're familiar with the way of it. You have younger siblings yourself, I take it?"

"One. She was much indulged by the whole family." No lonely towers or savage dismemberments for dear Calla.

"Much indulged is a good description of my own childhood as well. My whims and fancies were catered to. I was never expected to take the throne, which meant no one thought letting me do what I wanted would have any consequences." He exchanged an unreadable look with the huntsman beside him. This time, Gervase was the one who broke it off, turning back to me. "Perhaps your mistress and I can learn to get along, then. I can indulge her where she has been ignored, and she can ignore me where I have been indulged."

"I've heard of worse foundations for a marriage," I said cautiously. I had also heard of significantly better ones, but I wasn't sure how much contradiction the king would tolerate from a handmaiden.

He chuckled. "I spoke in jest. For the most part. We might do well by each other, if nothing else. She will receive the respect due to her as a queen. And I, as a king, am no longer able to evade my responsibilities."

"Perhaps," the lion grumbled, "you will even start taking your royal counselors seriously."

Gervase inclined his head in the lion's direction. "I take heed of your advice, Lion, as generations of kings have done before me." He smiled thinly. "The court would have a collective fit if I did not."

The lion sniffed. "As well they might. My wisdom, knowledge, and perception are of a superior nature, tempered by centuries of experience."

The king's final offhand remark to me was weighing on my mind. "Do you view your marriage to Princess Melilot as one of your responsibilities?" I asked.

He hesitated a long moment before replying. "My marriage to her was my father's last wish. I could not, in good conscience, gainsay it."

"He wanted you to have a magical protector," I said. "A sorceress."

He nodded. "The royal family of Skalla is known for its powerful magic."

"You might have asked for help from elsewhere instead." The huntsman, who had been silent for so long, had a bitter tone to his voice.

"I made a promise to a dying man, Jack," Gervase said heavily. "And was he wrong?"

"We've managed so far," the huntsman—Jack, I could say now—replied.

I'd been right about Gervase's reluctance. He had no greater desire for this marriage than I did. He, as much as I, was fulfilling a duty and hoping to make the best of it.

It was only to be expected, yet I was disappointed, nonetheless. Jonquil had found ardor and romance in her arranged marriage. Calla had wed her love. I would have to content myself with being useful. Except, of course, I wasn't even that. Behold, the great grower of hair.

"I suspect it's too late for second thoughts now," Gervase told Jack, before turning to me. "Am I right in doubting your queen would appreciate a broken courtship?"

"It would be a disaster," I answered honestly. "She doesn't enjoy having her plans foiled, and she likes being slighted significantly less. Your current troubles would seem a pittance in comparison. She might tear your castle apart stone by stone or turn the forest into a desert. As for you yourself, there is a good chance she would leave you blind, penniless, and wandering the wasteland for the rest of your days."

He took a sharp breath. "Are her daughter's powers as potent?"

"Not . . . as potent as that," I admitted.

"I confess to being somewhat relieved."

I wasn't convinced he should be. "Isn't it better for you the more powerful she is? I doubt you feel any safer now, with only me by your side to offer magical protection."

"Your mistress will prove her worth, I'm sure, even if she cannot turn Tailliz into a wasteland."

I made a noncommittal noise. It struck me as a bad time to tell him my "mistress" was neither what he expected nor what he wanted. He'd gotten a bad bargain in me. A very bad bargain indeed.

"And as for you," he continued, "I wouldn't worry unduly. No one knows where in the forest we've traveled. Nothing has happened to the hunting parties since we adopted Jack's strategy. There's no chance whatever that anything will happen today."

"I'm glad to hear it."

And that, of course, was the moment the monsters attacked.

CHAPTER EIGHTEEN

The Answer Lies upon Your Lips

They erupted out of the ground with the bone-shaking rumble of an avalanche. I caught a glimpse of something whitish and big before Poma squealed in fright and reared. Keeping my seat took all of my focus.

"Witch!" Jack screamed. "Is this your doing?"

I couldn't reply. I could barely stay on my horse. She bolted away from the threat while I clung desperately to her neck. Gentle mare she might have been, but maintaining her calm in the face of whatever had just happened was too much to ask.

As I struggled to regain control, I heard shouts and curses, thuds and cracks and booms. To my left, a huntsman spat a bright blue poison dart frog at a giant swinging fist. To my right, an arrow shattered against an eyeless, misshapen head.

One of the creatures stepped in front of us, and Poma came to a terrified halt, so abrupt I was nearly flung over her head. When I thumped back into the saddle, my gaze fixed on the two great columns of leg that blocked our way. My stare traveled up . . . and farther up.

It was at least ten times my height, and roughly in the shape of a man. It was made of unhewn rock, pale except where clumps of mud still clung to it. Moss and grasses dusted its shoulders, and a sapling had taken root on its elbow. Its great hand reached for me.

Two riders thundered past me on their stallions. The stone giant paused. One of the horsemen took the opportunity to duck under the enormous fist and slash at its leg with a sword.

Or tried to, anyway. His sword scraped across the stone with a shower of sparks. It didn't leave behind so much as a mark. A boulder-like head turned with a grinding of stone against stone. That massive hand came at him with an almost disinterested swat, like the paw of a lazy cat batting at a toy. With a crunch, the green-clad swordsman went flying off his horse.

"Jacqueline!" screamed Gervase from my other side. He turned his steed and dashed toward the fallen huntsman.

I blinked, and a half-formed understanding flickered across my mind. But it would have to wait. The towering monster had turned its attention to me.

Finally, my horse and I reached complete agreement as to the proper course of action. Poma wheeled around and galloped away as fast as she could.

Sapling Elbow pursued us. We'd managed to get a decent head start before it swung into motion, and its movements were ponderous, the massive slabs of stone that were its legs shifting only with reluctance. But it hardly mattered. Each of its strides ate up great swathes of land.

Chaos was exploding all around me. The giant rock creatures seemed to be everywhere, fighting one-sided battles with huntsmen and guards. Dogs ran underfoot, adding their barks to the cacophony. Armored men lay smashed on the ground like broken dolls. The air had grown bitterly chill, and a violent wind threatened to pull me off my saddle. Max and Kit were making their stand—Hat On Ear and The Nose Blower putting their powers to the test. No doubt they were doing their best, but the rock monsters were unaffected. They were insensible to the cold and too heavy to be blown over.

I reached the edge of the clearing. Poma swerved to avoid crashing headfirst into the trees. The creature chasing us drew closer. It had no need to dodge; oaks and maples toppled before it as it loped straight through them.

A huntsman pulled up beside me, bow in hand. He twisted around to shoot backward off his horse. Arrow after arrow cracked against the stone giant charging after me. His quiver hung flat, nearly empty.

"What are you doing?" I cried.

"Tryin' tae find a weak point."

"I don't think they have one!"

Clem muttered a curse. "Keep it awa' fae the king. Ye gang left, an' ah'll gang richt. It'll follow ye o' me."

I nodded and tugged on Poma's reins. Clem and I veered apart. Sapling Elbow hesitated, swiveling its head, choosing which of us to chase. Giving us precious seconds of extra time.

But when its great feet thudded forward, it chose to follow me.

I zigged and zagged through the trees. In the flurry I saw the lion, his spectacles askew. He raced at a monster, claws out, slashing. They did no more good than Jack's sword. Close by, three huntsmen rode in circles around a moss-speckled stone giant, just beyond the reach of its hammering fists. Thorny vines heavy with roses burst forth from the ground and twined up past their enemy's granite torso. For a moment, I was baffled, even wondering if I might somehow be responsible. Then I realized it must be another huntsman's power.

The vines burst apart, falling in shreds, as soon as those vast stone legs moved. Whoever had grown the roses, they'd failed to vanquish their foe.

I'd done no better. Fleeing for my life was as much as I'd been able to manage. Behind me, the thunderous footfalls of the creature in pursuit grew louder and louder, ringing the earth like a bell.

Could I grow my hair long enough to use as a snare? It snaked down my back as I thought about it, flowing past my waist to brush the saddle. But that would more likely rip my scalp off than be of any use.

So much for being the sorceress destined to save the king and the kingdom. Jonquil would have performed some astonishing feat of spell casting by now. Calla would have convinced a horde of moles to dig pits under the monsters' feet. Even Liam, with far less magic than me, would have figured out some clever way to exploit their weaknesses, and Gnoflwhogir would have . . . I don't know. Eaten them?

I was at a complete loss for a means of escape until I spied a stand of the enormous shaggy trees native to Tailliz topping a nearby rise, surrounding the hilltop like a henge, in staggered rings. They towered high above the smaller trees the stone giants smashed down with such ease.

The gaps between them were larger than I would have liked, but there was a chance they were narrow enough to suffice for my hastily improvised plan. I did my best to steer Poma in the right direction. Her hooves pounded on the frosting-over ground. She shot up the hill, a howling tailwind speeding us on. I guided her between the closest pair of great trees and heard a tremendous crash just after she slipped through.

The stone giant had smashed into the trees, unable to fit between them. The massive trunks shook, the treetops whipping to and fro in the heights. But they held firm. The trees were five times as tall as the monster and as thick around, with roots that twisted deep into the soil.

There was little opportunity to relish my escape. Poma decided she'd had enough. She threw me off with one mighty buck and fled. Kit's wind caught me and whipped me to the ground, flat on my back.

"Ow," I said, rather inanely. I blinked up at a sky gone white with clouds. It had begun to snow, stinging wet flakes driven near horizontal by the gale.

Something huge and gray hurtled toward me. I rolled out of the way moments before an immense stone hand smashed into the mud where I had been. I staggered to my feet and stumbled back as it groped for whatever part of me it could catch hold of.

The monster had managed to wedge a shoulder between the trees. Its long arm stretched out, the flexing fingers close enough that I saw bright flecks of quartz glittering in their tips. I shrieked and scuttled farther out of reach.

Then the hand flew away as something wrenched the monster backward, sending it tumbling down the hill.

I squinted against the blowing sleet as a huntsman poked his head out from behind the trees. I shouldn't have been able to tell him from the others, but as he strode closer, there was no doubt in my mind it was Sam.

The knuckles of both his hands were bloodied. The whole of his right side looked like a single massive welt. He grasped my shoulders as soon as he was within reach and paused for a moment, frowning.

"Is your hair different?" he asked.

"Really not the time."

"Right, sorry." He shook his head as if clearing his thoughts. "Are you hurt?"

"I'm fine. Thrown from my horse, but that's all. You?"

"Oh, I dismounted early on. Easier to punch things on foot."

"I meant, are you injured?"

"I'll live."

I restrained myself from yelling at him for battling monsters bare-handed again. I would yell at him later if we both managed to survive. "The one you threw—is it dead?"

"No. When I hurl them down, they just get right back up. Nothing I try does any lasting damage."

What weapons could be brought to bear against these indestructible creatures? "I don't suppose you brought any siege engines along?"

The ghost of a smile alighted on Sam's lips. "Sadly, no."

"Seems like an oversight."

"After today, I'll carry a trebuchet wherever I—"

He cut himself off when he noticed the expression on my face. Over his shoulder, I could see what was coming up the hill. Not just my original pursuer, Sapling Elbow, but also two more. Behind it was the moss-speckled one I'd seen attacked by roses and another with dark striations banded across its chest.

They didn't attempt to force their way through the too-narrow gap. Sapling Elbow pounded on the smallest of the trees in the outer ring, a youngish one scarce a hundred feet high, trying to smash it to pieces. Futilely, I hoped. Moss Speckle and Chest Bands circled the tree line, peering between the trunks. Hunting for a large enough break in the barrier. It wouldn't take them very long to find one. The trees weren't anything like a real fence and were giving us only a brief reprieve.

The young tree shuddered under Sapling Elbow's blows. Sam shouted to make himself heard above the pounding. "You should run. I'll try to hold them off for as long as I can—"

"Don't be ridiculous," I snapped. "I'm not leaving you alone to get trampled into bits."

He nodded but had no time to say anything else. Moss Speckle had found a way to squeeze through.

Sam charged before it was able to do much more than turn in our direction. He slipped his hands under its carriage-size foot. With a mighty heave, Sam threw the creature off-balance, toppling it over. By then, Chest Bands was rushing toward me. I dove aside just in time to evade being crushed beneath its heel.

A fist thumped down so close I was splattered with slush. I leapt back only to be caught on the side by the flat of its other hand.

The blow sent me flying twenty feet or more. I slid another ten when I landed, stopping just short of braining myself against a tree. My whole body throbbed; if nothing was broken, I'd be lucky.

There was a creak like an enormous rusty door being forced open. I blinked away the black dots swarming in my vision and saw Sapling Elbow had its arms wrapped around the tree blocking its path. With an earsplitting crack, the trunk began to tilt.

Sam skidded to a halt next to me. Behind him, Chest Bands was picking itself up. I hadn't seen Sam knock it over. Too much was happening all at once.

"All three of them will be here soon," he said, panting. "If you've been holding back any great feats of sorcery, now would be the time." He didn't look optimistic.

I wasn't hopeful myself. Even if I could dredge up some kind of enchantment, what would work against them? What weaknesses did a rock have? Not fire, not lightning. Clearly not snow or sleet. Strength hadn't broken them. Weapons didn't scratch them. I doubted that the mightiest of death curses would stop them, if I knew any. They had no blood to boil or bones to splinter.

The drunkenly tilting tree vanished from the line like an abruptly pulled tooth. Long seconds later, a crash jolted the ground as it fell somewhere below.

The ground will shake; the earth will quake. . . .

Sapling Elbow appeared in the empty space where the tree had been and stepped up to join its fellows. Three great slabs of animate rock marched forward through the pelting snow. Beside me, Sam braced himself, chin tucked to his chest, ready for the fight. They would be upon us in moments.

Your love one breath away from death . . .

His fingers brushed mine.

And clinging by his fingertips . . .

I curled my hand around Sam's.

My thoughts floated in a peculiar bubble of calm. I felt detached from the events around me, a dispassionate observer of my own terror. The stone giants seemed far away, their movements lethargic, as if they were walking underwater.

What good had Gnoflwhogir's warning been? There was nothing I could do. I wasn't powerful enough. And I had no way to increase what meager power I possessed. I did not have the Golden Key, or a hair plucked from a devil's tail, or . . .

Or . . .

If you would save him from the grave, / The answer lies upon your lips.

Maybe Liam had given me something useful in my dream after all—a clue, pressed against my cheek before he vanished.

"Do you think," I asked Sam, my voice sounding distant, as though I were listening to myself speak from somewhere off to one side, "that they can swim?"

"What?"

"Kiss me," I said.

He didn't hesitate a moment, turning even as their stone hands reached for us, pressing his lips against mine.

Become water, I thought.

And I did.

PART V

THE TWO INEXPLICABLE TOWERS

CHAPTER NINETEEN

Lacustrine Dreams

I had become a lake, vast and smooth and cool. Snow floated from the leaden sky and lit on my surface, melting and disappearing.

Deep within me, stone figures plummeted down, down, and farther down, vanishing into the crushing depths, sinking into the thick mud far below. Back into the earth that had birthed them.

My senses were slipping away from me, my thoughts turning into lake thoughts, water thoughts. Words and memories replaced by the slow churn of sun and wind and time.

From above me came alarmed honks and quacks as a flock of startled birds flew upward. Horses and dogs and hunters and guards had turned into ducks, geese, and a single bewildered swan I suspected was the king.

Oh. So that's where the birds came from when Jonquil did it.

As they spiraled into the sky, a goose detached itself from the group and splashed down onto me. It twisted its neck around to tuck its head between its wings and shut its eyes.

Most of what I was dissolved into the lap of waves against the shore.

The snow stopped.

Light came, and darkness, and light again.

Sometimes the goose left for a while, but more often than not it was there, dipping the paddles of its feet into me, grazing on the pondweed near my edges.

Leaves drifted across me. Rain made pockmarks on my skin, and the wind whipped it into white froth. More light and more darkness, more darkness and more light . . . over and over. I didn't keep track of how often. I had forgotten what counting was.

The snow returned, softer than the rain. A delicate lace of ice, thin and transparent as an insect's wing, spread along my shallows. Dense, murky fog crept up to my shoreline from the woods. The goose woke and cocked its head.

"If you think you're going to evade your marriage this way," the fog said, "you are sorely mistaken."

I didn't answer. I was busy reflecting the gray smear of the moon hidden behind a cloud.

"Turn back into a human at once," the fog huffed, sending streamers of vapor across my surface. "This has gone on long enough. I didn't raise you to spend your life as a pond."

A pond? That stirred a response from me. *I'm a lake. A deep one.* I had thermal layers. I had aphotic trenches where sunlight never reached.

"Yes, yes, very impressive. Your spell didn't go wrong. For once."

Of course it doesn't matter to you. She did the impossible on a routine basis. By her standards, this was nothing more than a parlor trick.

"I said it was impressive. Why do you always have to be so difficult?"

The goose honked angrily at the fogbank. But I remained silent. A lake doesn't speak.

"And now you're sulking. I never know how to deal with you when you're sulking."

A lake can only be a lake. Nothing else.

"Ignore me, then. I won't waste any more time on your stubbornness. Your sisters should be here as soon as the celestial spheres align. Maybe they can talk sense into you."

My stepmother roiled away. Good riddance. I relaxed back into the business of ebbing and flowing, my irritation floating away along with what little was left of my identity. Endless uncounted moments drifted past, and I settled further into lakehood, letting go of the last remnants of my nonlake self. Becoming only water.

Until other voices started prodding at me.

"Melilot? Melilot, are you here? Calla, do you see her anywhere?"

"No, I can't see anything but water. Why is she dreaming about water?"

"Are there any fish you can ask? Can you still do that in a dream?"

The two of them swam through me, around and around, their words becoming bubbles that floated to the surface and popped, releasing their meaning into empty air.

"Calla . . . I think she is the water. I think she's become a lake."

"Really? Good for her! She always wanted to."

"No, it's a problem. She's nearly all lake. There's almost no Melilot left. We have to turn her back."

The words roused something buried deep within me, a thought that refused to be silenced no matter how waterlogged it was. First the fog and now this. They couldn't ever let me be. They were convinced I was inept. Inadequate. Regardless of what I did.

Once more, like an involuntary reflex, an answer welled up from my depths.

I'm fine.

"Melilot? Is that you?" Calla. I vaguely recalled the name. The name of whatever was pestering me. She swam through the dark water, looking for the source of my voice, not quite understanding there was no source other than the water itself.

"Clearly you're not fine," said Jonquil. The other one. "You need our help. There's a ritual I know that might—"

Leave me alone.

"Look," she continued, paying me no mind, "just tell us where you were when you deliquesced. We'll get there as soon as we can."

You always do this.

"Do what? What are you talking about?"

You think I can't do anything. Both of you. All of you.

"That's not fair!" Calla burst out. "You're the one who's always belittling yourself. I don't feel that way, and I've certainly never said that!"

Then why are you here?

My sister paused. "Do you not want me to care about you?" She sounded bewildered and hurt. I tried my hardest not to feel guilty about it.

I want . . .

What did I want?

"Stop being ridiculous," Jonquil snapped. "You're in over your head, and you need us."

I didn't ask you to come.

My waters went still. The goose, puzzled by the sudden change, flapped its wings in agitation.

You should go.

My sisters swam through me, yelling to get my attention. Their voices grew louder, their motion more frenzied.

GO.

I washed them from my dreams. Out of the lake. Out of myself. They drifted through my surface, into the air, vanishing in a spray of droplets.

And I woke up.

CHAPTER TWENTY

What Is This Thing Called Love?

I came to consciousness slowly, watery thoughts dribbling out of my head until they were replaced by a human mind once more. At some point in the process, I noticed I had a splitting headache and, except for something warm pressed up against my side, I was freezing cold.

I couldn't tell exactly where the warmth was coming from, because I was having difficulty opening my eyes. It took me a while to understand the problem, because first I had to remember that I had a body and then that my body had eyes that could be opened. At that point, I tried to open them. And failed.

This caused me a moment of panic, until I realized the sensation was familiar. I'd encountered the same problem during my time on the plain of ice at the top of the world. My eyelids had frozen shut.

Have I mentioned how much I hate the outdoors?

My teeth ached from the cold, and the hairs in my nose had iced up as well, an irritating sensation something like being permanently on the verge of a sneeze. I pressed my hands against my eyes and waited for the heat of my body, little enough though there was, to melt the frost around my lashes.

"It was very odd," said Sam, close enough that I felt his breath on my cheek, "being a goose."

Well, that explained why my left side was less frozen than my right.

"Sorry," I told him.

"Better that than being mashed to a pulp. And I didn't say it was horrible. Just odd. I ate a lot of grass. Pounds and pounds of it, every day. It must be doing terrible things to my digestion now that I'm no longer a bird."

I was able to open my eyes at last. I blinked at him a few times. He and I were both half-covered in snow. We staggered to our feet.

"You'd think so," I said, brushing snow off my skirt and leggings, "but you probably won't have any problems. I doubt you'll throw anything up, even if you stuffed yourself so full that your liver turned into foie gras. It doesn't count somehow. Although if you'd injured your wing, you might have a broken arm right now."

He frowned and ran his fingers down his side. "Are you sure? The bruises I got from the stone creatures don't hurt anymore. I can't even feel my stitches pulling. They're gone, I think. I feel better than I did before I turned into a goose."

"Huh. Maybe you wouldn't have a broken arm, then."

"Why not?"

I shrugged. "Logic and magic don't exactly go hand in hand. And a good thing, too." I glanced around at our surroundings. "Otherwise, I'd have ended up killing a lot of innocent animals. By all rights, Lake Me should have drowned every squirrel on this . . . um."

We weren't on the hill anymore.

Instead of a rise ringed by massive trees, we were in a shallow dip on the bank of an icy, burbling brook. From the looks of things, we were still in the Tailliziani forest. But beyond that, I had no idea of our whereabouts. Lake Melilot had spanned miles and miles. Who knew where in that wide expanse we'd ended up?

Snow coated the ground and frosted the branches, and more snowflakes sifted through the treetops like fine sugar. "Why is it still so cold?" I asked, rubbing my upper arms and shivering. "Did Max lose his hat?"

Sam gave me an odd look. "Max flew off with the rest of them. Back to the castle, I'd imagine. It's winter."

"It's . . . what?"

"You were a lake for weeks. Maybe a month? I didn't keep track of sunsets and sunrises as well as I'd have liked; geese don't really understand numbers. But there were more than a few."

"Oh." Geese were better at counting than lakes, apparently. I remembered the light and the darkness, now that I thought about it more, and had dim memories of the air above me warming and cooling, wisps of mist steaming off me in the morning and vanishing as the day progressed. But I couldn't have said how many times it had happened. I certainly wouldn't have guessed a month.

Sam peered up into the sky. "I hope the others are all right. Have they been birds until now, too?"

"I don't know, honestly." I'd never achieved anything of this scope before and had no experience to draw from. It was entirely possible they'd turned back into people once they were far enough away. "They might be better off than we are."

The weather was going to be a serious problem. Neither Sam nor I was dressed for winter. It wasn't as bad as it might have been; Sam wore a green jacket over a green cambric shirt, and I had my good red hooded cloak. Better still, I was wearing more sensible footwear than the last time I'd had to tramp through these woods on foot. I doubted we'd freeze to death as long as we kept in motion.

But it didn't strike me as a wise idea to bed down for a night in the great outdoors if we could avoid it. On the plain of ice at the top of the world, I'd had a magic stone that kept me from dying of exposure while I slept. Nothing like that seemed likely to come to hand.

"Do you have any idea where we are?" I asked.

"None whatever. I take it you don't, either?"

"No." My sigh became a small white cloud in the frigid air. "We should try to find some kind of shelter." I looked around. No direction seemed more promising than any other.

"Downstream?" He motioned at the brook. "The burn here might run toward the sea. It could lead us to the castle."

I nodded my assent, and we set off, following the stream.

It was tough going, with the usual difficulties of fighting our way through a trackless wilderness made worse by having to slog through the snow. Often, we had to take circuitous routes, when the brook dove into a defile, or the banks were clogged with impassable undergrowth. We did our best to keep it within earshot so that we could find our way back.

And of course, every now and then, there were the creatures, peering at us from the bushes and trees. A beakless owl, its three cavernous mouths filled with the teeth of a lamprey. A fox with no eyes that felt its way forward with two long, whiplike antennae. An enormous mound of snoring fur in the bushes. We kept our distance from that one.

None of them attacked us—at least not yet.

"I've never seen anything like what happened when you turned into the lake," Sam said after a while. "You were there, and then you were water, and then you were everywhere. And I was a bird." He gave me a sideways glance. "That was no minor work of sorcery."

"It's more than I've ever managed before. And likely more

than I ever will again." There was no guarantee I'd be able to repeat my success. Magic doesn't merely defy logic; it doesn't behave in any orderly, reasonable manner. Casting a spell is more like trying to ride a bolt of lightning than it's like mixing measured ingredients to make a medicinal tincture. "And in this case, I had . . . certain advantages."

"Like what?"

Like the kiss. True Love's First Kiss, to be precise. A power that has been known to break mighty enchantments, revive the nearly dead, and amplify magic a thousandfold. It had been the wildest of desperate gambles. I hadn't really thought it would work.

I hadn't really thought about what it might mean.

And I still didn't know. Was Sam in love with me? Was I in love with Sam? Did we know each other well enough to say? Perhaps it meant we would fall in love at some later point. Or simply that we could fall in love. I'd heard of True Love's First Kiss happening for two people who had only danced together at a ball three times. Or being used to break a sleeping curse by a couple who had never exchanged a word before that very moment. Surely they couldn't have already been in love? I'd never considered the subject very deeply before. I'm not sure I'd believed it would ever come up.

Instead of answering Sam's question, I asked one of my own. "Why did you stay," I said, "when everyone else flew away?"

"Ah, well." Sam appeared to become fascinated by his boots crunching through the snow. "I thought you might need someone around when you came out of it. Or as much as a bird can think such a thing, anyway. I had to fight against the urge to migrate. Some days I would fly south for a few miles before I remembered."

"Well . . . thank you. I'm glad I'm not alone out here."

"It's no great sacrifice on my part. The king can make do with eleven hunters protecting him instead of twelve. For a while, at least." Despite what he said, he sounded troubled.

"He only had six when we were fighting the spider wolves," I pointed out.

"I know. It's only that before now, I haven't ever . . . Jack must be worried about me. The two of us have never been apart for very long. We've always been there to look out for each other."

"Jack," I said. "Jacqueline."

That brought Sam's gaze up from his boots. The snow was pouring down, puffy white pellets that clung to our clothing. The wind had picked up as well.

"You figured that out, did you?" said Sam.

"Hardly. The king called out her name in a moment of panic. She was his fiancée, wasn't she? Before he was engaged to . . ." I stopped myself before saying "me."

"Aye, she was."

"Are all of the hunters women in disguise?"

"Most. Not quite all."

"Jack kept a version of her name," I mused. "To keep things simple. Did the others? Is Harry short for Harriet? Max for Maxine? Kit for Kate and Clem for . . ." I had to puzzle over that one. "Clemence?"

"Clementine. She hates it."

"And what about Sam?"

"Just Sam. Nothing more. As I said, not *all* of us are women."

Conversation halted for a few minutes while we forced our way through a dense thicket. Some twisting plant with inch-long thorns had hidden itself inside, so the whole of our attention was spent detaching spiky vines from our clothes before we were both scratched bloody. Neither of us was entirely successful, and I was left with a red, dripping gash on my cheek.

When I dragged myself through to the other side, grabbing

Sam's hand to assist me, I asked, "So, is Jack your fraternal twin, then?"

Sam went still, and there was a long pause before he answered. "No," he said at length. "We're identical twins."

"Oh, of course." I dabbed at the blood on my face with my glove. Something in the line of Sam's shoulders relaxed ever so slightly.

In Skalla, it wasn't uncommon for someone to realize they weren't what everyone had assumed at the time they were born. But I doubted such things were treated with as much respect here in Tailliz, with its rigid gender roles enforced by the ruling class.

"Did Jack borrow your clothes, then?" I asked. "When she adopted her disguise?"

"At first. It helped that we're the exact same size."

We resumed our trek through the snow, ducking our heads as the wind blew heavy flakes into our faces. Four-legged sparrows regarded us with beady, faceted eyes. I pulled my cloak around me. The weather was getting grimmer as the day went on.

"Are any of the others men?" I asked.

"I've never polled the whole group." Sam sounded amused in spite of the cold. "Jules seemed extraordinarily happy to switch from skirts to breeches. But that doesn't necessarily mean anything."

"Jules—that's the frog spitter?"

"No, that's Jude," Sam corrected me. "Flowers spring up from the ground wherever Jules walks."

"I never did learn the names of all the duchess's siblings."

"Alex can eat anything, Nick can make anyone sneeze, Drew can cover tracks so well that no beast or bird can follow them, and Fred can make small windows into somewhat larger windows."

"That one . . . doesn't sound especially useful."

"It is if you want a somewhat larger window."

"Well," I said, "I can see why no one suspected their secret. Your abilities must distract everyone from anything else about you."

Sam grinned sourly. "For the most part, aye. Not entirely."

I mulled that over as we pushed through the shrubs along the bank of the creek. Who had figured out most of them were women?

"The lion," I realized. "That's what he's been testing for. How on earth did he come to believe peas on the floor would prove anything?"

Sam's laugh was almost a snort. "He has odd notions about how humans operate. According to the Doctrine of Lion, laddies stomp, but lassies prance, and . . . it's hard to explain. He's written a whole book about it. You should read it. It's hilarious."

"But why does he care? What does it matter?" I was bewildered—I knew it was deeply important to the lion, but I couldn't fathom why he would be concerned about the gender roles of an entirely different species.

"He's been told there are rules, and he thinks it's his job to impose them." Sam's mouth compressed into a thin line. "He's hardly alone in that."

We walked in silence for a long while after that. The clouds overhead darkened from light gray to charcoal; behind them, the sun must have been dipping low on the horizon. I had to clench my teeth to keep them from chattering as it grew colder. One of my boots had sprung a leak at some point, and my foot was thoroughly soaked. So much for better footwear.

Snow still plummeted from the sky, and the drifts were getting deeper. Soon, we'd have to start worrying about frostbite—or worse, unless our circumstances improved before nightfall.

Frostbite should be treated by moving the patient to a warmer area as soon as possible. Immerse the affected body parts in tepid water, if available, but never in extremely hot water. Severe cases of frostbite can lead to gangrene and may require amputation.

I tucked my hands into my armpits to keep them as warm as I could. We'd be in a great deal of trouble if we couldn't find a place to bed down. And in the vast, untamed wilderness, that didn't seem very likely.

CHAPTER TWENTY-ONE

The Not-Entirely-Uninhabited Ruin

My foot ached abominably, but at least that meant it hadn't gone numb. I steered my thoughts away from the possibility that it would have to be cut off if the situation worsened.

"So, why twelve?" I asked.

"What?"

"Why was it so important for Jack to find eleven duplicates? Or any duplicates, for that matter? You never did get around to telling me."

"Decoys."

"Right. Of course." It was obvious, now that I had enough pieces to put together. "Jack thought the assassin would target her, too, once she started defending the king. She wanted to confuse whoever it was."

"It was my idea, actually. Mine and Clem's. Jack was going to go off on her own, but we wouldn't let her. She finally agreed to let us come as long as she could be in charge of it all." He paused as we helped each other over a twisted tangle of roots. "It was supposed to just be the three of us, but then we met Kit and Harry and Max, and things got a wee bit out of hand."

"And then after the business with the duchess . . ."

"Things got very out of hand."

I stumbled over a tree root that arched just high enough above the ground to catch my foot, wrenching my ankle. I managed not to fall on my face, but after that my ankle complained when I put any weight on it. It was the same foot that was already half-frozen, and my limp grew more pronounced. Still better than injuring the other foot. Sam put a hand on my arm to steady me.

Our hike was growing more difficult as the darkness deepened. If I'd broken my ankle rather than spraining it, it would have been a disaster.

"Do you think there's any chance we'll find shelter soon?" I asked.

"We might." Sam's cautious tone belied the already-limited optimism of his words. "Even if we don't find the castle, someone might live nearby—the burn would be a good source of fresh water. There could be a hunter's lodge, or a hermit's hut, or—"

"A ruined tower!" I cried.

"I suppose," Sam said with more than a hint of skepticism. "Although I don't know why anyone would build a tower in the middle of the forest. No roads to guard, the visibility through the trees would be terrible—"

"No, I mean I see one. Over there." Between the trees, through the haze of falling snow, I'd caught a glimpse of a curved stone wall with a ragged top.

The remains of the round keep were nestled in a bend of the brook. It might have stood taller in the past, but at some point everything higher than about fifteen feet had been sheared off, with a slope of mossy irregular rocks fanning out from one side. It looked as if a giant had kicked it over. Possibly that was exactly what had happened.

"This makes no sense," Sam said. "What's it doing here?"

"Oh, you find all kinds of nonsensical things in the middle of a forest. Take gingerbread houses. Ridiculous place to put them. The ants get in after a day and never leave."

Sam regarded the structure dubiously. "Are you saying a witch might live in there?"

"Who knows? Either we go inside, or we spend the night in the snow. I just hope it doesn't belong to bears. They get annoyed if you sleep in their beds or eat their porridge." Unreasonably so, in my opinion. If you're perishing with hunger and find porridge that's been left to sit out all day long, I think it's fair to assume no one has any plans to eat it. Two out of the three bowls had been inedible anyway. But they tossed me out the window before I had a chance to apologize or explain.

The light had almost faded by the time we made our way inside. I was happy to see solid walls, although the ceiling had a large hole in it where a stone staircase, grooved in the middle by the passage of innumerable ancient feet, wound its way up the wall to the nonexistent upper floors. Between that and the gaps where the windows had been, it wasn't much warmer than the outside. A chandelier of icicles dripped from the remains of an arrow slit. But there was enough wall to keep the wind at bay and enough roof to keep the snowfall off our heads. In fact, other than some small drifts beneath the window holes, the place was surprisingly free of snow.

It was also, however, clearly inhabited. Although no one was present at the moment, there were signs of recent use. No bowls of porridge had been left unattended, which was a pity; we could have used a warm meal, stolen or otherwise. But tucked beneath the stairway, out of the way of any drafts, we found a bedroll of much more recent origin than the building itself, along with a few other odds and ends—blankets and pillows and a basin for water.

I walked over and poked at the bedroll, which proved to be exceptionally thick and soft.

"My goodness," I said, peering at it in the dim light. "Is this a feather mattress?"

Sam looked uneasy. "Surely we shouldn't stay here."

"I don't see that we have much of a choice." In another few minutes, the light would be gone. "Look, there's only a couple of possibilities. Maybe someone lives out here because they don't like a lot of company. If they object to us coming in out of the snow, we can deal with that when they get back. I think most people would understand our difficulty." Asshole bears aside.

"I suppose," said Sam.

"On the other hand, this could be a horrible trap meant to lure us in, and something awful is going to happen if we stay."

"What kind of something awful were you thinking?"

"Oh, the usual. Our legs get cut off if we don't fit the bed. Forced marriage to a beast. My firstborn child is demanded as payment for—"

"Those are your worries? I was more concerned about axe murderers."

"All right, ordinary axe murderers, then. But if that's the case, our options are either a horrible fate in here or a horrible fate out there." I gestured at the forest, now visible only in smudges of black and gray streaked with the dim whiteness of snow. "So I'd rather hold out hope that a kindly old hermit will twitter over us in the morning, since the only alternative is freezing to death."

"You have a point," he said, not looking happy about it. "All right. I'll take the floor, then."

"Take the floor for what?"

"To sleep on, obviously."

I stared at him. "It's icy-cold stone. That'll be awful. Why wouldn't you sleep on the bedroll?"

"Because I assumed *you* would be sleeping on the bedroll. And we're not . . . I mean, you and I . . ."

Silence hung in the air between us until I took in what he was getting at.

Then I burst out laughing.

"Oh, my goodness!" I said, gasping for breath. "Should I promise I'll safeguard your unwedded virtue?"

"Stop it." Sam was blushing, his pale cheeks turning a deep red. "It isn't that funny. It's just that we've not so much as had dinner together, and I didn't think—"

"This situation doesn't seem funny to you? At all?" I flung a dramatic hand to my forehead. "A snowstorm forced them together, and there was only . . . one . . . bed! What were they to do?"

Sam cracked a smile. "Well. When you put it that way."

"Honestly, I'm starting to wonder if mischievous fairies put all this here to embarrass you." I unpinned my cloak—too damp to be of any more use—and sat on the bedroll in question. It compressed under me but stayed springy as it took my weight. I bent over to pull my boots off, careful of my ankle. "That would explain how suspiciously convenient it is, don't you think? Ow!" I winced as my foot moved in a direction it didn't want to move.

"Let me help you with that." Sam knelt in front of me and eased the boot past my injury.

"Thank you," I said, leaning back on my elbows. "Look, you're not sleeping on the floor, and neither am I. Warmth is more important than other considerations right now. And surely I can't be that much of a temptation, can I?"

"Aye," Sam said, looking up and meeting my eyes. "You are."

My voice caught in my throat when I tried to reply. I found myself unable to tear my gaze from his.

"Sam," I choked out when the lull grew uncomfortable. "You should know . . ."

He knelt there, waiting for me to continue. It wasn't fair to keep it secret from him. Not when he had revealed so much of himself to me.

I had to let him know there could be no future for us.

"You should know," I said at last, "that I am affianced to King Gervase."

He let out a long sigh. "You're Princess Melilot."

"Yes."

"Why—" He answered his own question before I had a chance to. "Because someone is trying to kill you."

"Which means I'd very much appreciate it if you kept this to yourself."

"Of course." He sat back on the floor. I could barely see him in the darkness. About ten heartbeats passed before he asked, "Do you want to be married to him?"

"Not really. And he's in love with someone else." I cleared my throat. "It doesn't matter."

"It should."

"Yes." I shifted aside, making room on the narrow mattress. "Now come to bed. I'm cold."

There was a rustle of cloth as he shed his own wet clothing. I had a sudden, vivid memory of Jack refusing to let me remove Sam's shirt when I was stitching him up.

"Are you wearing a binder?"

"Yes."

He couldn't have had enough opportunities to take it off for any healthy length of time, given the situation with the lion and everything else. "If it's getting uncomfortable, you don't have to suffer for my sake. Just so you know."

Another rustle, and then he slid in next to me. I debated whether or not I should keep my distance, but the weather overcame any objections in short order. I wriggled in closer and tucked my head against his shoulder as he wrapped an arm around me.

"Were you planning to sleep in your mask again, too?" I asked.

After a moment, he reached up and removed that as well.

His face, I thought, was a very handsome one. Admittedly the light was dim, but I doubted my opinion would change in the morning. I wanted to brush my fingers across his freckles, but I didn't.

"What a mess," Sam said.

"Yes."

"Gervase is a perfectly nice fellow, by the way. For a long time, I expected he'd be a brilliant brother-in-law."

"I'm almost surprised Jack isn't the one trying to kill me."

"She wouldn't."

"Not unless she decides I'm the one behind everything."

"She won't. You saved our lives. Hers included."

"Oh, is that all it takes to get on her good side?"

Sam gave a low chuckle in reply. "You haven't been seeing her at her best. She's just frustrated and grasping at any straw. She has a good heart. Jack's always been my fiercest champion, you know. From the moment I told her about who I was, she wouldn't let anyone try to deny it. Even when it was taking our parents a much, much longer time to come around to the idea."

I pulled him the tiniest bit closer. "I'm glad she was there for you."

"Me, too."

I'd already known she wasn't at all a bad sort, in spite of her suspicions and accusations. Jack and her friends had saved me from the spider wolves. They hadn't been there by accident. They'd been looking for me. Jack had gone into the woods to protect a princess she had every reason to hate. In return, I appeared to have seduced her brother under false pretenses. In my defense, however, he was very, very warm.

Maybe I was the villain of this saga, after all. I hoped not.

"Can you sleep?" Sam asked.

"No."

I felt him turn toward me, though it was too dark to see him now. "Me, neither."

"What should we do, then?"

There was a long pause before he answered. "Tell me a story. It's your turn, I think."

"All right. A story about what?"

"You."

That seemed fair, all things considered. I took a deep breath and began.

CHAPTER TWENTY-TWO

The Tale of Melilot

Once upon a time, when the world was younger and the sky was a little bluer, a man and a woman in the Kingdom of Skalla wished more than anything to have a child. But that wish, alas, had never been granted. After many years and much discussion of foster care, adoption, or stealing an infant from its cradle in the dead of night—

"Wait, what?" said Sam.

"Oh, does that not happen in Ecossia?"

"No! Do folk steal bairns in Skalla?"

"Well, not so much anymore. Before the treaty, the fairies used to take babies and replace them with exact duplicates. Then it caught on, and everybody started doing it. It was a big problem."

After many years and much discussion, the woman at last discovered she was pregnant. By then she was advanced in age, and the pregnancy was not an easy one. In fact, she suffered greatly from cramping and soreness, reddened skin, and a troubling swelling in her legs. Both the woman and her husband were not unlearned in the ways of medicine, and they feared she was suffering from clots in her veins that might well lead to an untimely death.

Now, as it happened, not far from their cottage, close enough that they could see it through their window, there was a marvelous garden. Beyond the forbidding wrought-iron fence that surrounded it, the garden abounded with every plant imaginable. Flowers bright with all the colors of the rainbow, ripe and luscious fruit hanging off the boughs, herbs—

"No, hold on." Sam put a hand on my arm to stop me. "I'm still having trouble with the bairn stealing. Why would the fairies do that in the first place?"

"I have no idea. My sister's wife is a fairy, but she got all embarrassed when I asked her about it and wouldn't tell me."

"Your sister-in-law is a fairy? Like a wee fluttery butterfly fairy?"

"More like a six-foot-tall fairy with a massive sword."

"I'm impressed by your sister, then."

"She rides a dragon. They're evenly matched."

No one was brave or foolish enough to go into this garden, for it was on the grounds of a magnificent palace that belonged to the queen of Skalla. And if that wasn't enough to discourage trespassers, the queen happened to be a mighty and terrifying sorceress.

As the woman's pregnancy progressed, her condition worsened, and she became most miserably ill. They tried every remedy they could think of to thin her blood—teas brewed from turmeric, medicines made from an extract of feverfew, and many more. But none had any effect.

One day, she looked out the cottage window and saw that the garden bed nearest the fence had been left free of flowers for the season. It had therefore been planted with a luxurious crop of sweet clover. Sweet clover has a most astonishing ability to renew tired soil since, as everyone knows, it is a hardy, drought-tolerant, nitrogen-fixing plant with a warm-weather biomass production capability that exceeds even that of alfalfa.

Less well known, however, is the fact that sweet clover, properly prepared, can be made into an excellent remedy for blood clots. But the wise woman at the window knew this, and she likewise knew any plant that grew in the queen's garden must be potent with magic. She came to believe the only cure for her ailment lay across the garden fence.

Her belief strengthened with each passing day and grew into an obsession. "Fetch me some of the sweet clover from the queen's garden!" she belabored her husband.

"But the queen would surely object to such a theft," he protested, "and smite us with dark magic!"

"She will not miss a small patch of clover," the woman rejoined. "It's only grown to prepare the way for prettier plants. And if you do not bring me some, I am sure I shall die."

The man loved his wife very much and did not wish for her to die. *I'll fetch her some of the queen's sweet clover,* he decided, *no matter the cost.* And so that night, he clambered over the garden fence and tore a handful of clover out of the patch as quickly as he could. When he brought it home, they made a tincture of the leaves.

"Already I feel better," the woman claimed upon drinking it. "If I take this blood thinner daily for a period of three to six months, depending on presentation of symptoms, I am certain I shall be cured."

The man was not happy about this pronouncement. "Such

a course of treatment would be contraindicated during pregnancy," he objected, "due to the risk of osteocalcin inhibition causing lower fetal bone growth."

"The first trimester presents the greatest risk of teratogenicity, and I am already past that," she countered.

"This story includes a lot more about the side effects of medicinal plants than I would have expected."

"Yes, well." I shrugged. "I'm a doctor's daughter. I was taught to be thorough."

"It was magic sweet clover, though, wasn't it? Would that have any side effects?"

"Anyway, it's magic sweet clover," the woman reassured her husband. "It probably doesn't have any side effects. Don't worry so much."

"But even so, if we persist in our theft for that long, we shall surely be smited! Or smitten! Or smote! I am unsure of the correct participle."

"And if we do not," she uttered darkly, "I shall die."

And so it was that the man found himself climbing over the garden fence night after night. Each time, he would snatch a bit of clover, bring it home, and make a tincture of the fresh leaves. After many weeks passed without incident, he decided the queen either had not noticed or did not care.

Each day, his wife waxed healthier and healthier. And finally, several months later, they decided a single additional dose of the tincture would be enough to pronounce her cured. The clouds gathered ominously on that fateful night, and as the man set forth, the heavens unleashed a torrent, accompanied by flashes of lightning and crashes of thunder. Nonetheless, he once again sneaked into the garden, drenched to the skin but relieved to know he soon would need to thieve no more.

Of course, anyone who has ever heard a story before will

be unsurprised to learn what happened next. As he snipped off that final clump of sweet clover, rainwater cascading off the leaves, there was a blinding light and a deafening boom, and a hand thumped onto his shoulder. He turned his head, blinking away the glowing spots the light had left in his vision, to see the queen standing behind him. The rain touched neither her clothes nor her hair, as if her very presence was repellent to nature itself.

"So you are the thief who has been making off with my clover," she mused. "I believe it is time for some serious smitening."

"Oh, great queen, please let your justice be tempered by mercy!" he begged her, dropping to his knees with a splash as he landed in a puddle. "My wife is ill, and without your sweet clover, she would surely perish."

The queen hesitated and peered at his face. "Wait. Aren't you my next-door neighbor? The cute one?"

"Uh . . . yes? That is, our little cottage is indeed inexplicably adjacent to the forbidden magical garden of your grand palace."

We cannot know what passed through the queen's mind at this time. Perhaps his pleas moved her and softened her heart. Perhaps she reflected that he had been a good neighbor for many years until desperation forced him into theft. Or perhaps she was thinking not with her head but with a different body part altogether. Whatever the reason, she refrained from smiting him.

Do not, however, mistake her restraint for gentleness, for the next thing she told him shook him to his core.

"You shall not be smitterated this night," she decided, "and your wife may have however much of my clover she requires. But it is not in me to let a debtor escape without payment or allow an insult to go unanswered. In exchange for your lives, a life must be given to me. Someday, I will take your child as my own. I will care for it like a mother and train it in sorcery, for any child born under the influence of a magic herb will bear magic in its blood."

Having no alternative, the man conceded to her demand, and with a heavy heart he went home with the last handful of clover. While his wife might survive, he feared his child was lost to him.

Survive the woman did, and some time later, she gave birth to a healthy girl. Because of the unusual circumstances of the pregnancy, they decided to name the child Melilot.

"I'm not following," Sam said.

"Not following what?"

"Why Melilot?"

"It's another word for sweet clover. Like how some people say garbanzo bean, but other people call it a chickpea."

"You were named after the medicine your mother took when she was pregnant?"

"Listen, I was lucky. If she'd had a cold, I might have been named Sneezewort."

"Or Bastard Toadflax," Sam suggested. "Or Wormwood. Or Rapunzel."

"Bastard toadflax is badass. But rapunzel is basically an anemic parsnip. Awful."

"Agreed."

When the child was born, the queen came to visit the cottage, an event the new parents viewed with much trepidation. They felt certain the queen would take the baby as she had threatened to do that terrible night.

Much to their surprise, she did no such thing. Instead, she brought gifts—a bottle of fine wine for the parents and a pretty doll for the child. Accompanying the queen was her own daughter, the two-year-old princess Jonquil, who was named after the lovely rush daffodils that bloomed in the garden. Princess Jonquil's father had perished not long earlier in a tragic self-bifurcation incident—

"In a what?"

"Someone guessed his name, and he got so mad that he tore himself in two. It happens."

Sam shook his head decisively. "No, it doesn't."

"Well, it happens in Skalla."

"Skalla is a very strange place."

"Says the masked man who fights monsters with his fists."

The adults drank the wine and chatted while Jonquil frowned thoughtfully at the baby, and then the visitors departed with nary a hint about the queen's demand.

"Perhaps it has slipped her mind?" the man speculated.

The woman shook her head. "No matter how insignificant we may be, she cannot have forgotten the curse she laid upon our household. There is some plot afoot here. We should not drink the rest of the wine, and we should destroy this doll lest it do harm to our child."

They poured the dregs of the bottle on the ground and threw the doll into the fire. But the wine they had consumed caused them no ill effects, and the doll burned like an ordinary doll.

The queen came over to chat with her neighbors once every couple of weeks for the next few years, bringing gifts that were eventually accepted. Most often, she came with her own child in tow. Jonquil and Melilot began to play together once the younger girl was able to walk. They'd squeeze their way through the garden fence to view the marvelous flowers. Their parents discussed the noteworthy issues of the day, such as which farmhands were secretly kings and whether an alliance with the mermaid kingdom would put a stop to mute girls washing up onto the shore and causing a fuss.

Melilot's father came to look forward to these visits. Her mother, however, never fully trusted the queen.

"A sorceress does nothing unless it is to her own benefit, and neither does a monarch," Melilot's mother warned her. "Someday, she will try to take you from me. Be watchful and wary, and do not be deceived." Melilot listened and tried to do as her mother bade her.

But when Melilot was still very young, her mother died.

It would be a neater story if her death could be blamed on the queen—a spell, a curse, a dagger in the night. In later years, Melilot would wish she had the consolation of believing the queen was the cause of her mother's death, of having someone to blame. But she did not believe it. Her mother's death was as terrible and as prosaic as any ordinary death, with no hint of magic to it. No telltale bird proclaimed the queen to be a murderer; no flute made of bone revealed some hideous plot behind it all. Melilot's mother died of pneumonia, and this time neither medical skill nor special herbs were able to save her.

Soon after that—far too soon, in Melilot's opinion—her father began to woo the queen. Romancing her with his words, sending her small presents she could not possibly need. She accepted his attentions, and before long he informed Melilot they were leaving their warm, snug cottage and moving into the drafty stone palace next door. Her father was marrying the queen and would become her new consort.

"I am your mother now," the queen advised Melilot the day she arrived in the palace. "I will raise you as I raise my own child, and I shall teach you sorcery and all manner of secret things."

"You are not my mother," Melilot retorted. "My mother is dead."

"You are willful," the queen scoffed. "But you must learn to obey me nonetheless."

Less than a year later, the queen gave birth to another child, a girl she named Calla, after the beautiful lilies that bloomed in the garden.

"This is your sister," the queen informed Melilot the day the child was born. "Now that you and I are linked by blood, you must acknowledge I am your mother."

"You are not my mother," Melilot rebutted her. "My mother is dead."

"You are willful," the queen sneered. "But you must learn to obey me nonetheless."

Their quarreling grew constant. Her father stayed neutral whenever they fought, never weighing in—

"That must have stung."

"What? No. Why?" Startled, I spoke so loudly that Sam drew an inch or two away. We'd been huddled close together in the darkness, and I'd shouted almost directly in his ear. "It wasn't like he took her side," I continued in a quieter voice. And tugged him back again; cold air was already filtering into the gap between us.

"If you don't take sides in an argument between a parent and a child," Sam replied, "doesn't it basically mean you've sided with the adult? That's who has all the authority. It's not a fair fight."

I spent a few moments thinking about that. "Maybe," I said. I'd always laid the blame for the miseries of my childhood on my stepmother. It had never occurred to me that my father might have had some culpability as well, if only through inaction. "I'm sure he was trying his best," I told Sam. "Anyway, it hardly matters now."

The years passed by, one after another, and Melilot learned medicine from her father and also, albeit reluctantly, sorcery and statecraft from her stepmother—although she was never particularly good at either magic or politics. She grew to love Jonquil and Calla as sisters. But she always remembered the words of her mother, and she never gave the queen her trust.

Her father was sorely grieved by the rift between the two. It wore on him and aged him beyond his years. He grew frail and weary, and no one was shocked when, not so much as a decade after his remarriage, he followed his first wife into death.

"I'm sorry." Sam gave my shoulder a gentle squeeze. "About your father and mother, both."

"It's all right. It was years ago." After the slightest of pauses, I added, "But thank you, even so."

As always, Melilot blamed her stepmother for what had happened. Although this time, perhaps, not any more than she blamed herself.

"I am your only parent now," the queen observed to Melilot not long after the funeral. "Surely this is when you will admit I am your mother."

"You are not my mother!" Melilot shouted. "My mother is dead!"

The queen's frown was ominous. "When your father still lived, I allowed your willfulness to grow unchecked. I shall allow it no longer. You must learn to obey. Fetch me three pure white hairs from a unicorn's beard."

Melilot's jaw dropped open. "What?"

"You heard me. It is a simple task, no more than I would ask of any of my daughters. Do it, or you shall face whatever punishment I devise."

Fearing this punishment, Melilot did as her stepmother wished. She spent the next month tracking down a unicorn and convincing it to let her pluck its beard. When she returned, she scattered the hairs before the throne, declaring, "There! I have performed the task commanded of me by my queen. Now let me be in peace."

Her stepmother, however, was unsatisfied. "You have obeyed me once, but will you do so a second time? Fetch me the shadow of a candle flame."

Melilot stared. "Fetch you what?"

"You heard me. It is a simple task, no more than I would ask of any of my daughters."

"It most certainly is not!" Melilot contended. "You would never assign such an impossible quest to Jonquil or Calla!"

"Jonquil has already brought me the shadow of a clear pane of glass," the queen asserted, "while you were out frolicking with unicorns. She searches for the flame's shadow even now. If you wish to have any hope of finding it first, I suggest you make haste."

Not wishing to be outdone by her sister, Melilot did as her stepmother bade her.

The tasks continued as the years passed by—

"Where on earth did you find the shadow of a candle flame, though?"

"It turns out fire is less dense than the surrounding air," I explained, "which gives it a lower refractive index. So if you shine an even brighter light source on it, you'll see a dark region—"

"That's a lot less poetic than I would have expected."

"Trust me, it only takes one or two impossible quests before you become a firm advocate of victory by pragmatic technicality."

The tasks continued as the years passed by. Melilot was sent to copy an endless book, to capture the moon in a cup, to make bread from a stone. Sometimes her sisters went with her, and sometimes she went alone, setting forth on her own to seek wonders, find treasures, and match her wits against villains. The work was often tedious and always difficult. Her sorcerous skills did not develop at the same pace as her sisters', and she grew jealous of their easy, hereditary might. Although admittedly, Melilot's refusal to practice magic, in order to spite her stepmother, may have also contributed. Whatever the cause, she never came close to matching their magical prowess, and she was a greater failure still compared to the queen. Her sisters often had to bail her out of difficulties. Which only reinforced her feelings of inadequacy.

By the time she was sixteen years old, she was thoroughly sick of all this. And one day, when her stepmother attempted to shove her out on another ridiculous-sounding quest, Melilot refused.

Her stepmother paused in the middle of her instructions. "What did you say?"

"You heard me," Melilot growled at her. "I'm done. In case you hadn't noticed, there's an enemy army threatening our borders." For indeed, such was the case, although that threat has gone entirely unmentioned until this moment. "I think there might be more important things right now than finding a dragon's toenail for you."

The queen's eyes narrowed. "And if I say that there is not?"

"Then I would answer that you're not my mother, and you can't tell me what to do. You might have my sisters under your thumb, but not me. Not anymore. And you know what? I don't think there's going to be any of this 'punishment' you keep talking about. I'm calling your bluff."

At this, the queen pressed her lips together, nodded, and

promptly ordered Melilot to be confined in a tower deep within the trackless wilderness of Skalla. The tower had no doorway. The only opening in the sheer wall was a single small window at the highest possible point.

"That's terrible." Sam sounded appalled. "You must have been miserable."

I shrugged. "Some might say I got off lightly."

"I don't. Your queen built a doorless tower just to punish her daughter for disobedience. That's beyond excessive."

"Well, that wasn't the only reason she had it. It was a— Hm."

"What?"

"Possibly nothing. An idea that we might want to look into once there's enough light."

Every morning, Melilot's stepmother would stop by the base of the tower and call up to her, "Will you not let me in?"

Melilot would yell, "Do not mock me, you poisonous snake! You know full well there is no door."

For a full year, Melilot languished in the tower. Day after day she gazed upon the wilderness of Skalla. With little to occupy her time, she spent her days resenting her stepmother, resenting herself, and longing to be free.

"Why have you stopped?" Sam asked after a moment.

"That's the end."

"That can't be the end!" Sam sat halfway up. My head slid off his shoulder. "That's not a finished story. What happened next?"

"Nothing. It was a boring year in a tower. But I got out eventually, and now I'm here."

"You're skipping bits." He let his head fall back on the pillow.

"There isn't anything left to tell," I said as I resettled myself. "Some stories are like that."

"If you say so."

"I do."

But of course, I was lying.

CHAPTER TWENTY-THREE

Today When I Was on the Stair, I Saw a Room That Wasn't There

I woke up slowly, with a raw ache at the back of my throat. That didn't bode well. The trek through the frozen forest had taken its toll, and a single night of sleep had not been enough to stave off the effects.

At least I'd slept decently enough. The feather mattress was the most comfortable place I'd had to lay my head since leaving Skalla. Soft and cozy. Especially cozy since at some point during the night, I'd curled up even closer to the warm body next to mine; my cheek was still nestled in the crook of Sam's shoulder, but now my arm was flung across his chest as well. He snored softly and evenly, like a drowsy cat. In the morning light, his face was just as lovely as it had been at dusk. Lovelier, in fact, now that I could see it better.

I didn't want to move. In particular, I didn't want to move my arm. I wanted nothing more than to possessively drape my leg over him, too. There was, I thought, a solid argument to be made that it would be healthiest for me to spend the rest of the day snuggling in bed. Or possibly the rest of the week.

But a bladder is a harsh mistress, and no matter how warm Sam was, no matter how much my throat hurt, and no matter how cold it was outside the nest of blankets—and it was cold enough to sting—the urgent signals my body was sending could not be long ignored. Repressing a groan, I slid away from Sam and tottered to my feet. The frigid stone floor stabbed at my toes like a knife until I managed to get my boots on. My ankle was feeling better at least.

Outside, a perfect blanket of unbroken white covered the ground and clung to the limbs of the trees. It was almost eerily quiet. The snow had stopped, and the wind had died down, which meant I was able to take care of necessary business in relative comfort. "Relative" being a word doing a lot of heavy lifting in a situation where I risked literally freezing my ass off. The low morning sun was shining in a cloudless sky, making the snow glitter and glimmer, but it failed to provide much heat.

Sam was sitting up and blinking when I came back in. He'd just begun to get dressed and looked unfairly chipper considering the arduous journey we would need to resume that day. I still resented having had to get out of bed. But when he smiled shyly at me, an answering smile crept onto my own face nonetheless.

He looked down and away. My grin faded.

We were falling into a very deep and difficult place together, weren't we?

"We should probably get on our way," he mumbled at the floor as he tied his mask on. "It'll be hard going even without the snowstorm. The earlier we start, the more likely we are to find the castle before nightfall. I think we both could stand to have a hot meal in front of a roaring fire."

My stomach made a gurgling noise at the uncomfortable reminder I'd had nothing to eat all day yesterday. And for the month before that, technically.

We had no great reason to believe we were heading toward

the castle, though. Following the stream was a reasonable plan, but it didn't come with any guarantee of success. At least it meant we had a constant source of fresh water, although one so cold it made my teeth throb.

Sam was right that our chances would be better if we got an early start. But still . . .

"I want to check one thing before we go." My voice came out as a harsh croak. Sam glanced up at me in surprise. I swallowed, even though it hurt, and tried again. "It shouldn't take long," I managed more smoothly.

If I'd been my own patient, I would've prescribed a healthy dose of willow bark tea. Perhaps with some elderflower or lemon and honey. Then I'd suggest bed rest. Maybe we'd find a willow in the woods. Tea didn't seem likely, but I could chew on the bark.

"What did you have in mind?" Sam asked.

I walked over to the grooved stone stairs and looked up through the ragged hole in the ceiling above them. Through it, I saw only blue sky. "Shouldn't these stairs be completely covered in snow?" I asked. "There's only a little bit on them, near the windows. Why didn't any come in through the roof?" I should have noticed how strange that was last night, but I'd had other things on my mind.

Two furrows appeared on Sam's forehead. "That is odd. Perhaps it's some trick of the wind?"

"Perhaps," I agreed, testing the stairs with my foot. They didn't feel inclined to collapse under me, so I started trotting up. "But I don't think it is." Talking about my imprisonment the night before had reminded me of one of the customary reasons to build a tower in the middle of nowhere.

I kicked my way past the few stray clumps of snow and approached the top. As soon as my head broke the plane of the ceiling, the bright sky overhead disappeared.

In the ensuing dimness, before my eyes adjusted, I was startled by horrific screams and shrieks. My nose was assaulted by animal smells, fur and musk and carrion flesh. I almost stumbled backward in fright, which would have been a bad idea on a stairway, but then my vision cleared, and I glimpsed the cages.

I pulled my head back into quiet and light. "There's a whole invisible floor up here. This is a sorcerer's tower. Let's take a look."

"This is a what?" Sam frowned as he came to join me. "Is it safe to go up there?"

"Well, I wouldn't call any sorcerer's tower safe. But it looks like all the monsters are imprisoned."

"There are monsters." He sighed and shook his head. "Of course there are. Up we go, I suppose."

I strode into the hidden upper chamber, Sam at my heels. It was as ancient and broken as the one below; the stones of the walls were weathered and pitted, and the joints were pocked with holes where the mortar had crumbled, but there was even less snow—only a couple of sparse patches on the floor beneath the two narrow windows, resembling scatterings of spilled flour.

Dozens of cages lined the curving walls, row upon row of padlocks and iron bars, some of the enclosures so small a squirrel would barely fit inside, others stretching so high I could have stood on Sam's shoulders, and my head still wouldn't have reached the tops. More than half were filled with unnatural beasts.

The spider wolves were familiar from my own experience. Some of the others were ones I'd been told about, like the huge strange birds with serrated beaks and rings of thornlike protrusions sprouting from their heads. A furred, hooded serpent with feathery spines made a noise halfway between a growl and a hiss. Close against its body, dozens of tiny sharp claws clenched and unclenched as it slithered closer to the front of its cage.

The rest were ones I'd never seen or heard of before, writhing masses of tentacles, mandibles, and spikes. They tried to launch themselves at us as we passed, rattling the bars of their cages and howling in rage. Sam and I looked around warily, but the padlocks held firm. We didn't seem to be in immediate danger, as long as we stayed out of reach of any of the grasping limbs that poked through the bars.

These were not the harmless oddities we sometimes came across in the forest. These wanted blood.

"I understand why whoever lives here sleeps downstairs," I said.

The cages weren't the only furnishings in the room. A wooden chair sat before an ink-stained writing desk. Papers and quill pens lay scattered across it, along with a jumble of other paraphernalia—black candles, an ornate hand mirror with a silver frame, and what looked like the skull of a goat.

"How much of this tower is an illusion?" Sam asked, close to my ear so I could hear him over the howls. "Is it even as old as it looks?"

"Probably. The big tumble of fallen stone outside might just be set dressing, but I can feel drafts coming through the holes in the wall, so they're real enough. The furniture's in far nicer shape, though. My guess is that the place was built a long time ago, but a new sorcerer found it and moved in. They do that sometimes. Like hermit crabs. Saves the trouble of building one from scratch."

Sam put his hand through a window, as if testing whether it was truly there. "I still don't see why they'd build one in the first place. Is it really in case they ever need to imprison a maiden?"

"No. Well . . . maybe," I said, eyeing the cages again. Not every last one was currently occupied, after all. "But the one my stepmom stuck me in wasn't designed to keep me captive. It was adapted to the purpose. Mostly they're meant to be secret places—hard to get into or hard to find."

"Somewhere to experiment with magic," Sam murmured, lost in thought, "far from any prying eyes."

I nodded. "And they also"—I approached the desk—"make excellent hiding places for magical artifacts." I tapped the mirror with my fingernail.

"Hey!" it cried out. "Don't scratch me up!" The images on its surface rippled together to form the rough semblance of a face. Sam's eyes widened in surprise, and I allowed myself a small smile. I'd developed a keen sense for spotting enchanted knickknacks over the years. Admittedly, this one had been blatant enough that any pride was unwarranted. No one leaves a regular mirror lying around next to their goat skull.

"Sorry," I said.

"You should be." The mirror didn't seem much appeased by the apology. "I don't go around shoving my finger in your mouth, do I?"

"You don't have fingers. For that matter, you can't exactly go around anywhere, can you?"

"Not the point!"

While I'd been chatting with the looking glass, Sam had started shuffling through the papers on the desk. "It looks like the sorcerer kept notes."

I glanced over at the page he was holding, a sketch of a spider wolf. Leafing through, we found more of them—or rather, we found creatures that were almost spider wolves. Some had six legs, or no legs, or four pairs of tentacles instead. Octowolves? A few of the papers had notes scribbled in the margins: "Can't walk. Flopped around. Kill it and start over." "Poison bite?" On other pages were further sketches of different beasts.

One depicted a bipedal form with a boulder for a head. There was even a sapling whimsically drawn growing out of its elbow. Next to it was a note reading "Stone creatures—more difficult to destroy?"

This wasn't the work of some helpful soul, studying the creatures in order to better defeat them. This was where the monstrosities had been envisioned, created, tested, and refined into deadly predators. This was where my death had been planned.

"Who lives here?" I said to the mirror. "Who made these drawings and bred these creatures?"

It shouldn't be possible for a glimmering, abstract impression of a face to look so smug. "Powerful enchantments prevent me from revealing any information about my master."

Of course they did. Although, with my knowledge of magic, there was a chance I'd be able to break those enchantments. It might only take me five or six years of trial and error, if I got lucky.

"We need to let King Gervase know about this place," I told Sam, "as soon as we possibly can."

"You don't think we should stay here? Lie in wait for . . . whoever this is, catch them unawares?"

I shook my head, the bloodcurdling shrieks of the monsters echoing in my ears. "No, I don't think that would be a good idea. When we come face-to-face with this sorcerer, I'd much rather do it with the king's entire army at my back."

The face in the hand mirror scowled. "Don't you dare bring an army to my home. If you try it, my master will rip out your bones and dance in your blood."

"That's kind of why I want the army," I informed it before turning back to Sam. "We have to bring word of this place to the castle, and we have to do it quickly. Before the next attack."

He took a moment to stomp on a spiked tentacle that had snaked a hairbreadth too close to my foot. The creature howled in pain and whipped its injured limb back behind the bars of its cage. "What if we've been going in the wrong direction?" he asked. "It might take us days to find the castle. Weeks."

I was about to remark that we didn't have any better options when a thought struck me. "How did the sorcerer know where to attack us?"

"What do you mean?"

"The spider wolves could have been waiting to ambush me on the road. But how did the stone giants find the hunt at a random spot in the middle of the woods?"

Sam shrugged. "Magic, I suppose."

"Exactly."

A good rule of thumb when it comes to enchantments is that function follows form. A magical sword is meant to cut through something, whether that something is flesh, steel, or cheese. A magical harp will play bewitching music, and a magical goose will lay marvelous eggs of some kind. I have encountered exceptions to this rule—spinning wheels, as I've noted, are so easy to curse they can drop you into a coma rather than doing anything as sensible as producing golden thread. But the exceptions are rare. In general, if you know the purpose of a regular object, you can make a decent guess at what the magic version will do.

The purpose of a mirror is reflection. Creating an image of whatever's nearby.

The purpose of a magic mirror is scrying.

"Show us how to get to the castle," I said to the looking glass.

The glittering eyes glared at me. "No. You didn't say the magic words."

I grinned. You didn't grow up in my stepmother's household without learning that little trick. "Mirror, mirror on the wall—"

"I'm not on the wall!" it interrupted.

"Really? You're going to be a stickler about that?"

"Yes."

A pedantic mirror. Just my luck. "You're only delaying the inevitable, you know. Mirror, mirror on the desk . . ." Hm. Grotesque? Statuesque? No effective way of using either one sprang to mind. I glanced at Sam. "Can you think of something that rhymes with desk?"

He hesitated, thinking it over deeply, before saying, "Pesk?"

"*Pesk?*"

"Like pesky? Only without the *y*?"

"Doesn't look so inevitable now, does it?" the mirror said.

"We'll see about that," I growled, scooping the mirror up and holding it before me. I wanted to get this over with. Something that seemed to be made of tongues was throwing itself at its cage door so furiously that I worried about the lock. "Mirror, mirror in my hands, show me where the castle stands."

The mirror made a frustrated noise, and a perfect, clear image of the castle formed in the glass, snow coating the battlements and heraldic flags snapping in the wind. Not quite what we needed, but at least I'd managed to make it work. I lay the mirror at my feet.

"Mirror, mirror on the floor," I intoned, "show us to the castle's door."

"This is humiliating," it grumbled as pictures unspooled across it. At first my face appeared, just like an actual reflection, before the image swooped away from me, down the stairs, out the door, and into the woods, as if the path were being viewed by a bird in flight.

I tried to commit it to memory, making note of the direction and any landmarks I could see. The route veered from the stream, tracing a straight line through the heart of the woods. It was difficult to tell how long a journey it would be.

"I think I might be able to get us there, from that," Sam said.

"If not, we can check again along the way." I gathered up the protesting mirror, and I grabbed a handful of papers as well. "Let's take whatever evidence we can."

Sam picked up the rest of the notes. It would definitely be easier to use those as our proof than to bring one of the sorcerer's creations back with us. Even the little ones were too much of a risk. The old king, I remembered, had died of a poisonous bite. I had no wish to meet the same fate.

We hurried out, the cries of the monsters vanishing into silence the moment we left the secret chamber. I hoped when I returned, it would be to tear the whole place down.

CHAPTER TWENTY-FOUR

The Welcoming Committee

The skies remained clear, and the next leg of our journey was noticeably easier without a blizzard blowing into our faces. Shuffling through the deep snow made it an exhausting hike, nonetheless. I hadn't eaten in so long I'd stopped being hungry—never a good sign. Foraging seemed pointless. Little would be available, and even less would be visible, thanks to the previous day's storm.

More dangerous still, now that we'd traveled away from the stream, we had no ready source of fresh water. Snow makes a poor substitute—it draws heat from your body and ends up doing more harm than good. I considered attempting to turn into a puddle so Sam could drink from me, but he found the idea unsettling. I tried to reassure him that the water wouldn't turn back into my organs in his stomach, but that somehow only made things worse.

My sore throat had been growing more painful by the hour. And despite the cold, I had broken out in a fevered sweat. My hands shook. I wasn't able to hold them steady.

We were both somewhat buoyed, however, by the knowledge we were headed toward warmth and a meal. Traveling in a straight line was impossible in the dense forest, but we recalibrated our position with the looking glass whenever we worried we were getting off track. It provided this help unwillingly. Even more so since we were forced to put it in a variety of undignified positions in order to supply appropriate rhymes. ("Mirror, mirror on wet leaves, point us to the castle's eaves," and so on.)

Unfortunately, I had no luck in tricking it into telling us anything about its master, no matter how clever my attempts. I was particularly proud of "Mirror, mirror in the air, show your master in their lair," but Sam made me stop after that because I'd flung the mirror as high as I could, and he'd only just managed to catch it before it hit the ground. He rightly pointed out that a broken mirror wouldn't do us any good. We had to travel for the next mile or two with a looking glass insulting my intelligence, virtue, and parentage—the last of which grew increasingly improbable the longer the tirade continued. But I would have considered that a small price to pay if my ploy had worked.

Toward the end of the day, a final check of the mirror showed the castle less than half an hour's walk ahead. Tired, thirsty, ailing, and frozen as I was, I picked up my pace in anticipation.

Then an arrow thudded into a tree trunk scant inches from my face.

I was so surprised that I didn't scream, only stumbled to a halt, blinking in bewilderment.

"Clem!" Sam shouted. "What the hell?"

Three masked hunters stepped out from the shadows of trees like ghosts appearing from thin air. One—Clem, presumably—had her bow nocked, with the arrow trained on me. The other two could have been any of them.

"Hello, witch," the one in front greeted me.

"Sorceress," I corrected automatically, my voice hoarse and cracking. If I'd been given three guesses as to which hunter this was, I'd have said Jack for all of them.

Her eyes, hard and sharp as a pair of nails, locked on me as unwaveringly as Clem's arrow. "Come back to assess the damage? I think you'll find it wasn't as much as you hoped."

"What are you *talking* about?" Surely Jack didn't still imagine I'd been the one behind the assassination attempts? Not after I'd rescued them.

But other than Sam, I realized, no one could have known for certain I'd done that. Everyone else must have been left baffled by the appearance of the lake and their sudden transformation. If a month ago, Jack had thought I brought the stone giants upon us, she'd been given no reason to change her mind.

The three hunters watched me in tense silence. Silence that could snap at any moment into something dangerous.

"Look," I said. "I can explain—"

"Are you all daft?" Sam stepped in front of me, cutting me off. "Clem, put your bow down."

Clem's aim adjusted by a fraction of an inch. "Git oot th' way, Sam," she answered. "Till this gits sorted."

"There's nothing to sort!" Sam stared at his cousin in disbelief. "She didn't summon the monsters. She's the one who saved us!"

"You're not even making sense," Jack said. "No one saved us."

"She turned us into birds!" Sam shouted.

Jack's face twitched. "She was the one? You're certain?"

"I saw her do it."

"Thirty days as a goose," Jack growled. "A month trapped in that nightmare." So they hadn't changed back any earlier than we had. Useful information if I was ever able to cast the spell again. Although surviving Jack's rage would be a necessary first step toward that goal.

Sam was shaking his head. "You don't understand. If she hadn't—"

"The whole kingdom thought we were dead until yesterday morning. They thought the king was dead. They had to appoint a regent." She bared her teeth. "Did you hope for our deaths?" The question was directed at me. "Did you think I would get eaten by a fox? Or that Gervase would?" Her eyes flicked to Sam. "It nearly happened. I had to drive it off him. Hitting it with my wings. Where were you?"

I shivered—standing still let the cold creep up my feet. Clem's bow followed the motion like a reflection. Keeping a bowstring taut for that long takes astonishing strength. She must have had an arm like an iron bar.

"Dinnae shift." Her tone was empty of any emotion. "Ah'll shoot afore ah let ye cast anither spell."

I'd no doubt she could do it, too. Not that I'd be able to cast much of anything without the benefit of True Love's First Kiss. "Clem," I rasped, my throat raw and aching. Speaking felt like shoving my words through a grater. "You saw me run from those creatures. Do you really think I brought them down on us? I did . . . the thing I did so we could get away."

Her aim didn't waver, but her voice did, ever so slightly. "Ah dinnae ken whit tae think."

With a valiant effort, I refrained from screaming. It wouldn't have done my throat any favors.

And although I wasn't eager to admit it, as misdirected as Jack's ideas might have been, they weren't completely without cause. She was suspicious of me because I had been behaving suspiciously, from practically the first moment we had met.

Enough was enough. It was time to come clean.

"There's a very simple explanation for everything I've done." I took a painful swallow and then at last admitted, "I am Princess Melilot."

There was a moment of profound silence.

Then Jack laughed. "No, you're not."

"Yes, I am," I replied crossly. That wasn't the response I had been hoping for.

"Then, when we met you in the forest, where were your servants? Your guards? What became of your carriage? You were alone and unaccompanied. It makes no sense."

My own words, flung back at me. Had I lied too well for my own good? "They were . . . they were teeth," I tried to explain. "And a pumpkin . . ."

Jack took a step closer, her hand on her sword hilt. "I've been wondering what you did with the real Princess Melilot." Her voice was almost a whisper. "She still hasn't arrived. I wasn't looking forward to her wedding day, but that was no fault of hers. She didn't deserve death."

"I didn't kill her!" Shouting hurt just as much as I'd thought it would. I grimaced in pain and dropped my voice to a scratchy mutter. "Me, I mean. I didn't kill myself."

"Jack." Sam moved to interpose himself once again, his eyes flicking between Jack and the arrow still targeting me. "She really is the princess. She told me yesterday."

"She told you." Jack sighed. "Sam, has it crossed your mind you might be ensorcelled?"

Sam's mouth dropped open. His face turned the dark red of beet juice. "I might be *what*?"

Clem looked thoughtful. "Jack haes a point."

"No," Sam said. "That's absurd."

Jack stepped in closer, until their faces were only inches apart. "You've been mooning over her since the moment you saw her—"

"Oh, that's rich," her brother interrupted, "coming from you!"

"—even though she's been lying about who she is, she forgot to mention she's a witch—"

"Sorceress," I protested.

"—and after she turned us into birds, you abandoned me to go traipsing off after her!"

"Because I'm supposed to follow along behind you, right?" Sam said. "So that Jack gets to be the hero, like always. Jack gets to have the grand romance. No one else can have a story of their own."

"You're not having a romance!" Jack shouted. "You've been enchanted!"

"The first lassie or laddie I've ever had feelings for, the first one, and you can't handle it, is that it?"

"Will you for one second listen to what I've been—"

"All of you stop!" I yelled at the top of my lungs. The words stabbed my throat like a knife. "Stop it right now!"

Much to my surprise, they did, turning to look at me warily.

"If you'd just give me a chance to tell you what happened," I managed to say with what was left of my voice, "then everything will become clear."

They waited, tense but expectant. I took a moment to choose the best place to begin. It matters how stories are told. I needed to tell one that was true. Lies had only led to distrust. I decided to start with a woman kneeling in her stepmother's throne room, waiting for the latest in a long, long series of impossible demands.

There's no way to know what would have happened if I'd been able to tell the story. Before I had a chance, the mirror in my hand butted in to make its version of events known.

"Don't trust her!" it bellowed. "She stole me! She's a liar and a thief!"

Too many things happened at once.

I was so startled I dropped the looking glass. It shrieked as if I'd hurled it off a cliff. Clem's arm tensed, her arrow tracking the mirror as it fell. Jack whipped out her sword, more out of surprise than anything else. But Sam leapt forward and grabbed

Jack's shoulder, his fist cocked back for a punch. Protecting me from his sister. Jack looked so shocked it was almost comical.

That was when the third hunter, the one who'd stood by so quietly I'd almost forgotten about her, put her hand to her nose and closed one nostril, blowing through the other.

Oh, it's Kit, I thought inanely. *The Nose Blower.*

Only the faintest brush of a breeze touched my face, but the wind plucked Sam right out of the snow, leaving only a deep pair of footprints behind. He went tumbling end over end until, dozens of feet away, his head slammed into a tree. Someone started screaming; I think it might have been me. If it still hurt my throat, I didn't notice.

Jack and I both raced over to Sam. Behind us, Clem was yelling at Kit, and Kit was yelling right back as the wind subsided. Half-buried in a snowdrift, the mirror continued to hurl accusations: "She means to gather an army! I heard her say it! And she broke into my house and shoved me in a pile of leaves and dropped me in the snow! I could have broken! You all saw it!"

I knelt next to Sam. His eyes were open but didn't seem to be focused on anything. They slid past me. "Prinzzess?" he murmured.

He turned and retched, little coming up except greenish strings of bile that dripped onto the white snow.

Concussion, I thought. *Prescribe rest. Apply ice to any bumps or swelling. Observe symptoms closely in case they worsen over time. Check to see if the pupils are of unequal size; bleeding in the brain can be deadly. . . .*

Jack dropped to her own knees on Sam's other side, her face gray. "I swear," she hissed, "if he's been hurt because of you, I'll—"

"You're blaming me?" The fury welling up within me was something I hadn't felt in a long, long time. Not since my stepmother had condemned me to the tower. The anger was like a physical force, a boiling black cloud swelling inside my body. It dimmed the edges of my vision. The tree beside us creaked, as if something was bending the trunk. Other trees joined the chorus, rustling, crackling.

"Are you nimble, Jack?" I whispered. She didn't answer; she'd gone quiet. "Are you quick? If you start running now, do you think you can escape my wrath?"

My hair twitched and lifted, blown by an unseen wind. Moving and growing, twining its way toward Jack's pale, exposed throat.

"That's enough o' that."

I looked up to see an arrow pointed at my eye. Clem was standing only a few feet away. Behind her, a sour-faced Kit kicked at the snow.

"Kit didnae mean tae hurt Sam," Clem said. "So please stoap doin' . . . whitevur it is ye're doin'."

"What . . . ? I didn't . . ." I blinked, and my vision cleared, the dark blurriness vanishing. The sound of straining wood died away. The reaching tendrils of my hair dropped; it had grown long enough to spread out around me on the ground. It would brush my ankles when I stood. "I wasn't going to . . ." My voice trailed off.

Had the trees slid closer to us?

There was a more important matter to attend to. "We have to get Sam to the castle," I told Clem. "He needs treatment."

"Aye." She nodded. "We kin figure oot th' rest efter."

Kit and Jack managed to get Sam upright and stumbling forward, supported on both sides. At some point, I didn't fully notice when, Jack picked up the looking glass, which was still mumbling dire warnings about me. I was somewhat distracted by the fact that while Clem lowered her bow, she kept it strung and ready at hand.

I couldn't blame her. If I'd wanted to make a case for my innocence, I doubted I could have done a worse job. Although I still wasn't sure exactly what I'd been doing. Or how. There'd been no kiss this time to enhance my abilities. What had just happened?

I'd have to be more convincing at the castle. Or at least less terrifying than when I'd threatened Jack. Never in my life had I sounded more like my stepmother.

Maybe I had learned something from her after all.

PART VI

MIRROR, MIRROR

CHAPTER TWENTY-FIVE

A Fevered Imagination

At first, I thought I was hallucinating the lion on the other side of the bars, pacing back and forth outside my prison door. Then I remembered there really was a lion living in the castle. Although that didn't necessarily mean this one *wasn't* a hallucination. If you imagined there was a toad sitting on your head that would eat your face if you told a lie, it wouldn't mean every face-eating head toad was imaginary. They're quite real, as it happens. I once met someone who had one. It was inconvenient; he was never able to find a hat that fit properly.

Now I was hallucinating a toad on my head.

High fever, I thought. *Elevated skin temperature, shivering, sweating. Delirium and confusion. Recommendations—keep the patient hydrated. Prepare willow bark tea. In severe cases, cool the patient in a bath.*

My throat actually felt a bit better than it had. It was only everything else that felt worse. I regretted not chewing on any willow trees when I'd had the chance.

"Tell me who your confederates are," the toad said.

The stone walls of my cell shimmered and swam, as if distorted by a heat haze. I wasn't hot, though. I was cold, very cold, unless I touched my palm to my forehead. That was so hot it burned.

Through the one small window up near the ceiling, I could see nothing but a slice of dark night sky. Never before had I so longed for the power to make a window into a somewhat larger window. At least the one in my stepmother's tower had a nice view.

Stone surrounded me on three sides of my narrow cell. On the fourth was a row of iron bars serving as the door. In the dim light beyond, a stairway built from the same stone as the walls spiraled upward into the unknown. I vaguely remembered being dragged down it, but my memory did not stretch to whatever might have lain above.

The undulating walls were making me nauseous. I had already thrown up once—two times? More? However many times it had been, I'd managed to get most of it into the bucket someone had left in the corner, but the whole cell reeked of vomit.

"Tell me who your confederates are," the toad repeated. "Is it the women? The women in disguise?"

"I don't have any confederates," I told it. "I didn't do anything. Get off my head."

"If you reveal your allies, the king may yet have mercy." It wasn't the toad talking. The toad wasn't real. It was the lion. It shoved its muzzle closer to the bars and peered at me through its spectacles. Lion real, toad fake. I had to remember that.

The whole room pulsed, closing in and drawing back, like lungs. The scattering of straw across the floor shifted and writhed. Or no, wait. Those were insects. They'd left bite marks all over my legs. So they were actually there, crawling around, not just in my mind. Weren't they?

I closed my eyes. If I was lucky, the insects would be gone

when I opened them. "I'm not who you think I am. I'm the princess of Skalla."

"Thare wis a time whin ah micht hae believed ye," someone said.

I cracked one eye open and saw a masked hunter squatting on her heels outside my cell. The lion was gone.

"Ah wis hauf-convinced ye were tellin' th' truth. Till we fun th' sketches. Drawings o' th' monsters ye created."

A weak stream of winter sunlight trickled through the window, brightening the room from dark to dim. Dust motes danced a slow pavane in the beam. I wondered if sunrise had somehow come while I blinked. It didn't make me feel any warmer.

"Those drawings aren't mine. I told . . ." Who had I told? The lion? Gervase? I wasn't sure I'd had a chance to talk to Gervase. "I told someone. I found them. We have to go there before—"

"That's nae whit yer mirror's bin saying."

"That isn't my mirror!" I wrapped my arms around my legs and shuddered. It was so very, very cold in the cell. I pressed my forehead against my knees. "Clem, listen—"

"I'm not Clem. I'm Jack."

I tried to fix my blurry gaze on the hunter. She was still squatting on her heels outside my cell. "If you're trying to drive me insane," I said, "you may be a bit late."

"Is that why you did it?" Jack grabbed the bars, her grip so hard her knuckles turned white. "You're mad? Is that your excuse?"

"That was a joke, Jack. Do you have any sense of humor?"

I lay back and watched the arched ceiling heave and flow like the shore of a lake. I'd been a lake, once. It had been peaceful. When bugs crawled over me, they'd made tiny ripples. They hadn't hunted for fresh portions of my flesh to bite. I raised my head to glare at them, but I couldn't see any; I only felt them scuttling across my skin.

"I just want to know why," Jack said. "I want to know what possible reason you could have had to try to kill Gervase. To kill his family. To kill the Skallan princess."

"Oh, the Skallan princess and I have issues going way back," I murmured.

Jack pounced on that, once again missing the joke. "Why did you hate her? Why do you hate Gervase?"

"I don't hate him. I don't hate anybody."

"Well, I hate you!" she shrieked at me. I whipped around at the change in tone and regretted it when agony stabbed through my head. "I hate you for what you've done to Jack! Her love for Gervase is beautiful and pure, and they'd be married by now if it wasn't for you."

The hunter I'd thought was Jack spat a toad at me through the bars. It thumped into my chest and flopped onto the floor.

"You're not real," I muttered at it as it hopped around the cell. "The lion is real. You're not."

Ignoring me, it speared something small and skittering with its tongue and swallowed it with a satisfied crunch.

"Could you please just tell me," I said, turning to the masked hunter, "if Sam is all right?"

"Who's Sam?" Angelique asked.

The sky outside the window was dark again. They were changing day and night on me. To keep me disoriented, no doubt. But they'd have to do more than that if they wanted me to talk. I'd been held prisoner by better than them. I'd been locked in the shifting prison of the Shadow King and entombed beneath the ice by the Queen of the Northern Snows. A bit of petty trickery wasn't going to make me spill my secrets.

Come to think of it, the joke was on them. I didn't remember which secrets they wanted me to spill.

"Excuse me," I said to Angelique, and crawled over to throw up again in the overflowing bucket. I vomited until my torso felt hollow and wrung out.

"I've been doing my best to help you," she said as I collapsed onto the floor, panting and sweating. "You've made it rather difficult. Everyone is frightened of your powers. The hunters say you were the one who turned them into birds. That you moved the very trees to attack them."

"That's an exaggeration." They'd only slid in a little bit closer when I'd threatened Jack.

"Gervase wants to execute you in some suitably horrible way."

"Thrown in a barrel of poisonous snakes? Forced to dance in red-hot iron shoes until I perish? Roasted to death in my own child-cooking oven?"

Angelique seemed puzzled. "You have a child-cooking oven?"

"No. You'll have to use someone else's."

I looked around for the door leading out, but I couldn't see it. Someone had hidden it. I peered into the dark corners in case they'd made it very, very small.

Angelique cocked her head to one side, watching me. "I've argued with my brother day and night, trying to convince him to let you live."

"Really? You and I barely know each other."

"You've . . . become like a sister to me. Truly." She paused, waiting for me to fill the silence. I didn't know what she wanted me to say. "Looking at the state of you," she went on, "you might not survive long enough for him to kill you."

My back ached. My head ached. So did my stomach. Even my toes ached. "If I died right now, I'm not sure I'd mind."

The toad bit me on the face.

I swatted at it, and it fell to the floor with a thump. *That was uncalled for,* I thought as I pulled myself up into a sitting position, cradling my injured cheek. *You weren't supposed to bite me unless I lied.* Well, perhaps I had lied, a little. But you'd think a magical toad would know the difference between deception and hyperbole.

There was no sign of the toad when I looked around. A rat, however, was scampering away. Was that what had bitten me? It occurred to me that toads weren't noted for having sharp teeth.

Rabies transmission from rats is rare, I reminded myself. *Symptoms of rabies include fever, headache, agitation, paranoia, hallucinations— Wait, am I already rabid? No. I'm not afraid to drink water. That's the telltale symptom.*

If I do have rabies, I'll fall into a coma and die. There is no known cure. Death is all but inevitable two to ten days after first presentation of symptoms.

But I don't have it.

I did not feel reassured.

Angelique had vanished. She'd probably taken the toad with her when she left. Did she really think of me as a sister? I supposed I would be her sister, once I married Gervase. But she didn't know that, did she? Or no, I'd told everyone who I was. Only no one believed me. So did that mean Angelique thought of the person that she thought was pretending to be the person who was going to be her sister as her sister?

"Hey," I said to the rat. "Hey. Do you know my sister? My half sister."

Where was Calla? Shouldn't she and Jonquil have arrived in my dream by now? Maybe I wasn't dreaming hard enough. Maybe I wasn't dreaming.

It probably didn't make any difference. I'd yelled at them and thrown them out the last time they'd shown up. I regretted that now. I didn't want to be executed with them hating me.

The rat paused a few paces from me, poised on its haunches with its forepaws in the air. A pair of eyes like black beads stared in my direction. Its hairless tail was raised like a whip. I suspected it was waiting until I fell asleep so it could try for another bite. It'd serve the damn thing right if it caught rabies from me.

"You must know my sister," I said. "She's a friend to all animals. Calla of Skalla."

I had never noticed how well that rhymed before. *The name of my sister is Calla of Skalla. She rode to the gala upon an impala.*

The rat tilted its head at almost the same angle as Angelique had tilted hers. I hoped that meant it was listening.

"You need to take her a message from me," I whispered. It was time to swallow my pride, even though my throat felt too dry to swallow anything. "Tell her I'm in trouble. That her sister Melilot is in trouble and needs help." Maybe she would come if I asked, despite what I'd said to her.

The rat licked its forepaws and began grooming its face like a cat. It couldn't have ignored me more plainly if it were . . . well, if it were a cat. So much for that idea.

No one was coming to save me. They would never know I'd needed saving.

"This is quite the mess you've gotten yourself into," my stepmother said.

"That I've gotten myself into?" I staggered to my feet. "You sent me here!"

"It was so simple. Get married, I said. I know you like to spite my wishes, but you've been rather extreme about it this time."

She was as blurry and wavery as the stone walls and flickered from place to place around the room like a fluttering moth. Magic. Everything my stepmother did was stuffed full to bursting with magic. She could hardly lift a finger without leveling a kingdom. Small wonder she viewed me as insignificant.

"Real mothers don't browbeat their daughters when they're sick," I complained. "They give them soup."

"Do they?" She reached out and tapped her fingers against my forehead. Through my forehead. I felt them wriggling around inside my skull.

"What are you doing?"

"Checking to see whether you will die of your illness if you are left here any longer. Death by fever in a jail cell is too ignominious a fate for one of my own." Her fingers stretched within me and spread through the rest of my body, wrapping around my organs, poking at my gallbladder and spleen. "I cannot compete with your rosy memories of your first mother. Who, incidentally, was more likely to categorize your maladies than offer you comfort. 'Note the symptoms of extreme delirium in this feverish patient.' As if you were a diagram in a medical text instead of her daughter."

"Don't you talk about my mother," I mumbled around the fingers in my throat. Was that true? Had my mother been more cold and detached than I liked to believe? My memories of her had faded with time, but I had the uncomfortable feeling it might be accurate. Not that I was about to admit it. "Your own bedside manner is nothing to brag about."

"Never good enough for you, no matter what I do," she said under her breath. After a final, uncomfortable rearrangement of my intestines, she withdrew her hands. There was a sucking sound followed by a pop as they parted from me. "There's no need to fetch you home. You'll be fine."

"Keep your sticky fingers out of my brain."

"Is soup what you truly want from me? Then here." She proffered me a steaming bowl. "Have some soup."

I grabbed it and threw it at her face.

She dissolved into hundreds of outraged, croaking toads. One of them hopped onto my head and settled in as if taking up residence.

"Confess your crimes!" the lion roared.

"You again?"

I looked at the window. The sky was a medium gray. Perhaps it wasn't day or night. What if there was nothing out there at all?

"I have been trying my hardest to convince the king not to execute you. It would be easier to make my case if there were any semblance of cooperation on your part." The lion squinted at me. His spectacles had slipped down his muzzle. "Is that a toad on your head?"

"Yes. It was my stepmother. A huntsman spit it on me, and then it turned into a rat." That had made perfect sense until I said it aloud.

The lion huffed and ignored my ravings. "If you do not reveal your co-conspirators among the so-called huntsmen—"

"What is your problem with them, anyway?" I lurched to the bars, grabbing hold of them to keep myself upright. "Female lions hunt. Lionesses. They hunt more than the males do, don't they? You should be thrilled. Hurray for the humans, acting more like lions!"

"I am a centuries-old magical talking lion," he answered. "Not some common savannah trash. And even if I were, it would make no difference. Humans are not supposed to behave like lions. They are supposed to behave like humans. As the guardian of the laws and traditions of this country—"

"Well, see, that's your problem right there. Centuries-old traditions fall out of date. I woke a princess from an enchanted sleep once, and she used lead paint in her eyeliner and thought arsenic was good for your complexion. Get with the times."

"I am with the times!" He prowled forward until his face was mere inches from mine, separated from it only by the bars of the cell. "I wrote the book on humans. *The* book."

"I bet it's poorly sourced and derivative."

"CONFESS YOUR CRIMES!" Hot lion breath washed over me as he shouted. Fangs as long as dagger blades were crammed into his mouth.

"I haven't committed any crimes." Only my grip on the bars kept me from falling over. I shouldn't have talked so much. It was tiring. I certainly should never have bothered to argue with him. "I'm the princess of Skalla," I mumbled at the floor.

"I know," said Angelique.

I looked up to find her face as close to mine as the lion's had been. A faint smile curled the edges of her mouth.

"You do?" My voice sounded weak and thready.

"Of course." She trailed one hand down the bars, almost but not quite touching mine. "Only a true princess has trouble sleeping if a pea is hidden beneath her mattress. And once I found out you were a sorceress, well—everyone knows about the Skallan royal family. It's the reason you're here, after all." There was a sound like a flock of birds fluttering their wings, and suddenly she was standing next to me, dabbing at my wounded cheek with a damp cloth. "I was suspicious from the very beginning, naturally. Why would a mere handmaiden arrive in a magic carriage?"

The cool, wet linen was so soothing I almost moaned. "Are you really here?" I asked.

"Why are you surprised? I have my ways of getting where I want to go."

"Oh. Your ring of keys. You have one for the dungeon? Then why don't you let me out, if you know I'm telling the truth?"

She shook her head. "It isn't that simple. I might believe you, but convincing everyone else is trickier." Her smile tightened. "It would have been easier when I was regent, even as reluctant as they were to accept my rule. I suppose I have you to thank for my thirty days on the throne."

"You're welcome, I guess."

"I'm doing what I can for you." She gave my cheek a final delicate wipe and leaned in close. "In the meantime, is there anything that would make you more comfortable?"

"A feather bed?" My thoughts oozed through my head like thick syrup. "A cup of willow bark tea? With honey, if you can manage it. Or how about a bath? I'd love a bath."

"A bath," she mused. "Perhaps that could be arranged. Do you need someone to soap your back?"

I blinked. "Are you . . . are you flirting with me?"

"Certainly not!" the hunter snapped.

I peered through the bars, looking everywhere, trying to find Angelique again, but she was gone. I wanted to punch the wall in frustration, but I'd only hurt my hand. Or miss. "Where does everyone keep going?"

"Flirting with you?" the hunter said. "Hardly. You've got vomit on your shirt, and something's been chewing your face. Also, I despise you."

The temperature in the cell had dropped precipitously. Snow drifted in through the window. The bars felt like ice under my hands.

I let go and stepped away before my sweat could freeze. "Put your hat on, Max. It's like an icebox in here."

"I'm not Max," she said sullenly. "I'm Kit."

"Oh." It wasn't supernaturally cold. It was just winter in an unheated prison. "How's Sam doing? No one's told me."

"He . . ." Kit hesitated. "He fell unconscious not long after we got back to the castle. He isn't waking up."

"What?" That was bad. That was very bad. I had to get out. I had to do something. "I need to see him! Now!" There had to be a treatment, a cure, if only I could examine him, if only I could leave this place and go somewhere I could think. "Will you let me see him?"

"You're not getting anywhere near him!"

"It wasn't me who blew him into a tree, Kit!"

"I'm not Kit," the hunter said.

I put my hands against my face, pressing the palms into my eyes. "I was right. You really are trying to drive me mad."

"I should tell Gervase to put you to death," she said. "He'd do it, if I asked him."

"Ah. Jack." I wasn't able to speak above a whisper at this point. "That is you, isn't it?"

"Your name is the one in question here. First Clover, now Melilot. Who will you claim to be next?"

"Tell me something. Are you more worried that I might be here to murder Gervase or that I might be here to marry him?"

She didn't answer.

I peered at her through spread fingers. "Murdering your rival isn't very heroic. It wouldn't be living up to the name you've taken. You're the one who chose to call yourself Jack."

She flinched back from the bars. "I had good reasons for coming to Tailliz in disguise."

"Oh, I know. So did I."

"That's hardly the same—"

"Isn't it?" I shrugged, my hands falling from my face. "But really, it doesn't matter what your reasons were. Whether you started as a Jacqueline, a John, or a Gnoflwhogir, you can't turn away from it now. Once you take on the mantle of a Jack, you've put yourself into the story."

I could barely keep my eyes open. So I stopped trying. My lids fell like lead weights, and I sank to the floor.

Something urgent still tugged at me. "Sam needs treatment," I said, my voice scarcely audible even to myself. "I can help. You have to let me out." No one answered.

My cheek stung where I'd been bitten. I'd just have to hope it wouldn't become infected. At least Angelique had cleaned it. If I hadn't imagined her; the seduction attempt at the end was giving me serious doubts about her reality.

I heard footsteps, ringing louder and louder as they approached. A key turned in the lock with a clank, and the barred door creaked open.

Someone stepped beside me. I didn't look up to see who it was.

"I'm not sure what I should do with you," Gervase said. "All of my advisers except Jack have said I should execute you. If only for turning me into a swan. Which was . . . strange."

I shuddered in the cold, my legs pulled up to my chest. There seemed to be a weight pressing my head against the floor.

"But I'm still uncertain," he continued. "I'm not sure what's true and what isn't."

That made two of us.

He said nothing for so long I thought he was gone. Or that he'd never been there to begin with.

But then he said, "Why is there a toad on your head?"

When I didn't answer, he left. The door slammed closed with a resounding clang that echoed across the cell. His footsteps grew quieter until they were gone.

I was alone. Trapped, with no way to help Sam and no way to help myself. With nothing to do but lie on the hard stone floor and listen to the silence.

CHAPTER TWENTY-SIX

Prison Breaking

After an unknown number of days locked in the dungeon, I awoke one morning with no bodily miseries more pressing than a runny nose. I lifted a hand to the bite mark on my cheek and found it scabbed over. There was no feeling of heat or pain as I poked at it. It itched a bit. I refrained from scratching.

My fever had broken, and my wound remained free of infection. Sometimes the body is more resilient than expected, needing nothing more than time to heal. Of course, other times, the mildest of untreated illnesses can become a death sentence. If the disease had descended into my lungs, my tale might have ended early. Pneumonia took my mother. Even the bite was no joke. Rabies might never have been a serious danger, but sepsis can kill someone who shrugs off other illnesses.

I'd been lucky. And there may have been those who'd hoped I wouldn't be. No doubt some of my jailers would have breathed a sigh of relief if I'd quietly expired and spared them the trouble.

I stood and stretched. My joints and spine popped audibly.

Half of my body was cramped, and the other half tingled painfully as my sluggish blood resumed circulation. A beam of bright winter sunlight shone through the window. It looked hard and cold enough to chip with a chisel.

Out of the corner of my eye, I saw something moving. Startled, I turned to find the toad hopping about in the corner by the bucket.

"Oh," I said. "You're real, then."

It replied with a croak that resembled a long, loud burp and returned to hunting for insects in the straw. I searched for any piece of my shirt clean enough to wipe my nose on. How was I going to occupy my time now that I had enough presence of mind to be bored?

The building shuddered.

I stumbled and fell to the ground, catching myself on my forearms, barely keeping my face from smashing into the flagstones. A cloud of dust filtered down from the ceiling.

Something flashed past the window outside, briefly cutting off the light. I couldn't make out what it was. There was a rumble and a crash like a giant bowling a strike with a boulder, and the building shook again. A crack crept up through the mortar and widened. The metal bars groaned as if in pain. Was the whole place about to collapse on top of me?

I missed the time when I could have convinced myself it was all a hallucination.

As I picked myself up, one of the hunters came rushing down the stairs. Jack, I was almost sure. By this time, I could recognize a particular kind of intentness in her expression. She was running so quickly she skidded down the last few steps, coming close to toppling over at the bottom. She held an unsheathed sword in one hand. As soon as she steadied herself, the gleaming length of it was pointed at me.

"Are they yours?" she asked. "Call them off!"

"Call off who? What's going on?"

Her mouth twisted beneath her mask. She darted forward. I backed away from the bars, worried she might try to stab me then and there.

Instead, she fished a key out of her jerkin and twisted open the lock.

When she wrenched at the cell door, though, it didn't move. The walls had been bent askew, and the door was stuck fast.

"Help me," she snarled. "Unless you want to be trapped in there when the roof caves in."

I threw myself at the door and pushed while she pulled. With both of us straining, the door crept open an inch. And then another. Finally, it sprang free.

With the sound of a thundercrack, the room jumped a foot to the left. A stone slab the size of a wheelbarrow fell from the ceiling. It broke in two on the floor. One wall of the prison leaned inward, angled like a drunkard on the verge of collapse.

"We need to leave," the hunter said. "Now." She grabbed my arm and tugged me toward the spiral staircase. I delayed only long enough to scoop up the toad; it seemed cruel to leave it behind. The hunter pulled more insistently. This time I staggered after her, nearly tripping on my own hair—it still brushed my ankles.

Wherever she was taking me, I doubted it could be worse than staying behind.

The stairway had buckled and warped. We had to clamber over rubble and jump over the odd stair that had broken off and tumbled into the depths. More thuds and booms sounded outside. As well as what might have been screams.

At the top of the first flight, the hunter cursed. An archway had collapsed, blocking the corridor beyond with stone rubble. Dust billowed around the debris, still settling from its fall.

"Any chance we can crawl over it?" I asked. "Or find a way through?"

"There's no time. We'll have to go farther up."

The toad squirmed and wriggled in my grip. I clutched it closer as I followed the hunter up the increasingly precarious stairway. I took her word for it that there was another exit. I hadn't paid much attention to details when I'd been unceremoniously tossed into the dungeon, half off my head with fever.

A set of five steps in a row had broken off. We'd climbed over their shattered fragments a floor below. Here, there were only stubs stubbornly clinging to the side of the stairwell. We pressed against the wall and picked our way across sideways, careful of our footing on the narrow surface. I slipped halfway through. I would have fallen if the hunter hadn't grabbed my shoulder and shoved me against the wall.

The disquieting noises from outside were growing louder. The toad was thrashing spasmodically, doing its level best to escape my grasp. I don't know why it was so bent on committing toad suicide on the rocks below.

Once we'd cleared the broken stairs, we went around another turn and stepped through an arch into the morning sunlight. And also, as it turned out, straight into a war.

We had emerged at the top of the castle wall. Across the bay, monsters were arrayed along the seashore.

Hundreds of them.

Many were indistinguishable because of the distance, although I could make out the distinctive scuttle of the eight-legged spider wolves. Others were hard to miss, like the misshapen giants made of stone and the huge worm whose maw was an abyss filled with curving teeth. There were six-winged bats walking on wrinkled elephant legs. Oversized leopard-like animals with thorns poking out of their flesh. A roiling, wriggling mass I thought might be a pack of the poisonous furred snakes.

The toad fought its way free of my suddenly nerveless fingers. It plopped to the ground and hopped away as rapidly as possible.

On the mainland, the walls of the gatehouse had been smashed to pieces. Their stones lay scattered across the beach, the great doors torn from their hinges and cast aside. The only reason the horde hadn't swarmed across the bridge was that the bridge was half-demolished. The broad, graceful arches extended from the castle out to empty air. Beyond, only a few pilings remained, lapped by the surging waters of the bay. It crossed my mind that the castle's defenders might have shattered it themselves as a delaying tactic.

The monstrous army, however, had hardly been thwarted. Shrieking beasts flew overhead, diving and attacking with their talons and fangs. A soldier on the wall flailed in the claws of a massive half bird, half weasel. It lifted him a dozen feet into the air before an arrow took the creature in the eye and sent them both crashing down. The larger monsters across the water were hurling whatever they could find—rocks on the shore, masonry from the gatehouse, uprooted trees. The tower I'd been imprisoned in, the one nearest to the castle gates, had been hit more than once. The roof was partly staved in by a pine tree, and the whole upper structure tilted at an alarming angle.

I looked into the courtyard, expecting death and devastation in the packed grounds, bodies crushed under boulders or torn to pieces by flying horrors. To my surprise, little of the damage appeared to have reached the masses below. Soldiers were ushering the villagers out of the unroofed area and into the castle buildings.

The reason for the courtyard's relative safety became evident when a thrown boulder seemed to hover in midair before being blown back against the stone giant that had hurled it. It slammed into the monster's granite shoulder, sending sharp fragments of rock flying from both. Not far from us, a masked hunter raced back and forth along the wall. She held one nostril shut and blew through the other whenever she saw something hurtling her way. On a different part of the wall, a hunter with a bow led a cohort of archers. They turned any winged foes into pincushions if they ventured too near.

But even with Kit and Clem doing everything they could—and with the other hunters surely using their tricks to defend the castle as well—the wall underfoot shuddered as a missile flew under Kit's guard. In the very next moment, a hapless archer was snatched off the walkway by a dark cloud of tentacles and feathers. It shot straight up in the air, and then blood splashed the ramparts as it wrung the archer's body like a dishrag.

It was only a matter of time before the defenders were overwhelmed by sheer numbers. Or until the enemy found another way to get over the wall. Across the bay, some enormous rodent, four times my height if not more, slipped into the water and began paddling across. It made it halfway to the castle before Clem was able to redirect the archers and a shower of arrows thudded into its back. Howling in agony, the creature turned back and swam for shore.

I peered at its retreating shape. "That's a hamster," I said.

"Are they yours?" the hunter beside me asked once again. "Did you summon them here?"

Definitely Jack. Of course it was Jack. I swung around to face her. "No, they're not mine! They nearly dropped the tower on my head."

"They might be trying to rescue you," she said, not sounding convinced of it herself. "Kill the king and get you out in one fell—"

"Jack," I cut her off, shaking my head in disbelief. "Think about what you've seen me do. If I wanted Gervase dead, I'd have drowned him. And you right along with him."

"You . . ." Her voice trailed off. She looked thunderstruck. Had that really never occurred to her? To any of them?

My magic had turned them into birds to protect them. If I hadn't cared, they'd have sunk into my vast depths along with the stone giants, until the air bubbled up from their lungs.

"So you don't control them," Jack said. "You can't call them off." She slumped, deflated, her sword dangling limply at her side.

She'd been hoping I was the one behind it, I realized. I'm not sure she ever truly believed it was me, in her heart. But as long as the possibility existed, there'd been someone tangible, present, she could accuse. Now, once again, there was no one. Nothing but month after month of incomprehensible attacks. They'd taken their toll.

"Jack, listen—" I began. But then something with a segmented body and too many membranous wings grabbed me by the shoulders and yanked me off the wall.

CHAPTER TWENTY-SEVEN

Ice Capade

I shrieked. The creature shook me like a dog killing a squirrel as it swerved left and right to evade the arrows zipping past. I tried to think up some means of escape, but all I managed to do was thrash in its grip. I couldn't form a single coherent thought.

As the monster dodged, Jack leapt onto the battlements. She lashed out with her sword, the blade passing so close to my face I saw my nose reflected in it. It bit deep into the creature's carapace. A spray of ichor fanned out to join the other stains on my clothes. The flickering wings halted, their strident buzzing silenced. We dropped together, straight toward the jagged rocks at the island's edge.

A hand grasped my wrist, nearly wrenching my arm out of its socket. I swung sideways and smashed face-first into the wall. My scream was cut off as the breath was forced out of my lungs. The insectoid thing hung from me for a moment, its claw still hooked on the edge of my cloak. Then the cloth tore, and the creature continued its final descent.

"If you could find a way to climb up," came Jack's strained voice from above me, "I'd appreciate it."

I looked up to see her braced on a crenellation, trying her hardest to hold my weight with one arm. I scrabbled to find handholds and footholds. After a moment, I managed to get my fingers over the lip of the wall. With a great heave, Jack pulled me up and over. We both collapsed on the walkway, panting for breath.

"Thank you," I said.

Jack gave a weary shrug. "I've been told it's important I live up to my name."

Behind us, an errant boulder slipped past Kit's breath. It smashed into the tower. The roof disintegrated, showering rocks and timbers into the stairwell.

Just before the collapse, a black bird had launched itself from the highest window. I frowned as it banked and flew off into the distance. The first faint glimmerings of a suspicion began to form in my mind. Something that someone had said to me didn't quite add up.

Jack dragged herself to her feet. As I started to do the same, a blurry figure dashed up to us and gibbered something in a voice too fast to decipher.

"Take your leg off or talk slowly, Harry," Jack said. "We didn't get a word of that."

The blur resolved into the oddest of the masked hunters as she detached her leg and cradled it in her arms. "Sorry. Have a message for you. Summons from the court."

"I already know about it," Jack said. She jerked her chin in my direction. "I'm trying to get her there in one piece."

Harry shook her head, bouncing on her foot as if impatient to be moving again. "It's changed. Not just her. All the hunters, too."

"What?" Jack's eyebrows shot up into her messy bangs. "Has Gervase lost his mind?" She gestured at the ongoing battle.

I could make out other hunters in the mix now, wherever the fighting was thickest. One had wrapped a horn bird in a mass of morning glory vines. Its struggles were weakening as the pretty flowers choked the life out of it. Another hunter appeared to be grabbing not-quite-bats out of the air and shoving them into her mouth, which was open wider than seemed possible.

"We're the only reason the castle is standing!" Jack said. "The moment we leave the wall, it's over."

Harry shrugged. Jack drew in a breath and closed her eyes. Her face scrunched up in thought.

I tried to catch sight of Sam, hoping he'd recovered since Kit had brought me the bad news, and I'd find him tossing monsters around like so many matchsticks. He was nowhere to be seen. But that didn't mean anything, did it? A thousand small skirmishes were being waged on every side of the castle, far more than I could take in at a glance. He might be fighting in any one of them. He might be.

"Where is—"

Jack's eyes popped open. "We'll make them pause the assault first. Tell Kit and Max to meet me here. Everyone else needs to concentrate on picking off as many of the fliers as possible. Hurry!"

Harry had reattached her leg before Jack finished speaking, shifting back into a blur and zipping off along the walkway while the last word was still echoing in the air. Jack turned and looked over the parapet. The seething carpet of furry snakes had gathered close to the wrecked gatehouse. The broken walls shielded them from arrows as they slithered into the water.

I pushed my other concerns aside, at least for the moment. "How are you going to stop them?"

"With a terrible plan that probably won't work. Unless . . . By any chance, do you have anything spectacular to contribute?" She kept her voice casual, but I heard the urgent hope underneath. "As long as it doesn't turn me into a bird again."

"I don't know." I'd have said no, but after what I did when Sam was injured—whatever it was—I wasn't sure anymore. "Maybe if I had some time to think about it?"

"Time isn't something we really—"

She broke off as Kit sprinted up to us, panting with effort. Max, her telltale hat pulled slantwise over her ear, wasn't far behind.

"What do you want?" Kit asked between wheezy breaths, clutching at her side as she skidded to a stop. "Every moment I waste here, a rock might sail through."

Jack pointed at the bay. "Make a wave. As big as you can."

"Why—"

"*Now*, Kit!"

Kit's expression stayed sour as she held one nostril shut and blew through the other. The great wind of her breath whistled down to the water. The dark surface below rippled and undulated, gathering into humps and troughs. Waves started rolling toward the mainland, chunks of ice slipping over them as they crossed the frigid bay. They grew in size, each cresting higher than the one before. The first rose tall enough to engulf a child, the next a horse, the next a house.

"Keep going," Jack urged.

Kit's face turned red as she blew harder. The waves began to break against the shore. The furred serpents paused. Every new crash sent the surf farther and farther across the beach.

"Higher!" Jack said.

With a final phlegmy snort, Kit expelled whatever breath remained in her lungs. It created a sudden depression in the water, nearly deep enough to hold the castle itself. As she dropped her hand from her nose and gasped desperately for air, a massive wave reared up, twice as large as the one that preceded it. The great swell of water advanced like an avalanche, casting a long shadow over the creatures that stared at it from the opposite shore.

"Will that really help?" Kit sputtered. "The big ones might not even topple over!"

"Max," Jack said, ignoring Kit, "when it breaks—"

"I know." The hunter whipped off her hat. "I'm on it."

The temperature dropped. Goosebumps rose on my skin, and the ichor staining my dress crystalized. Max set her mouth in fierce concentration.

"Everyone get back!" Jack shouted. We stumbled away from the hatless hunter as the vapor in the air around her froze into glitter.

Solid ice fanned out from the rocks at the base of the wall. As it spread, every bump and ripple in the water became trapped in motionless sculpture. The ice shot across a bay already on the point of freezing, the dark water transforming into an expanding semicircle of white, racing its way to the opposite shore.

Some of the monsters turned and ran, but it was already too late. The wave was moving too fast. As it neared the shore, the top of it curled, foamed, and came crashing over their heads.

And it froze there, the ice overtaking the wave just before it collapsed, sealing the enemy in a frozen prison.

Max jammed her hat back on her head, and I clenched my chattering teeth to a halt.

Jack nodded at the other hunters. "All right. Let's go find out what they want with us at court."

"Did you just win the battle?" I asked. The flying monstrosities had evaded the ice and were harrying the archers, but one by one, they were meeting their ends.

Jack shook her head. "Hardly. Listen."

Deep booms issued forth from the mound of ice. The glistening surface was crazed with cracks. Small at the moment but widening as we watched.

"I hope I froze a few of them solid," Max said. "But it won't be all of them. And those rock things won't care. They'll break it, given enough time."

"Enough time is what I was hoping for," Jack told her. "The archers can hold out as long as no one's throwing boulders at them."

"And then what?"

"There must be a reason we've been summoned. Maybe Gervase has a brilliant plan. Or the lion. Or anyone."

I didn't see why any brilliant plans on offer wouldn't have been sent as part of Harry's message. But military strategy hadn't been an emphasis of my eclectic education, so I held my tongue. Perhaps it could only be explained using charts or those toy soldiers you push around a map with a little rake. Which still wouldn't explain why I had been invited. I supposed a summons to the Great Hall meant I had permission to be there this time, at least.

We made our way to the nearest ladder, dodging the extended claws and tentacles of winged horrors as we went. Clem met us at the top, firing arrows one after another. Her quiver had scarcely any left. Things I didn't have time to look at thudded to the ground around us, pierced through.

"This 'ud better be important," she snarled as she slung her bow across her back and grabbed the rungs. "If tis some courtier wha wants a report, he's gittin' an arrow thro' th' knee."

We slid down the ladder. The evacuation was still in progress when we reached the bottom. We pressed through the remaining villagers more slowly than any of us would have liked. Kit raised a hand to her nose but lowered it at a headshake from Jack. And thank goodness—using a hurricane to blow the crowd apart would have been ill-advised, to say the very least.

I could sympathize with Kit's impulse, though. The stone fists resounded like distant thunder whenever they smashed against the ice. As we forced our way forward, step-by-step, I pictured fissures spreading, frozen outcrops breaking free and splashing into the lake.

When we reached the entrance of the Great Hall, the rest of

the hunters were already there, waiting with poorly concealed impatience. Or not quite the rest of them—a hurried count brought me only to eleven.

My hopes fell. I knew who was missing. "Where's Sam?"

"Still unconscious," one of them said. Fred or Kit or Jules or I really didn't care. A coma lasting so long was a bad sign. A very bad sign.

"I need to take a look at him." My fingers clenched tight in my hair. "I have to—"

"Later," said the hunter, laying a sympathetic hand on my shoulder. "There's no time."

"My brother's strong. He'll recover." Jack's voice wavered ever so slightly. She wasn't any more certain of that than I was. "The chirurgeon has prescribed a course of care."

"The chirurgeon's cures are bloodletting and dung!" I shrugged away the hand and tried to leave, but a few of the others grabbed me and pulled me into the Great Hall along with the rest of them. I barely restrained myself from lashing out at them with my fists.

I didn't want to be there. I wanted to make sure Sam wasn't being bled white, though there'd be little enough else I could do for him. The recommended treatment for a coma is to wait, do nothing, and hope the patient wakes.

I have always hated the recommended treatment for a coma.

The hall was as packed full of Tailliziani noblemen as it had been before. Now, however, there was a pervasive undercurrent of fear. The murmurs were sharper, angrier. As I struggled free of the hunters' grip, I heard furious shouts echo from the other side of the room. In spite of the chill weather, there was a sharp aroma of sweat beneath the nobles' perfume. Sweat and something else. Something uncomfortably familiar.

It pulled at me, whatever it was. I took a few involuntary steps. The hunters kept pace with me.

The nobles fell silent and parted before us as we neared. Their expressions were strange and grotesque—leering grins; rage-filled snarls; terrified, wide-eyed stares. When they watched us pass, I could practically feel their gazes searing my skin.

As we approached the far side of the hall, the shouts resolved into words. ". . . must return them to the wall at once!" Gervase yelled, red-faced with fury as he came into view, angrier than I had ever seen him before. "This castle will fall if we don't—"

"The castle will fall if we fail to expose the traitors in our midst!" the lion bellowed back at him. His mouth was close enough to Gervase's head to swallow it with a snap of his fangs. "This simple test—"

"Is preposterous! It makes no sense! Why would any woman be compelled—"

"THEY WILL!" the lion roared. "IT'S IN MY BOOK!"

The last of the noblemen moved out of the way, revealing what had been hidden. It had been placed beside the wall, a few feet from where Gervase and the lion were embroiled in their quarrel.

A spinning wheel.

I finally recognized the familiar scent for what it was—not a scent at all, truly, but a feeling, a presence. The air was thick with dark magic.

I'd spent much of my childhood feeling that same disquieting prickle across the hairs on the back of my neck. I half expected to see my stepmother somewhere in the room, brewing a potion or chanting an incantation under her breath. But this felt indefinably different from her magic; its flavor wasn't the same, perhaps, or its color. My stepmother hadn't cast this spell.

"They will approach the spinning wheel because it is the nature of human women to spin," the lion said in a calmer tone. "This is scientific fact based on observations and interviews with the women in this very castle. The deception of your supposed huntsmen will at long last be revealed."

"Nonsense!" Gervase snapped. "This has gone far enough. A

messenger will be sent to countermand your ridiculous summons. And once this siege has been lifted, Lion, you will no longer . . ." He paused, noticing that the rest of the Great Hall had gone quiet. As he turned, frowning, his eyes fell upon the twelve of us marching across the chamber, our footfalls echoing in the otherwise silent room.

The spinning wheel was the locus of the enchantment. It practically pulsed with power. The light was dimmer around it, the shadows deeper. Who had set the spell on it? The lion? He was watching with a smug expression on his muzzle as we drew ever closer to it. But that didn't seem right. If he was capable of this, why hadn't he done it before? The peas had been ordinary peas.

"Jack?" Gervase said, sounding perplexed. "Jack, what are you doing?"

She took another step and didn't answer. I tried to answer for her, to give a warning, but my mouth wouldn't open. The magic kept me silent.

The spell targeted us; that much was obvious. The noblemen, the lion, Gervase—they were ignoring it. Only the hunters and I were driven by the compulsion. But that couldn't be all there was to it. A spell that was only intended to make us touch a spinning wheel wouldn't have needed to be so powerful, so dark. Something else was going to happen when we put our hands on it.

A curse. Spinning wheels were used for the worst curses possible. Death, destruction, decay. Endless pain. Eternal sleep. No matter what enchantment had been cast on it, it could be nothing good.

But even if I knew the exact spell, its weaknesses and strengths, I'd never be able to unravel it before we set if off. We were mere paces distant from the spinning wheel. Gervase still looked puzzled, but he made no move to stop us.

A dozen right feet lifted up, swung forward, dropped. A

dozen left feet did the same. I couldn't speak, couldn't stop, couldn't run away from it.

It occurred to me, however, that running toward it might be an option.

The spinning wheel wanted me to approach, after all. It wanted me to succumb to its lure. I tried to pick up my pace, and my feet responded.

I gathered as much speed as I could and threw myself on top of it. I felt a sharp pain as the spindle stabbed into my thigh, but wood broke beneath me with a satisfying crunch.

Breaking the enchantment had been beyond me. But breaking the enchanted object? That would do. The spell had been mighty, but the spinning wheel itself had not. It hadn't been made to bear weight. The dark magic leaked out of it, the shadows receding, the air becoming easier to breathe.

But to break it, I'd had to touch it.

I heard shouts, questions, but they seemed to be coming from a great distance.

And then I stopped hearing anything at all.

CHAPTER TWENTY-EIGHT

Strange Reflections

I couldn't say how long I'd been wandering through the maze of mirrors.

They lined the walls, ceiling, and even the floor, broad rectangles of glass fitted snugly one after another, separated only by their thin golden frames. The corridors branched, split, and dead-ended at random intervals. The difficulty of spotting the twists and turns was exacerbated by the occasional clear pane of glass that I smacked into face-first. Which was, I thought, just plain mean.

Counting my footsteps proved useless as a way of determining how much time was passing—no matter how hard I concentrated, the numbers looped, became meaningless, and vanished from my head. There seemed to be no time in this place. Or it was outside of time.

Once upon a time, a woman found herself trapped in the once upon a time.

At least I didn't become hungry or thirsty no matter how far I walked—a good thing since there was nothing to eat or drink.

I likewise did not become fatigued or feel any need for rest, so I strode on and on without ever sleeping.

When I grew bored of calling for help, I switched to muttering grumpily. Then I sang snatches of every song I could remember. When I at last fell silent, no other voice took the place of my own, and I had nothing left to do but gaze into the mirrors as I passed.

At first, there was nothing much to see—only my own image repeating endlessly into the distance. My hair was a long, tangled snarl. My clothes had seen better days. And the scabbed-over bite mark on my cheek was doing me no favors. After some unknown number of turns, however, the mirrors began to reflect someone else. Someone not quite me.

She looked like me. Or, rather, they looked like me, for there was a different version in every pane. There was a Melilot in a fancy ball gown, pink and blue with leg-of-mutton sleeves. A Melilot in tattered rags. A Melilot in a gleaming suit of armor. A Melilot in a dress dripping with so many diamonds the cloth could not be seen. My hair showed up straightened, braided, long, short, and once shaved off, leaving me smoothly bald. I saw a Melilot with scars like Jonquil's at her neck and wrists. A dead Melilot, her flesh half-decayed from her bones. An empty mirror where I thought, perhaps, I had never been born.

"If you're trying to disturb me," I remarked to a reflection with sharp teeth, curved claws, and backward-facing feet, "you're going to have to do better than that. An ogre once took me to see his collection of human skeletons in amusing poses. He was very proud of it. It was a family heirloom."

As if in response, a mob of angry strangers stepped into the frame and began poking at sharp-toothed me with torches and pitchforks. My mirror image opened her mouth wide and leapt on one of them, tearing his throat out with a spray of blood. She was remarkably nimble for someone with feet pointed in the wrong direction.

All right, so it was a *bit* disturbing.

From then on, the mirrors stepped up their game; instead of reflecting me as I wasn't, they showed me scenes from lives I had never lived. Down one set of corridors, I watched my stepmother cast a dish of lentils into the fireplace and command me—her mouth moving silently—to count them while she and my sisters went to a party. Then my birth mother, somehow turned into a tree, gave me a makeover. In a different passage, I saw myself and all twelve hunters sneaking off to an underground kingdom to dance the night away. Around a turn, Gervase was giving me the freedom of the entire castle except for one forbidden room with a temptingly locked door. Familiar stories. But none of them my own.

I saw myself sent off to marry a monster. A prince. A queen. A bear. I saw myself severing the head from my sister Jonquil's dragon, forcing her to act as my servant, and claiming her bride, Gnoflwhogir, as my own. At the end of that hallway, I sat on the obsidian throne of Skalla, wearing a dress the color of midnight and sipping something far too red from a bone-white cup. I don't know how long I stood staring at that image. I'd like to say it was entirely in horror, but some small part of me was fascinated as well. Here was a Melilot who'd never again be forced to kneel before her stepmother.

Eventually I backed away and chose a different route, passing through a long gallery of Sams and me—or would that be Sams and mes? Samses and meses? There was a Sam slaying a deer and cutting out its heart so he could pretend it was mine. Next to it was a Sam taking an axe to a spider wolf that was dressed in an old-fashioned nightgown and sleeping cap. I wasn't even in that mirror, unless the unsightly bulge in the spider wolf's abdomen meant something I didn't care to think about.

Sam as my captive; Sam as my captor; Sam capitulating, capricious, capable, captivating . . .

"I wish you were really here," I murmured at the mirrors.

One of the Sams, green masked, turned to look at me sharply. "You can talk?" he asked.

My jaw dropped open. "Sam?"

"This is amazing!" he said, bouncing on his heels in excitement. "You're the first voice I've heard in . . ." He stilled, his brow furrowing. "Can you hear me? Can you respond? Or are you another kind of . . ." He motioned his head toward a mirror where he knelt before a me reclining on some kind of chaise lounge made of skulls. Neither of us was wearing very much.

I stepped forward and reached out a tentative hand to his face, more than half expecting to touch nothing but cold glass. Instead, I felt warm, solid flesh. He inhaled a shuddering breath.

"You're real," I said, amazed. "How are you— Eep!" I had no breath to say anything further because he'd wrapped me in his arms and squeezed me tight.

"You're here. You're really here. I thought I'd never, ever—" He paused and drew back, loosening his hold enough for me to inhale. "Wait. Are you dead? Because I've been wondering if I might be dead."

"I don't think so." I'd considered the possibility. But this wasn't the way Jonquil had described death. She had, naturally, spent some time dead when she was decapitated, and she'd never mentioned a maze of inaccurate mirrors. "The last I heard," I told Sam, "you were only unconscious."

"Oh. Am I . . . dreaming, then? I suppose that's reassuring. But does that mean you're nothing but a dream?" He looked rather put out by the idea.

"No." I shook my head. "I'm here. I've been cursed. I'm not sure exactly how. Eternal sleep is pretty standard, though. So if you're dreaming, maybe I . . . stepped in with you, somehow?" I glanced at his hands, which were resting on my hips. "Um. Not that I mind, but there's ichor on my clothes, among other things, and you're most likely getting it all over you."

"I don't care. Also, dream ichor probably doesn't stain."

"Good point."

He gathered me up in his arms again, rather more carefully this time around. "I missed you."

I closed my eyes and rested my chin on his shoulder.

Soon after, we walked through the corridors hand in hand, both of us reveling in the presence of another person after so much silence. It wasn't long before we were telling each other about everything that had happened since we last laid eyes on each other. I let him know about my imprisonment, the siege, and the spinning wheel. He didn't remember much after Kit had blown him into the tree; he had dim recollections of walking back to the castle, and he'd been here ever since.

Wherever "here" was. I wasn't convinced we were trapped together in a shared dream. Everything was far too consistent and logical. The mirrors stayed what they were, and Sam was what he was. There was nothing like the tooth tunnel or the amorphous dream lover, and I didn't feel at risk of suddenly becoming naked.

That took my thoughts in the direction of the possible benefits of getting naked, if I was fated to be trapped in this place with Sam forever. Surely "the bride is wandering for eternity in an endless maze" would be a good reason to cancel a wedding. A wedding that had to have been on shaky ground already, after the groom had thrown me into a dungeon. But I refrained from ripping anyone's clothes off.

For the moment.

We stopped to watch a scene play out in one of the floor mirrors. A rooster that somehow resembled Sam, a cat that had my eyes, a hound with Clem's hangdog look, and a donkey (that looked like a donkey) were trying to play musical instruments, most of which were not well designed for hooves and paws. I winced as the donkey decided the best way to get a noise out of a violin was to stomp on it. The strangest of the stories always seemed to appear in the mirrors on the floor for some reason.

"Mirrors, mirrors all around," I said. "We are lost. Can we be found?"

Nothing changed in any noticeable way. On the floor before us, the animals scared a group of robbers out of a cottage. Either these weren't the sort of mirrors that could answer questions, or they thought they were already answering.

"Are you certain we're not dead?" Sam asked.

"No." If I put Jonquil's experience aside, the theory had some compelling aspects. It's the most likely outcome for a coma that lasts for more than a few days, and death curses are as common as sleep curses. "But if this is the afterlife, it certainly isn't anything I expected."

"What did you have in mind? Castle in the clouds? The big rock candy mountain?"

My sister had explained it as a sort of blank nothingness, like the silence that comes when you close a book. I'd always found that depressing. "Maybe not those, but also not"—I gestured around—"this."

"I see what you mean."

"But on the bright side, even if we are dead, it isn't necessarily irreversible."

Sam turned to give me a questioning look. "It isn't? I was under the impression that 'irreversible' was part of the definition."

"Not always. Especially if it's the result of a curse. What's done unnaturally can generally be undone in the same way."

"But I wasn't cursed. I bashed my skull against a tree."

"I . . . suppose that's true, yes. Although, I mean, Kit's breath isn't exactly natural, but is that what killed you? If it killed you. Or was it the blunt force trauma that resulted from it? I'm not sure how that would count."

Such is the irrational and disorganized nature of magic. You could never be certain which way it would go in a situation like this.

Sam watched cat me, rooster him, and the other animals celebrate their victory in the robbers' house. Eating the dinner that had been left on the table, drinking ill-gotten fine wine, and making merry. "So if we broke the curse, it's possible you might vanish from this place while I remained."

"It's possible," I agreed. "But it doesn't matter, does it? We have no idea how to break the curse, anyway."

"We could . . . try the traditional method, couldn't we?" He blushed. "It's nothing we haven't done before."

I paused. Would that work?

I had always assumed curse breaking was another effect of True Love's First Kiss, which was no longer available to the two of us. But was I absolutely positive that was the case? I remembered my earlier doubts about true love having formed between strangers who had never spoken. And for that matter, I recalled instances of curses being broken by other, let's say, kiss-adjacent methods. One woman had woken up from an enchanted sleep when she gave birth to twins. Remember how I said necrophiliac princes are the worst? Yeah.

But that did imply first kisses might not be the only way to break a spell. Perhaps our second one would work.

Or would work for me.

"That could end up trapping you here," I said. "Alone. Forever."

"You'd rather we both stayed?" He spread his arms wide, toward the endless, silent mirrors.

The scene below us had changed. Now I was a hot coal leaping out of a fire, landing next to a piece of straw that resembled Sam and a bean that looked like my sister Calla. You'd think it would be difficult to tell who was meant to be who, but it wasn't subtle. The bean had Calla's nose.

They came to a river and tried to cross. It didn't go well. The straw caught fire, and the coal fell in the water, going out with a hiss. The bean split in two and had to be rushed to surgery, but it ended up fine. Hurray for the bean.

"Would it be so bad, if we never escaped?" I asked. "We're not going to starve. And we'd always have someone to talk to." Although doing anything naked together would, unfortunately, also be precluded under this plan. There was too much chance it would count as kiss adjacent.

He looked down, thinking it over.

In the mirror, I was a bird in Sam's mouth. He swung an axe at me and cut off his own head. Then Sam was my magic cook pot, but I didn't know how to make him stop cooking, so I drowned the whole world in porridge. Other scenes followed. I don't know how many. How long did we stand there without speaking, in that place without time?

Sam turned his gaze to me again. "You said an army of monsters has gathered. They're trying to murder my sister and my cousin and my friends. Even if Jack's been a bit of an arse lately, she's still my sister."

I nodded slowly. "Your fiercest champion."

"Yes. If we can go back, we need to. And if you can go back alone, I want you to. Help them. Please."

I couldn't think of any way to argue. Or rather, I couldn't think of any argument I was willing to make. None that weren't selfish compared to what Sam was begging me to do.

"All right," I said quietly. "If that's what you want. All right."

Sam put his hands on my shoulders and took a final long look at me, his eyes tracing the contours of my face.

Then he leaned forward and kissed me.

I had thought my eyes were open, but I found myself opening them anyway.

I spent a moment disoriented—I'd been standing up, and now I was lying down. But I was still being kissed, a pair of parted lips pressing firmly against my own.

"Sam?" I tried to ask, but it came out more like "Srrgm?"

The face in front of mine pulled away.

"I honestly wasn't sure that would work," Angelique said with a tired smile, sitting back on her heels. "Welcome back to the world of the living."

PART VII

EVERY VILLAIN NEEDS A MONOLOGUE

CHAPTER TWENTY-NINE

The Glass Menagerie

A quick glance around showed me we were in the sorcerer's tower, the chamber that was invisible from the outside. The cages were mostly gone, and the few that remained held smallish monsters, perhaps juveniles. There was a snarling undersized spider wolf that looked to be barely out of puppyhood (or spiderlinghood). A writhing nest of tiny furred snakes poked their heads out between the bars, raising their feathery spines and flexing their claws.

The rest of the cages had been replaced by a circle of see-through rectangular boxes with hinged lids. Each one just large enough to hold a single person inside.

Glass coffins. It made sense. Curses always work better when they keep to the traditional forms. The spinning wheel to cast my consciousness adrift and the coffin to receive my emptied body. The spell must have brought me straight to it. How long had I been trapped here in a box, comatose?

I was lying in the only one with the top open. I didn't take the time to count them, but it looked to be somewhere around a dozen or so. At an educated guess, thirteen—enough to display the inert forms of twelve hunters and one inconvenient Skallan princess.

Angelique stood patiently while I made my assessment of the room. When I returned my attention to her, I couldn't help but notice her eyes were bloodshot, and the shadows beneath them had deepened. Her face looked a shade too pallid and a little damp. She struck me as being desperately in need of a good night's sleep.

"We should talk," she said. "I have a proposal I think might be of interest to you."

I wasn't keen to hear it. My suspicions had been confirmed, and with the taste of my first kiss with her still fresh on my lips, there might be something I could do about it.

It was time to see how she really felt about me.

"Drown," I told her, and dissolved into water.

Her eyes widened and her smile vanished. Quick as a striking snake, she grabbed the coffin lid and slammed it shut.

If I still had a mouth, I would have laughed. My waters swelled and rose, preparing to burst the glass, flood the tower, rise over the treetops, and—

Nothing happened.

I filled the coffin, but it didn't shatter. Had I merely managed to become a large puddle?

"Nothing can get out when the lid is closed," Angelique said. "Not wind or water, fire or frost. I enchanted it myself. You might as well change back."

My thoughts were once more dissolving into the languid roil of water. If I didn't pull myself together now, I might very well be stuck that way for another month. I didn't much fancy the idea of spending it locked in a box.

Think of human things, I told myself. *Hands. Feet. Hair in desperate need of a brush. The feel of my tongue pressed against the back of my teeth. Lips. Kissing. You can't kiss without lips.*

Dragging my flesh back together felt like sculpting jelly. Somehow, I forced my fluid shape to congeal into a panting body. My clothes remained soaking wet, and a thin stream of water trickled from my hair and pooled at the base of the coffin.

I glared at Angelique. Being taken out of one cage only to be stuck into another was extremely tiresome. "I see you prepared for me."

"You, and the chilly one, and the strong one, and the others." The glass muffled her voice, but if I listened closely, I was able to make out what she was saying. "I have to say, you attacked me more quickly than I expected. Drowning's such a nasty death, too. What if I came here on a daring rescue mission and was about to spirit you to safety?"

"You didn't. And you weren't."

"No."

She waited expectantly.

It wasn't as if I would gain anything by keeping silent. "The timing of the siege was strange. Why didn't it begin when the hunters were helpless birds? Why only after you stopped being regent? So I started putting together some of the other little signs. Like how you knew about the pumpkin coach when I hadn't told anyone."

"You hadn't?"

"No. The hunters never saw it. I pretended I'd come without one."

"My own fault. I assumed too much honesty from you, even though I knew you were a liar." She heaved a little sigh.

"And then, of course, there was the spinning wheel."

"Ah, yes. Thank you for the idea, by the way. Not the first you've given me. It's why I think we might work so well together." When I didn't respond, she added, "How is it that the curse only brought you? I was hoping to acquire a full set of hunters, too. You should have all been compelled to prick yourselves on the spindle."

I fidgeted in the close, damp confines, trying to find a more comfortable position. There really wasn't one. "I smashed it."

"Pity."

"Is the lion your collaborator or just a dupe? Were the peas yours, too?"

"I'd love to tell you everything. I think you might enjoy it better if you weren't in such a cramped space. Will you promise to behave?"

It seemed unwise to let her know I probably wouldn't be capable of repeating the lake trick right then if I wanted to. The lingering traces of her kiss had surely faded.

I squirmed onto my side so I could look at her more directly. "How do you know I would keep any such promise?"

"You might not," she replied. "However, do you know what happens to someone if they're interrupted midway through turning into a lake?"

"I . . . don't, actually."

"Neither do I." She smiled sweetly. "If we can have a civilized conversation, neither of us will have any need to find out."

Could she do that? Bring a spell to a halt in the middle of the casting? I'd never heard of such a thing. There was no doubt she was powerful—she had bred hundreds of monstrosities in her tower and ripped the stone giants out of the earth itself. I'd felt the touch of her spell work, and it had been no petty curse. She was one of the mightiest sorceresses I'd ever met. Perhaps as mighty as my stepmother.

If I was going to try anything, I would need to pick my moment with care. "All right, I promise. No drowning."

"Good." She opened the lid and set it carefully down. "Come out and have a seat. I'd like to tell you a story."

"A story?" I stood, arching my back to get the kinks out. When I stepped out of the coffin, the shallow water at the bottom rippled back and forth. I thought about the castle by the sea. How long would it be before it fell? Or had it fallen already, while I wandered through the maze of mirrors?

"There," she said. "That's better, isn't it?"

My red cloak dripped onto the stone floor. Frankly, it had benefited from the rinse. It wasn't as good as Jonquil's clothes-cleaning spell, but at least the water had washed some of the ichor out.

"What kind of story?" I asked.

"I don't know yet." She considered. "Perhaps it will turn out to be a love story."

"My favorite." I looked out a window. Outside, there was nothing but trees and snow. The room was warm, although there was no glass to keep out the chill, and no fire had been lit within. More of her magic.

I brushed my hair out of the way so I could sit on the sill, bringing the whole sodden heap of it forward over my shoulder. I fidgeted with it, fussing at the tangles, as if undoing a few of the knots would make any difference.

"Go ahead," I said. "I'm listening."

CHAPTER THIRTY

The Tale of the Evil Sorceress

Once upon a time, a child was born to the royal family of Tailliz. This was a great disappointment to her parents and considered by most everyone to have been a dreadful waste of time and effort.

The queen, you see, was getting on in years. So was the king, but no one really cared about that. The queen's fertility, on the other hand, had been the talk of the kingdom for nearly two decades. Or more accurately, her lack of fertility. The nation gossiped nonstop about the miscarriages, the stillbirths, the cradle deaths, and the queen's stubborn inability to become pregnant again after every such embarrassment, sometimes for years at a stretch. This was considered a grave problem for the king, for the royal bloodline had shrunk over the centuries until he and his wife had become the bottleneck for any future generations. He had no brothers, uncles, nephews, cousins, or even distant relations who might be hastened home to plop their rear ends on the throne should the worst come to pass.

But finally, when the king had all but given up hope, the queen not only became pregnant but also brought the child to term; and the child survived not only the day of its birth but also the week, and the month, and soon enough the year. Unfortunately, the child was a girl.

For the Kingdom of Tailliz had an ancient rule, and the rule was this: Women cannot inherit the throne. The origins of this rule were unknown even to the lion who was the keeper of the laws and traditions of the kingdom—although he had his theories and wrote a ridiculous book about them.

The king bided his time for a few years, holding out hope, perhaps, that the queen might yet produce a son out of some unexpected orifice. But no such son sprang forth, so the king at last went to seek advice from the lion.

"I am in dire need of an heir," the king apprised his counselor, "and the queen has proven intransigent in this regard. Is there some method by which I might birth one on my own?"

"That is biologically unlikely," the lion opined. "As I have conclusively proven, humans only reproduce asexually under conditions of extreme stress, usually when their fruiting bodies are triggered to spore by fire." He eyed the king suspiciously. "Didn't you say you read that chapter?"

The king grunted in lieu of giving an answer. "I would rather not be lit on fire. What are my other options? Could I find a less incompetent queen?"

"Marrying a second spouse while not yet unmarried from the first spouse is a practice known as philately," the lion divulged. "It is, I fear, forbidden by the ancient laws of Tailliz."

The king mulled that over for a great deal of time before he spoke again. "What if the first spouse is no longer alive when the second wedding occurs? Marriage is invalidated by death, is it not?"

"It is," the lion hesitantly agreed. "But spousal murder, while not historically unknown in Tailliz, is . . . frowned upon."

"Frowned upon?"

"Severely frowned upon," the lion confirmed.

"Well, that's no good either, then!" the king groused. "I detest being frowned upon. It appears I am out of options."

"Hm. Possibly not. Are you familiar, perchance, with the ritual known as 'divorce'?"

Once the lion had explained the meaning of the word and how it might best be accomplished under Tailliziani law, the king was overjoyed. They talked long into the night, plotting and planning. For divorce in Tailliz was only allowed if an iron-clad reason could be found for it, and a lack of male offspring had been deemed insufficient. Which meant it was imperative that a different reason be either discovered or invented.

And so it was that wild rumors began to circulate through the court—rumors that the queen held regular tea parties with demonic horse-size rabbits, that she was a porcelain doll animated by clockwork, that she floated three inches above her bed at night babbling in an unknown tongue. Only one of these things was true, but it mattered little. By the time the king declared his marriage null and void, few were surprised and most were relieved. The princess was a notable exception, but no one paid any mind to what she thought.

The former queen was sent packing to a distant estate, where she died some years later in bewildered obscurity. In the meantime, the king remarried, selecting a bride from a line of minor nobles noted primarily for their fecundity; she was herself the seventh of twelve siblings, which he took as a promising sign. And indeed, in rapid succession she popped out an heir, a spare, and an extra pair. Then she died of a chill, and no one cared. She had served her purpose, everyone agreed, most admirably.

"So you see," Angelique said, "we have a great deal in common."

"We do?" I remained dubious. The last time I was in this tower, I'd realized my father hadn't been the perfect parent I had always imagined, but he never would have cast off my mother like a broken shoe.

"Two princesses," she continued, "who weren't ever meant to sit on their parents' thrones—"

"Oh, that." I shrugged. "Not being in line for a throne isn't exactly unique. Most people endure it all their lives. It's hardly a good enough reason for a 'We're not so very different, you and I' speech."

"Do most people also live in the shadow of their stepmother's natural children, eternally envious of the bright future that will never be theirs?"

"Is that how you see me?" She was still missing the mark, I thought. If I was envious of my sisters, it wasn't because of their place in the order of succession. I'd never been one to spend my days scheming for power and scrambling for a crown.

Then I remembered the Melilot in the mirror with her bone-white cup, and I wondered if Angelique had come nearer to the truth than I wanted to believe.

I leaned against the window embrasure, narrowing my eyes. "You seem to know more about the Skallan royal family than most. Not even Gervase had heard I wasn't the queen's daughter by birth."

She smiled. "We have far more in common than that."

The princess grew up largely ignored. Of her brothers, only the youngest and least important bothered to spend any time with her, following her about and pestering her with questions. Or at least, he did until she was old enough to be sequestered in the women's wing. If not for one unexpected event, she might have been content to rule over her petty fiefdom of storytelling and embroidery, for she was still the king's daughter and at the top of the only hierarchy open to her.

But then, one night, she exploded a mouse.

It is fortunate that the creature surprised her when she was alone, for at that time she had neither understanding nor control of her powers. All she knew was that her bedroom had been invaded by a rodent, and she hated it and wanted it gone. In an instant, its tiny body bulged, distended, and then inverted, spraying the wall with blood.

Intrigued, the princess stepped forward to examine what she had wrought. The mouse corpse, she found, had been not merely exsanguinated but transformed. Tentacles sprouted where its tiny ears had been. Its paws were clubby stumps of bone, and its tail had grown a spike that glittered like metal in the candlelight. Needless to say, she was delighted. She wished for nothing more than to do it again.

There was no one she could turn to for instruction. Sorcery was unknown in Tailliz, and the sole magical being was the lion, who was, frankly, a buffoon. So she began to practice on her own, in secret. The secrecy came not from fear or shame; it came, rather, from a desire to have something for herself, at least for a while. Something that made her more than the superfluous child of a failed mother. She harbored vague dreams of dazzling her father with her talents, but that, she felt, should wait until she perfected them.

Her experiments started out innocently enough. Oh, a beloved cat or poodle might have vanished on occasion, with much weeping and wailing from this Yvette or that Yvonne, but sacrifices are necessary in the pursuit of knowledge. And imagine the joy the princess felt as her knowledge and ability increased. The triumph when an animal survived a transformation for the very first time. The thrill when she took a rat and a centipede and squashed them together to form something new.

As her powers grew, and her creations became larger,

fiercer, and more difficult to dispose of, she wondered whether the time was growing ripe to reveal her abilities. But one day, she watched her younger brothers from behind a wooden screen as they prepared for a fraternal hunting expedition—a rare event because they did not like one another overmuch—and she could not help but notice they were all, compared to her, wholly inadequate.

The eldest of them was vain, boastful, and talentless, loudly proclaiming how many animals he would bring home from the forest, although he never managed to return with more than a scrawny hare. The next eldest was whiny, weak, and cowardly, a spindly fellow who sniffled in the cold and was so frightened of his own horse he could barely sit astride. The third eldest was dull as a brick, a slack-jawed mannequin with little to say and none of it worthwhile. The youngest of the brothers, Gervase, had no flaws so obvious, but he was hardly out of boyhood, a blank slate upon which anything might yet be written.

And as they rode out of the castle gate with great fanfare and cheering, it occurred to her to ask herself: Why should any of them rule? Why should the throne go to a braggart, a poltroon, a dolt, or a stripling while someone of much greater talents was swept aside?

Indeed, she wondered, why not her?

Attaining such an ambition would take years, but patience she had in abundance. She increased the scope and scale of her experiments, cultivating a reputation for frequent illnesses in order to obtain time and privacy. Eventually her creations grew too large and dangerous to hide within the castle, so she dared to turn her transformative powers on herself. The first attempt nearly killed her, but within a few months, she had perfected a method of slipping away from the castle unseen, so she might continue her practices deep in the woods. There, no one would stumble over the corpses of her failures or into the teeth of her successes. Or at least, they would not do so before she was ready.

"Am I supposed to find this relatable?" I asked. "Because I'm still not seeing all of these great similarities between us."

"No? Am I the only one here who concealed the truth about herself to achieve her ends?"

"I did that to protect myself. From you."

"We are two women not content with the lives laid out for them. Two sorceresses of vast and dangerous power. Two liars."

I shifted uncomfortably. Even more so than before, this was striking closer to home than I would have liked. Especially the part about not being content with the path I'd been set on. "I've never exploded any mice," I said.

"Oh, you should try it," she told me. "It's great fun."

The princess spent many years learning her craft. No longer content with mere animal transformation, she scoured the land for books of arcane lore. Books she memorized and then burned. She used what she learned to conceal her laboratory from sight, further lessening the risk of discovery—although not, as it later turned out, enough to prevent it entirely.

"I've been wondering why you didn't turn the whole thing invisible. We'd have walked right past it."

She looked rueful. "I tried that at first, but then I couldn't find it myself."

Her research took so long that her youngest brother grew up, traveled far, fell in love, and brought his fiancée back to the castle. But the fiancée was discontented by her days in the women's wing after a life in the hills and moors of her own country. The prince, in his turn, was distressed by his inability to spend time with his love after their passionate courtship, conducted under the customs of another land. They decided to return to Ecossia, and they had little intention of ever coming to Tailliz again. Perhaps if they'd stayed away, they would have lived happily for the rest of their days, without struggle or strife. But this was not to be.

For the sorcerous princess judged herself ready to enact her plans.

Regardless of her dabbling in other enchantments, her twisted creatures remained the centerpiece of her magic and her greatest pride. At last, they had grown large enough and deadly enough to kill at her command.

She targeted the oldest of the brothers first, largely because she liked him least. While he led a hunt through the woods, talking incessantly of his skill at slaying beasts, she set beasts upon him that proved him more prey than predator. She had bred them from timber wolves and huntsman spiders. So much effort! So many failures! In the beginning she was only able to produce tiny useless, hairless wolves, bursting from their egg sacs and scuttling out the windows. Or grotesque mistakes whose chitinous legs were unable to support their lupine bodies; they collapsed and died within a day. At long last, though, she achieved her vision—monsters of dangerous elegance and deadly speed. And she watched from the treetops as they tore her brother and his hunting party into bloody shreds.

Their deaths were blamed on the unknown dangers of the forest. Thanks to the escape of some of the princess's lesser experiments, strange creatures had been spotted lurking there for years. They had come to be regarded as a predictable hazard. Even her failures provided unexpected benefits.

But the next brother was so frightened by the incident he refused to step outside the castle walls. Indeed, he spent most of his days cowering in terror within his rooms. He ventured forth to take the air upon the battlements only once each day. So the princess unleashed a bird she had bred from a shrike and a thornbush. So much effort! So many failures! She'd made bleeding horrors rooted to the ground by their talons, shrieking their despair. Or feathered shrubs capable of nothing more violent than tickling a foe who chanced to fall into one. At long last, though, she achieved her vision—a monster that could fly like a butcher-bird and stab like a knife. And she watched from a window as it bore her brother off and impaled him in midair on its spiky head.

The king and his remaining sons began to suspect something was amiss. But the next brother was easily misled. It took nothing but a few carefully planted rumors of a secret sorcerer's lair—*The best lies*, the princess thought, *have a ring of truth*—and he stormed off into the forest, heedless of any danger. Upon his arrival at the rumored spot, he fell into the hole where the princess had concealed her cross between an antlion and a regular lion.

Disturbed as I might have been by the current narrative, my curiosity compelled me to ask, "What do you call that? A lion-antlion?"

"An antlionlion, actually."

I tried to imagine what such a thing might look like. "I didn't see any of those at the siege."

"I didn't use any. They're wonderful against someone foolish enough to walk directly into a pit, but they're of limited usefulness otherwise."

The king himself was cannier than his children, and by this time he refused to venture out for any reason. It took weeks before the princess was able to secrete an assassin beneath his bed—a deadly mix of a cobra, a devil firefish, and a duck-billed platypus. You don't want to know what the failures looked like. But the final success was a snake with fur and fins that combined the venom of three different species in a single bite.

The king's guards dispatched the creature before it had time to sink its fangs into him more than once, but the damage had already been done. The poison worked its way through his system, condemning him to a slow, painful death. He clung to his life just long enough to summon his last remaining son and issue a final command. To protect the royal line, he ordered, Gervase must break off his engagement and instead marry a sorceress from a foreign land, a woman with magic potent enough to defeat whatever enemy had been plaguing their family.

Upon his father's death, Gervase was crowned, albeit with some reluctance on the part of the council of nobles. They feared he might have picked up distasteful foreign customs during his years abroad, but having no other alternative, or so they thought, they allowed the coronation to proceed. To their dismay, he soon defied convention by seeking out his older sister for conversation. Gervase was distraught by the death of his father and his estrangement from his beloved; he didn't much like being kept apart from the only relative he had left. Not long after he was crowned, he created a new administrative position for her with considerable say in affairs of state, adding her to his privy council and giving her a ring of keys to symbolize her freedom to move about the castle.

This caused much consternation, but it was a great boon to the princess's machinations. Where before she had thought to slay the entire council of nobles in order to clear her way to the throne, now another pathway had been opened for her. She could win the nobles over to considering her as a suitable regent if Gervase ever happened to die.

"None of Gervase's actions inclined you to be more charitable to him?"

"Should I have groveled at his feet in exchange for a pittance?" Angelique scoffed. "I want the throne. I can't afford to be fainthearted."

However, for the first time since her plan had been set in motion, the princess began to worry. The old king's scheme had born fruit, and a sorceress was on her way from another kingdom to wed Gervase. The princess was fearful this would bring all her hard work to naught, but she resolved to be patient. The journey was long, and it would take some weeks for her opponent to arrive—time during which she could ingratiate herself with the lords and prove herself invaluable to the functioning of the kingdom before she killed her brother.

Her delay in committing fratricide proved to be her one great mistake. For while she bided her time, a dozen mysterious huntsmen arrived from a distant land, masked, dressed in green, and identical in appearance. They presented themselves at court, and Gervase brought them into his service. The princess, of course, recognized that they all looked somewhat like Gervase's former fiancée, but she didn't trouble herself over it. She did wonder exactly what he was doing with twelve identical copies of his beloved in fancy dress, but it was surely no business of hers.

Not until they made it her business, that is. For when the princess sent her spider wolves to slay Gervase while he was out hunting—and the ridiculous man did insist on going hunting, despite the danger—they were pierced by dozens of arrows before they could venture close, and the hunting party returned unharmed.

The serpents she sent next were frozen to death. Her thorn birds were blown out of the sky. Again and again, while she watched from the trees, the hunters defeated every creature she pitted against them with strength, or with speed, or with poisonous frogs.

Before long, she stopped being able to find the hunters. They took twisty paths through the woods to evade her attacks. When she tried to pursue them in her transformed state, she discovered their tracks had been covered so well no beast or bird was able to follow. The princess spent many days crafting a magic mirror that would let her lead her bestial armies to her victims once more.

Even so, she was starting to grow desperate. She thought if she managed to murder the actual ex-fiancée, the others might give up, but neither she nor her magic mirror could tell them apart from one another. It probably didn't help that the princess could not for the life of her remember the former fiancée's name.

It occurred to her that the laws that had stymied her own advancement might help her now. She began to circulate rumors that the so-called huntsmen were, in fact, women in disguise. Much to her delight, the lion latched on to these tales and decided it was his duty to expel them from the kingdom.

In the meantime, her magic mirror informed her a visitor was soon to arrive from Skalla. So while the lion laid his plans to expose the hunters, the princess set a trap for the new arrival, planning to slay her before she ever set foot in the castle. If both proved successful, the way would at last be clear for another swift regicide.

But at that point everything went a bit pear-shaped.

The hunters were on the alert for attacks against the Skallan and came to her rescue. Soon after, the lion's first attempt at revealing the hunters' secret proved to be disastrously nonsensical, doing more harm than good to his own cause. Thereafter, events unfolded that need not be recounted to one who lived through them. Events that saw the princess given the regency—her hard work cozying up to the nobility paying off—only to see it wrenched away after only a month. Her plans were foiled once again, her hiding place discovered, and her magic mirror snatched by thieves.

But these events also led, at long last, to the rival sorceress lying entirely in the princess's power, asleep for all eternity in a coffin made of glass. No longer a problem, no longer a threat.

And yet.

The princess could not help feeling a certain kinship with the woman in the glass coffin. From everything she had pieced together, sought out, or overheard, their stories were far from dissimilar. Both of them forced into roles they did not seek, subject to authorities who cared little for them.

She already had hints of how powerful they might become if they combined their power and knowledge. An offhand comment by the other sorceress led the princess to envision ripping monsters from the living rock of the earth, her most powerful creations yet.

"It did?" I wasn't exactly sure what comment she meant.

"You told me you had problems getting past statues. Remember?"

"No." I must have been talking about the sphinxes. They'd certainly been a pain to deal with.

Another conversation with the Skallan interloper turned the princess's eye to the utility of the humble spinning wheel; armed with that knowledge, she manipulated the lion into setting a better trap for her foes. All this had occurred while they were working at cross-purposes. What might they accomplish if their goals were the same? Who could stand against them?

The princess lifted the coffin lid and kissed her captive's lips, wondering even as she did if what lay between them would be strong enough to break the curse. Unsure what she was feeling for this woman who had thwarted her, fought with her, and flirted with her.

And as she pulled back from the kiss, she heard the other woman's breath catch and saw her eyelashes flutter.

She had kissed the sleeping girl, and the sleeping girl had awoken.

CHAPTER THIRTY-ONE

Hairbreadth Escapes

"So," Angelique said, gazing at me expectantly, "would you consider a partnership?"

"What kind of partnership did you have in mind?"

The corners of her lips twitched into a small, coy smile. "We can work that out over time. But you seem to have infected me with your foreign notions. I don't think I'd mind if you were awake the next time we kissed."

"I'm . . . not sure." I hadn't come up with any reasonable escape plans. Unwisely, I'd gotten caught up in her story instead.

"Whyever not?" She came nearer, closing the distance between us. "You must see the benefits."

I shrank back, but I had nowhere to go short of throwing myself out the window. Around us, the few monstrous creations left in their cages gibbered and shrieked.

"For one thing," I said, "I think you might be, you know . . . evil."

She stopped midstride.

Then she chuckled. "Well, if the glass slipper fits, I'm happy to wear it."

I blinked, surprised. "You are?"

"I've murdered most of my family. I understand that's a lot to take in." She moved in so close that our knees were almost touching. "But you must see I had my reasons. You know what it's like here. All of us restricted to our little wing. Kept out of the light so we don't get any ideas."

"Locked in a tower." My throat was suddenly dry, and the words came out as a whisper.

"I'm hardly the first person to kill for a crown. They weren't going to give it to me any other way." She put her hands on the sill, one to either side of my hips, and leaned forward. "I'd be shocked if any rulers haven't left a few corpses behind them. I'd wager your stepmother has, to keep hold of her throne. Why does she deserve it any more than I do?" Her face was a scant inch from my own. "Or more than you do? Come to Castle Tailliz with me. It surely can't withstand the both of us."

The castle still stood, then. I hadn't been trapped in the glass coffin as long as I'd feared.

Angelique lowered her lashes. "I know you feel something for me. My kiss wouldn't have woken you otherwise."

Was that true? I hardly knew anymore.

She was right about my stepmother. I was well aware of what she'd done to crush any threats to her rule. I remembered watching a prince tumble from my tower window, falling so far and so fast into the rosebushes. It was unlikely he'd survived very long, wandering blind in the wilderness. My stepmother had kept her life at the cost of his. Although the blame couldn't be shouldered by her alone—I'd played my own role in it.

I didn't like to tell that part of the story.

I'd be lying if I said no trace of me was tempted by Angelique's offer. Two sorceresses united, with a kingdom to call their own. We would have enough power to stand against anyone who might oppose us—the nobles, the lion, perhaps even my stepmother if she objected to her plans being disrupted.

And who was to say she would care? I had been sent to wed the ruler of Tailliz, and here was a would-be ruler of Tailliz, waiting on my answer. One who had kissed me and perhaps truly meant it, which was more than Gervase had ever done. If whatever I felt for Sam could never come to anything outside the realm of dreams and stories, if my ultimate choice was either a queen with a ruthless streak or a king who loved someone else, then the queen with a ruthless streak might at least view me as a valuable ally instead of a curse. Not to mention that I couldn't deny a certain justice to her cause. Forever set aside in favor of her brothers. Her mother's life ruined. Both of them trapped in a kingdom where women were locked away and ignored. In her place, I might have fought back just as fiercely. There were far worse reasons to overthrow a government, even if the only brother who'd ever listened to her was condemned along with the rest.

There was, however, one important subject her tale had not addressed.

"Why do you want to be queen?" I asked.

She pulled back slightly. "What on earth do you mean?"

"You must have a reason beyond it being denied to you."

"I thought that would be obvious." She tilted her head, peering at me like a bird. "Wealth. Power over everyone else. Instant obedience to our whims. Anything we want brought to us the moment that we want it."

"Is that all?"

"That's everything, surely. That's why kings and queens exist, so others might serve them. Who would rather serve than be served?"

"I see."

It wasn't an unusual opinion. In my travels, I had seen despots of every type. I'd heard every version of Angelique's argument—that this was simply the way of things, that the only options were to be in command or to be commanded.

But I could not help but think of my stepmother's kingdom, where ogres no longer sucked the marrow from human bones and the fae folk had stopped stealing babies. To defy her, thieve from her, or insult her was to risk terrible punishment, but during the years of her rule, her people had thrived and prospered, protected from all predators except my stepmother herself. Angelique had not once given a thought to the villagers crowded into the castle courtyard or the soldiers defending the walls, facing horrible death by tooth, tentacle, and claw.

I have made many mistakes in my life and undoubtedly will do so again, but I was not about to ally myself with a woman who somehow managed to be *even worse* than my stepmother.

I threaded my fingers into my hair. Since no reasonable escape plans were coming to mind, I'd have to try an unreasonable one.

"Do you know," I asked, "what happens to someone stopped midway through growing out their hair?"

"No." She sounded baffled. "What?"

"Probably nothing much." I threw the whole tangled mass of it toward her and commanded it to grow.

Grow *fast.*

It shot out with enough force to knock her off her feet. Within seconds, it filled up the room, pressing up against the monster cages and through the bars as the creatures inside howled and shied back from the snaking strands.

Keep going, I commanded my hair. *More.*

I'd never tried anything like this before, and I hadn't been sure it would work. But hair growth was the first magic I'd mastered and still the one I was best at. If there was anything I could command without a devil's hair, the Golden Key, or True Love's First Kiss, it would be this.

I didn't dare let my concentration drop. By this time I no longer saw anything but my own tresses, the whole of my vision a wall of snarled brown curls. The monsters screamed, and the stone walls groaned with the strain as the hair took up all the room in the chamber and continued to pack more densely, seeking space that wasn't there. It pressed against me, threatening to push me out the window.

I let it.

The moment I was outside, the noises cut off. Frigid air hit me like a slap. I dropped a short distance and stopped with a jolt that threatened to rip my scalp off.

Above me, my hair pulled taut, rising straight up until it vanished into thin air. To all appearances, I was dangling from nothing above the ruined building where Sam and I had spent the night. Whatever spell Angelique had used to make the upper floor invisible and inaudible, it was a strong one.

The tug on my scalp became more uncomfortable with every passing second. I focused on lowering myself to the ground. As I did so, the air in front of me began to glow with a golden, misty light. It quickly spread to the stone building below. The entire structure must have been a magical construct of some kind, and my hair, still expanding within it until the very stones cracked, was breaking the spell. I sped up my descent, not wanting to find out what would happen if it reverted to its original form while I kicked in midair.

Just as my feet touched the earth, the tower collapsed in on itself, twisting and shrinking until it was an acorn that hovered in the air for a fraction of a section before dropping into the snow. Twenty feet of hair fell around me, sheared off at the end by the vanished window but heavy enough to land with a thump even so. I was relieved that I'd been spared from being crushed under the thousands of pounds of it that had vanished along with the tower. Without question, I hadn't thought this plan all the way through.

Angelique was nowhere to be seen. Had she suffocated in my runaway locks, or been transformed into an oak seed? Or simply been crushed to death when the spell broke, compressed to the size of an acorn?

I was still wondering when a huge dark bird, easily twice my size, dove out of the sky with an ear-piercing cry. Its talons reached for my neck.

I barely managed to fling myself out of the way before it could rip out my throat. As it hurtled past, I saw that it had Angelique's warm brown eyes, narrowed in fury.

Her offer of an alliance had not extended past my second attempt to kill her.

She reached the edge of the clearing that used to house the tower and wheeled around for another go. Out of ideas, good and bad alike, I gathered my hair in my arms and ran.

My effort was doomed from the start. I still had too much hair dragging behind me, catching on roots and shrubs. Even if I'd had the means to cut it off, she could fly faster than I could run. I'd stumbled no more than a few feet out of the clearing when the bird's shrieking cry sounded just behind me.

Then something narrow and bright flew past my head. I heard a thud of impact as I dove to the ground. With a flutter of wings, the bird changed course, veering up to the treetops.

I glanced up. A huge sword was sticking out of a tree, vibrating like a plucked guitar string. Who had thrown a sword?

"Would you pull that out?" came a familiar voice from behind me. "I want to kill the evil bird."

I whipped my head around to see my sister-in-law, Gnoflwhogir, large as life and twice as green. She was balancing awkwardly on one leg and looking very grumpy about it.

"I'd do it myself," she continued, "but these annoying boots would carry me away. What have you done with your hair?"

My brain was beginning to catch up with the situation. I finally recognized the distinctive magic boots she was struggling not to use by accident. A single step would send her far into the distance. I couldn't remember the last time my stepmother had let someone borrow the seven-league boots.

"How did you get here?" I asked. "How did you find me?"

"A cranky magic mirror told me. But the sword? Now? Because the evil bird is—"

She broke off, her gaze flicking upward as Angelique shot toward her like a stooping hawk. Gnoflwhogir cursed, shifted her weight, and hammered her fist forward. It connected with an audible crack against Angelique's head. The bird tumbled into the underbrush.

"Sword!" Gnoflwhogir shouted, turning her eyes back to me.

I rose to my feet and tugged on the hilt. The blade was stuck fast in the tree.

"That's not a bird, by the way." I braced my foot against the trunk and pulled harder.

"It looks like a bird."

"She's a sorceress. She can probably look like whatever she wants."

"Oh." A pensive look crossed her face. She fingered her necklace of left ears fretfully. "I should have brought my witch-slaying axe."

A familiar hissing growl came from the woods around us. A few of the young furred snakes poked their heads out of the underbrush. They flared their hoods at us, and feathery spines rose from their bodies like the fluffed-out fur of an angry cat. They must have been small enough to escape their cage and weave their way through my hair. A disquieting thought.

Gnoflwhogir turned sharply to see what was making the noise. She nearly lost her balance, windmilling her arms in a desperate attempt to keep from toppling over. I wrenched her claymore free at last and tossed it to her as soon as she stopped wobbling.

"These snake things," she said, snatching her weapon out of the air, "do they die if you stab them?"

"Probably." More of them slithered into view. I retreated as rapidly as I could without tripping on my own hair. "But there are an awful lot of them, and a single bite might be deadly." Were the juveniles as dangerous as the adults? I wasn't eager to find out. Out of the combined venoms of a cobra, a devil firefish, and a platypus, one would probably kill us even if the others didn't.

Gnoflwhogir bared her teeth in a grimace. She swung her huge claymore as easily as someone else might brandish a knife. With a quick shift of her weight, she settled into as good a fighting stance as she could manage on one leg. I scurried behind her since it seemed like the safest place to be. Somewhere deeper in the woods, I was sure, Angelique was watching.

"I will fight you, enemy snakes!" Gnoflwhogir shouted. "You are many and I cannot move, so horrible death shall be our fate! But I will do battle with you nonetheless!"

Dozens of them darted closer, surprisingly fast. She chopped at one and then another. Her claymore blurred into a streak of bright metal. In moments, half of the monsters had been bisected, strange blue-green blood leaking onto the ground. But there were simply too many. Only one had to find an opening. And as she slashed at a serpent to her right, one on her left struck to kill, lunging at her exposed ankle.

Its fangs snapped closed on air when a dragon caught Gnoflwhogir in its claws and yanked her up and out of the way.

"Light them up!" Jonquil shouted from her seat on the dragon's back. It bent its sinuous neck into the shape of a question mark and disgorged a burst of flame. The fire scorched bark and leaves and fur, and it left the snakes dead or fleeing in its wake.

Behind Jonquil sat Calla, and behind Calla sat Liam, clinging to his wife and looking rather airsick.

My family had come.

"The snakes aren't the worst threat!" I yelled. "There's an evil killer bird!"

I gestured toward where I had last seen Angelique. Jonquil obligingly turned her dragon's head in that direction and sent another stream of fire into the trees. There was a startled squawk, and something dark fluttered up and out of sight.

"Here!" Jonquil flew the dragon low to the ground and reached out a hand. "Hop on!"

I grabbed hold and swung myself up as they passed. Calla shifted to let me on and took a firm hold around my waist. "Get us out of here!" I said.

"I'm having a definite sense of déjà vu." Jonquil grinned at me before turning her attention back to her dragon, encouraging it to greater heights and faster speeds. My hair streamed behind us like a banner.

"Fine, leave me down here like a handbag!" Gnoflwhogir called up from her uncomfortable position clenched in the dragon's grasp. "It is not at all demeaning for a proud warrior!"

"*Little* busy escaping from the evil right now, darling," Jonquil said through gritted teeth. The dragon banked hard to the left. Jonquil peered over her shoulder for any sign of the dark bird following us, maintaining her sidesaddle perch without apparent difficulty.

The air was bitter cold, but the dragon was a furnace, the fire in its belly keeping me warm. Calla's grip turned into the quick squeeze of a hug, before she reached up to bat my fluttering locks out of her face. I tried to gather it all up again. The pair of goldfinches nesting on her head chirped in my ear. "I missed you," she said.

"Missed you, too." I half expected to feel some lingering resentment over having to be saved by my sisters again, but none came. Other than the night I'd spent with Sam in Angelique's tower, it was the first time since I'd been attacked by the spider wolves that I felt safe. "How did you— LOOK OUT!"

Out of the corner of my eye, I'd seen movement. One of the furred snakes was creeping up to Liam, pulling itself along the dragon's back with its little claws, nearly in striking distance. It must have hooked on when they picked me up. Jonquil began chanting the syllables of some spell. I couldn't imagine she would complete it in time.

The furred snake stopped as Liam thrust a small hissing animal at its face. He was clutching Calla with one white-knuckled hand, but with the other he had pulled a furious mongoose from her skirt pocket.

The furred snake scrabbled backward in fright and lost its grip on the slick dragon scales. With a whistling shriek, it slid over the side and dropped until it vanished far below. The words of the spell died on Jonquil's lips.

The danger gone, I looked around, but the dark bird was nowhere to be seen.

"Natural enemy of cobras," Liam explained, glancing down at the forest, then away again, shutting his eyes.

"Good job, Lord Thrombwobbley," Calla told the mongoose. It leapt to her shoulder and made proud chittering noises. Liam took the opportunity to wrap both his arms tightly around her.

"Lucky thing he came along," I said.

"Not lucky at all," Liam replied, his face buried in his wife's back. "I told Calla to bring him."

"Really? Why?"

His lifted his head, his eyes opening the barest fraction. His expression changed from one of nausea to one of puzzlement. "In case we met any dangerous snakes, of course."

From experience, I knew there was little point in continuing that line of questioning. In any case, the magic mirror tied to his belt chose that moment to make its presence known. "I was rooting for the devilserpent fireplatyfishes," it said in a bitter tone. "But no one asked my opinion."

"Where did you get that?" It occurred to me there were a number of other questions I should really be asking. "When did you get to Tailliz? How did you know I was being attacked?" I glanced around at all of them, trying to put the puzzle together but lacking far too many pieces. "What's going on?"

"I don't know," the mirror said. "I was brought here under protest."

Calla rapped her knuckles against its frame. "Shut up, mirror," she said. "It's a bit of a long story. Why don't you go first?"

"All right." My own story was hardly a short one. It felt like ages had passed since my tooth guards were attacked on the forest road. "Things started going wrong," I began, "when I was about a day's journey away from Castle Tailliz. . . ."

CHAPTER THIRTY-TWO

My Family Weighs In

When I finished giving an abbreviated account of everything that had happened since my arrival in Tailliz, the others fell silent. Calla absentmindedly stroked the mongoose. The goldfinches, whom she had introduced as Carduelis C. Carduelis and Beaky, blinked drowsily on her head.

We were flying toward the castle. A brief landing had let Gnoflwhogir pull off the seven-league boots and take a more dignified seat—and she'd done me the favor of cutting off most of my hair with her claymore. Cutting hair with a sword is awkward at best, but the haircut she gave me was still better than the hideous ragged mop the chirurgeon had left me with.

"We should have come sooner," Jonquil said at length.

"No, we shouldn't!" Calla scolded her. "We talked about this, remember? Only when she asks from now on."

"Look, I'm . . . I'm sorry for yelling at you when I was a lake," I told them both. "You were right. I was in trouble. Am in trouble."

Jonquil shook her head. "You had every cause to say what you did."

"You were just trying to help."

"I knew how you felt," Calla said, "but I kept interfering anyway."

I fumbled for words. "If you hadn't . . . I don't want to be ungrateful—"

"That's not what I meant!" She looked horrified. "We should trust you to know—"

"Stop it!" Gnoflwhogir shouted. "You three are giving me a headache."

Into the ensuing quiet, Liam said, "She's not wrong. Trying to out apologize one another isn't going to solve anything."

Calla muttered her embarrassed agreement, and after a moment, Jonquil and I did, too.

Underneath us, the forest of Tailliz was a vast patterned carpet of evergreen needles and white snow, spreading out toward the dim, bluish mountains far to the north. The gargantuan trees pierced through the canopy like the upthrust spears of a disorganized army, but even they were far below. The thin, freezing wind of the upper air swept through our clothes, leaving me grateful for the heat of the dragon.

"So, this sorceress," Jonquil said. "Does she have a weakness?"

"I don't know." It wasn't uncommon for those steeped in magic to have some kind of tragic vulnerability. If they melted when you threw a glass of water at them, that made for a rather easy fight. But if you had to find their heart, which was concealed in an egg inside a duck inside a hare in a locked chest buried under an oak tree, then things got rather complicated. I had never figured out my stepmother's weakness, if she had one.

"We will stab her, then," Gnoflwhogir said. "Stabbing is everybody's weakness."

"I have a more important question," Calla broke in. "Tell me about Sam. Is he cute?"

I couldn't keep the disbelief out of my voice. "Really? That's your question?"

"Monsters attack you all the time," Jonquil pointed out, not unreasonably. "Sam is the first person you've sounded so much as vaguely interested in since that dreadful prince Mother had to throw into a rosebush."

"Well, it hardly matters," I snapped. "I'm engaged to someone else."

Jonquil and Calla exchanged A Look, which didn't seem fair, since I was closer in age to either of them than they were to each other, and they therefore had no business whatsoever exchanging Looks that were meaningful to each other but completely unreadable to me.

"He's not unattractive," I said. "He has a face. Blue eyes, red hair, freckles."

"Oh, *that's* who was in the dream!" Liam said. I rolled my eyes.

Gnoflwhogir glared at the others, her patience at an end. "All this is irrelevant."

"Yes!" I was pleased to be moving on at last. "Thank you. Can we—"

She turned the glare on me. "Appearance means nothing. How is he in battle? Is this Sam capable of slaying your foes?"

"He's— Wait, I told you what he did against the spider wolves and things. Weren't you listening to my story at all?"

"No," Gnoflwhogir admitted. "It was very long."

I tried to take a steadying breath, but the thin air rendered it ineffective. "He's supernaturally strong. And extremely good at slaying foes. All right?"

"Excellent," said Gnoflwhogir. "I agree with your sisters. Take him as your mate."

I buried my face in my hands. Between my fingers, I saw Jonquil and Calla exchanging another Look.

I didn't want to think about Sam, because it made me queasy

with anxiety. I had no idea whether he'd recovered from his head injury. Or perished in the siege. "Would you please just tell me how you found me?"

"We used this." Liam lifted the looking glass. It caught the sun and flashed a painfully bright blaze of reflected light.

"Unhand me, you cretin," it snarled.

I considered that half an explanation, at best. "That only raises more questions! Where did you get hold of that? And when? And how did you end up saving me in the nick of time?"

"Well," Calla said, "I first heard you were in trouble when a beaver splashed its way over to me while I was asking some aardvarks to redirect a river. The beaver told me it had heard from a fox who heard from a bear who heard from a swallow who heard from a rat that my sister had been imprisoned in a foul dungeon in the Kingdom of Tailliz."

"Oh," I said. "So I did talk to the rat? I wasn't sure that really happened."

"Yes, of course you did. I said I'd only come if you wanted me from now on, and I meant it. Anyway, I dropped everything I was doing—"

"Wait, what had you been doing?" I asked. "Why did you need to redirect a river?"

"Because if I gave the river spirit her waterfall back, she'd agree to give me the casket of gold dust I needed to trade the bridge troll for the magic goatskin that a woman made of twigs—"

"I get the idea. Go on."

"So I went home and told Liam that your intended husband was a horrid villain—"

"He wasn't!" I interrupted. "Isn't."

"Yes, he is," the mirror said. "Beastly person. He stands in the way of my master's triumph."

I frowned at it. "You're biased." Vaguely rude images swirled within the depths of the reflection.

"It was a fair assumption at the time," Liam said. "Anyway, when Calla let me know what was going on, I told her we would need the seven-league boots, so we went and borrowed them from your mother."

"Stepmother," I corrected him. "How long did it take you to pry those out of her?"

Calla shrugged. "Not long. I just told her I wanted them, and she handed them over. She didn't even ask why."

I opened my mouth, and then I closed it again without speaking. Remember my trip across the plain of ice, where my hair froze to the ground every night? Before I went, I'd spent a full hour begging my stepmother for those boots. She'd said no.

"You planned to use the boots to get to Tailliz?" I asked, rather proud of the fact I'd said it calmly instead of yelling something incoherent and profane.

"No," Liam said. "Only one of us would have been able to come that way. But I thought we might want to have them on hand if you ever ended up fighting a magic bird in the woods."

A sliver of sea appeared far ahead of us, a thin line of blue-gray interrupting the endless expanse of green and white. I strained to catch sight of the castle, but I couldn't make it out yet.

"They came to Gnoflwhogir and me next," Jonquil said, "and told us you were in trouble, so I offered them a ride to Tailliz on dragonback."

"And I offered my sword"—Gnoflwhogir drew the weapon in question and waved it threateningly—"so I could stab whoever needed stabbing."

Jonquil ducked as the tip of the claymore passed uncomfortably close to her head. "We flew to Tailliz as quickly as possible, pausing only for the usual reasons—battles against air pirates, gryphons, that sort of thing. When we arrived at the castle, though, it was under heavy assault."

"We weren't sure which side we should be on, at first," Calla said. "Neither was anyone else. The monsters threw rocks at us, but when we approached the castle, the guards tried to shoot us full of arrows."

"You did make your approach on a dragon," I reminded her.

Jonquil sniffed. "That's no reason to be rude. I was about to blast everyone with dragon fire, but then a masked fellow in green hopped up onto the ramparts and asked if we were your sisters. I said yes and demanded you be set free from the dungeon, and he said you weren't in the dungeon anymore and asked if we could please go find you. Then he said, 'Here, use this,' and he threw the magic mirror at us. Nice throw—a hundred feet at least."

"It wasn't nice at all," said the mirror. "I might have cracked against the stones. I might have fallen into the sea."

"He threw it?" I asked. "You're sure? It wasn't, say, blown on a sudden wind or fired out of a bow somehow?"

"Definitely a throw," Calla replied. "Overhand, like a spear toss. Why?"

My breath caught, and something in my chest clenched tight. Sam. Sam was awake. Sam was alive. I didn't say anything. I didn't want Calla and Jonquil to trade their Look a third time.

"We dodged and weaved our way out of the battlefield," Calla continued when I stayed silent, "and landed in the woods. We decided we should give the mirror to Liam because he's the cleverest. But although he asked question after question, using every rhyme he could think of, it refused to show us anything."

"Mirror, mirror on my knee," Liam murmured. "Mirror, mirror by my boot. Mirror, mirror in the mud."

"My humiliation," the mirror said, "knows no bounds."

"I was in an invisible room," I told them. "I don't think it was able to see me until I got out."

Calla nodded, startling awake the goldfinches. "That makes sense. From our end, it looked like you weren't anywhere in existence, and then suddenly you popped into being and were attacked by a bird. Liam figured out exactly where you were—"

"Mirror, mirror with an attitude," he said, "pinpoint longitude and latitude."

"—and Gnoflwhogir grabbed the boots."

"So I could get there and start the stabbing," Gnoflwhogir explained, somewhat unnecessarily.

The castle appeared at last, a blunt thumb of stone poking up out of the gray sea. Jonquil peered at it, adjusting the dragon's heading, then glanced back over her shoulder. "The rest of us followed along after, and everything else you already know. Normal family rescue operation."

"Well, thank you for coming. And also for helping out now, even though they shot arrows at you."

"Of course. Something needs to be done about that sorceress." Calla shuddered, holding Lord Thrombwobbley close. The mongoose wriggled in her too-tight grip. "Those monsters she's been making . . . I tried to talk to some of them, when we were in the woods. There's nothing there. They're not real anymore. Like walking corpses. Puppets stitched together with resentment and animated by magic. All the forest animals are terrified it will happen to them. It's horrible."

As the castle loomed larger, I saw that the gate to the courtyard had been shattered by boulders, and the walls were breached in several places, talus slopes of rubble tumbling into the sea out of holes that looked like vast bite marks. The remains of the ice prison littered the shore, thousands and thousands of glittering white chunks bobbing in the surf. The monsters had broken free.

And they had launched a new plan to reach the half-destroyed bridge. Stone giants were getting on their hands and knees in the shallow water of the bay, lumbering into place one after another, their backs forming a broad causeway the other creatures could use to stride, leap, or squirm their way across. There were more of the stone giants now, a few dozen at least. No doubt every rock formation in the surrounding area had been recruited to Angelique's cause.

I recognized one with a sapling growing out of its elbow. Plunging them into a lake had never been more than a temporary solution. They were hardly going to drown.

Archers stood on what was left of the battlements, the distance making them tiny as finger puppets. They fired arrows too small for us to see at the cloud of gnat-like flying creatures surrounding them. An armed host had assembled at the ruined remains of the gate. Perhaps a hundred tin soldiers on toy horses, preparing to face the coming onslaught. A miniature lion paced impatiently to and fro.

At the very front, spread out across the ranks, were a dozen figures clad in green, one of them mounted and the rest on foot.

"Can this dragon go any faster?" I pleaded.

"Hold on." Jonquil whispered something to the dragon, and it angled downward, its wings flexing as it slanted into a long dive. "So. We're up against slashing claws, poisonous bites, stabby birds, invulnerable rocks, and what looks like an enormous hamster. Anything else?"

"I'm not sure." I scanned the forested ground racing past, looking for any holes that might house an antlionlion. I didn't see any, but something about the woods didn't look quite right. For a moment, I tried to convince myself the movement might be caused by the wind. But it didn't take me long to abandon that idea as wishful thinking.

"Are those trees," I asked, "walking onto the beach?"

PART VIII

SIEGE PERILOUS

CHAPTER THIRTY-THREE

When Plants Attack!

The colossal trees had pulled their roots out of the ground and were striding toward the sea. High up on their trunks, luminous green eyes had opened in the bark. Below them, mouthlike hollows widened and howled.

I remembered the stories of kingdoms toppling when trees started walking. I could see why. The behemoths beneath us were hundreds of feet tall, dwarfing even the stone giants. Trees of that size would barely need to attack the castle; it would crumble beneath them if they tripped and fell on it.

This was magic at the level of the grandest spells I had seen my stepmother cast. Angelique was pulling out all the stops. She had to be testing her powers to their limits.

Unless she didn't have any limits. Possibly the only thing hampering her had been the lack of a proper sorcerous education. If that was the case, she was learning quickly. Which meant things were likely to go poorly for the rest of us.

Our descent brought us uncomfortably close to the highest

branches. They swung to and fro, stretching and bending into reaching arms. Their twig fingers grasped at the empty air.

"These tree things," Gnoflwhogir said, "can we chop them down?"

"I doubt it," I told her. Their trunks were as broad as a barn. Even with Gnoflwhogir's comically oversized sword, it would take days to make a significant dent.

"Let's try fire, then!" Jonquil prodded her dragon, and it exhaled a stream of flames onto the nearest tree, charring the bark and setting the needles alight. The tree took a step back, flailing its limbs in an attempt to put itself out. But the damage looked insignificant compared to its great bulk, and there were plenty more trees where that one came from.

More of them turned their attention to us, shambling nearer with murderous intent. They knocked down their lesser cousins in their fury. The dragon banked away from one tree only to get closer than I liked to another.

"DUCK!" I shouted. We bent low as a gnarled wooden appendage swept overhead, trying to scrape us off the dragon's back.

Liam reached up and jabbed something into it as it passed. The tree shrieked and whipped its arm away. The dragon dropped into a steep dive, and the cries of the tree faded into the distance.

We passed the edge of the forest. The abandoned buildings of the town seemed to leap up at us with dizzying speed.

"What did you use?" I asked.

"Copper nail." Liam's face was tinged green as he stared at the rapidly approaching ground. "Trees hate them."

"Why did you have a copper nail?" I said.

"In case we met an angry tree, of course."

Why did I bother to ask?

"I'd better hop off here," Calla said. The dragon was flying low, skimming the beach, well out of range of the reaching branches high above. Ahead of us, the monstrous army was scrambling onto the still-forming stone-giant bridge. "I'm going to the forest to rally some troops."

"Wait!" I said, but it was already too late; Calla swung both legs over to one side of the dragon and slid off, Lord Thrombwobbley clutched in her arms. She landed on the beach and scurried into the forest. The goldfinches fluttered along in her wake.

"I should go with her." Liam sounded less than thrilled by the idea of jumping off, but he pulled a handful of copper nails out of his pack. "I can protect her from the trees."

"You're going to do what?" said the mirror. "Hold on a minute. I'm very fragile."

Liam ignored the looking glass and, trying hard to conceal his expression of stark terror, followed after his wife.

"Don't break my faaaaaaace!" the mirror screamed as they dropped.

"Now it is my turn." Gnoflwhogir readied her claymore. "I will attack the monsters from the rear. They will be crushed between the two sides."

Jonquil heaved a long-suffering sigh. "Crushed between the army of Tailliz and . . . you? Darling—"

"Away!" Gnoflwhogir leapt off the dragon, thumping onto the ground at the edge of the surf. Without pause, she rushed in the direction of the monstrous army, her great sword waving in the air.

The dragon flew on, over the blue-gray water. The wind of its passage cut a wake through the waves.

"Do you ever wonder," Jonquil asked me after a moment, "if our entire family is insane?"

"It's crossed my mind from time to time, yes."

She gazed off in the direction her wife had gone. "You and I should help out the defenders as best we can, I suppose." Twin lines of worry creased her brow.

"I'm sure she'll be fine," I reassured her.

"Oh, I know. It isn't that. It's only . . ."

I waited for more and began to grow concerned when it didn't come.

"Jonquil. What's wrong?"

"It doesn't matter, I—" She broke off to chant a lengthy phrase in language that hurt my ears as a scabrous warthog with four mismatched wings hurtled toward us. When she finished, its body swelled until it was nearly spherical and then burst like an overfilled bladder. "It's not important," she went on. "Forget about it."

I knew an evasion when I heard one. "I'm not— Look to your right!" She turned to where I pointed and directed a jet of dragon flame at a whirling, buzzing monstrosity. "I'm not going to let this go," I finished.

Her shoulders hunched ever so slightly, creeping up toward her ears. "It's nothing. It's just, there she went, charging straight into danger again, and here I am, staying behind on the back of my dragon again, and I can't help but wonder if . . ."

It was easy to forget that my sisters needed my support, too, sometimes. Even during the most perilous of situations. Maybe especially then. "Gnoflwhogir adores you. For exactly who you are." I laid a hand on her wrist, where the scar encircled the joint. "And she knows what you'd do for her, if it came down to it. You don't have to prove it to her over and over again. She knows."

Jonquil gave me only a single stiff nod in answer, but where my hand rested, her arm felt a little less tense. The dragon snapped at a thorn bird that flew too close, and a mess of blood and feathers plummeted into the sea with a faint splash.

"Well," my sister said. "I do, in fact, intend to stay here on dragonback. Light whatever I can on fire, cast every spell I can think of on the rest. You?"

Staying with Jonquil would have been the smartest option. I

wasn't even sure what else I could really do. No True Love's First Kisses would be mine for the taking here, not unless far more people found me irresistibly attractive than I was willing to believe. If I spent the battle clinging to a dragon, then at least I wouldn't be in everybody's way.

Nonetheless . . .

"Take me to the castle gates," I said. "Out on the bridge. Next to those hunters in green."

She gave me a fond look. "Completely mad. All of us."

Word must have gotten around that the dragon was on their side—or on my side, anyway—because we weren't peppered with arrows as Jonquil steered it to the front line of the coming battle.

"Take care," she said as we dipped low enough for me to heave myself off without breaking a leg.

"You, too." I gave her a quick kiss on the cheek. "See you when this is over." Or so I hoped.

I jumped.

CHAPTER THIRTY-FOUR

The Lines Are Drawn

My landing was less than graceful, but at least I hit the bridge—what was left of it—rather than the water. I wobbled unsteadily on my feet for a moment before I found my balance. The dragon turned and raced off, spewing a gout of fire into the air like a fountain.

"It's aboot time ye shawed up," grunted a hunter in green.

"Hello, Clem," I said. "Lovely to see you, too."

"Hae ye git ony magic tricks tae save th' day?"

"Not really, no."

I didn't have time to say anything more before I was swept up in a pair of very strong arms.

"Hi," said Sam.

I relaxed in his embrace. "I missed you." He didn't have a single weapon on him, not so much as a paring knife. "Are you about to fight monsters unarmed?"

"It's worked for me so far."

"No, it hasn't."

"You changed your hair again," he observed.

"Hacked off with a claymore. Is it flattering?"

"It's . . . a unique look."

I would have liked to stay that way, pressed up against him, my head on his shoulder. It would have been nice to hold each other until the monsters completed their bridge of stony bodies.

Instead, someone cleared their throat next to us, and we remembered our circumstances. All of them. We sprang apart like guilty teenagers.

Gervase was mounted on a great roan stallion, and the king's eyes flicked first to me, then to Sam, and then to the hunter riding to his left, the only one of the twelve on horseback. Given that her hand was laid on the king's elbow, I was confident it was Jack. On Gervase's other side, the lion scowled, his tail swishing back and forth.

Gervase returned his gaze to me. "I have come to understand you are, in fact, my bride-to-be."

"Oh. Um, yes," I said. Sam remained silent, staring fixedly at the ground. "Sorry for the deception," I added.

"Surely, I'm the one who should apologize," Gervase said.

"Whatever for?"

The king's eyebrows hitched up. "For . . . falsely imprisoning you?"

I fluttered my hand in a vague gesture of unconcern. "No worries. I mean, yes, it was horrible—"

"I hate to interrupt," Jack said acidly, "but is right now *really the time*?"

We all turned to look out into the bay. The stone-giant bridge had almost finished assembling itself. Rock scraped against rock as they clambered over one another in an effort to close the final gap. A horde of unnatural creatures readied themselves to swarm over us. The trees weren't bothering with the bridge. They had reached the water and were slowly wading across, an inexorable, unstoppable force.

The archers on the battlements above us kept the thorn birds from snatching up any soldiers, and the dragon flew over the enemy lines, spitting fire. From its back, Jonquil cast her spells, and blinding bolts of lightning cracked into their ranks. And also, I'm sure, somewhere on the shore, a fairy princess with a claymore was making her fearsome charge, planning to single-handedly carve her way through the monsters one by one.

I had my doubts any of it would make much of a difference in the end. Even the dragon was doing little damage. It had to pull up too often to avoid the grasp of a threatening branch or the raking claws of an enormous hamster.

"I only wish I knew why," Gervase said behind me. "What is the cause of this? Who hates us so much?"

He still had no idea. I should have said something earlier. "It's your sister. Angelique wants to kill you and rule in your stead."

I risked a backward glance. He didn't look particularly surprised. Only sad. "And so, having failed to murder me," he murmured, "she will murder the kingdom and rule over . . . nothing."

The lion harrumphed. "This is what comes of giving a woman a taste of power. I warned you when you appointed her to high office—"

"Lion," Gervase snapped, "shut up."

His animal counselor stopped short, looking affronted. Jack smirked.

"General Jack," Gervase continued, turning to her, "the field is yours."

So Jack had been promoted from hunter to general. She straightened in her seat. Something with tentacles and bat-like wings splatted to the ground beside her, its single eye pierced by an arrow. Jack's horse shied away a step, whuffing nervously, its breath stirring my hair. The thought of Poma drifted across my mind. I hoped she'd made it home from the forest. Although on second thought, considering the imminent conflict, I hoped she was anywhere but here, happily living the free life of a wild mare.

"All right," Jack said, addressing the troops. "You know what you need to do. If anything gets past us"—she gestured to the other hunters—"it's your job to stop them. You and the archers are our last lines of defense. Keep everything out. No matter what."

A hundred soldiers saluted her, gauntlets clanking against their helms. She didn't have to say what would happen if a single monster made its way past them. The refugee villagers were hiding in what remained of the castle. Easy prey.

Jack's gaze landed on her eleven identical duplicates, in their masks and boots and cloaks of green. "That makes us the first line of defense. Sorry if this wasn't what you expected when we set out from Ecossia."

She was met by a chorus of dismissive voices as they all spoke at once.

"Not the first army we've ever—"

"—kin say ah expected muckle worse—"

"—hard could it be to fight a tree—"

"—still better than living with the duchess!"

She gave them a wry grin and drew her sword from its sheath.

"As for you, witch—" Jack began.

"Sorceress," I corrected her.

"Do whatever you can. If nothing else, protect my brother."

I nodded, and my hand found Sam's as Jack rode to the edge of what was left of the bridge. A few of the hunters stepped up beside her, one with her hand at the side of her nose, another busily fastening on her leg. The rest arrayed themselves wherever they thought they might do the most good. The lion, to give him what credit he might be owed, stepped to the forefront as well. As did Gervase, bringing his mount alongside Jack's. It struck me as perhaps not the best place for him, but time would tell soon enough whether it was heroism or foolishness. Often the only difference is how the story ends.

In front of them, a final stone giant was laying itself in place with a series of bone-rattling thumps, like an unbalanced millstone.

"The odds don't seem to be in our favor," I remarked.

"They don't," said Sam.

"You should kiss me."

"Will that help?" He looked optimistic.

I shook my head. "No. But you should kiss me anyway."

Heedless of my fiancé mounted nearby or the army of unnatural creatures on their way, Sam drew me close. His lips were warm and soft against mine.

And then the final piece of the monstrous bridge crashed into place, and the enemy was upon us.

CHAPTER THIRTY-FIVE

The Battle Is Joined

The monsters had learned the hunters' tricks and tactics. They dug their claws into the rock as the wind picked up and fluffed out their fur as the temperature dropped.

Nonetheless, the gale and the frost made a serious dent in their ranks as Kit and Max pressed on with their assault. Scores of the creatures were frozen to death where they stood. More were blown off the backs of the stone giants and tossed into the frothing, icy sea. And those who managed to make their way closer found the hunters had learned much about them, as well.

Harry dashed into their ranks, the knife in her hand scarcely more visible than a patch of haze. She left bloody streaks behind her wherever she went. Teeth gnashed at her but closed on nothing, too slow to catch her as she passed. In her wake, Jack and Gervase rode side by side. They carved their way through with flashing swords, their horses' hooves smashing the skulls of any furred snakes that slithered underfoot. Whenever something dreadful threatened them, one of Clem's arrows pierced its throat.

On our left flank, half a dozen hunters scrambled up the fur of the huge hamster. To my horror, it began grabbing them with its claws and stuffing them into its cheek pouch. But abruptly, its mouth wrenched wide open. It strained its muscles, trying to close its jaw to no avail. One of the hunters in its cheek must have been Fred, turning the only available window into a somewhat larger window. A few of the victims clambered out, but one was stuck wrestling with the hamster's tongue until another made a gesture and the giant rodent sneezed. The last hunter tumbled out—covered in phlegm and saliva but otherwise no worse for wear—and was caught by the rest of them.

From that point on, I saw little more than was directly beside me. No doubt other hunters were doing battle using flowers, or frogs, or whatever abilities they had. But they were hidden beyond the wall of matted fur and glittering scales closing in around me. The noise was deafening—roars and screams, screeches and clangs. Charred carcasses, their wings still trailing smoke, dropped from the sky as Jonquil and her dragon did their work overhead. The stench was overwhelming, a choking mix of foul breath and burnt hair. There was a flash of tawny fur when the lion drew near. His spectacles flew from his face as he bit the neck of a skittering hyena beetle and broke its spine. The great cat leapt away again and vanished from my sight.

Sam stayed close to my side. He moved like a whirlwind, picking up a spider wolf and using it as a club to bash the creatures on every side. When it snapped its teeth at him, he threw it at a pair of bloated red lizards, and all three went hurtling over the edge of the bridge. His fists smashed into jaws. His feet lashed out to snap the legbones of anything with legs. Within moments, we were both splashed with blood and ichor.

Even more ichor than before, in my case. I vowed that if I survived this, at some point I would find a change of clothes.

I cursed myself for not thinking to borrow a weapon before

the battle began, when I had the chance. I guarded Sam's back as well as I was able. Something purple, bat-winged, and leech-like attached itself to his shoulder. I yanked it off, threw it to the ground, and crushed it under my bootheel. It shrieked like a furious teakettle as it died. I hoped it hadn't been venomous.

He flashed me a smile while he punched an eel crab in what might have been its face. It hardly seemed worth thanking me for—he'd probably saved my life a dozen times in the last minute; I'd managed to kill a bug.

I stomped on any small assailants I saw after that. I may have killed dozens that way, but it didn't affect their overall numbers much. An endless supply of creatures loped across the stone-giant bridge, slavering in anticipation of joining the bloodshed.

They leapt and crawled over the bodies of their dead, tearing into the guards defending the gates. The melee looked more like an overpacked crowd. Monsters and soldiers jammed together so tightly there was barely room to raise a sword.

But then there was a thinning of ranks in the monsters in front of us, a certain sense that their attention was no longer entirely directed toward the castle. And soon, there were large enough gaps for me to see what was hitting them from behind.

A green-skinned swordswoman with a claymore as long as her body, a tailor with a fistful of copper nails, and my younger sister with a whole flock of birds nesting in her hair. Behind them was an army of thousands. Their warriors thundered across the stone-giant bridge, crashing into the rear of those monsters left on it.

Bears and elk and squirrels and hawks. Foxes and rabbits and sparrows and voles. The animals of the forest had rallied to my sister's call, and they appeared to be very, very angry.

They smashed their way through the packed monstrosities, butting them off the bridge with antlers and horns, biting, tearing, or simply barreling through. And if you don't think a vole is particularly frightening, then you've never seen a few hundred of them claw their way up a creature's legs and commence chewing.

Their unnaturally made cousins fought back, but their line bent and broke under the onslaught. The hunters and soldiers continued to press them from our side. The creatures were caught between two armies, left with nowhere to escape except the sea. And I'd have bet anything that Calla had arranged for a greeting party of sharks and pikes in the water below. I was beginning to have hope the day would soon be won when the stone giants stood up.

Their monstrous allies and the forest animals alike showered off their backs into the bay. Calla and Liam and Gnoflwhogir fell along with them. I only had a short time to worry about their fate. The giants advanced on the castle, the bridge made of their bodies dissolving back into individual shapes as more and more of them broke away to join the march. They'd remained so still I had nearly forgotten them. I wondered what had caused them to join the battle now, at the cost of so much of their own army. The answer came soon enough.

The first of the great trees reached the edge of the island, the circle of its grasping limbs rising so high above the waterline that it overtopped the cliff. They had spent their time wading across the bay, and now they were here. Many of their crowns were on fire. Jonquil's dragon set yet another alight as it neared. They paid the flames no mind, having learned what negligible damage they would do. These were trees that could treat a lightning storm as beneath their notice, a forest fire as a minor inconvenience.

They gathered on all sides, making no effort to climb the cliff. But if the trees chose not to break the walls with their toppling weight, as I had feared, they had no need to. Their limbs had enough reach to rip the castle apart stone by stone. Or pluck us up into the air and tear us to pieces, one after another.

The stone giants began pulling themselves onto the bridge. Whoever the trees didn't slaughter, the giants would grind beneath their feet.

The rest of Angelique's army had never been important. An opening sally to tire us out and draw blood until the actual attack began. An attack that would ignore everything we threw at it, be it swords and arrows or ice and wind. The land itself, the rocks and the trees, had been roused to destroy us.

"I don't suppose," Sam said, "you could turn into another lake?" He had grabbed two of the remaining spider wolves, one in each fist, and bashed their heads together as they scrabbled at him.

"On a bridge?" I asked. Even if I succeeded, there'd be no point. "I'd drain into the sea and wash away."

He grimaced, tossing the spider wolves aside. "Then I guess we'll have to do this the hard way."

CHAPTER THIRTY-SIX

Clash of the Titans

The lion was the first to fall. He threw himself at a stone giant, claws extended, mouth open wide in a roar. The giant batted him aside like a child's ball, with a sickening crunch of breaking bone when the granite hand slammed into his body. I couldn't see where the lion fell, whether on the bridge or over the edge. I didn't know whether he was dead or merely injured. Either way, it boded poorly for the rest of us.

Harry skidded to a halt when a tree limb swung in front of her, rendering herself plainly visible for a bare moment as she stopped to reverse direction. But another writhing bough barred her way from behind, too, and a third to the side. Soon they formed a net surrounding her, drawing her ever closer to the gaping wooden maw beneath the tree's green glowing eyes. A whip-thin branch wrapped itself around her leg and yanked it off. Harry was no longer a vibrating blur, just a one-legged woman struggling to escape from a deadly trap. Arrow after arrow thudded into the tree trunk. They had no more effect than fleabites.

The air stilled as the howling wind ceased. I wondered what was happening to Kit, and Max, and the others. In only seconds, the tide of the battle had turned against us.

A slablike foot kicked Gervase's horse out from under him. He went tumbling to the ground. Jack slashed at the stone giant's leg but only dulled her blade. A ball of fire from overhead engulfed the giant as the dragon flashed past. A bolt of lightning followed, along with a deafening crack of thunder. They burned off the lichen mottling the giant's shoulders but achieved nothing else. Jack swung her sword again and again, trying her best to keep the creature away from the king as he rose unsteadily to his feet. She did not see the branches stretching nearer until one pierced her shoulder like a spear.

Sam bellowed with rage at the sight of his sister sliding from her mount, dark blood soaking her tunic. He charged the stone giant and slammed his shoulder into its ankle. A fissure broke open in the monster's leg, exposing paler rock beneath. A second blow knocked the giant off the bridge. A branch thicker than a pillar swung at Sam's head. He ducked beneath it. Another thrust at his chest, and he clapped his arms around it, stopping it cold. His muscles strained as he fought the might of the tree.

With a deep, resounding snap, the branch broke off. Amber sap dripped from the stump as it withdrew.

I hurried toward him, wanting to help but unsure how. Not even Clem's arrows were flying anymore. The dragon was nowhere to be seen. Sam had become the last line of defense. The only one standing in front of the ordinary soldiers, who had no more hope of victory against these creatures than they would have had against an avalanche.

They closed in around him. He put up a valiant fight, smashing bark and sending more of the giants toppling.

But then he tripped over a slithering branch. Before he could recover his footing, a stone fist cracked into his temple. He did not drop so much as fly backward, hurled in an ungraceful arch. He thudded to the ground almost at my feet.

I jolted to a halt. Blood oozed down the side of his face. It formed little rivulets that flowed off his cheek in a waterfall of slow, constant drips. His chest rose and fell raggedly, but his eyes didn't open, and he didn't stand up.

A second concussion, received before the effects of the first fully subside, can have severe consequences. The words fluttered across my brain, as emotionless and dry as a footnote in a medical text. *Swelling of the brain is sometimes seen even in young, healthy patients. This can lead to vomiting, seizures, and cardiac arrest. . . .*

Something red and scalding pulsed at the base of my skull, sending jarring shocks into my spine. Thundering stone feet and grasping tree limbs reached for me, but I heard nothing besides a shrill, clanging noise whose source I couldn't name.

I screamed.

Rock became crazed with cracks. Trees shuddered and twisted, showers of bark scattering across the castle walls.

I kept screaming, unable to stop even if I'd wanted to. The stone giants shattered, collapsing into heaps of gravel. The trees split and burst, toppling over with great splashes that threw water all the way up onto the bridge.

I screamed and screamed as gravel became pebbles and as pebbles became powder. I didn't need True Love's First Kiss anymore. Maybe I never had.

Maybe I just needed to be sufficiently motivated.

Sharp talons raked across my shoulders. I gasped in shock and then fell silent.

The clanging noise vanished. I nearly fell over. My body felt heavy, my limbs no longer responding as they should. The magic had drained out of me like water from a sieve. It had taken almost every last reserve of strength I had along with it.

I coughed in the dust that was all that remained of the stone giants. It filled the air in a thick mist, obscuring everything more than a few feet distant into smeary shadows.

A large, dark bird landed in front of me. Its legs and wings lengthened and thickened; its beak shrank and curved. Feathers transformed into hair and smoothed themselves into a gown.

"I'm impressed," Angelique said. "Truly, I am. I suppose that's the benefit of a rigorous magical education."

"What did you do to me?" I rasped.

"Interrupted your spell. Remember? I warned you."

I did my best to draw myself up straight. "You were too late. You've lost."

She quirked an eyebrow. "Have I? Who's left to defeat me? You can barely stand after that display."

"And what about you?" I asked. She was swaying on her feet. For all her bravado, if she'd been tired before, now she was on the point of collapse. "You've been pouring out spells the whole day. How's your head feeling?"

"I was faking the headaches."

I snorted. "No, you weren't. You're in agony." Her face was pinched, her eyes narrow with pain. She'd fooled me about many things, but I knew what someone looked like when their head hurt so badly they could barely see.

"It doesn't matter. I still have a few tricks up my sleeve." She held her hand out to me, palm up. She shook her arm, and a tiny creature with far too many legs skittered out from her sleeve and clung to her finger. "I'm not convinced you do anymore."

I wasn't confident I had the strength left to grow my hair a single inch. But surely someone remained with the power to oppose her. Where were my sisters and their spouses? I had to have stopped Angelique's creatures in enough time to save them. I must have. And she couldn't have killed every last one of the hunters. Could she?

Sam lay at my feet in mute contradiction to my hopes.

If the swelling causes the brain to herniate, then death is the most likely outcome, usually within minutes.

It was possible that as we spoke, his brain was squeezing itself out through the opening in his occipital bone, where the spinal cord enters the skull.

The tiny monster in Angelique's hand looked at me with dark, liquid eyes as she brought it closer.

In the swirling dust behind her, a shadow moved.

"I'm rather proud of this one," she said. "Scorpion mated with a blue-ringed octopus."

I carefully didn't look at the figure making its way toward us. I kept my eyes on the little abomination.

"What does it do?" I asked.

"First the sting causes paralysis, then it dissolves your internal organs. Very tricky to get it right. It took hundreds of tries."

"I think I could outrun you." I wasn't sure of that. My feet felt as heavy as blocks of lead.

Angelique shrugged. "Go ahead."

I didn't move. Whether or not I was capable of running, I had no way to carry Sam with me. There was still a chance he would live.

"Or you can stay and let it bite you, if you'd rather," she said. "It's a pity, really. You taught me so much. I honestly thought that you and I had something—"

She gasped. Her expression became one of perplexity, as if she had been presented with a riddle she couldn't quite solve. She glanced down at the steel blade protruding from her chest. When she opened her mouth to say something, blood came out, first in a dribble and then in a flood. Angelique dropped to her knees, slid off the sword, and fell over sideways.

"Stop trying to kill my boyfriend," the hunter behind her said.

Jack dropped her sword, and it clattered to the ground. Her tunic was so drenched with her own blood it looked red rather than green. After a bleary, unfocused look in my direction, she collapsed on top of Angelique.

Angelique remained motionless, not so much as an eyelash fluttering.

Stabbing had been her weakness after all.

CHAPTER THIRTY-SEVEN

Happily Ever After

First things first. The scorpion octopus had fallen from Angelique's hand. I eyed it warily.

The creature flopped in my general direction. It moved awkwardly, flinging its tentacles ahead and then rolling over them in a kind of drunken zigzag. A light breeze sprang up, stirring the dust. The little monster lost its balance and tripped over its own limbs.

I frowned. Was this really the deadly killer she'd described? She hadn't used it in any of her assassination attempts. Could it have been a bluff? A failed experiment or one not yet ready for use? Perhaps she'd wanted nothing so much as for me to panic and run.

I didn't care to find out. I stomped on it. It squished beneath the thick leather of my boot with a satisfying crunch. No sting penetrated the sole; I was not stricken with paralysis, nor did my internal organs dissolve.

The breeze had picked up, gradually dispersing the haze. I

wondered if Kit had survived or if it was simply the weather. Finding out would have to wait—I had patients in front of me. I took a breath to steady my nerves and tried to give the situation a calm assessment, as my mother and father had taught me.

Angelique was dead. Jack's sword had pierced straight through her heart. She hadn't even been slain by magic, no curse that might be reversed. There was nothing I could do for her.

While my impulse was to attend to Sam, there was hardly anything to be done for him. Either his brain was swelling inside his skull, or it wasn't. If it wasn't, he might wake and be fine in a couple of minutes. If it was, he would die.

That left Jack. I stumbled to her side and rolled her off Angelique's corpse. A quick initial examination told me little. Her blood-soaked tunic made it impossible to find the injury. I tore it open, ripping it from the neck to the bottom. If I had qualms about exposing her long-held secrets, I suppressed them. One of my earliest lessons had been that hesitation could cost a life.

She'd been speared just above the armpit. Blood flowed from her wound in uneven spurts, a bright red gout, then a trickle, then another gout.

Bright red blood in time with her heartbeat means an arterial bleed. Survival time without intervention depends on location and severity but can generally be measured in minutes. As a first step, stanch the blood flow by applying pressure.

With nothing to use as a disinfectant, I slid two fingers into the wound and pressed. The blood slowed and then stopped.

So far, so good. Now what? I needed proper equipment to manage more than that.

Jack's eyes cracked open. I was surprised she was conscious. The rate of bleeding suggested the artery had been nicked instead of severed, but even so, she'd been lucky to remain alive for so long. She must have had the stamina of a mule.

"What are you doing, witch?" she asked.

"Sorcer—" I stopped. It wasn't worth it. "I'm keeping you from bleeding to death."

"With a spell?"

"With my fingers."

"Will that work?"

"Maybe. Call it fifty-fifty?"

"Oh." She did nothing but breathe for a few moments, then added, "Thank you." Her eyelids drifted closed.

The dust had mostly cleared. I wasn't sure if anyone was looking in our direction, and I couldn't afford to turn around to check. Too much movement and I might let up on the pressure. She'd lost far too much blood already.

I was about to cry for help when a figure stumbled up to us. I risked a glance upward, worried it might be a monster that had somehow survived the battle.

Gervase stared at Angelique's corpse, a complicated expression crossing his face before he schooled it into stillness. His eyes then went to Jack, and he reddened as he took in her torn garments, averting his gaze for a moment before bringing it back. I didn't find the blood-soaked torso of a hemorrhaging patient particularly arousing myself, but Tailliz has some odd notions about feminine modesty.

He dropped to his knees at Jack's side and took her hand. The engagement ring she had never removed lay gleaming on her finger.

"Don't jostle her!" I snarled.

He ignored me. "Jack," he said. "Jacqueline. I love you. I have always loved you. Now that the kingdom is safe from . . . from my sister, I will accept no other as my bride, and, uh . . ." His voice trailed off, his eyes finding mine, acknowledging my presence at last.

"Let's sort that out later," I said. "Fetch me a—"

Jack snapped awake. "I stay on as general, too."

Gervase blinked. "What?"

"She's not in any condition to talk," I told him. "Really, you need to—"

"Queen and general," Jack growled, sounding more irritated than anything else. "The soldiers will follow me. I saved the kingdom."

Gervase sat back on his heels, her hand still held in his own. His lips were pursed in consideration. "The council of nobles will have a fit."

"They can bite my arse," Jack said. "Let them protest to their troops. See how far they get."

"The lion—"

"Important as this conversation might be," I said tightly, "I am currently preventing her blood from leaving her body *using only my hands.*" Was this the third inappropriately timed heart-to-heart of the day? Although to be fair, I'd been responsible for the ones I'd had with Gervase and Jonquil. "None of this will matter unless someone can bring me—"

A vast dark shadow passed over us, cutting off the sunlight. The dragon alighted, so close we were dimly reflected in its gleaming scales. Seawater cascaded off it. It flapped its wings to dry them, spraying all of us with a shower of droplets.

On its back was my entire family. Jonquil had rescued Calla, Liam, and Gnoflwhogir from the waves. Calla had so many wet, shivering animals clinging to her that she resembled a haystack made of damp fur. The rest were soaked to the skin, and they looked much the worse for wear from a staggering variety of cuts, bruises, and burns.

Liam leapt off the dragon before the others had gotten their bearings and rushed over to me, something held in his outstretched hand.

"Needle and thread?" he offered.

"Yes!" I grabbed them with my free hand. "I don't suppose you have any disinfectant, too?"

He passed me a bottle full of something strong enough to

make my eyes water. I smiled in thanks, and he gave me a quick nod and spun back around, holding out his arms to assist his wife and in-laws down.

"Now," I said, "if someone would just—"

"How can I help my sister?" Sam asked from behind me.

I permitted myself a fraction of a second to revel in the sound of his voice, to feel the knot in my chest unravel. He was awake. He was alive. Again and again he had risked himself at my side, and again and again he had returned to me.

But I tucked those feelings away for later. "Clean your hands with what's in the bottle, and then put your fingers right where mine are. Apply pressure." Considering who I was talking to, I added, "Normal human pressure. Don't dislocate her arm."

More blood that Jack could ill afford to lose leaked out when I removed my hand, but Sam's fingers replaced mine almost instantly. I threaded the needle, tied a quick knot, and used what was left in the bottle to disinfect everything I could.

"Don't die on me now, Jackie," Sam said.

"Doing my best," she grunted, wincing as I pierced her flesh and drew the thread through.

"We'll talk of your position at court later," Gervase said. "Once we know that you—"

"Queen and general," she said. "The other hunters get knighted. As their true selves."

"How are you even awake?" I muttered.

She grinned through the gore that spattered her face. "I'm relentless. That's my talent."

"That's not a talent," Sam said. "You're just too pigheaded to give up. On anything. Ever."

Jack turned to Gervase. "And no more women's wing."

"Stop moving!" Stitching her up was a tricky enough procedure as it was.

The king seemed to be rather at a loss. "My love, I don't say you're wrong. But . . . must we discuss it right at this moment?"

"Now's the perfect time. Darling." She gazed up at him with wide eyes. She would have been the complete picture of a smitten damsel if not for a certain strained tension at the corners of her mouth. And all the blood, of course. "I might be dying. Fifty-fifty chance. Ask the witch. You can't refuse a dying wish."

He rocked back as if slapped. "That's . . ."

"Fair?" she finished for him. "Promise me."

Gervase looked grim. "Can I? You remind me I am already on the verge of forsaking my last such promise."

"Oh, for goodness' sake," I said as I tried to pierce a lip of ragged flesh without tearing it further. "Obviously I'm not going to marry you. You love someone else. I love someone else." Sam's breath caught as my hand brushed against his. "Sam, move your fingers to the left, would you? No more than a hair."

"That's very well to say," Gervase replied. "But will not the queen of Skalla devastate my lands, and turn the forest into a desert, and leave me blind, penniless, and wandering the wasteland for the rest of my days?"

"Yes, if you refuse me. But you're not. I'm refusing you. King Gervase of Tailliz, I find I cannot honor our marriage pledge. I'm terribly sorry. It's not you, it's me. Any punishment will be mine alone to bear."

"And what will that punishment be?" Sam asked. "What will your stepmother do to you?"

"I'll handle her," I said.

"But—"

"I will." Somehow. "Your Majesty, I reject you entirely. Find someone else."

Gervase hesitated no more than a moment. "All right," he told Jack. "I promise. All of it."

"Took you long enough," she grumbled. "Fine. We're re-engaged."

"Then I am yours, and you are mine," Gervase said, "and nothing shall ever part us again."

Her hand tightened around his. I'd have taken it for a sign of passion, if it hadn't been accompanied by a sharp gasp while I finished off a stitch. Maybe it was romantic, even so. Certainly I'd have wanted Sam to be the one holding me if I lay bleeding.

"I love you," Gervase proclaimed.

"I love you more," Jack avowed.

"That is impossible. There can be no love that is greater than mine."

"My love *is* impossible. Love you more than . . . greatest amount of love . . . one person could feel." Her face was pale, and her eyes fluttered shut again. The pain and the blood loss were taking their toll, but she rallied enough to flash another grin at him. "I win."

His answering smile looked somewhat worried. "You cheated."

"You still. Lost." Jack's voice was a whisper, barely escaping her lips. "Suck on your loss. Loser."

I tied off a final knot and might have collapsed on the ground myself if Sam hadn't steadied me. "Done," I said. "Get her feet elevated above her head. And keep her warm. We'll need to monitor her lips and her fingernails. It's a bad sign if they turn blueish. But if infection doesn't set in—which is a big if, we need to watch for that carefully—then I think there's a good chance that she, uh . . ." My voice trailed off. Now that my attention wasn't entirely on my patient, I noticed there were a lot more people around us than when I had started. "I mean, that he . . ."

My family was there, of course, in front of a wet, sleeping dragon. Jonquil and Liam were looking at me with some concern—had they overheard my intention to defy my stepmother again?—while Calla's gaze seemed focused on the way Sam's arm was wrapped around my shoulders. Gnoflwhogir was prodding Angelique's corpse with her foot. I'm not certain she knew who Angelique was; stabbed bodies always attract my sister-in-law's attention.

But the rest of the hunters had also crowded around us—the quick count I made showing all of them alive, astonishingly enough—along with a host of soldiers. The commoners and noblemen from inside the castle were standing at the back of the pack, straining to see what was going on. Everyone, it appeared, had poured out onto the remains of the bridge and gathered around our little group, talking in a great confusion of murmured conversations punctuated by shouts and questions. Everybody was speaking at once, about the king, about the hunter he was now holding in his arms, about Angelique's body, about the dragon snoring tiny jets of fire, even about me.

While I tried to make sense of the cacophony, the lion limped forward, keeping his weight off a broken leg, muscling aside soldiers and huntsmen until he reached the king. His tawny fur was matted with blood.

Squinting nearsightedly, he glared at Jack, taking in everything revealed by the tunic I'd torn to shreds.

"*Now* do you believe this is a woman?" he asked Gervase.

A thousand rejoinders flitted across the king's face in an instant. In the end, though, he simply said, "Yes, Lion. You were right all along."

"Right about her, maybe," Sam muttered under his breath. "Wrong about so much else, it's impossible to keep track."

If the lion heard this at all, he chose to ignore it. He huffed a hot breath over us and hobbled away with the expression of immense self-satisfaction that only a cat can ever truly achieve.

PART IX

AFTER HAPPILY EVER AFTER

CHAPTER THIRTY-EIGHT

Picking Up the Pieces

Once the confusion that followed the fight had subsided, the first thing I did was procure a change of clothes. Half of my garments were so tattered they fell to shreds as soon as I unlaced them. My good red cloak was in need of repair again, and my leggings had become so stiff with filth I had to cut and peel them off, like paring a fruit. At some point during the process, I fell asleep.

I stayed on at the castle in the wake of the great battle, tending to Jack and other patients. And fending off the chirurgeon, who remained adamant that bloodletting was the proper treatment for every ailment, including blood loss. I tried to be as good a doctor as my parents. And perhaps a little kinder to my patients than my mother might have been.

There were casualties among the knights and archers, but on the whole the defenders had gotten off rather lightly, all things considered. Each of the hunters had an unlikely story of a hairbreadth escape from death, stories that grew more unlikely with each retelling. Jack had been the most severely wounded, although none of them had escaped unscathed.

Harry's reaction to her leg getting eaten took me by surprise. I sought her out the day after the fight and asked if she wanted my help acquiring and fitting a prosthesis to replace the limb that had been devoured by a tree.

She shrugged. "No, thanks. I'm used to it. I'll just wait until I grow another one." And then she hopped away.

My family embarked for Skalla after only a short rest. Calla needed to resume whatever quest she had been on when my plea for help had interrupted her, and Jonquil had duties as well. Not to mention they needed to return the seven-league boots, which were out on the briefest of temporary loans.

While Jonquil prepared the dragon for flight, Calla gave me a hug, the chipmunk curled up on her shoulder taking the opportunity to nibble on my hair.

"Take care of yourself," she said. "And come home soon."

"You don't think I should run as far as I can, as fast as I can?" I asked. "Maybe cross the sea? Or find a nice deep cave to hide in?"

She considered. "The kingdom of rabbits is surprisingly well protected. But you'd have to marry a rabbit."

"I'll take a pass on that one, then."

"We'll talk to the queen," Liam said. "Maybe we can convince her to go easy on you."

"Maybe." I wasn't optimistic.

"I hope she kills you," the mirror muttered from his belt. "If she doesn't, I will. I'll shatter on your floor and stab your toes with my shards. In death, I shall have my revenge." Similar dire pronouncements had issued from it nonstop since the battle, so it had been generally agreed that the mirror should be taken to Skalla and added to my stepmother's collection. I wished them joy of each other.

The dragon reared up, causing a minor panic on the castle

walls. "Time to go before they start pelting us with arrows again," Jonquil said. "No one wants a restless fire-breather lingering about."

"I could stay here," Gnoflwhogir offered. "In case anyone else wishes to murder Melilot. I can murder them first."

"I couldn't possibly part you from Jonquil for so long," I insisted hastily. Fortunately, she acquiesced without further comment, and soon they all departed on dragonback.

In the weeks that followed, when not preoccupied with medical care, I spent much of my time with Sam, who had made a full recovery. In fact, after enough time had passed that I judged my patients were all healing nicely and capable of surviving my absence, Sam and I sequestered ourselves in the first empty room we found. I was pleased to discover that after everything we'd been through, whatever reservations he'd held about sharing a bed before marriage were long gone.

We did not emerge for a day and a half. Except once.

"Where are you going?" Sam asked when I started putting my clothes on.

"I'm going to filch a better mattress from the women's wing. We're going to want to sleep sometime, and straw bedding won't make that easy for me."

"There's been little enough sleeping so far."

I smiled. "We can't keep doing this forever."

"Hm." He brushed his lips across my neck, and I considered taking my clothes right back off again. "We'll see."

When we came up for air, I was prepared for disapproval from the Tailliziani—I had a response ready involving peculiar foreign customs—but to my surprise, there weren't any comments. Well, none aside from Clem expressing surprise we hadn't made ourselves too sore to walk. I wondered if the pair of us were so far outside the local expectations that we had become effectively invisible—if they did not know what to make of us, so they elected not to make anything of us at all.

Change came slowly to Tailliz as the weeks turned into months. The refugees began to decamp back to the village, one small boat at a time launched from the end of the broken bridge. Meanwhile, stonemasons, engineers, and architects had assembled to begin repairs. Preparations for the royal wedding were also underway, albeit with a different bride. The wedding date was delayed to allow a suitable period of mourning for Princess Angelique. Gervase donned black and spoke little of her. No one discussed the fact that his bride-to-be had slain his sister.

The reforms Gervase introduced to fulfill his promise to Jack caused upheavals in the court. But Jack had not been mistaken about the loyalties of the troops. They would hear no word against her or the other hunters, and the nobles found themselves compelled to support the continued leadership of General Jacqueline, along with the knighting of the rest. Thus Detachable Leg became Sir Harriet, The Nose Blower became Sir Katherine, Hat On Ear became Sir Maxine, and so on. Sam simply became Sir Sam, and Clem insisted on being Sir Clem and said she would put an arrow "richt in th' lug" of anyone who called her Clementine.

I hoped it would not be long before any ill feelings about them were overcome by the obvious benefits they offered. Tailliziani shipping would surely profit from a knight who could generate wind at will, and the kingdom's architecture was already demonstrating the advantages of somewhat larger windows. But prejudice is not subject to common sense, so I supposed only time would determine which of the two would win out. If I were a betting woman, though, I'd have wagered on the outcome that favored the hunters.

One holdout for the old ways of Tailliz was, unsurprisingly, the lion. His complaints were relentless, and he interrupted every council meeting to air them. Which meant the few I was invited to, as a sort of general consultant on magic, dragged on endlessly. At least I was permitted to attend. The ban on women in the Great Hall had been one of the first rules to be disposed of.

"Haven't you read chapter fifty-seven?" he moaned for what must have been the twentieth time. "This proposal is directly contradicted by footnote seventeen!"

After several weeks of this, Gervase had reached the limit of his patience. "Then your book is in need of revision!" he snapped.

The lion tottered up to the throne, one of his forelegs still wrapped in a cast that smelled of piss and onions; he insisted on being treated by the chirurgeon. "In need of revision?" He peered at the king. His lost spectacles had not yet been replaced, so he thrust his muzzle close.

Gervase drew back from the lion's breath as politely as possible. "If reality opposes your book, then clearly it is your book that—"

"Are you," the lion rumbled, "commissioning a second edition?"

The king paused. "I . . . suppose?"

"Well, I don't know if I really have the time." The lion's eyes were agleam with excitement. "That would require a great deal of work. But I have accumulated new material over the years, and I suppose theories must be reexamined now and again. Perhaps I was overhasty in declaring humans a species of spider. They may be somewhat closer to frogs. . . ." With a three-legged leap, he sprang past the astonished nobles, presumably to begin work immediately.

"Frogs," I said. "Why? Because the humans who croak the loudest receive the greatest rewards?"

"I have no idea," the queen-to-be remarked from Gervase's side. She shifted uncomfortably in her chair; her wound was infection-free and mending well, but it still pained her. "Honestly, that went better than I expected."

"I'm not sure I'd agree," the king said. "We're going to have to read it once he's done."

Another pocket of resistance to change was much more surprising to me—the Yvettes and Yvonnes. A few of the younger ones came out of the women's wing to mingle with society, but most of them remained cloistered in spite of their newly inaugurated freedoms. Toward the end of my stay at the castle, I began to wonder why, so I made my way to the sewing circle to find out.

"Oh, you're back," Eldest Yvette said when I arrived, acting for all the world as if I had been gone for no more than a few unremarkable days. "I've heard tell you're a princess."

"Yes," I admitted. "I'm sorry for the deception."

She glowered at me. "You should have said. Princesses have no business using a spinning wheel."

So saying, she thrust a half-finished bonnet into my hands with the clear expectation that I would sit in my accustomed spot and commence chain stitching. So I did. And before I had a chance to ask any questions, one of the Yvonnes started a story.

"Once upon a time," she said, "when the world was younger and the air smelled a little sweeter, there was a young girl who lived in a village near a forest. Her grandmother, who loved the girl dearly, had given her a hooded cape of red velvet and warned her always to be wary of wolves. . . ."

I attended for a number of days, sewing and listening to folktales, before I gleaned what the difficulty was from snatches of conversation.

"All very well to say we can go," one grumbled on the third day, "but go where? And do what?"

"I don't think it's safe," said another.

"Princess Angelique could have told us whether—"

This last comment was silenced with a sharp glance.

"We are not to speak of her," said Eldest Yvette, "by royal command."

That caught me by surprise. I had noticed Angelique was seldom spoken of after her death, but I hadn't been aware Gervase had ordered silence.

The Yvettes and Yvonnes, I realized, had been cast adrift. No one had told them anything more than that they were free to leave the women's wing. No provision had been made to ease their departure or explain what was expected of them. The person they would have trusted to lead them had been cut down with a sword and accused of murder, and now they couldn't even discuss it.

I resolved to talk to Jack about helping them find their place in the kingdom; she wasn't from Tailliz, and I didn't think she'd realized there was any need for it. I certainly hadn't.

For my own part, I could, perhaps, do one thing for them—explain what Angelique had done and why. I was not one of Gervase's subjects, so I decided his decree did not apply to me.

And I had heard the tale from the princess herself.

"Once upon a time," I began. It was the first time I had joined the storytelling there. A head or two turned in my direction, but most of them continued spinning or sewing. No one stopped me, though, so I went on. "Once upon a time, when the world was younger and the laws were a little crueler, a child was born to a king and a queen. This was a great disappointment to the king and was considered a terrible waste of time and effort by most everyone in the land. The queen, you see, was getting on in years. So was the king, but no one really cared about that. . . ."

CHAPTER THIRTY-NINE

Fairy-Tale Wedding

Since I would be traveling by ordinary means, rather than on the back of a dragon, I had to wait until the mountain passes were clear before making the trip to Skalla—which meant I could justify delaying long enough to attend the royal wedding in the spring. Sam and I both wanted to see his sister married to her true love at last. In part because it would be the final proof that I wasn't the one getting married to him.

The castle was still under repair, and the wedding procession through the courtyard occasionally had to detour around unstable, roped-off areas. There was a brief downpour in the early afternoon, and everyone got damp, which made me feel somewhat smug. They should have listened when I suggested a backup plan in case of rain.

The ceremony as a whole was elaborate, opulent, and astonishingly dull. Jack appeared to have had no better luck requesting changes than I had. She'd been shoved into a dress with a train that required most of the other hunters to trail behind her holding it off the ground. It had a hem so tight she had to shuffle along, rather like the flightless black-and-white birds I'd sometimes found nesting on the plain of the trackless ice. She would have tripped if so much as a single pebble hadn't been cleared from the route, and suddenly I realized why the lion had been so certain peas on the floor would make an infallible woman detector. I would have to explain it to him, for the new edition.

When the interminable preliminaries were done with and the couple exchanged vows, the crowd applauded and cheered—loudly in the case of the assembled soldiers and villagers, but the nobility exhibited something closer to restrained politeness. I was pleased to see a few of the Yvettes and Yvonnes scattered about the crowd. More and more of them had been venturing out of the women's wing since Jack had begun consulting with them about their needs. Rehousing and retraining had been offered to those who desired it. And some had found themselves better suited to their new circumstances than they'd assumed; Eldest Yvette was already in popular demand as a storyteller.

The feast that followed the ceremony was as sumptuous as could be managed, considering the meager winter stores were at their lowest ebb. Decorative pastries had been made with the scant remains of the flour, sugar, and dried fruits. Thanks to the hunts, there was still venison, but the whole castle was thoroughly sick of venison by then. The chefs had done their best to supplement the game meat with whatever vegetables could be foraged in the early spring. Everyone was looking forward to the coming months, when more would be in season, and the eventual harvest that would presumably proceed unthreatened by horrible monsters. Even Sir Alexandra, the hunter who could eat anything, was tired of dining on rubble and twigs.

Sam and I took full advantage of the limited variety on offer. I was nibbling on the wing of a cake shaped something like a deformed gryphon when the king and queen detached themselves from a crowd of well- and ill-wishers and made their way over to us. This required considerable maneuvering and more than a bit of shoving from the hunters wrangling her train.

"Congratulations on your marriage, Your Majesty," I said. "And . . . Your Other Majesty."

"Hi. How's the cake?" Jack asked, eyeing the sculptured confection with skepticism.

"Awful," I admitted. "It's mostly fondant, and it's got raisins in it. Still makes for a nice change. Want some?" I offered her a forkful.

She took it, chewed, made a face, and kept chewing.

"You look bonnie," Sam told her.

Her face grew even sourer, and she mumbled something as she chewed that sounded vaguely like "Can't walk" followed by a rude word.

"I understand you'll be leaving us soon," Gervase said. He made a gesture that took in both Sam and me.

"Yes," Jack said, swallowing. "Since she was unable to steal my bridegroom, she's stealing my brother instead."

"Oh, hush," Sam said. "You know I had to practically beg her to take me along. Days and days of 'It's not safe!' and 'My stepmother is an evil sorceress-queen!'"

"Well, she is," I pointed out. Again. "You'll be in terrible danger."

"You, too. We're going together," Sam said firmly. "That's what couples do."

Small smiles lit on the faces of Jack and Gervase at that, and they twined their fingers together. The hero and heroine, content in their happy ending. Good for them. I could only hope the secondary characters in their story would do as well. No one ever bothers to mention the fate of the helpful companions or the ex-fiancées.

"It's about time, really," Jack told Sam. "I've had quite enough of you following me around like a lost puppy. Go have a romance of your own."

"I'll miss you, too," he answered, and leaned forward to kiss her on the cheek. She released Gervase's hand and embraced her brother tightly.

All things considered, maybe Sam had graduated out of helpful-companion status. He wasn't one of Jack's decoy duplicates anymore. And he was certainly my hero.

Speaking of the decoy duplicates, by this time the other hunters had abandoned Jack's train and pushed through the crowd to the table, considerably impeded by their billowy bridesmaids' dresses—in matching forest green, of course. It wasn't as surprising a sight as it might have been a few months earlier; several of them, although not all, had taken to wearing gowns or skirts when they weren't out hunting. I'd overheard a couple discussing how glad they were to be growing their hair out and how much of a relief it was to be perceived as women again. To which another had replied that the chance to have short hair and put on a pair of breeches was the whole reason they'd been so eager to run off with Jack in the first place. During the wedding procession, I'd noticed that one of the hunters—Jules?—had already cut, resewn, and modified their bridesmaid's dress until the bottom half had effectively been turned into a pair of wide trouser legs. I wondered if I was seeing a new fashion in the making.

They all pressed in close to us, a cluster of uncannily similar faces bidding their goodbyes to Sam and me. The masks were long gone by then, but I still had trouble telling most of them apart. The duchess's six siblings could have been the exact same person at slightly different ages.

"May the wind be ever at your back," one of them said.

"Keep warm," said another.

"I wish you a swift journey," said a third, who might have been standing on a single leg; the swathes of green skirts made it difficult to tell.

The one in the trouser dress handed me a rose and then

stepped aside to make way for one with tears streaming down her face. "I was wrong about you," she said. "This is so romantic." She pressed a small, beautiful frog into my hands. It was patterned like a harlequin with splotches of yellow, orange, red, blue, and green.

An overlapping chorus of farewells followed, which sometimes grew muffled as Sam insisted on hugging them all close, one after another. Just as that was quieting down, one of the hunters drew herself up, spat on the floor, and said, "Ah hawp ye twa eejits dinnae die oan th' road."

We left early the next morning, hungover but lighthearted. The bridge to the shore remained broken, so we took a skiff across the bay to the town. Travel to and fro had been a tremendous pain all winter, and more than one disgruntled engineer had asked whether it had been absolutely necessary for me to smash all the stone giants into powder rather than leave a few corpses around to use in rebuilding projects. I apologized and said that next time, I would refrain from taking such rash action and let everybody get murdered instead. That usually shut them up.

The horses the king and queen had gifted us were waiting in the town—a piebald stallion for Sam and for me, Poma. She'd been found cropping grass at the edge of the forest only a few days after I had turned into a lake. I fussed over her greatly as soon as we were reunited, which she calmly ignored, although she seemed to bear me no ill will for placing her in dangerous straits on our previous outing.

Though we were caught in bad weather more often than not, this time without even a carriage to keep it off our heads, the journey was pleasant. Partly because I'd had the foresight to bring along a bedroll stuffed with goose down, which meant I got a good deal more sleep than I usually did when I was traveling. Not all of Angelique's approaches to problem-solving had been terrible.

But mostly, it was a better trip because of Sam. I didn't mind getting drenched in a sudden storm quite so much if he was there to complain about it with me. I began to enjoy seeing the sunrises and sunsets, the wildflowers and the clouds, the ancient oaks looking embarrassed by their tiny baby leaves, bright green and delicate as lace. Sam was much better company than an entourage of animated teeth.

On perhaps our third night of travel, we took shelter beneath a willow tree, lying on the bedroll and listening to the patter of raindrops making their way from leaf to leaf in the forest. A stream burbled nearby, overfull with runoff snowmelt. In another day or two, we'd be out of Tailliz altogether, leaving the trees behind and crossing the plains. Making our way to the rolling hills that would slowly rise until they became the mountains of Skalla.

We'd lain in silence for some time before he asked, "Are you sure you want to go home?"

I propped myself up on my elbows but didn't reply for a moment. A little way off, Poma and the stallion companionably chomped on a patch of dandelion greens, heedless of the rain.

"I'll have to confront her sooner or later," I said at last. "Might as well make it sooner."

"Do you, though?" he asked, sitting upright and turning to face me. "What if we, I don't know, went across the sea?"

"To Ecossia?"

"Farther if we have to. To unknown lands."

East of the sun, I thought. *West of the moon.* I shook my head and lay back against him, feeling his warmth. "She came to me when I was a lake. When I was locked in the dungeon, too, I think. My sister found me in my dreams, and my stepmother is far craftier than Jonquil. I suppose there's a chance we'd escape her notice if we made our way back to the mirrored hallways, but . . . I don't much care for that idea."

"No. Especially not if we'd have to curse ourselves into comas."

"Dangerous to leave your body lying around like that," I agreed. "You might wake up being kissed by some weirdo."

"Ugh." He tossed a pebble into the stream. We listened to the plunk. "If your stepmother did come to find you, maybe you could fight her off."

"Me? I'm—"

"The mightiest sorceress I've ever seen."

My first impulse was to argue, to deny it. True, I'd defeated a sorceress of astonishing power no more than a few months ago, but there were a hundred reasons that didn't make me a match for my stepmother. I couldn't imagine her being foolish enough to exhaust herself, for one thing. And I'd had help fighting Angelique and her army. The rest of my family. The king's soldiers. A dozen hunters with supernatural powers.

But I'd done it. I'd screamed until rocks shattered and trees cracked.

"Hm," I said.

Sam stroked my hair, unconcerned that it was as wet as a dishrag.

"You know, you never did finish that story," he said. "The one about you."

"The story I told you had ended?"

"Aye. I'd like to hear the rest of it."

I was silent for a long minute. There was only the sound of the rain.

And then I said, "All right."

CHAPTER FORTY

The Tale of the Princess in the Tower

Once upon a time, when the world was younger and I was a little angrier, a wicked sorceress-queen imprisoned her stepdaughter in a tower deep within the trackless wilderness of Skalla. The tower had no doorway. The only opening in the sheer wall was a single small window at the highest possible point.

Every morning, Princess Melilot's stepmother would stop by the base of the tower and call up to her, "Will you not let me in?"

And Melilot would yell, "Do not mock me, you poisonous snake! You know full well there is no door."

Her stepmother remained unfazed by this. "Surely any daughter of mine can use magic to grant her visitors entry." Then she would turn and depart.

Melilot spent her first month in the tower raging.

She spent the second month moping.

She spent the third month crushed by unutterable boredom.

In the fourth month, she turned her mind to the problem at hand.

At first, she focused her efforts on mighty feats of magic that proved to be far beyond her capabilities. She attempted to summon a powerful gale to bear a visitor aloft to her window, but after weeks of effort, she managed to create no more than a light breeze.

She attempted to command roses to twine up the tower and form a ladder of vines that a visitor might climb—for she did not much mind the idea that her stepmother might prick herself on a thorn or two—but after many days, she was only able to make a few squat rosebushes sprout around the base of the tower. The rosebushes thrashed their canes threateningly, for they had been made in a rage, and the rage remained. But their reach was short, and they were certainly useless for approaching the window.

Melilot attempted to turn herself into a vast lake, as her sister Jonquil had once done, in the hopes that any visitors could swim to her window. It also crossed her mind that she might employ this method to flow out of the tower and escape. But it mattered not; at the time, she was able to become nothing greater than a puddle.

But one day, almost as an idle thought, she willed her hair to lengthen, and to her great surprise it responded, cascading first to her waist and then to her ankles before spilling onto the floor. Although she had mastered nothing else, she had at least mastered this.

Sam glanced down at me; my head was in his lap by that point. "Nothing else?" he asked. "You altered the winds and grew violent plants and turned yourself into water."

"Only a little bit."

"You transformed your entire body into liquid 'only a little bit'?"

"Can we argue about this when I'm done with the story?"

"All right." Sam sighed and gave me a wry grin. "At least I finally know why your hairstyle keeps changing."

"You never figured that out? I told everyone!"

"Not me. I thought you were just fashion-forward."

"So much that I stopped to redo my hair in the middle of a pitched battle?"

"Fashion doesn't wait on circumstance."

The next morning, when her stepmother called up to her, Melilot flung a great waterfall of hair out her window.

"I suppose that will work," her stepmother sniffed. "Brace yourself. This is likely to hurt." She dug her hands into the masses of brown curls and scaled her way up the tower.

Once the queen was safely inside, Melilot pulled her endless length of hair back through the window and massaged her aching head. Hair climbing, she reflected, was unlikely to become a popular mode of transportation.

"Might I have visitors now," she implored her stepmother, "since I have fulfilled your wishes?"

"Indeed you may," the queen conceded. "And here I am."

Melilot scowled. "I had hoped I could see my sisters."

"Your sisters are off on the quest you refused to undertake. When they return, perhaps I will allow you to see them, if you find some way to let them in that's more sensible than this hair nonsense."

Melilot was deeply incensed and shouted bitter curses as soon as her stepmother had left the tower and was well out of earshot.

Thereafter, the queen came to visit every morning, shouting, "Melilot, Melilot, let down your hair!" After she climbed up, she would stay to chat, drink tea, and bring news from the world outside, including the fact that the invading army was pressing ever deeper into Skalla—

"The what, now?" Sam asked.

"There was an enemy army attacking Skalla at the time. I'm sure I mentioned it in the first half of the story."

"Did you? I don't remember that."

"Well, to be fair, there's been a lot going on since then."

Melilot was surprised by how much time the queen was spending with her given the dire situation. Nevertheless, her resentment toward her stepmother grew with each passing day, especially since the hair climbing continued to be awkward and irritating, although much less painful once Melilot came up with the idea of winding it around the window handle first.

Then one afternoon, nearly a year into her imprisonment, a voice other than the queen's called her name from the base of the tower. She stuck her head out the window and saw a man she had never met who was dressed in the clothing of a prince.

"Melilot, Melilot!" he thundered at the top of his lungs. "Let down your hair!"

Unsure what to make of this, Melilot wound her hair around the handle and tossed it out.

"Who in the world are you?" Melilot interrogated him. "And why have you come here?"

"A few nights past, while riding through the wilderness, I spied you at your window," he cooed as he made his way up. "I immediately fell in love with you from afar. However, seeing as your tower has no doorway, I despaired of ever finding a way to enter and meet you. Each night since then, I have approached to admire your beauty and curse my lot. But today, I chanced to arrive in the morning and saw a mysterious woman ascend the walls by means of your glorious hair. And I vowed I would do likewise." He squeezed through the window and bowed before her.

Melilot, as you might recall, was sixteen years old, so she believed every word he said. Soon the prince won Melilot's very first kiss. Not long after that, he won even more.

A week passed by with her stepmother visiting every morning and the prince stopping by each afternoon. He spoke of love, and he frequently described the future life he planned for them together in the distant kingdom he left curiously unnamed. He paid her many compliments, especially for the long and beautiful locks of her hair. They broke off such talk only to curse the queen for imprisoning Melilot in the tower and mistreating her throughout her life. She confessed her fury at her stepmother as she had never done before, not even to her sisters.

All the while, his whispered words evoked heady fantasies in Melilot's mind—a future far from Skalla, in which she would no longer be at the mercy of the queen's whims. Soon enough, Melilot wanted nothing more than to escape the tower and run off with him.

"A ladder of sufficient height would be too bulky for my horse. But perhaps I could bring you a length of silk each time I arrive," the prince proposed. "You can weave them into a rope in secret, and when it's ready, you shall descend it, and then together we will ride away from this place."

Melilot was puzzled. "Wouldn't it be easier just to bring a pair of scissors? We cut off my hair, tie a knot, and both climb out?"

"My idea would make a more thrilling story," the prince huffed.

"But with mine, we could leave earlier—as soon as tomorrow night!"

The prince hesitated and bit his lower lip, weighing his words before he allowed them forth. "I perceive one great flaw with either plan. Is not your stepmother a powerful sorceress?" he pointed out. "No matter when we leave, would she not bend the very elements themselves to hunt us down and capture you once again? I care little for my own life, but I would not see you imprisoned for the rest of your days."

"That is true," Melilot acknowledged. "What, then, should we do?"

"I can see no other option. We must kill your stepmother."

Melilot blinked. "Kill my stepmother?" she echoed.

"Tomorrow, when I come to your tower, I shall come armed!" he attested. "I will stay the night, until the queen comes to see you in the morning. While you toss down your hair, I shall hide by the window, and as she comes through, I will cut off her head. The very sword we use to slay her shall serve to shear off your hair and provide our escape."

He gave her a kiss and departed until the morrow, leaving behind nothing but the memory of his words.

The following morning, when the queen came to visit, she found Melilot curiously silent. She was used to hearing, at the very least, barbed rejoinders from her stepdaughter and did not know what to make of this uncharacteristic reticence. After a few minutes of one-sided conversation, the queen frowned. "What is amiss?"

Melilot did not look up from her teacup. "I'm pretty sure I've been seduced by the leader of the invading army."

The queen raised her eyebrows. "You've been what?"

It was the first time her stepdaughter could ever recall the queen looking surprised.

"He's been stopping by every afternoon," Melilot continued, each word dropping from her lips like a leaden weight. "I suppose he learned there was little love lost between us and sought me out to see what advantage he might gain. He plans to assassinate you when you arrive tomorrow."

"Ah." The queen finished her tea and set the cup in the saucer with a clink. "Then I imagine we shall have to deal with that today."

"I'm sorry your first boyfriend turned out to be a deceitful murderer." Sam laid his hand over mine.

I laced our fingers together. "It wasn't great. At least he didn't get me pregnant."

That afternoon, the prince came at the appointed time. "Melilot, Melilot," he rhapsodized as usual, "let down your hair!" When the mass of curls came tumbling down the side of the tower, he scrambled up, a great sword strapped to his back.

As he approached the window, however, Melilot was nowhere to be seen. Her hair, he saw, had been snipped from her head and knotted to the window handle. Almost as if his plan had already been enacted. But it proved to be someone else's plan entirely. For waiting for him within the tower was the queen.

"I don't believe we've been formally introduced," she greeted him as he dangled below her, clinging to the rope of hair, "but I hear you've been seeing my daughter."

The prince reached for his sword, but before he had a chance to draw it, the queen undid the knot that held the hair in place.

Hidden in the wasteland nearby, Melilot watched him scream as he plummeted down and down and down, landing in the rosebushes Melilot had grown at the base of the tower with her magic. They cushioned his fall to the extent that he did not die, but they thrashed and attacked him, the wicked thorns piercing his eyes. Cursing his fate, he stumbled away blind into the vast wilderness surrounding the tower, and for all anyone knows, he wanders there still.

But it is far more likely he died there, lost and alone.

Melilot thought her stepmother, in her anger at the princess's foolishness, might cast her out to wander the wilderness as well. But she did not. Instead, some days later, freed from the tower, Melilot gazed out from a palace balcony while her sister Jonquil routed the leaderless enemy soldiers almost singlehandedly, mounted on the back of a dragon. The quest to retrieve a dragon's toenail had been fulfilled, and the result was a complete victory over the opposing army.

From behind her, as the dragon breathed fire on the invading troops, she heard her stepmother's voice.

"I hope," the queen whispered, "you have learned something from this."

Melilot laughed bitterly. "I have learned I will be punished if I disobey you. I have learned I am weak in magic and easily deceived. And I have learned I am the least of your children. Is that the lesson you sought to teach me?"

"No." The queen seemed to be speaking directly into Melilot's ear, so quietly she could still scarcely be heard. "But at least you have finally called yourself my child."

Melilot whipped her head around.

But the queen had already vanished, as if she had never been there at all.

My story lapsed into silence. Sam held me close until we both fell asleep to the rustle of leaves in the soft spring rain.

CHAPTER FORTY-ONE

Sweet and Savage Clover

"So," Calla said, "we've been dropping hints for the past few weeks—"

"Subtle hints," Liam added.

"—that we think she should go easy on you. That it wasn't your fault, and you can hardly be blamed if Gervase was in love with someone else."

"But also that it wasn't his fault."

"Or anyone's fault, really, except maybe the evil princess's, since she's already dead."

Liam's thumbs were tucked into his pockets, his fingers tapping fretfully against his legs. Although his discomfort might have been attributable to the swarm of bees clustered around Calla's head. "We tried not to push the evil-sorceresses-are-the-problem thing too hard, though," he said. "We thought that might, um, backfire."

They'd met us in the gardens at the base of the palace. They must have been keeping an eye out because Sam and I had barely dismounted before they ran up to us, already spouting plans before we had a chance to so much as say hello. It was a bright, clear day, and the gardens were in full spring blossom, the pansies and daffodils aglow with color, the air scented by rosemary and mint. Scattered cherry blossom petals dusted the paths. A few of the nearby beds had been planted with white or sweet clover to rest the soil.

Calla had placed a few flowers in her hair, and a cloud of bees hovered over them contentedly. Liam was brave enough to stay within striking distance, but Sam's stallion had backed away, pawing at the ground nervously. Sam murmured soothing nonsense in the horse's ear to calm him down. Poma, who had judged the bees to be a less noteworthy threat than murderous stone giants, regarded the scene with tranquil disinterest. But for my part, I decided to forgo giving Calla a hug.

There was a rustle in the bushes nearby, and Jonquil and Gnoflwhogir emerged from one of the narrow, winding pathways, cherry blossoms clinging to their shoes.

"We've been explaining to Mother that it wasn't your fault—" Jonquil began.

"I think we got the gist of it," I said. "How's it been going?"

There was a long pause, filled with the buzzing of bees, while the four of them eyed one another.

"I have a backup plan," Gnoflwhogir said.

"Does it involve stabbing?" I asked.

She looked affronted. "You think this is my only idea? Of course not stabbing."

"Sorry."

"First, I will light everything on fire—"

"Maybe I should talk to her," I said, "before we try anything too rash."

Gnoflwhogir sniffed and swatted at a bee that had ventured too close. I flinched in reflexive sympathy, but it didn't sting her. Maybe it didn't dare.

Sam had managed to calm his horse. "Do you want me to go with you?" he asked.

"I think I should face her alone," I said. "But I wouldn't mind if there was someone waiting for me outside the door." I took a steadying breath. "Shall we?"

"Wait." Liam plucked a sprig of clover off a stalk and pressed it into my hands. "Take this."

It was, I saw, the rarer four-leaf kind. I twirled it between my thumb and forefinger. "And what will this do?"

"Do?" He looked surprised. "Nothing, hen. It's for good luck."

"So," Gnoflwhogir said, "once the fire is lit, I will shout, 'Look! An invisible army is attacking!'"

"Darling, we've talked about this." The fraying patience of Jonquil's voice suggested it had been discussed many, many times. "How could you see an invisible army?"

"You can't. That's the point!"

Sam and I climbed up the stairs that wound back and forth outside the palace, inching our way up to the dizzying height of the main gate. The others stayed below to talk Gnoflwhogir out of her ill-advised rescue plan. We left them mid-argument, my sister-in-law doggedly lighting and relighting a torch even though Jonquil summoned a wind to blow it out every time.

I ran my hand along the smooth stone of the walls. Unbroken and unmortared, carved out of the mountain in a single piece. As familiar as everything was, I felt distanced from it all, like I was visiting a place I hadn't seen since childhood. This was hardly the first time I had returned to the palace after months away. But this time, everything seemed irrevocably changed.

"WHO DARES TO BEG FOR AN AUDIENCE WITH—"

"It's me," I told the guards.

"OH, HI, MELILOT," Humba yelled. "LONG TIME NO SEE."

"AND WHO'S THIS DELICIOUS MORSEL?" Femus's single eye looked Sam up and down. "MIND IF I STEAL A BITE?"

"YES, INDEED," Humba agreed. "WOULDN'T MIND GRINDING HIS BONES TO MAKE MY BREAD."

Sam cracked his knuckles. "Try it. We'll see who ends up a loaf of sourdough."

"OH, I LIKE HIM," Femus said.

I put a hand on Sam's shoulder. "Settle down. They're joking. They don't eat people anymore."

Sam looked at me askance. "Anymore?"

"Is Her Royal Unpleasantness inside?" I asked hastily. The last thing I wanted was for a fight to break out between Sam and the ogres. *Although,* I thought rather smugly, *if it came to that, I'd put my money on Sam.*

"SHE'S BEEN EXPECTING YOU," Humba told me. The ogres hauled open the massive doors, which made their usual earsplitting screech as they scraped against the floor.

I sighed. "Of course she has. Play nice while I'm in there. Talk about, um, stuff that strong people talk about."

"WHAT DO YOU BENCH?" Femus asked obligingly.

"Horses, usually," said Sam. I could tell he was distracted, his gaze following me as I slipped through the doorway.

"DO YOU TRACK YOUR MACROS? EVER SINCE I STOPPED DEVOURING HUMAN FLESH, I'VE BEEN HAVING TROUBLE GETTING ENOUGH PROTEIN—"

The doors were pulled shut behind me with a dull, reverberating boom.

Most of my confidence evaporated as I crossed the wide gulf of the throne room. My bootheels clicked on the mosaic tiles, the images of teeth and eyes and scales, bone white, night black, corpse blue, pus yellow, the colors as vivid as the day they were set into the floor. In the distance, a figure waited, silent and still on the obsidian throne. I rubbed the four-leaf clover between my fingers, hoping it really was lucky. It released a pleasant scent, like hay or new-mown grass. Sweet clover. Melilot.

Had I been overhasty in refusing Gnoflwhogir's offer of a rescue should it all go wrong? Or for that matter, rejecting Sam's suggestion that I never come back to Skalla in the first place? We might have tried, at least—done our best to hide from her. Perhaps I could have convinced a raven to conceal us in an egg, or a fish to swallow us whole, or a fox to turn us into sea hares. I'm sure it would have taken my stepmother at least a day to find us.

Hiding in an egg is extremely uncomfortable anyway. Don't even ask about the smell of fish innards or the exceedingly dull daily routine of a sea hare.

I had, somehow, walked the entire distance to the throne and stood at the point where I should prostrate myself before her. My knees nearly flexed out of automatic habit, but I forced them still. This time, I would face her standing upright.

After a few moments of awkward silence, the queen remarked, "You're very bold today."

Be bold, be bold. But not too bold. How bold was just bold enough? "Why not? You're going to punish me for my disobedience anyway."

Her head inclined a bare fraction. "You have returned to me unmarried, in defiance of my direct instructions."

"I have."

"Your sisters tell me I should be merciful. That you are blameless. That King Gervase is blameless. That my plans have been stymied, yet somehow no one is to be held accountable. Is that what you say?"

"No."

There was a downturn at the edges of her lips, hardly a movement at all. "Then what do you say? Are you the one at fault? Should you be punished?"

Be bold. "Try it," I said. "We'll see who ends up a loaf of sourdough."

She blinked. "What?"

"I mean, um . . ." I coughed. "It was my decision not to marry Gervase. I don't accept your right to judge me for it, though. So if you want to test your powers against my own, go right ahead."

I tensed, readying myself.

My stepmother's eyes narrowed. "Are you certain about this?"

"No," I admitted. "But I've traveled far and survived a great deal, and the last time a powerful sorceress went against me, she died, and her works crumbled into dust." I took a deep breath and curled my fingers into fists. "Take your chances if you dare."

She nodded gravely and leaned back against her throne. "Well. It's about time."

I frowned. "About time for what?"

She relaxed, looking for all the world like she was sprawled across an armchair. "For you to start living up to your potential."

"For . . . No." I shook my head. "Don't even try it. You can't possibly be claiming everything you did was for my own good."

"Of course it was. If you've traveled far, who sent you there? If you've survived a great deal, who put you in harm's way? Who pushed you toward that powerful sorceress you defeated? When you refused to grow in your magic, who locked you in a tower until you had no choice? Why would I have done any of that, if not for your benefit?"

"Because you're spiteful and cruel!" I shouted. My hair rose on an invisible wind, lengthening and reaching for her, sparks crackling from it. "And manipulative, and . . . and I do not believe you imprisoned me because you were *trying to be a responsible mother*!"

The throne room shook. Crevasses broke open in the floor, radiating out from where I stood. The sharp scent of sulfur puffed up from below. Someone started pounding on the stone doors.

The queen smiled thinly. "You're calling me your mother now? I suppose that's better than the soup bowl to the face I got the last time I saw you."

I stared at her. The rumbling and shaking stopped.

I dropped six inches to the ground—I hadn't noticed I'd been floating—and nearly twisted my ankle. The stench of sulfur lingered in the air.

Had she been hurt I wouldn't call her my mother?

"Are you planning to continue?" she asked. "Or does this sorcerous duel stop at the need to make repairs to the floor?"

I hadn't thought of her as someone who could be hurt.

I'd never really seen her as a person. More a force of nature, like a storm or a forest fire. A disaster that struck without reason or care. Omnipotent and merciless.

I'd told myself a story about a mother and father who were perfect in their loving kindness and a wicked stepmother driven purely by malice. But it hadn't been a fair comparison, because it wasn't true, not completely. My parents, I was coming to realize, had their flaws. And my stepmother was more complicated than I'd been willing to admit.

There were many accusations I could fairly level against the queen. She was indeed manipulative. She was also ruthless, autocratic, intransigent, demanding, and overly secretive. But that wasn't the whole of it.

Ogres in her kingdom no longer ate human flesh. The fairies no longer stole children. The people of Skalla were peaceful and prosperous, and while they might quake in terror at the thought of stealing a peach from her garden, my father had escaped with his sweet clover unscathed.

I had seen what a truly mad and evil sorceress looked like, and it wasn't the woman on the throne in front of me.

"Locking someone in a tower is terrible pedagogy," I said. "Just the absolute worst. Bitter resentment doesn't encourage learning."

"Nothing else was working." She sounded almost plaintive. Less the almighty queen, more the woman who'd fallen for the doctor next door and found herself raising a rebellious stepdaughter. A memory stirred of a voice in a prison cell. *Never good enough for you, no matter what I do.*

"What wasn't working?" I asked. "Sending me off on an absurd quest to trap lightning in a bottle? Or to find an acre of land between the sea and the shore?"

"Yes."

I rubbed the bridge of my nose and sighed. "Queen Hellebore." When was the last time I had called her by her name? I couldn't remember. "Maybe you could have asked for my help, if you needed it."

Because of course she had. She'd needed, and wanted, my help, along with Jonquil's and Calla's. It was obvious now that I'd given it a moment's thought. She acted as if she were holding the kingdom together all by herself, but then she sent her children off to find dragons and tooth guards and magical tools. Even my latest misadventure had deposited another magic mirror, obnoxious though it might have been, into her arsenal of enchanted artifacts.

"That is the last thing I could have asked for." The words came out slowly, as if reluctant to leave her mouth. "A queen cannot ever show weakness."

"Being terrifying isn't the same thing as being strong."

"It is for me." She fixed me with her gaze. It was as disconcerting as always. "I am not only a queen but a sorceress. I will be seen as terrifying whether I wish it or not. No other path is open to me. So I must be as terrifying as possible, if I am to rule."

"To rule," I repeated flatly. "So why were you like that with your daughters, too?"

The slightest of tremors crossed her face, a crack in her façade, like stone splintering. Then it was gone. I'd never noticed how much effort it took her to steady those dark, carved-basalt features—Jonquil's face with Calla's eyes. What had it cost the queen to keep up that front at all times? I knew what it had cost me.

"If you couldn't ask for my help," I told her, "then you might have tried asking what I wanted. Or showing I could trust you. Or just letting me miss my mom."

She didn't answer.

Maybe she wasn't driven by spitefulness and cruelty. Maybe it was more complicated than that. But whenever I'd pushed against her, the only thing she'd known how to do was push back harder. She could see a thousand thousand futures, and she'd still had no idea what to do with a grieving seven-year-old girl.

I turned on my heel and walked away. "I'm leaving."

"I haven't been the worst of mothers," she called out after me. "I did my best. Have you forgotten our morning teas together? Or how I saved you from that prince?"

Even now, she wouldn't acknowledge the whole truth of it. "You misremember, my queen. I saved *you.*"

"What exactly are you leaving?" she asked, speaking more softly. "The throne room? The palace? Skalla?"

I paused for only a moment. "I don't know yet."

When I reached the bronze doors, they had already been wrenched halfway open. On the other side, Sam had Femus in a choke hold with one arm and was fending off Humba's mighty fists with the other. The ogre froze mid-swing when I stepped forward.

"Are you all right?" Sam asked.

"Fine," I said. "Is there a problem here?"

"Oh, no," he reassured me, releasing Femus, who gasped with relief. "Not anymore, at least. They wouldn't let me in when the palace started shaking. They were very nice about it, but—"

"STANDING ORDERS," Humba screamed apologetically.

"NO ONE IS TO INTERRUPT WHEN THE QUEEN IS IN PRIVATE CONFERENCE."

Although all three looked rather bruised, there didn't seem to be any hard feelings; the ogres spent the next few minutes thanking Sam profusely for his tip about whey protein. I suspected they'd rather enjoyed the break in their routine.

It wasn't until we were halfway down the stairs, well out of earshot of any curious eavesdroppers, that Sam asked, "How did it go?"

"Surprisingly well," I told him. "I'm not going back to the tower. She and I are both still alive. And . . . I understand her a little better than I used to, for what it's worth."

"Good."

"Yes, I thought so, too."

My stepmother wasn't all-knowing, after all. And far from all-powerful. Which meant that she wasn't the only person I'd been comparing to an illusion. Suddenly, I had a lot less to live up to.

It was very freeing.

"So," Sam said, "what happens now?"

I contemplated my answer as we made our slow way to the garden. If I wasn't obeying the queen's whims any longer, I could go anywhere. Do anything. If I undertook quests in the future, they would be of my own choosing. And they would not involve trapping lightning in a bottle. That one nearly killed me. I can still taste copper on my tongue during bad storms.

"I might like to travel for a while," I said. "Visit a few places without any royal commands compelling me."

"You hate traveling. You complained about the rain the whole way here."

"I did not."

"You did."

"All right, yes, I hate traveling," I admitted. "But I do like reaching a destination. Want to show me around Ecossia? I've never been there."

Sam smiled. "I'd love to. And where after that?"

"Who knows?"

"East of the sun and west of the moon?"

"It's not that great," I said. "The trolls aren't good company, and the food is terrible."

I would come back to Skalla someday, I had no doubt. My family lived there. Perhaps it would just be for a visit, if I fell in love with Ecossia's windswept moors as strongly as I'd fallen for Sam. Or perhaps we'd return to Skalla after years away and clean out the little cottage where my father and mother had lived. I could offer my skills as an apothecary. Or a sorceress.

"Once upon a time," I murmured, "when the world was younger and the horizon was a little wider, a princess ran off with a huntsman into the great and boundless unknown. . . ."

"Sounds like an intriguing story," Sam said.

"It does, doesn't it?"

I linked my arm through his and clutched the four-leaf clover in my hand. Sam and I stepped into the garden, where the rest of my family waited to hear my tale.

It didn't feel like I was walking into happily ever after. Not exactly. Those are reserved for the ends of stories, and this was the beginning.

Author's Note

When the first pandemic lockdown began in 2020, I thought it wouldn't be much of a problem for me. I already worked from home. And my writing had been going well; my debut novel, *Love Bites,* was about to be published, and I'd just finished the final edits on the sequel, *Bleeding Hearts*. It didn't seem like anything would keep me from working as usual.

I hadn't counted on the, you know, creeping existential dread.

After months without writing a single word, I decided to start reading fairy tales. Why fairy tales and for what purpose? I wasn't entirely sure. At least it was doing something instead of nothing. My vague plan was pretty much:

Step one: Read fairy tales.

Step two: ???

Step three: Write book.

I began with the Grimm brothers' collections, going through them story by story. And they were wonderful. Wild, weird tales, many of them with roots thousands of years old, dating back to the earliest storytelling traditions. Some I'd known for almost my entire life, and some I'd never heard of before—including one called "The Twelve Huntsmen."

I was immediately fascinated by it. Identical duplicates! Queer subtext! Gender tests set by a talking lion! I found myself particularly intrigued by the most minor character in the story, a princess who's sent out to get married and then unceremoniously sent back home again, without having a chance to say a single word about it. What, I wondered, did she make of the bizarre scenario she'd been thrown into? So I started writing her story, which eventually became *This Princess Kills Monsters.*

In the end, dozens of fairy tales from many different sources were referenced in one way or another within this book. The biggest influences by far, however, remained what I began with—the classic German folktales collected and edited by Jacob and Wilhelm Grimm in the volumes of *Kinder- und Hausmärchen* ("children's and household tales"), first published in 1812 and continually revised and expanded until 1857. It should be noted that the Grimm brothers gave no credit to the women who told them the stories, although they are now known to have included Henrietta Dorothea Wild, Wilhelmine von Schwertzell, Marie Hassenpflug, Jeanette Hassenpflug, Amalia Hassenpflug, Dorothea Viehmann, and Jenny von Droste-Hülstoff, among others.

Several Grimm fairy tales are recounted, adapted, expanded, or affectionately satirized over the course of *This Princess Kills Monsters.* "The Twelve Huntsmen" ("Die zwölf Jäger" in German) is, as already mentioned, the inspiration for the entire text. More directly, it serves as the basis for the chapter titled, "The Tale of the Twelve Hunters, as It Has Been Inaccurately Recorded." Similarly, I took the Grimm story "How Six Men Got On in the World" ("Sechse kommen durch die ganze Welt") and split it in two pieces, which were then transformed into "The Tale of How Two Became Six" and "The Tale of the Duchess's Challenge." The best-known tale I adapted was "Rapunzel" (titled the same in both German and English), which became both "The Tale of Melilot" and "The Tale of the Princess in the Tower." The partial story Eldest Yvette tells is an only slightly altered version of "The Six Servants" ("Die sechs Diener").

I added to and embellished the original stories significantly; the Grimm brothers' version of "The Twelve Huntsmen" is only about a thousand words long. I also changed the plots and characters however I needed to fit the book I was writing and cut significant sections when necessary. There's a long digression about filling a giant bag with treasure in "How Six Men Got On in the World" that I didn't have any reason to include. However, many of the basic plot elements in the "storytelling" chapters of the book come directly from the Grimm tales, and there are more than a few passages in those chapters where the language remains close to the original German (so, for example, "a room that had an iron floor, and iron doors, and windows set with iron bars" can be traced back to "einer Stube, die hatte einen Boden von Eisen, und die Türen waren auch von Eisen, und die Fenster waren mit eisernen Stäben verwahrt").

Since my German is rather rusty—I spoke it well enough to get by when I lived in Germany over a decade ago, but I haven't had to use it regularly since—I'm also indebted to the marvelous nineteenth-century English translations of the Grimm stories by Margaret Raine Hunt, published in 1884 under the title *Grimm's Household Tales*. Several of her turns of phrase have made their way directly into this book, most notably "face, figure, and size" for the German "Angesicht, Gestalt und Wuchs" but also "you shall dance about in the air" ("sollt ihr sämtlich in der Luft herumtanzen") and "I will care for it like a mother" ("ich will für es sorgen wie eine Mutter"), as well as various other small phrases and words—sometimes simply because, for instance, "small mountain" is really the only reasonable translation for "kleiner Berg," so we both made use of it.

Both *Kinder- und Hausmärchen* and *Grimm's Household Tales* are works in the public domain.

Acknowledgments

My first thanks go to the collectors, editors, and tellers of classic folktales and the authors of classic literary fairy tales. Of those whose names are known, there are far too many to list here, but some of the ones whose work had an influence on this book are Jacob and Wilhelm Grimm (and the uncredited women who told them the stories—see the author's note for some of their names), Margaret Raine Hunt, Charles Perrault, Madame d'Aulnoy (Marie-Catherine Le Jumel de Barneville), Hans Christian Andersen, Joseph Jacobs, Andrew Lang, Gabrielle-Suzanne Barbot de Villeneuve, Jeanne-Marie Leprince de Beaumont, Giambattista Basile, and Alexander Nikolayevich Afanasyev.

No book is written in a vacuum, and there are innumerable people who helped this one along the way. Many, many thanks are owed to:

My parents, Mark Herman and Ronnie Apter, who read me my very first fairy tales.

Everyone who offered me critiques and advice while the

book was in early drafts. Beth Biller, who was the first person other than me to see any of it. Rogue Writers Edinburgh, especially the late Peter Muego. Manu Shadow Velasco. Sarah Lawrie, for her help with Scottish dialect. And throughout the writing process, the members of the Happy Fun Sunday Writers Group—Armarna Forbes, Whitney Curry Wimbish, and Jack Jackman.

My agent, Michelle Hauck, for support and enthusiasm that began when she started reading the prologue and never flagged. Also Victoria Selvaggio, owner of Storm Literary Agency, for her invariably astute and useful help.

My editor, Katy Nishimoto, for her keen insight, boundless energy, and excitement about the book.

Everyone at the Dial Press and Random House who helped make this happen, including Whitney Frick, Andy Ward, Avideh Bashirrad, Debbie Aroff, JP Woodham, Cassie Vu, Donna Cheng, Vanessa DeJesus, Corina Diez, Cara DuBois, Nathalie Mairena, and Alexis Flynn.

© KATE HAAG PHOTOGRAPHY

Ry Herman has held a variety of jobs, including submissions editor, theatrical technician, and one position that could best be described as typing the number five all day long. They are bisexual and genderqueer. Their hobbies include weight lifting, playing tabletop role-playing games, and reading as many books as humanly possible. For many years, Herman was primarily a playwright, and they've also worked as an actor and director. They performed at the Edinburgh Fringe Festival in 2018 and 2019. Although born in the United States, Herman is now a permanent resident of Scotland.

ryhermanwrites.wordpress.com
X: @ry_herman
Instagram: @kyrademon
Bluesky: @ryherman.bsky.social

About the Type

This book was set in Caslon, a typeface first designed in 1722 by William Caslon (1692–1766). Its widespread use by most English printers in the early eighteenth century soon supplanted the Dutch typefaces that had formerly prevailed. The roman is considered a "workhorse" typeface due to its pleasant, open appearance, while the italic is exceedingly decorative.